English Country House Murders

Other Anthologies available in Large Print:

ENGLISH COUNTRY HOUSE MURDERS

A Large Print Anthology

Edited and Introduced
by Thomas Godfrey

G.K.HALL &CO.
Boston, Massachusetts
1991

Published in Large Print by arrangement with
The Mysterious Press.

G. K. Hall Large Print Book Series.

Set in 16 pt. Plantin.

Library of Congress Cataloging-in-Publication Data

English country house murders / edited and introduced by Thomas
    Godfrey.
        p.   cm.—(G.K. Hall large print book series)
    ISBN 0-8161-5089-3 (large print)
    1. Detective and mystery stories, English.   2. Country homes—
Fiction.   3. Country life—Fiction.   4. Manors—Fiction.
5. Large type books.   I. Godfrey, Thomas, 1945–
[PR1309.D4E46   1991]
823'.087208—dc20   90-46934

Acknowledgments

"The Fordwych Castle Mystery" from *Lady Molly of Scotland Yard*. © 1910 by Emmuska Orczy. Reprinted by permission of A.P. Watt Ltd. acting for the Estate of Emmuska Orczy and Joan Orczy-Barstow.

"The Blue Scarab" from *The Blue Scarab* by R. Austin Freeman. © 1924. Renewed 1951. Reprinted by permission of A.P. Watt Ltd.

"The Doom of the Darnaways" by G. K. Chesterton from *The Incredulity of Father Brown*. © 1926. Reprinted by permission of Dodd, Mead Inc.

"The Shadow on the Glass" from *The Mysterious Mr. Quin* by Agatha Christie. © 1930 by Agatha Christie Mallowan. Renewed 1957. Reprinted by permission of Aitken, Stone Ltd. and G. P. Putnam's Sons Inc.

"The Queen's Square" from *Lord Peter* by Dorothy L. Sayers. © 1933 by Dorothy Leigh Sayers Fleming. Renewed 1961 by Lloyds Banks Ltd. Executors. Reprinted by permission Harper & Row Publishers Inc. and David Higham Assoc. Ltd.

"Death on the Air" by Ngaio Marsh. © 1939 by Ngaio Marsh. Reprinted by permission of Harold Ober Assoc. and Aitken & Stone Ltd. agents for the estate of Ngaio Marsh.

"The Same to Us" by Margery Allingham. © P&M Youngman Carter Estate. First published in *The Daily Express* 1934. Reprinted by permission Curtis Brown Ltd. and John Stevens Robling, American Literary Executor.

"The Hunt Ball" by Freeman Wills Crofts. © 1943 by the American Mercury Inc. Renewed. Reprinted by permission A.P. Watt Ltd.

"The Incautious Burglar" AKA "A Guest in the House" from *The Man Who Explained Miracles*. © 1940 by John Dickson Carr. Reprinted by permission Harold Ober Assoc. and David Higham Assoc. Ltd.

"The Long Shot" by Nicholas Blake (C. Day Lewis.) Reprinted by permission of Sterling, Lord Literistic Inc.

"Jeeves and the Stolen Venus" by P.G. Wodehouse. First published in *Ellery Queen's Mystery Magazine*. Reprinted by permission of the Wodehouse Trust, J. Peter Lobbenberg, Trustee; A.P. Watt Ltd.; and the Hutchinson Publishing Group.

"Death in the Sun" by Michael Innes. © 1964 by J.I.M. Stewart. Reprinted by permission Dodd, Mead Inc. and Victor Gollancz Ltd. on behalf of the author.

To a trio of ladies who have influenced the mysteries of my life:

Janet Barber Godfrey Alspach
Rae Walters Barber
Doris Barber Parr

With thanks

Acknowledgments

To my publishers

    Lesley Omara for the idea

    Otto Penzler for his guidance and use of the Penzler collection

To Valerie Vanaman for her reading and researching

To my wife, Kathy, for her advice and tolerance

To my sons, Brian, Calvin, and Sam, who did not see much of me while all this was afoot

To the patient whose prescription was accidentally made out to Ethel Lina White because a good idea struck me at the end of an examination

CONTENTS

INTRODUCTION

Of all the civilized pleasures given to man, what can compare to a rattling good English Country House Mystery?

There you are, after a harrowing day with over-ripe household bills or baby nappies, fatigued and spent. You retire to a comfortable seat in a secluded corner with a new Country House Mystery. You open the cover and suddenly you are transported to a splendid baronial manor and tea with Lord and Lady Ferncliffe, who never paid a bill or changed a nappy in their lives. The conversation among the *cognoscenti* has just turned to the season in "Monte" when Sir Percy slumps forward in his chair before the fire, his cup of Earl Grey heavily laced with laudanum. Messy business, this. But not to worry, the local authorities are in on the case. An arrest is said to be imminent.

Later that night at the costume ball, all is temporarily forgotten as you glide around on the dance floor with a guest list culled from Debrett's. Upstairs Helena Cavendish, toast of the West End, engages in a secret tryst with Colonel Nigel Smythe-Balfour while in the library his wife, Felicity, daughter of Sir Randolph Cross (rumoured next in line at the Exchequer), lies dead from a nasty blow to the temple.

Most perplexing. Obviously the local man on the case has no idea what has happened. Are we to believe Simon Agate's alibi that his arrival at Ferncliffe Hall was delayed by a puncture?

And who was that shadowy figure seen leaving the gardener's shed earlier in the afternoon?

And what of that business about Cecily Fairchild being the champion arm-wrestler at Miss Thornhill's Academy for Girls?

Is there another murder in the offing? Can you puzzle it all out before the Great Detective?

And so the magic is worked.

The English Country House Mystery, which sprouted from Romantic literature at the end of the nineteenth century, was a logical extension of it. From the seeds of Godwin's *Caleb Williams* and Dickens's *Bleak House*, it had its first flowering in Collins's *The Moonstone* and produced its greatest bouquet in the tales of Sherlock Holmes.

Later, the Country House tradition blossomed in dazzling profusion with the stylized tales of Agatha Christie and her generation of early-twentieth-century mystery novelists. After World War II, as England rebuilt, economic reality moved the English Country House into the National Trust or onto the auction block, and its inhabitants into flats or out of the country.

With this passing, English mystery writing moved to intimate character study on a more modest scale. The Age of Nationalization produced a new variety of writers, modern stylists like P. D. James, Ruth Rendell, Margaret Yorke, and Celia Fremlin. The scope and sweep of the classic English Country House novel diminished, fading away with the colliers, cotillions, and chauffeurs that populated it, relics of a Golden Age.

But readers' enthusiasm for this form did not fade. Christie's books sold in greater quantity. New generations had great fun rediscovering Lord Peter Wimsey and Father Brown on television and again in print. Sherlock Holmes's and Miss Marple's popularity helped keep alive a Great English Fantasy, and took its cozy appeal all over the globe.

Will it die? I doubt that an insatiable readership will let it. These little packets of quiet pleasure have rewarded readers now for over a century. Today, they accompany many a traveler to the seaside, to the country, to the mountains, to the Orient, on round-the-world cruises, or just down the corridor to the W.C. And its appeal to the writer? Right now someone somewhere is preparing to do in poor Sir Percy again with his home computer.

How to define the English Country House Mystery? The question asserted itself as I set off to assemble the collection in hand. Exhaustive reading, exhaustive thinking, disclosed the following set of axioms:

1. Authentic English Country House Mysteries are written by authentic English writers. Americans, even Canadians, may study the form and give it a go, but they invariably give themselves away as pretenders to the tradition.

2. Any self-respecting English Country House Mystery must include a crime. Murder, of course, is the crime of choice, as it gets the reader's at-

tention most easily. Jewel robberies and unexplained disappearances follow, in that order.

3. Multiple crimes make for a jollier story, although mass murder and gory violence, graphically described, are to be deplored. (Ditto shooting sprees and kinky tortures.)

4. Poison is the prescribed means for eliminating victims in English Country House Mysteries. The alternative is a good solid wallop on the head. (I find defenestration shockingly under-utilized and commend it to new practitioners of the art. It is tidy, certain, and fleetingly picturesque. It can be dealt with in one sentence, allowing the author to get on quickly with more important matters, like the solution.)

5. The nature of the crime must be puzzling. The identity of the perpetrator must be unknown for as long as possible. The deduction of this identity should involve genuine reasoning ability. Rules of fair-play-with-the-reader must apply (the Marquis of Ellery Queen's-bury Rules).

It is far better that the solution to the crime be ridiculously contrived, and that it rely on the perpetrator's and detective's knowledge of Egyptian hieroglyphics or the average yearly rainfall in Katmandu, than that it be too simpleminded, allowing the reader to figure it all out by page two.

6. The crime must be solved by a detective, whether professional or amateur. Anyone can be designated by the author to be the detective, even one of the suspects, the victim, or the perpetrator himself.

7. A superior English Country House Mystery has the detective in attendance or on the scene moments after the crime is committed.

8. The crime, whether attempted or successful, should take place in the house or on the grounds. If events take the investigation elsewhere, the earliest possible return to the house is in order.

9. Police involvement in the investigation is irrelevant unless the detective is a police official.

10. Some attempt must be made to tidy up any loose ends as quickly as possible once the deduction has been made. Stretching and squeezing are permitted. ("Ah, well, Inspector, I knew I could eliminate the Reverend Mr. Falmouth immediately because of the glass eye, even though he was obviously the one who turned the clock back an hour, unwittingly allowing the murderer who, of course, had to be under three feet tall and a crack shot with a crossbow as well as having an intimate knowledge of the chemical properties of antimony . . ." etc., etc.)

11. Characterization is not important in the English Country House Mystery so long as the reader can keep everyone straight in his or her mind. It is not important that Lady Bracknell be a rounded, believable character. It *is* important that she be easily distinguished from Lady Billows.

12. The puzzle, the challenge to the reader, is paramount. There are no tears for the victim, no anguish for the falsely accused, no jeers for the perpetrator once revealed. It is vital that the reader be able to close the book and get back to carrying out the dustbin immediately, unburdened by any lingering emotional involvement. (Though one can be still pondering how the murderer knew that the victim would be in the study alone at eight that evening.)

13. Cultural concerns may occupy the writer, but social injustices are never to intrude. Reformers and radicals in English Country House Mysteries are invariably cranks or eccentrics brought in for a bit of color. Any writer in this medium who devotes pages to the plights of pensioners, failure of the National Health Service, or discussions of the merits of capital punishment has missed the point and will soon find himself without a readership, or a publisher.

14. The crime must take place in a proper English Country House.

As to that:

Rules of the House

A. The main setting must be a well-defined residence apart from surrounding real estate.

B. The larger the house, the better. Do not be put off by terms like "small" or "cottage." What was described in 1900 as a small cottage may well house the entire population of the Falkland Islands today.

C. The house should be well out of the city, if not actually in the countryside. Remember that what once struck an author as a secluded address far from the rigours of city life could now be a stop on the Jubilee Line.

D. There must be significant grounds attached. An English Country House worth consideration will include extensive gardens. Outbuildings like a guest house or a greenhouse or stables are added features to be admired. A maze offers lovely attraction to dead bodies.

E. There must be servants present, at least one of whom lives in residence. (There must be someone to be aroused to call the police and confuse issues later. "Oh, no, mum, begging your pardon, Sir Charles did not retire for the night at ten o'clock. I found him blotto in the pantry at two A.M. when I went to get the rat poison you requested.")

A butler is the preferred servant. A maid adds cachet to a mystery. A cook is often useful, especially if she suspects something and ends up dead. Secretaries, chauffeurs, and ill-defined householders are always to be welcomed in the proper English Country House Mystery.

Warning: Servants are *not* to be directly implicated in actual crimes. Only a poor constructionist would attempt to market a mystery in which the butler did it. (Unless, however, the butler was masquerading as the owner of the house, the local constable, or Mrs. Thatcher.)

F. It is crucial that the house have character. It need not be a pleasing character. Baskerville Hall was rather grim. Manderley was decidedly threatening.

G. The author is to be praised if secrets, curses, or prophecies attach themselves to the house or its residents. A ghost is permissible. A history of old crimes on the estate is bliss, especially if unsolved.

H. Do not neglect the importance of weather. Stormy or unpredictable weather is divine. A house in a sunny location where the rain never pours, the fog never creeps, or the mist never shrouds is to be shunned literarily. A cliff falling off to the seacoast may make an acceptable substitute for bad (that is, good) weather.

I. The pedigree of an English Country House Mystery is always found in its show of wealth. Jewelry and old paintings have proved themselves commendable ways of displaying one's wealth because they are so easily stolen. Moreover, their disappearance is always of immeasurable concern to the occupants.

J. An English Country House Mystery is to be considered stylish if a large social gathering occurs at the house during the telling of the tale.

K. In a proper English Country House, the telephone system does not function reliably.

Two final, important observations:
- Someone is always lying about his or her past in a true English Country House Mystery.
- No one named Lefty has ever appeared in an English Country House Mystery.

There are, of course, many exceptions to all these rules (except the last), as well as accepted variants. We shall encounter both in the pages that follow.

The stories have been arranged in developmental, roughly chronologic, sequence. We begin with an appearance by Sherlock Holmes, still the beacon by which all that happens in the English Country House Mystery is guided. Then follow some early accounts, showing the influences of Walpole, Burns, and other Romantic novelists. Then several classical accounts, from the rivals of Sherlock Holmes through the work of one of the last great ladies of the English mystery, Christianna Brand.

Some important variants are interspersed, most notably: the inverted story, in which the perpetrator and his methods are known, and the means of detection alone engages us; the Country House Mystery as humor and satire, with P. G. Wodehouse's Jeeves as the pluperfect servant ensnared in the crime; the English Country House Gothic Thriller, in which whodunit and how are subordinated to scaring the stuffing out of the poor reader.

At the conclusion, there are a few end-of-the-cycle Country House Mysteries where the postwar realities mentioned above assert themselves quite strongly. The Country House is present, the Mystery is present; but the characters are different, and their relationship to the setting is altered.

And then, a sweet to conclude: Holmes again, in a final bow to the tradition.

For those readers I will inevitably disappoint with my choice of tales and authors, a sincere apology. The possibilities were limitless, the limitation of space painful.

In the cases of Christie and Conan Doyle, I freely confess choosing works that were lesser known but still distinguished. I could have filled the book with their stories alone.

And now with that long-winded ordeal behind us, it's time we were off. Nappies and bills aside, please. We're booked (so to speak) for tea with Dame Agatha and Lord Peter. All the right people will be there: Sir Pelham, Dame Ngaio, Sir John, Baroness Orczy, and even the Poet Laureate and Master of the King's Musick. Mr. Holmes and Dr. Watson have promised to pop in. We are in for a grand time. There we are . . . a nice spot of Earl Grey brewed fresh for you.

That's right.

Just make yourself comfortable.

Scones in hand?

Affairs in order?

Let us begin. . . .

Sir Arthur Conan Doyle
(1859–1930)
THE ADVENTURE OF THE ABBEY GRANGE

No figure in English literature is so universally recognized as Sherlock Holmes. Modeled after one of Dr. Doyle's medical professors, Holmes is a man of thought as well as action, a shrewd and accurate observer with a keen imagination and flair for invention. In short, he is all that the successful detective must be. He appeared in one of the first and greatest of all English Country House Mysteries, that "curious business about the dog in the night-time" at Baskerville Hall. And now he bids us join him on yet another Country House adventure.

What is Holmes's appeal?

His ingenuity

His independence?

His strongly held values?

His romantic flair and sense of the occasion?

His Edwardian setting, so comfortable, cozy, and civilized?

His ability to make penetrating deductions from commonplace observation?

Memories of Basil Rathbone's indelible interpretation on the screen?

Wit tells us it is all of these things and more, for

Holmes has strong appeal for many different readers. All in all it is a very satisfying blend, suitable to any taste.

It was on a bitterly cold night and frosty morning, towards the end of the winter of '97, that I was awakened by a tugging at my shoulder. It was Holmes. The candle in his hand shone upon his eager, stooping face, and told me at a glance that something was amiss.

"Come, Watson, come!" he cried. "The game is afoot. Not a word! Into your clothes and come!"

Ten minutes later we were both in a cab, and rattling through the silent streets on our way to Charing Cross Station. The first faint winter's dawn was beginning to appear, and we could dimly see the occasional figure of an early workman as he passed us, blurred and indistinct in the opalescent London reek. Holmes nestled in silence into his heavy coat, and I was glad to do the same, for the air was most bitter, and neither of us had broken our fast.

It was not until we had consumed some hot tea at the station and taken our places in the Kentish train that we were sufficiently thawed, he to speak and I to listen. Holmes drew a note from his pocket, and read aloud:

"Abbey Grange, Marsham, Kent,
"3:30 A.M.
"My dear Mr. Holmes:
    "I should be very glad of your immediate assistance in what promises to be a most re-

markable case. It is something quite in your line. Except for releasing the lady I will see that everything is kept exactly as I have found it, but I beg you not to lose an instant, as it is difficult to leave Sir Eustace there.

"Yours faithfully,

"Stanley Hopkins.

"Hopkins has called me in seven times, and on each occasion his summons has been entirely justified," said Holmes. "I fancy that every one of his cases has found its way into your collection, and I must admit, Watson, that you have some power of selection, which atones for much which I deplore in your narratives. Your fatal habit of looking at everything from the point of view of a story instead of as a scientific exercise has ruined what might have been an instructive and even classical series of demonstrations. You slur over work of the utmost finesse and delicacy, in order to dwell upon sensational details which may excite, but cannot possibly instruct, the reader."

"Why do you not write them yourself?" I said, with some bitterness.

"I will, my dear Watson, I will. At present I am, as you know, fairly busy, but I propose to devote my declining years to the composition of a textbook, which shall focus the whole art of detection into one volume. Our present search appears to be a case of murder."

"You think this Sir Eustace is dead, then?"

"I should say so. Hopkins's writing shows considerable agitation, and he is not an emotional man. Yes, I gather there has been violence, and that the body is left for our inspection. A mere suicide would not have caused him to send for me. As to the release of the lady, it would appear that she has been locked in her room during the tragedy. We are moving in high life, Watson, crackling paper, 'E. B.' monogram, coat-of-arms, picturesque address. I think that friend Hopkins will live up to his reputation, and that we shall have an interesting morning. The crime was committed before twelve last night."

"How can you possibly tell?"

"By an inspection of the trains, and by reckoning the time. The local police had to be called in, they had to communicate with Scotland Yard, Hopkins had to go out, and he in turn had to send for me. All that makes a fair night's work. Well, here we are at Chiselhurst Station, and we shall soon set our doubts at rest."

A drive of a couple of miles through narrow country lanes brought us to a park gate, which was opened for us by an old lodge-keeper, whose haggard face bore the reflection of some great disaster. The avenue ran through a noble park, between lines of ancient elms, and ended in a low, widespread house, pillared in front after the fashion of Palladio. The central part was evidently of a great age and shrouded in ivy, but the large windows showed that modern changes had been carried out, and one wing of the house appeared to be entirely new. The youthful figure and alert, eager face of Inspector Stanley Hopkins confronted us in the open doorway.

"I'm very glad you have come, Mr. Holmes. And you, too, Dr. Watson. But, indeed, if I had my time over again, I should not have troubled you, for since the lady has come to herself, she has given so clear an account of the affair that there is not much left for us to do. You remember that Lewisham gang of burglars?"

"What, the three Randalls?"

"Exactly; the father and two sons. It's their work. I have not a doubt of it. They did a job at Sydenham a fortnight ago and were seen and described. Rather cool to do another so soon and so near, but it is they, beyond all doubt. It's a hanging matter this time."

"Sir Eustace is dead, then?"

"Yes, his head was knocked in with his own poker."

"Sir Eustace Brackenstall, the driver tells me."

"Exactly—one of the richest men in Kent— Lady Brackenstall is in the morning-room. Poor lady, she has had a most dreadful experience. She seemed half dead when I saw her first. I think you had best see her and hear her account of the facts. Then we will examine the dining-room together."

Lady Brackenstall was no ordinary person. Seldom have I seen so graceful a figure, so womanly a presence, and so beautiful a face. She was a blonde, golden-haired, blue-eyed, and would no doubt have had the perfect complexion which goes with such colouring, had not her recent experience left her drawn and haggard. Her sufferings were physical as well as mental, for over one eye rose a hideous, plum-coloured swelling, which her maid, a tall, austere woman, was bathing assiduously with vinegar and water. The lady lay back exhausted upon a couch, but her quick, observant

5

gaze, as we entered the room, and the alert expression of her beautiful features, showed that neither her wits nor her courage had been shaken by her terrible experience. She was enveloped in a loose dressing-gown of blue and silver, but a black sequin-covered dinner-dress lay upon the couch beside her.

"I have told you all that happened, Mr. Hopkins," she said, wearily. "Could you not repeat it for me? Well, if you think it necessary, I will tell these gentlemen what occurred. Have they been in the dining-room yet?"

"I thought they had better hear your ladyship's story first."

"I shall be glad when you can arrange matters. It is horrible to me to think of him still lying there." She shuddered and buried her face in her hands. As she did so, the loose gown fell back from her forearms. Holmes uttered an exclamation.

"You have other injuries, madam! What is this?" Two vivid red spots stood out on one of the white, round limbs. She hastily covered it.

"It is nothing. It has no connection with this hideous business to-night. If you and your friend will sit down, I will tell you all I can.

"I am the wife of Sir Eustace Brackenstall. I have been married about a year. I suppose that it is no use my attempting to conceal that our marriage has not been a happy one. I fear that all our neighbours would tell you that, even if I were to attempt to deny it. Perhaps the fault may be partly mine. I was brought up in the freer, less conventional atmosphere of South Australia, and this English life, with its proprieties and its primness, is not congenial to me. But the main reason lies in the one fact, which is notorious to everyone, and that is that Sir Eustace was a confirmed drunkard. To be with such a man for an hour is unpleasant. Can you imagine what it means for a sensitive and high-spirited woman to be tied to him for day and night? It is a sacrilege, a crime, a villainy to hold that such a marriage is binding. I say that these monstrous laws of yours will bring a curse upon the land—God will not let such wickedness endure." For an instant she sat up, her cheeks flushed, and her eyes blazing from under the terrible mark upon her brow. Then the strong, soothing hand of the austere maid drew her head down on to the cushion, and the wild anger died away into passionate sobbing. At last she continued:

"I will tell you about last night. You are aware, perhaps, that in this house all the servants sleep in the modern wing. This central block is made up of the dwelling-rooms, with the kitchen behind and our bedroom above. My maid, Theresa, sleeps above my room. There is no one else, and no sound could alarm those who are in the farther wing. This must have been well known to the robbers, or they would not have acted as they did.

"Sir Eustace retired about half-past ten. The servants had already gone to their quarters. Only my maid was up, and she had remained in her room at the top of the house until I needed her services. I sat until after eleven in this room, absorbed in a book. Then I walked round to see that all was right before I went upstairs. It was my custom to do this myself, for, as I have explained,

Sir Eustace was not always to be trusted. I went into the kitchen, the butler's pantry, the gun-room, the billiard-room, the drawing-room, and finally the dining-room. As I approached the window, which is covered with thick curtains, I suddenly felt the wind blow upon my face and realized that it was open. I flung the curtain aside and found myself face to face with a broad-shouldered elderly man, who had just stepped into the room. The window is a long French one, which really forms a door leading to the lawn. I held my bed-room candle lit in my hand, and, by its light, behind the first man I saw two others, who were in the act of entering. I stepped back, but the fellow was on me in an instant. He caught me first by the wrist and then by the throat. I opened my mouth to scream, but he struck me a savage blow with his fist over my eye, and felled me to the ground. I must have been unconscious for a few minutes, for when I came to myself, I found that they had torn down the bell-rope, and had secured me to the oaken chair which stands at the head of the dining-table. I was so firmly bound that I could not move, and a handkerchief round my mouth prevented me from uttering a sound. It was at this instant that my unfortunate husband entered the room. He had evidently heard some suspicious sounds, and he came prepared for such a scene as he found. He was dressed in nightshirt and trousers, with his favourite blackthorn cudgel in his hand. He rushed at the burglars, but another—it was the elderly man—stooped, picked the poker out of the grate and struck him a horrible blow as he passed. He fell with a groan and never moved again. I fainted once more, but again it could only have been for a very few minutes during which I was insensible. When I opened my eyes I found that they had collected the silver from the sideboard, and they had drawn a bottle of wine which stood there. Each of them had a glass in his hand. I have already told you, have I not, that one was elderly, with a beard, and the others young, hairless lads. They might have been a father with his two sons. They talked together in whispers. Then they came over and made sure that I was securely bound. Finally they withdrew, closing the window after them. It was quite a quarter of an hour before I got my mouth free. When I did so, my screams brought the maid to my assistance. The other servants were soon alarmed, and we sent for the local police, who instantly communicated with London. That is really all that I can tell you, gentlemen, and I trust that it will not be necessary for me to go over so painful a story again."

"Any questions, Mr. Holmes?" asked Hopkins.

"I will not impose any further tax upon Lady Brackenstall's patience and time," said Holmes. "Before I go into the dining-room, I should like to hear your experience." He looked at the maid.

"I saw the men before ever they came into the house," said she. "As I sat by my bedroom window I saw three men in the moonlight down by the lodge gate yonder, but I thought nothing of it at the time. It was more than an hour after that I heard my mistress scream, and down I ran, to find her, poor lamb, just as she says, and him on the floor, with his blood and brains over the room. It was enough to drive a woman out of her wits, tied there, and her very dress spotted with him, but she never wanted courage, did Miss Mary Fraser of Adelaide, and Lady Brackenstall of Abbey Grange hasn't learned new ways. You've questioned her long enough, you gentlemen, and now she is coming to her own room, just with her old Theresa, to get the rest that she badly needs."

With a motherly tenderness the gaunt woman put her arm round her mistress and led her from the room.

"She has been with her all her life," said Hopkins. "Nursed her as a baby, and came with her to England when they first left Australia, eighteen months ago. Theresa Wright is her name, and the kind of maid you don't pick up nowadays. This way, Mr. Holmes, if you please!"

The keen interest had passed out of Holmes's expressive face, and I knew that with the mystery all the charm of the case had departed. There still remained an arrest to be effected, but what were these commonplace rogues that he should soil his hands with them? An abstruse and learned specialist who finds that he has been called in for a case of measles would experience something of the annoyance which I read in my friend's eyes. Yet the scene in the dining-room of the Abbey Grange was sufficiently strange to arrest his attention and to recall his waning interest.

It was a very large and high chamber, with carved oak ceiling, oaken panelling, and a fine array of deer's heads and ancient weapons around the walls. At the further end from the door was the high French window of which we had heard. Three smaller windows on the right-hand side filled the apartment with cold winter sunshine. On the left was a large, deep fireplace, with a massive, overhanging oak mantelpiece. Beside the fireplace was a heavy oaken chair with arms and crossbars at the bottom. In and out through the open woodwork was woven a crimson cord, which was secured at each side of the crosspiece below. In releasing the lady, the cord had been slipped off her, but the knots with which it had been secured still remained. These details only struck our attention afterwards, for our thoughts were entirely absorbed by the terrible object which lay upon the tiger-skin hearthrug in front of the fire.

It was the body of a tall, well-made man, about forty years of age. He lay upon his back, his face upturned, with his white teeth grinning through his short, black beard. His two clenched hands were raised above his head, and a heavy, black-thorn stick lay across them. His dark, handsome, aquiline features were convulsed into a spasm of vindictive hatred, which had set his dead face in a terribly fiendish expression. He had evidently been in his bed when the alarm had broken out, for he wore a foppish, embroidered nightshirt, and his bare feet projected from his trousers. His head was horribly injured, and the whole room bore witness to the savage ferocity of the blow which had struck him down. Beside him lay the heavy poker, bent into a curve by the concussion. Holmes examined both it and the indescribable wreck which it had wrought.

"He must be a powerful man, this elder Randall," he remarked.

"Yes," said Hopkins. "I have some record of the fellow, and he is a rough customer."

"You should have no difficulty in getting him."

"Not the slightest. We have been on the look-out for him, and there was some idea that he had got away to America. Now that we know that the gang are here, I don't see how they can escape. We have the news at every seaport already, and a reward will be offered before evening. What beats me is how they could have done so mad a thing, knowing that the lady could describe them and that we could not fail to recognize the description."

"Exactly. One would have expected that they would silence Lady Brackenstall as well."

"They may not have realized," I suggested, "that she had recovered from her faint."

"That is likely enough. If she seemed to be senseless, they would not take her life. What about this poor fellow, Hopkins? I seem to have heard some queer stories about him."

"He was a good-hearted man when he was sober, but a perfect fiend when he was drunk, or rather when he was half drunk, for he seldom really went the whole way. The devil seemed to be in him at such times, and he was capable of anything. From what I hear, in spite of all his wealth and his title, he very nearly came our way once or twice. There was a scandal about his drenching a dog with petroleum and setting it on fire—her ladyship's dog, to make the matter worse—and that was only hushed up with difficulty. Then he threw a decanter at the maid, Theresa Wright—there was trouble about that. On the whole, and between ourselves, it will be a brighter house without him. What are you looking at now?"

Holmes was down on his knees, examining with great attention the knots upon the red cord with which the lady had been secured. Then he carefully scrutinized the broken and frayed end where it had snapped off when the burglar had dragged it down.

"When this was pulled down, the bell in the kitchen must have rung loudly," he remarked.

"No one could hear it. The kitchen stands right at the back of the house."

"How did the burglar know no one would hear it? How dare he pull at a bell-rope in that reckless fashion?"

"Exactly, Mr. Holmes, exactly. You put the very question which I have asked myself again and again. There can be no doubt that this fellow must have known the house and its habits. He must have perfectly understood that the servants would all be in bed at that comparatively early hour, and that no one could possibly hear a bell ring in the kitchen. Therefore, he must have been in close league with one of the servants. Surely that is evident. But there are eight servants, and all of good character."

"Other things being equal," said Holmes, "one would suspect the one at whose head the master threw a decanter. And yet that would involve treachery towards the mistress to whom this woman seems devoted. Well, well, the point is a minor one, and when you have Randall you will probably find no difficulty in securing his accomplice. The lady's story certainly seems to be corroborated, if it needed corroboration, by every detail which we see before us." He walked to the French window and threw it open. "There are no signs here, but the ground is iron hard, and one would not expect them. I see that these candles in the mantelpiece have been lighted."

"Yes, it was by their light, and that of the lady's bedroom candle, that the burglars saw their way about."

"And what did they take?"

"Well, they did not take much—only half a dozen articles of plate off the sideboard. Lady Brackenstall thinks that they were themselves so disturbed by the death of Sir Eustace that they did not ransack the house, as they would otherwise have done."

"No doubt that is true, and yet they drank some wine, I understand."

"To steady their nerves."

"Exactly. These three glasses upon the sideboard have been untouched, I suppose?"

"Yes, and the bottle stands as they left it."

"Let us look at it. Halloa, halloa! What is this?"

The three glasses were grouped together, all of them tinged with wine, and one of them containing some dregs of beeswing. The bottle stood near them, two-thirds full, and beside it lay a long, deeply stained cork. Its appearance and the dust upon the bottle showed that it was no common vintage which the murderers had enjoyed.

A change had come over Holmes's manner. He had lost his listless expression and again I saw an alert light of interest in his keen, deep-set eyes. He raised the cork and examined it minutely.

"How did they draw it?" he asked.

Hopkins pointed to a half-opened drawer. In it lay some table linen and a large corkscrew.

"Did Lady Brackenstall say that screw was used?"

"No, you remember that she was senseless at the moment when the bottle was opened."

"Quite so. As a matter of fact, that screw was *not* used. This bottle was opened by a pocket screw, probably contained in a knife, and not more than an inch and a half long. If you will examine the top of the cork, you will observe that the screw was driven in three times before the cork was extracted. It has never been transfixed. This long screw would have transfixed it and drawn it up with a single pull. When you catch this fellow, you will find that he has one of these multiplex knives in his possession."

"Excellent!" said Hopkins.

"But these glasses do puzzle me, I confess. Lady Brackenstall actually *saw* the three men drinking, did she not?"

"Yes; she was clear about that."

"Then there is an end of it. What more is to be said? And yet, you must admit, that the three glasses are very remarkable, Hopkins. What? You see nothing remarkable? Well, well, let it pass. Perhaps, when a man has special knowledge and special powers like my own, it rather encourages him to seek a complex explanation when a simpler one is at hand. Of course, it must be a mere chance about the glasses. Well, good-morning, Hopkins.

15

I don't see that I can be of any use to you, and you appear to have your case very clear. You will let me know when Randall is arrested, and any further developments which may occur. I trust that I shall soon have to congratulate you upon a successful conclusion. Come, Watson, I fancy that we may employ ourselves more profitably at home."

During our return journey, I could see by Holmes's face that he was much puzzled by something which he had observed. Every now and then, by an effort, he would throw off the impression, and talk as if the matter were clear, but then his doubts would settle down upon him again, and his knitted brows and abstracted eyes would show that his thoughts had gone back once more to the great dining-room of the Abbey Grange, in which this midnight tragedy had been enacted. At last, by a sudden impulse, just as our train was crawling out of a suburban station, he sprang on to the platform and pulled me out after him.

"Excuse me, my dear fellow," said he, as we watched the rear carriages of our train disappearing round a curve, "I am sorry to make you the victim of what may seem a mere whim, but on my life, Watson, I simply *can't* leave that case in this condition. Every instinct that I possess cries out against it. It's wrong—it's all wrong—I'll swear that it's wrong. And yet the lady's story was complete, the maid's corroboration was sufficient, the detail was fairly exact. What have I to put up against that? Three wineglasses, that is all. But if I had not taken things for granted, if I had examined everything with the care which I should have shown had we approached the case *de novo* and had no cut-and-dried story to warp my mind, should I not then have found something more definite to go upon? Of course I should. Sit down on this bench, Watson, until a train for Chiselhurst arrives, and allow me to lay the evidence before you, imploring you in the first instance to dismiss from your mind the idea that anything which the maid or her mistress may have said must necessarily be true. The lady's charming personality must not be permitted to warp our judgement.

"Surely there are details in her story which, if we looked at in cold blood, would excite our suspicion. These burglars made a considerable haul at Sydenham a fortnight ago. Some account of them and of their appearance was in the papers, and would naturally occur to anyone who wished to invent a story in which imaginary robbers should play a part. As a matter of fact, burglars who have done a good stroke of business are, as a rule, only too glad to enjoy the proceeds in peace and quiet without embarking on another perilous undertaking. Again, it is unusual for burglars to operate at so early an hour, it is unusual for burglars to strike a lady to prevent her screaming, since one would imagine that was the sure way to make her scream, it is unusual for them to commit murder when their numbers are sufficient to overpower one man, it is unusual for them to be content with a limited plunder when there was much more within their reach, and finally, I should say, that it was very unusual for such men to leave a bottle half empty. How do all these unusuals strike you, Watson?"

"Their cumulative effect is certainly considerable, and yet each of them is quite possible in itself. The most unusual thing of all, as it seems to me, is that the lady should be tied to the chair."

"Well, I am not so clear about that, Watson, for it is evident that they must either kill her or else secure her in such a way that she could not give immediate notice of their escape. But at any rate I have shown, have I not, that there is a certain element of improbability about the lady's story? And now, on the top of this, comes the incident of the wineglasses."

"What about the wineglasses?"

"Can you see them in your mind's eye?"

"I see them clearly."

"We are told that three men drank from them. Does that strike you as likely?"

"Why not? There was wine in each glass."

"Exactly, but there was beeswing only in one glass. You must have noticed that fact. What does that suggest to your mind?"

"The last glass filled would be most likely to contain beeswing."

"Not at all. The bottle was full of it, and it is inconceivable that the first two glasses were clear and the third heavily charged with it. There are two possible explanations, and only two. One is that after the second glass was filled the bottle was violently agitated, and so the third glass received the beeswing. That does not appear probable. No, no, I am sure that I am right."

"What, then, do you suppose?"

"That only two glasses were used, and that the dregs of both were poured into a third glass, so as to give the false impression that three people had been here. In that way all the beeswing would be in the last glass, would it not? Yes, I am convinced that this is so. But if I have hit upon the true explanation of this one small phenomenon, then in an instant the case rises from the commonplace to the exceedingly remarkable, for it can only mean that Lady Brackenstall and her maid had deliberately lied to us, that not one word of their story is to be believed, that they have some very strong reason for covering the real criminal, and that we must construct our case for ourselves without any help from them. That is the mission which now lies before us, and here, Watson, is the Sydenham train."

The household at the Abbey Grange were much surprised at our return, but Sherlock Holmes, finding that Stanley Hopkins had gone off to report to headquarters, took possession of the dining-room, locked the door upon the inside, and devoted himself for two hours to one of those minute and laborious investigations which form the solid basis on which his brilliant edifices of deduction were reared. Seated in a corner like an interested student who observes the demonstration of his professor, I followed every step of that remarkable research. The window, the curtains, the carpet, the chair, the rope—each in turn was minutely examined and duly pondered. The body of the unfortunate baronet had been removed, and all else remained as we had seen it in the morning. Finally, to my astonishment, Holmes climbed up on the massive mantelpiece. Far above his head hung the few inches of red cord which were still attached to the wire. For a long time he gazed upward at it, and then in an attempt to get nearer to it he rested his knee upon a wooden bracket on the wall. This brought his hand within a few inches of the broken end of the rope, but it was not this so much as the bracket itself which seemed to engage his attention. Finally, he sprang down with an ejaculation of satisfaction.

"It's all right, Watson," said he. "We have got our case—one of the most remarkable in our collection. But, dear me, how slow-witted I have been, and how nearly I have committed the blunder of my lifetime! Now, I think that, with a few missing links, my chain is almost complete."

"You have got your men?"

"Man, Watson, man. Only one, but a very formidable person. Strong as a lion—witness the blow that bent that poker! Six foot three in height, active as a squirrel, dexterous with his fingers, finally, remarkably quick-witted, for this whole ingenious story is of his concoction. Yes, Watson, we have come upon the handiwork of a very remarkable individual. And yet, in that bell-rope, he has given us a clue which should not have left us a doubt."

"Where was the clue?"

"Well, if you were to pull down a bell-rope, Watson, where would you expect it to break? Surely at the spot where it is attached to the wire. Why should it break three inches from the top, as this one has done?"

"Because it is frayed there?"

20

"Exactly. This end, which we can examine, is frayed. He was cunning enough to do that with his knife. But the other end is not frayed. You could not observe that from here, but if you were on the mantelpiece you would see that it is cut clean off without any mark of fraying whatever. You can reconstruct what occurred. The man needed the rope. He would not tear it down for fear of giving the alarm by ringing the bell. What did he do? He sprang up on the mantelpiece, could not quite reach it, put his knee on the bracket—you will see the impression in the dust—and so got his knife to bear upon the cord. I could not reach the place by at least three inches—from which I infer that he is at least three inches a bigger man than I. Look at that mark upon the seat of the oaken chair! What is it?"

"Blood."

"Undoubtedly it is blood. This alone puts the lady's story out of court. If she were seated on the chair when the crime was done, how comes that mark? No, no, she was placed in the chair *after* the death of her husband. I'll wager that the black dress shows a corresponding mark to this. We have not yet met our Waterloo, Watson, but this is our Marengo, for it begins in defeat and ends in victory. I should like now to have a few words with the nurse, Theresa. We must be wary for a while, if we are to get the information which we want."

She was an interesting person, this stern Australian nurse—taciturn, suspicious, ungracious, it took some time before Holmes's pleasant manner and frank acceptance of all that she said thawed her into a corresponding amiability. She did not attempt to conceal her hatred for her late employer.

"Yes, sir, it is true that he threw the decanter at me. I heard him call my mistress a name, and I told him that he would not dare to speak so if her brother had been there. Then it was that he threw it at me. He might have thrown a dozen if he had but left my bonny bird alone. He was forever ill-treating her, and she too proud to complain. She will not even tell me all that he has done to her. She never told me of those marks on her arm that you saw this morning, but I know very well that they come from a stab with a hatpin. The sly devil—God forgive me that I should speak of him so, now that he is dead! But a devil he was, if ever one walked the earth. He was all honey when first we met him—only eighteen months ago, and we both feel as if it were eighteen years. She had only just arrived in London. Yes, it was her first voyage—she had never been from home before. He won her with his title and his money and his false London ways. If she made a mistake she has paid for it, if ever a woman did. What month did we meet him? Well, I tell you it was just after we arrived. We arrived in June, and it was July. They were married in January of last year. Yes, she is down in the morning-room again, and I have no doubt she will see you, but you must not ask too much of her, for she has gone through all that flesh and blood will stand."

Lady Brackenstall was reclining on the same couch, but looked brighter than before. The maid

22

had entered with us, and began once more to foment the bruise upon her mistress's brow.

"I hope," said the lady, "that you have not come to cross-examine me again?"

"No," Holmes answered, in his gentlest voice, "I will not cause you any unnecessary trouble, Lady Brackenstall, and my whole desire is to make things easy for you, for I am convinced that you are a much-tried woman. If you will treat me as a friend and trust me, you may find that I will justify your trust."

"What do you want me to do?"

"To tell me the truth."

"Mr. Holmes!"

"No, no, Lady Brackenstall—it is no use. You may have heard of any little reputation which I possess. I will stake it all on the fact that your story is an absolute fabrication."

Mistress and maid were both staring at Holmes with pale faces and frightened eyes.

"You are an impudent fellow!" cried Theresa. "Do you mean to say that my mistress has told a lie?"

Holmes rose from his chair.

"Have you nothing to tell me?"

"I have told you everything."

"Think once more, Lady Brackenstall. Would it not be better to be frank?"

For an instant there was hesitation in her beautiful face. Then some new strong thought caused it to set like a mask.

"I have told you all I know."

Holmes took his hat and shrugged his shoulders. "I am sorry," he said, and without another word we left the room and the house. There was a pond in the park, and to this my friend led the way. It was frozen over, but a single hole was left for the convenience of a solitary swan. Holmes gazed at it, and then passed on to the lodge gate. There he scribbled a short note for Stanley Hopkins, and left it with the lodge-keeper.

"It may be a hit, or it may be a miss, but we are bound to do something for friend Hopkins, just to justify this second visit," said he. "I will not quite take him into my confidence yet. I think our next scene of operations must be the shipping office of the Adelaide-Southampton line, which stands at the end of Pall Mall, if I remember right. There is a second line of steamers which connect South Australia with England, but we will draw the larger cover first."

Holmes's card sent in to the manager ensured instant attention, and he was not long in acquiring all the information he needed. In June of '95, only one of their line had reached a home port. It was the *Rock of Gibraltar*, their largest and best boat. A reference to the passenger list showed that Miss Fraser, of Adelaide, with her maid had made the voyage in her. The boat was now somewhere south of the Suez Canal on her way to Australia. Her officers were the same as in '95, with one exception. The first officer, Mr. Jack Crocker, had been made a captain and was to take charge of their new ship, the *Bass Rock*, sailing in two days' time from Southampton. He lived at Sydenham, but he was likely to be in that morning for instructions, if we cared to wait for him.

No, Mr. Holmes had no desire to see him, but

would be glad to know more about his record and character.

His record was magnificent. There was not an officer in the fleet to touch him. As to his character, he was reliable on duty, but a wild, desperate fellow off the deck of his ship—hot-headed, excitable, but loyal, honest, and kind-hearted. That was the pith of the information with which Holmes left the office of the Adelaide-Southampton company. Thence he drove to Scotland Yard, but, instead of entering, he sat in his cab with his brows drawn down, lost in profound thought. Finally he drove round to the Charing Cross telegraph office, sent off a message, and then, at last, we made for Baker Street once more.

"No, I couldn't do it, Watson," said he, as we reëntered our room. "Once that warrant was made out, nothing on earth would save him. Once or twice in my career I feel that I have done more real harm by my discovery of the criminal than ever he had done by his crime. I have learned caution now, and I had rather play tricks with the law of England than with my own conscience. Let us know a little more before we act."

Before evening, we had a visit from Inspector Stanley Hopkins. Things were not going very well with him.

"I believe that you are a wizard, Mr. Holmes. I really do sometimes think that you have powers that are not human. Now, how on earth could you know that the stolen silver was at the bottom of that pond?"

"I didn't know it."

"But you told me to examine it."

"You got it, then?"

"Yes, I got it."

"I am very glad if I have helped you."

"But you haven't helped me. You have made the affair far more difficult. What sort of burglars are they who steal silver and then throw it into the nearest pond?"

"It was certainly rather eccentric behaviour. I was merely going on the idea that if the silver had been taken by persons who did not want it—who merely took it for a blind, as it were—then they would naturally be anxious to get rid of it."

"But why should such an idea cross your mind?"

"Well, I thought it was possible. When they came out through the French window, there was the pond with one tempting little hole in the ice, right in front of their noses. Could there be a better hiding-place?"

"Ah, a hiding-place—that is better!" cried Stanley Hopkins. "Yes, yes, I see it all now! It was early, there were folk upon the roads, they were afraid of being seen with the silver, so they sank it in the pond, intending to return for it when the coast was clear. Excellent, Mr. Holmes—that is better than your idea of a blind."

"Quite so, you have got an admirable theory. I have no doubt that my own ideas were quite wild, but you must admit that they have ended in discovering the silver."

"Yes, sir—yes. It was all your doing. But I have had a bad setback."

"A setback?"

"Yes, Mr. Holmes. The Randall gang were arrested in New York this morning."

"Dear me, Hopkins! That is certainly rather against your theory that they committed a murder in Kent last night."

"It is fatal, Mr. Holmes—absolutely fatal. Still, there are other gangs of three besides the Randalls, or it may be some new gang of which the police have never heard."

"Quite so, it is perfectly possible. What, are you off?"

"Yes, Mr. Holmes, there is no rest for me until I have got to the bottom of the business. I suppose you have no hint to give me?"

"I have given you one."

"Which?"

"Well, I suggested a blind."

"But why, Mr. Holmes, why?"

"Ah, that's the question, of course. But I commend the idea to your mind. You might possibly find that there was something in it. You won't stop for dinner? Well, good-bye, and let us know how you get on."

Dinner was over, and the table cleared before Holmes alluded to the matter again. He had lit his pipe and held his slippered feet to the cheerful blaze of the fire. Suddenly he looked at his watch.

"I expect developments, Watson."

"When?"

"Now—within a few minutes. I dare say you thought I acted rather badly to Stanley Hopkins just now?"

"I trust your judgement."

"A very sensible reply, Watson. You must look

at it this way: what I know is unofficial, what he knows is official. I have the right to private judgement, but he has none. He must disclose all, or he is a traitor to his service. In a doubtful case I would not put him in so painful a position, and so I reserve my information until my own mind is clear upon the matter."

"But when will that be?"

"The time has come. You will now be present at the last scene of a remarkable little drama."

There was a sound upon the stairs, and our door was opened to admit as fine a specimen of manhood as ever passed through it. He was a very tall young man, golden-moustached, blue-eyed, with a skin which had been burned by tropical suns, and a springy step, which showed that the huge frame was as active as it was strong. He closed the door behind him, and then he stood with clenched hands and heaving breast, choking down some overmastering emotion.

"Sit down, Captain Crocker. You got my telegram?"

Our visitor sank into an armchair and looked from one to the other of us with questioning eyes.

"I got your telegram, and I came at the hour you said. I heard that you had been down to the office. There was no getting away from you. Let's hear the worst. What are you going to do with me? Arrest me? Speak out, man! You can't sit there and play with me like a cat with a mouse."

"Give him a cigar," said Holmes. "Bite on that, Captain Crocker, and don't let your nerves run away with you. I should not sit here smoking with you if I thought that you were a common criminal, you may be sure of that. Be frank with me and we may do some good. Play tricks with me, and I'll crush you."

"What do you wish me to do?"

"To give me a true account of all that happened at the Abbey Grange last night—a *true* account, mind you, with nothing added and nothing taken off. I know so much already that if you go one inch off the straight, I'll blow this police whistle from my window and the affair goes out of my hands forever."

The sailor thought for a little. Then he struck his leg with his great sunburned hand.

"I'll chance it," he cried. "I believe you are a man of your word, and a white man, and I'll tell you the whole story. But one thing I will say first. So far as I am concerned, I regret nothing and I fear nothing, and I would do it all again and be proud of the job. Damn the beast, if he had as many lives as a cat, he would owe them all to me! But it's the lady, Mary—Mary Fraser—for never will I call her by that accursed name. When I think of getting her into trouble, I who would give my life just to bring one smile to her dear face, it's that that turns my soul into water. And yet—and yet—what less could I do? I'll tell you my story, gentlemen, and then I'll ask you, as man to man, what less could I do?

"I must go back a bit. You seem to know everything, so I expect that you know that I met her when she was a passenger and I was first officer of the *Rock of Gibraltar*. From the first day I met her, she was the only woman for me. Every day of that voyage I loved her more, and many a time

29

since have I kneeled down in the darkness of the night watch and kissed the deck of that ship because I knew her dear feet had trod it. She was never engaged to me. She treated me as fairly as ever a woman treated a man. I have no complaint to make. It was all love on my side, and all good comradeship and friendship on hers. When we parted she was a free woman, but I could never again be a free man.

"Next time I came back from sea, I heard of her marriage. Well, why shouldn't she marry whom she liked? Title and money—who could carry them better than she? She was born for all that is beautiful and dainty. I didn't grieve over her marriage. I was not such a selfish hound as that. I just rejoiced that good luck had come her way, and that she had not thrown herself away on a penniless sailor. That's how I loved Mary Fraser.

"Well, I never thought to see her again, but last voyage I was promoted, and the new boat was not yet launched, so I had to wait for a couple of months with my people at Sydenham. One day out in a country lane I met Theresa Wright, her old maid. She told me all about her, about him, about everything. I tell you, gentlemen, it nearly drove me mad. This drunken hound, that he should dare to raise his hand to her, whose boots he was not worthy to lick! I met Theresa again. Then I met Mary herself—and met her again. Then she would meet me no more. But the other day I had a notice that I was to start on my voyage within a week, and I determined that I would see her once before I left. Theresa was always my friend, for she loved Mary and hated this villain

30

almost as much as I did. From her I learned the ways of the house. Mary used to sit up reading in her own little room downstairs. I crept round there last night and scratched at the window. At first she would not open to me, but in her heart I know that now she loves me, and she could not leave me in the frosty night. She whispered to me to come round to the big front window, and I found it open before me, so as to let me into the dining-room. Again I heard from her own lips things that made my blood boil, and again I cursed this brute who mishandled the woman I loved. Well, gentle-men, I was standing with her just inside the win-dow, in all innocence, as God is my judge, when he rushed like a madman into the room, called her the vilest name that a man could use to a woman, and welted her across the face with the stick he had in his hand. I had sprung for the poker, and it was a fair fight between us. See here, on my arm, where his first blow fell. Then it was my turn, and I went through him as if he had been a rotten pumpkin. Do you think I was sorry? Not I! It was his life or mine, but far more than that, it was his life or hers, for how could I leave her in the power of this madman? That was how I killed him. Was I wrong? Well, then, what would either of you gentlemen have done, if you had been in my position?

"She had screamed when he struck her, and that brought old Theresa down from the room above. There was a bottle of wine on the side-board, and I opened it and poured a little between Mary's lips, for she was half dead with shock. Then I took a drop myself. Theresa was as cool as ice, and it was her plot as much as mine. We must make it appear that burglars had done the thing. Theresa kept on repeating our story to her mistress, while I swarmed up and cut the rope of the bell. Then I lashed her in her chair, and frayed out the end of the rope to make it look natural, else they would wonder how in the world a burglar could have got up there to cut it. Then I gathered up a few plates and pots of silver, to carry out the idea of the robbery, and there I left them, with orders to give the alarm when I had a quarter of an hour's start. I dropped the silver into the pond, and made off for Sydenham, feeling that for once in my life I had done a real good night's work. And that's the truth and the whole truth, Mr. Holmes, if it costs me my neck."

Holmes smoked for some time in silence. Then he crossed the room, and shook our visitor by the hand.

"That's what I think," said he. "I know that every word is true, for you have hardly said a word which I did not know. No one but an acrobat or a sailor could have got up to that bell-rope from the bracket, and no one but a sailor could have made the knots with which the cord was fastened to the chair. Only once had this lady been brought into contact with sailors, and that was on her voyage, and it was someone of her own class of life, since she was trying hard to shield him, and so showing that she loved him. You see how easy it was for me to lay my hands upon you when once I had started upon the right trail."

"I thought the police never could have seen through our dodge."

"And the police haven't, nor will they, to the best of my belief. Now, look here, Captain Crocker, this is a very serious matter, though I am willing to admit that you acted under the most extreme provocation to which any man could be subjected. I am not sure that in defence of your own life your action will not be pronounced legitimate. However, that is for a British jury to decide. Meanwhile I have so much sympathy for you that, if you choose to disappear in the next twenty-four hours, I will promise you that no one will hinder you."

"And then it will all come out?"

"Certainly it will come out."

The sailor flushed with anger.

"What sort of proposal is that to make a man? I know enough of law to understand that Mary would be held as accomplice. Do you think I would leave her alone to face the music while I slunk away? No, sir, let them do their worst upon me, but for heaven's sake, Mr. Holmes, find some way of keeping my poor Mary out of the courts."

Holmes for a second time held out his hand to the sailor.

"I was only testing you, and you ring true every time. Well, it is a great responsibility that I take upon myself, but I have given Hopkins an excellent hint, and if he can't avail himself of it I can do no more. See here, Captain Crocker, we'll do this in due form of law. You are the prisoner. Watson, you are a British jury, and I never met a man who was more eminently fitted to represent one. I am the judge. Now, gentlemen of the jury, you have heard the evidence. Do you find the prisoner guilty or not guilty?"

"Not guilty, my lord," said I.

"Vox populi, vox Dei. You are acquitted, Captain Crocker. So long as the law does not find some other victim you are safe from me. Come back to this lady in a year, and may her future and yours justify us in the judgement which we have pronounced this night!"

Wilkie Collins
(1824–1889)
A MARRIAGE TRAGEDY

A fellow novelist and close friend of Charles Dickens, Wilkie Collins is the man who transformed Victorian melodrama into detective fiction. A later fancier of the art, T.S. Eliot, described Collins's The Moonstone *(1868) as "the first, longest, and best of modern English detective novels." It wasn't, strictly speaking, but the sentiment will do. Other significant works include* The Woman in White *(1860) and the oft-collected tale "A Terribly Strange Bed." The tale in hand first appeared in* Harper's Magazine *in October 1858 and includes—appropriately—a detective, Mr. Dark, and the auspicious setting of Darrock Hall.*

Chapter I

It rained all Monday, all Tuesday, all Wednesday, all Thursday. My tutor, who never went out if he could possibly help it, and who cared for nothing so long as he had his books with him, was proof against the miserable weather, and was not even polite enough to agree with me when I complained of it. I, who was reading with him for my college examination, found my spirits so seriously affected by the incessant rain that I resolved, unless the sky cleared at the end of the week, to propose that we should depart forthwith from the little Cumberland watering-place which we had unfortunately selected as the place of our temporary abode.

Friday came. The morning began with some gleams of watery sunshine; but toward noon the clouds gathered again, and down came the rain as persistently as ever, just as I had made up my mind to take a holiday, and had got my hat on to go out. In sheer desperation I resolved to adhere to my original intention, let it rain as it might. Leaving my tutor with his eternal books on one side of him, and his eternal snuff-box on the other, I descended to the ground-floor of the inn at which we were staying, and sent for the landlord.

"I have been waiting for the weather, in this horrible climate of yours, four whole days," I said, "and I mean to wait no longer. Get me a horse, or a gig, or any conveyance you possess, and tell me where I am to go to get rid of the sight of that waste of drab-colored sand in front of the window, and of that changeless strip of dreary gray sea beyond it."

The landlord—a very intelligent and very good-humored old man—laughed, and said that he had a gig and horse at my disposal, if I was really determined to take a drive in the rain.

"Order the gig," I answered, "and tell me which direction I am to take. Are there no sights in the neighborhood?"

"No, Sir," was the unpromising reply. "No sights that I know of."

"What! no old house any where inland!" I exclaimed. "No great family seat in this part of the country that strangers are allowed to see!"

The landlord's face changed a little, I thought. He looked away from me, and his hand trifled rather uneasily with the curtain of the parlor-window at which we were standing.

"The only family house in these parts," he said, "is Darrock Hall. And that has been an empty house for some years now."

"A fine, ruinous, dreary old place, no doubt?" I said. "Just the sort of house I should like to see. Order the gig, and send somebody with me to show me the way to Darrock Hall."

"You would only be disappointed when you got there, Sir," said the landlord, shaking his head gloomily. "It's neither a fine place nor an old place. Darrock Hall is nothing but a square stone house, and it wasn't standing a hundred years ago. So far from the place being at all ruinous, it is now being altered and put into thorough repair. They say there's a new lead mine been discovered near; and a strange gentleman—one of the sort they call speculators in London—has taken the Hall, and means to work the mine right down under it, as I am told."

"Well," I said, "if there is nothing to see at the Hall, I can look at the mine. I must drive somewhere, and I may just as well go there as any where else in this rain. How far off is it?"

"Nigh on eleven miles," said the landlord. "The road goes round about so that no stranger could find it, and the last three miles are all up hill."

"Is there nobody who could go with me in the capacity of guide?" I asked.

"Nobody who can be spared just now," replied the landlord, "unless it's myself. And I—" He stopped, and looked at me doubtfully.

"And you," I rejoined, finishing the sentence for him, "are not quite young enough to risk getting wet through with impunity?"

"No," he said. "It's not that. People who live in Cumberland don't mind rain. I'll go in the gig, if you specially wish it. But, to be plain with you, Sir, there isn't a place in the neighborhood I wouldn't sooner drive you to than Darrock Hall."

"Indeed! May I ask why?"

"Well, Sir, when I was a young man I lived in service at that house; and certain things happened there which have made the sight of the place, since that time, not over-pleasant to my eyes. It was a frightful business, Sir; and I was mixed up in it."

These words made me naturally anxious to know what had happened at the mysterious family mansion. I abstained from giving any expression to my feeling of curiosity; but I suppose my face must have betrayed me, for the landlord pursued the subject of his own accord.

"You mustn't suppose it is any thing I have reason to be ashamed of," he said. "So far as I am concerned, I came out of the matter with all possible credit and advantage to myself. If that same miserable business hadn't happened at the Hall, I doubt whether I should ever have had the money to take this inn."

"Do you mind telling me about it?" I asked.

38

"That is to say, if the circumstances are of a nature to be communicated to a stranger?"

"They could not be kept a secret at the time," said the landlord; "and there is no need to keep them a secret now—for none of the people who were concerned in the affair are left alive excepting me and one other person living in London. But it is rather a long story, Sir."

"I shall not think any the worse of it on that account," said I. "Tell me all about it, and I will put off the drive in the gig, and give up my visit to Darrock Hall."

The landlord placed a chair for me and took one for himself, apparently very much relieved by the assurance that my last words had conveyed to him. After the usual prefatory phrases of apology for his own defects as a narrator, he began his story, which I shall repeat here, as nearly as possible, in his own words.

The first place I got, when I began life by going out to service, was not a very profitable one. I certainly gained the advantage of learning my business thoroughly, but I never had my due in the matter of wages. My master was made a bankrupt, and his servants suffered with the rest of his creditors.

My second situation, however, amply compensated me for my want of luck in the first. I had the good fortune to enter the service of Mr. and Mrs. Norcross, in which I remained till I changed my station in life, and took this inn. My master was a very rich gentleman. He had the Darrock house and lands in this county, a fine estate also in Yorkshire, and a very large property in Jamaica, which produced, at that time and for some years afterward, a great income. Out in the West Indies he met with a pretty young lady, a governess in an English family, and, taking a violent fancy to her, married her, though she was a good five-and-twenty years younger than himself. After the wedding they came to live in England; and it was at this time that I was lucky enough to be engaged by them as a servant.

I lived with my new master and mistress three years. They had no children. At the end of that period Mr. Norcross died. He was sharp enough to foresee that his young widow would, most likely, marry again; and he bequeathed his property so that it all went to Mrs. Norcross first, and then to any children she might have by a second marriage, and, failing that, to relations and friends of his own. I did not suffer by my master's death, for his widow kept me in her service. I had attended on Mr. Norcross all through his last illness, and had made myself useful enough to win my mistress's favor and gratitude. Besides me she also retained her maid in her service—a French woman named Josephine. Even at that time I disliked the foreigner's wheedling manners, and her cruel, cunning face, and wondered how my mistress could be so fond of her as she was. Time showed that I was right in distrusting this woman. I shall have much more to say about her when I get further advanced with my story.

Meanwhile I have next to relate that my mistress broke up the rest of her establishment, and, taking me and the lady's maid with her, went to travel on the Continent. Among other wonderful places, we visited Paris, Genoa, Venice, Florence, Rome, and Naples, staying in some of those cities for months together. The fame of my mistress's riches followed her wherever she went; and there were plenty of gentlemen, foreigners as well as Englishmen, who were anxious enough to get into her good graces and to prevail on her to marry them. Nobody succeeded, however, in producing any very strong or lasting impression on her; and when we came back to England, after more than two years of absence, Mrs. Norcross was still a widow, and showed no signs of wanting to alter her condition.

We went to the house on the Yorkshire estate first; but my mistress did not fancy some of the company round about, so we moved again to Darrock Hall, and made excursions from time to time in the lake district, some miles off. On one of these trips Mrs. Norcross met with some old friends, who introduced her to a gentleman of their party bearing the very common, uninteresting name of Mr. James Smith. He was a tall, fine young man enough, with black hair, which grew very long, and the biggest, bushiest pair of black whiskers I ever saw. Altogether he had a rakish, unsettled look, and a bounceable way of talking which made him the prominent person in company. He was poor enough himself, as I heard from his servant, but well connected—a gentleman by birth and education, though his manners were so free. What my mistress saw to like in him I don't know; but when she asked her friends to stay with her at Darrock, she included Mr. James Smith in the invitation. We had a fine, gay, noisy time of it at the Hall—the strange gentleman, in particular, making himself as much at home as if the place belonged to him. I was surprised at Mrs. Norcross putting up with him as she did; but I was fairly thunderstruck, some months afterward, when I heard that she and Mr. James Smith were actually going to be married! She had refused offers by the dozens abroad, from higher, and richer, and better-behaved men. It seemed next to impossible that she could seriously think of throwing herself away upon such a hare-brained, headlong, penniless young gentleman as Mr. James Smith.

Married, nevertheless, they were, in due course of time; and, after spending the honeymoon abroad, they came back to Darrock Hall. I soon found that my new master had a very variable temper. There were some days when he was as easy and familiar and pleasant with his servants as any gentleman could be. At other times some devil within him seemed to get possession of his whole nature. He flew into violent passions, and took wrong ideas into his head, which no reasoning or remonstrance could remove. It rather amazed me, considering how gay he was in his tastes, and how restless his habits were, that he should consent to live at such a quiet, dull place as Darrock. The reason for this, however, soon came out. Mr. James Smith was not much of a sportsman; he cared nothing for in-door amusements, such as reading, music, and so forth; and he had no ambition for representing the county in Parliament. The one pursuit that he was really fond of was—yachting. Darrock was within sixteen miles of a seaport town, with an excellent harbor; and to this accident of position the Hall was entirely indebted for recommending itself as a place of residence to Mr. James Smith.

He had such an untiring enjoyment and delight in cruising about at sea, and all his ideas of pleasure seemed to be so closely connected with his remembrances of the sailing trips he had taken on board different yachts belonging to his friends, that I verily believe his chief object in marrying my mistress was to get the command of money enough to keep a vessel for himself. Be that as it may, it is certain that he prevailed on her, some time after their marriage, to make him a present of a fine schooner yacht, which was brought round from Cowes to our coast-town here, and kept always waiting ready for him in the harbor. His wife required some little persuasion before she could make up her mind to let him have the vessel. She suffered so much from sea-sickness, that pleasure-sailing was out of the question for her; and, being very fond of her husband, she was naturally unwilling that he should engage in an amusement which took him away from her. However, Mr. James Smith used his influence over her cleverly, promising that he would never go away without first asking her leave, and engaging that his terms of absence at sea should never last for more than a week or ten days at a time. Accordingly, my mistress, who was the kindest and most unselfish woman in the world, put her own feelings aside, and made her husband happy in the possession of a vessel of his own.

While my master was away cruising my mistress

had a dull time of it at the Hall. The few gentle-folks there were in our part of the county lived at a distance, and could only come to Darrock when they were asked to stay there for some days to-gether. As for the village near us, there was but one person living in it whom my mistress could think of asking to the Hall; and this person was the clergyman who did duty at the church, one Mr. Meeke. He was a single man, very young, and very lonely in his position. He had a mild, melancholy, pasty-looking face, and was as shy and soft-spoken as a little girl—altogether, what one may call, without being unjust or severe, a poor, weak creature, and, out of all sight, the very worst preacher I ever sat under in my life. The one thing he did, which, as I heard, he could really do well, was playing on the fiddle. He was un-commonly fond of music—so much so that he often took his instrument out with him when he went for a walk. This taste of his was his great recommendation to my mistress, who was a won-derfully fine player on the piano, and who was delighted to get such a performer as Mr. Meeke to play duets with her. Besides liking his society for this reason, she felt for him in his lonely po-sition, naturally enough, I think, considering how often she was left in solitude herself. Mr. Meeke, on his side, when he got over his first shyness, was only too glad to leave his lonesome little par-sonage for the fine music-room at the Hall, and for the company of a handsome, kind-hearted lady, who made much of him and admired his fiddle-playing with all her heart. Thus it happened that, whenever my master was away at sea, my mistress and Mr. Meeke were always together, playing duets as if they had their living to get by it. A more harmless connection than the connection between those two never existed in this world; and yet, innocent as it was, it turned out to be the first cause of all the misfortunes that afterward happened.

My master's treatment of Mr. Meeke was, from the first, the very opposite of my mistress's. The restless, rackety, bounceable Mr. James Smith felt a contempt for the weak, womanish, fiddling little parson; and, what was more, did not care to conceal it. For this reason Mr. Meeke (who was dreadfully frightened by my master's violent language and rough ways) very seldom visited at the Hall, except when my mistress was alone there. Meaning no wrong, and therefore stooping to no concealment, she never thought of taking any measures to keep Mr. Meeke out of the way when he happened to be with her at the time of her husband's coming home, whether it was only from a riding-excursion in the neighborhood or from a cruise in the schooner. In this way it so turned out that whenever my master came home, after a long or short absence, in nine cases out of ten he found the parson at the Hall. At first he used to laugh at this circumstance, and to amuse himself with some rather coarse jokes at the expense of his wife and her companion. But, after a while, his variable temper changed, as usual. He grew sulky, rude, angry, and, at last, downright jealous of Mr. Meeke. Though too proud to confess it in so many words, he still showed the state of his mind clearly enough to my mistress to excite her indignation. She was a woman who could be led any where by any one for whom she had a regard; but there was a firm spirit within her that rose at the slightest show of injustice or oppression, and that resented tyrannical usage of any sort perhaps a little too warmly. The bare suspicion that her husband could feel any distrust of her set her all in a flame, and she took the most unfortunate, and yet, at the same time, the most natural way, for a woman, of resenting it. The ruder her husband was to Mr. Meeke, the more kindly she behaved to him. This led to serious disputes and dissensions, and thence, in time, to a violent quarrel. I could not avoid hearing the last part of the altercation between them, for it took place on the garden-walk, outside the dining-room window, while I was occupied in laying the table for lunch.

Without repeating their words—which I have no right to do, having heard by accident what I had no business to hear—I may say generally, to show how serious the quarrel was, that my mistress upbraided my master with having married from mercenary motives; with keeping out of her company as much as he could; and with insulting her by a suspicion which it would be hard ever to forgive, and impossible ever to forget. He replied by violent language directed against herself, and by commanding her, in a very overbearing way, never to open the doors of the house again to Mr. Meeke. She, on her side, declared, in great anger, that she would never consent to insult a clergyman and a gentleman in order to satisfy the whim of a tyrannical husband. Upon that he called out, with a great oath, to have his horse saddled directly, declaring that he would not stop another instant under the same roof with a woman who had set him at defiance; and warning his wife that he would have her watched in his absence, and would come back, if Mr. Meeke entered the house again, and horsewhip him, in spite of his black coat, all through the village. With those words he left her, and rode away to the sea-port where his yacht was lying. My mistress kept up her spirit till he was out of sight, and then burst into a dreadful scream-ing passion of tears, which ended by leaving her so weak that she had to be carried to her bed like a woman who was at the point of death.

The same evening my master's horse was ridden back by a messenger, who brought a scrap of note-paper with him, addressed to me. It only con-tained these lines: "Pack up my clothes, and deliver them immediately to the bearer. You may tell your mistress that I sail to-night, at eleven o'clock, for a cruise to Sweden. Forward my let-ters to the Post-office, Stockholm."

I obeyed the orders given to me, except that relating to my mistress. The doctor had been sent for, and was still in the house. I consulted him upon the propriety of my delivering the message. He positively forbade me to do so, that night; and told me to give him the slip of paper, and leave it to his discretion to show it to her, or not, the next morning.

The messenger had hardly been gone an hour when Mr. Meeke's housekeeper came to the Hall with a roll of music for my mistress. I told the woman of my master's sudden departure, and of the doctor being in the house. This news brought

Mr. Meeke himself to the Hall in a great flutter. I felt so angry with him for being the cause— innocent as he might be—of the shocking scene which had taken place, that I exceeded the bounds of my duty, and told him the whole truth. The poor, weak, wavering, childish creature flushed up red in the face, then turned as pale as ashes, and dropped into one of the hall chairs, crying— literally crying fit to break his heart! "Oh, William!" says he, wringing his little frail, trembling, white hands, as helpless as a baby. "Oh, William! what am I to do?"

"As you ask me that question, Sir," says I, "you will excuse me, I hope, if, being a servant, I plainly speak my mind notwithstanding. I know my station well enough to be aware that, strictly speaking, I have done wrong, and far exceeded my duty, in telling you as much as I have told you already. But I would go through fire and water, Sir," says I, feeling my own eyes getting moist, "for my mistress's sake. She has no relation here who can speak to you; and it is even better than a servant like me should risk being guilty of an impertinence, than that dreadful and lasting mischief should arise from the right remedy not being applied at the right time. This is what I should do, Sir, in your place. Saving your presence, I should leave off crying, and go back home and write to Mr. James Smith, saying that I would not, as a clergyman, give him railing for railing, but would prove how unworthily he had suspected me by ceasing to visit at the Hall from this time forth, rather than be a cause of dissension between man and wife. If you will put that into proper language,

Sir, and will have the letter ready for me in half an hour's time, I will call for it on the fastest horse in our stables, and, at my own risk, will give it to my master before he sails to-night. I have nothing more to say, Sir, except to ask your pardon for forgetting my proper place, and for making bold to speak on a very serious matter as equal to equal, and as man to man."

To do Mr. Meeke justice, he had a heart, though it was a very small one. He shook hands with me, and said he accepted my advice as the advice of a friend; and so went back to his parsonage to write the letter. In half an hour I called for it on horse-back, but it was not ready for me. Mr. Meeke was ridiculously nice about how he should express himself when he got a pen into his hand. I found him with his desk littered with rough copies, in a perfect agony about how to turn his phrases delicately enough in referring to my mistress. Every minute being precious, I hurried him as much as I could, without standing on any ceremony. It took half an hour more, with all my efforts, before he could make up his mind that the letter would do. I started off with it at a gallop, and never drew rein till I got to the sea-port town. The harbor-clock chimed the quarter past eleven as I rode by it, and when I got down to the jetty there was no yacht to be seen. She had been cast off from her moorings ten minutes before eleven, and as the clock struck she had sailed out of the harbor. I would have followed in a boat, but it was a fine starlight night, with a fresh wind blowing; and the sailors on the pier laughed at me when I spoke of rowing after a schooner-yacht which had got a quarter of an hour's start on us, with the wind abeam and the tide in her favor.

I rode back with a heavy heart. All I could do now was to send the letter to the Post-office, Stockholm.

The next day the doctor showed my mistress the scrap of paper with the message on it from my master; and an hour or two after that, a letter was sent to her in Mr. Meeke's handwriting, explaining the reason why she must not expect to see him any more at the Hall, and referring to me in terms of high praise, as a sensible and faithful man who had spoken the right word at the right time. I am able to repeat the substance of the letter, because I heard all about it from my mistress, under very unpleasant circumstances so far as I was concerned. The news of my master's departure did not affect her as the doctor had supposed it would. Instead of distressing her, it roused her spirit, and made her angry; her pride, as I imagine, being wounded by the contemptuous manner in which her husband had notified his intention of sailing to Sweden, at the end of a message to a servant about packing his clothes. Finding her in that temper of mind, the letter from Mr. Meeke only irritated her the more. She insisted on getting up, and as soon as she was dressed and down stairs, she vented her violent humor on me, reproaching me for impertinent interference in the affairs of my betters, and declaring that she had almost made up her mind to turn me out of my place for it. I did not defend myself, because I respected her sorrows and the irritation that came from them; also, because I knew the natural kindness of her nature well enough to be assured that she would make amends to me for her harshness the moment her mind was composed again. The result showed that I was right. That same evening she sent for me, and begged me to forgive and forget the hasty words she had spoken in the morning, with a grace and sweetness that would have won the heart of any man who listened to her.

Weeks passed after this, till it was more than a month since the day of my master's departure, and no letter in his handwriting came to Darrock Hall. My mistress, taking this treatment of her more angrily than sorrowfully, went to London to consult her nearest relations, who lived there. On leaving home she stopped the carriage at the parsonage, and went in (as I thought, rather defiantly) to say good-by to Mr. Meeke. She had answered his letter, had received others from him, and had answered them likewise. She had also, of course, seen him every Sunday at church, and had always stopped to speak to him after the service. But this was the first occasion on which she had visited him at his house. As the carriage stopped, the little parson came out, in great hurry and agitation, to meet her at the garden-gate.

"Don't look alarmed, Mr. Meeke," says my mistress, getting out. "Though you have engaged not to come near the Hall, I have made no promise to keep away from the parsonage." With those words she went into the house.

The French maid, Josephine, was sitting with me in the rumble of the carriage, and I saw a wicked smile on her face as the parson and his visitor went into the house together. Harmless as

Mr. Meeke was, and innocent of all wrong as I knew my mistress to be, I regretted that she would be so rash as to despise appearances, considering the situation she was placed in. She had already exposed herself to be thought of disrespectfully by her own maid; and it was hard to say what worse consequences might not happen after that.

Half an hour later we were away on our journey. My mistress staid in London two months. Throughout all that time no letter from my master was forwarded to her from the country-house.

When the two months had passed we returned to Darrock Hall. Nobody there had received any news in our absence of the whereabouts of my master and his yacht.

Six more weary weeks elapsed; and in that time but one event happened at the Hall to vary the dismal monotony of the lives we now led in the solitary place. One morning the French maid, Josephine, came down after dressing my mistress, with her face as pale as ashes, except on one cheek, where there was a mark as red as burning fire. I was in the kitchen at the time, and I asked what was the matter.

"The matter!" says she, in her shrill broken English. "Advance a little, if you please, and look with all your eyes at this cheek of mine. What! have you lived so long a time with your mistress, and don't you know the mark of her hand yet!"

I was at a loss to understand what she meant, but she soon explained herself. My mistress, whose temper had been sadly altered for the worse by the trials and the humiliations she had gone through, had got up that morning more out of humor than usual; and in answer to her maid's inquiry as to how she had passed the night, had begun talking about her weary, miserable life in an unusually fretful and desperate way. Josephine, in trying to cheer her spirits, had ventured, most improperly, on making a light, jesting reference to Mr. Meeke, which had so enraged my mistress that she turned round sharp on the foreigner, and gave her—to use the common phrase—a smart box on the ear. Josephine confessed that the moment after she had done this, her better sense appeared to tell her that she had taken a most improper way of resenting undue familiarity. She had immediately expressed her regret for having forgotten herself, and had proved the sincerity of it by a gift of half a dozen cambric handkerchiefs, presented as a peace-offering on the spot. After that, I thought it impossible that Josephine could bear any malice against a mistress whom she had served ever since she had been a girl, and I said as much to her when she had done telling me what had happened up stairs.

"I! Malice!" cries Miss Josephine, in her hard, sharp, snappish way. "And why, and wherefore, if you please? If my mistress smacks my cheek with one hand she gives me handkerchiefs to wipe it with the other. My good mistress, my kind mistress, my pretty mistress! I, the servant, bear malice against her, the mistress! Ah, you bad man, even to think of such a thing! Ah, fie, fie! I am quite ashamed of you!"

She gave me one look—the wickedest look I ever saw—and burst out laughing—the harshest laugh I ever heard from a woman's lips. Turning away from me directly after, she said no more, and never referred to the subject again on any subsequent occasion. From that time, however, I noticed an alteration in Miss Josephine; not in her way of doing her work, for she was just as sharp and careful about it as ever, but in her manner and habits. She grew amazingly quiet, and passed almost all her leisure time alone. I could bring no charge against her which authorized me to speak a word of warning; but, for all that, I could not help feeling that if I had been in my mistress's place I would have followed up that present of the cambric handkerchiefs by paying her a month's wages in advance, and sending her away from the house the same evening.

With the exception of this little domestic incident, which appeared trifling enough at the time, but which led to very serious consequences afterward, nothing happened at all out of the ordinary way during the six weary weeks to which I have referred. At the beginning of the seventh week, however, an event occurred at last. One morning the postman brought a letter to the Hall, addressed to my mistress. I took it up stairs, and looked at the direction as I put it on the salver. The handwriting was not my master's; was not, as it appeared to me, the handwriting of any well-educated person. The outside of the letter was also very dirty; and the seal a common office-seal of the usual lattice-work pattern. "This must be a begging-letter," I thought to myself as I entered the breakfast-room and advanced with it to my mistress.

She held up her hand before she opened it, as

a sign to me that she had some order to give, and that I was not to leave the room till I had received it. Then she broke the seal and began to read the letter. Her eyes had hardly been on it a moment before her face turned as pale as death, and the paper began to tremble in her fingers. She read on to the end, and suddenly turned from pale to scarlet, started out of her chair, crumpled the letter up violently in her hand, and took several turns backward and forward in the room, without seeming to notice me as I stood by the door. "You villain! you villain! you villain!" I heard her whisper to herself many times over, in a quick, hissing, fierce way. Then she stopped, and said on a sudden, "Can it be true?" Then she looked up, and seeing me standing at the door, started as if I had been a stranger, changed color again, and told me, in a stifled voice, to leave her and come back again in half an hour. I obeyed, feeling certain that she must have received some very bad news of her husband, and wondering, anxiously enough, what it might be. When I returned to the breakfast-room her face was as much discomposed as ever. Without speaking a word she handed me two sealed letters. One, a note to be left for Mr. Meeke, at the parsonage; the other, a letter marked "Immediate," and addressed to her lawyer in London, who was also, I should add, her nearest living relation.

I left one of these letters and posted the other. When I came back I heard that my mistress had taken to her room. She remained there for four days, keeping her new sorrow, whatever it was, strictly to herself. On the fifth day the lawyer from London arrived at the Hall. My mistress went down to him in the library, and was shut up there with him for nearly two hours. At the end of that time the bell rang for me.

"Sit down, William," said my mistress when I came into the room. "I feel such entire confidence in your fidelity and attachment that I am about, with the full concurrence of this gentlemen, who is my nearest relative and my legal advisor, to place a serious secret in your keeping, and to employ your services on a matter which is as important to me as a matter of life and death."

Her poor eyes were very red, and her lips quivered as she spoke to me. I was so startled by what she had said that I hardly knew which chair to sit in. She pointed to one placed near herself at the table, and seemed to about to speak to me again, when the lawyer interfered.

"Let me entreat you," he said, "not to agitate yourself unnecessarily. I will put this person in possesion of the facts; and if I omit anything, you shall stop me and set me right."

My mistress leaned back in her chair and covered her face with her handkerchief. The lawyer waited a moment, and then addressed himself to me.

"You are already aware," he said, "of the circumstances under which your master left this house; and you also know, I have no doubt, that no direct news of him has reached your mistress up to this time?"

I bowed to him, and said I knew of the circumstances so far.

"Do you remember," he went on, "taking a letter to your mistress, five days ago?"

"Yes, Sir," I replied; "a letter which seemed to distress and alarm her very seriously."

"I will read you *that* letter before we say any more," continued the lawyer. "I warn you beforehand that it contains a terrible charge against your master, which, however, is not attested by the writer's signature. I have already told your mistress that she must not attach too much importance to an anonymous letter; and I now tell you the same thing."

Saying that, he took up a letter from the table and read it aloud. I had a copy of it given to me afterward, which I looked at often enough to fix the contents of the letter in my memory. I can now repeat them, I think, word for word.

"Madam" (it began),—"I can not reconcile it to my conscience to leave you in total ignorance of your husband's atrocious conduct toward you. If you have ever been disposed to regret his absence, do so no longer. Hope and pray, rather, that you and he may never meet face to face again in this world. I write in great haste and in great fear of being observed. Time fails me to prepare you as you ought to be prepared for what I have now to disclose. I must tell you plainly, with much respect for you and sorrow for your misfortune, that your husband *has married another wife*. I saw the ceremony performed, unknown to him. If I could not have spoken of this infamous act as an eye-witness, I would not have spoken of it at all.

"I dare not acknowledge who I am, for I believe Mr. James Smith would stick at no crime to revent himself on me if he ever came to a knowledge of the step I am now taking, and of the means by which I got my information. Neither have I time to enter into particulars. I simply warn you of what has happened, and leave you to act on that warning as you please. You may disbelieve this letter, because it is not signed by any name. In that case, if Mr. James Smith should ever venture into your presence, I recommend you to ask him suddenly what he has done with his *new wife;* and to see if his countenance does not immediately testify that the truth has been spoken by

"Your Unknown Friend."

Poor as my opinion was of my master, I had never believed him to be capable of such villainy as this; and I could not believe it, when the lawyer had done reading the letter.

"Oh, Sir!" I said; "surely that is some base imposition? Surely it can not be true?"

"That is what I have told your mistress," he answered. "But she says, in return, that—"

"That I feel it to be true," my mistress broke in, speaking behind the handkerchief, in a faint, smothered voice.

"We need not debate the question," the lawyer went on. "Our business, now, is to prove the truth or the falsehood of this letter. That must be done at once. I have written to one of the clerks, who is accustomed to conducting delicate investigations, to come to this house without loss of time. He is to be trusted with any thing, and he will pursue the needful inquiries immediately. It is absolutely necessary, to make sure of committing no mistakes, that he should be accompanied, when he starts on his investigations, by some one who is well acquainted with Mr. James Smith's habits and personal appearance; and your mistress has fixed upon you to be that person. However well the inquiry may be managed, it will probably be attended by trouble and delay. It may necessitate a long journey, and it may involve some personal danger. Are you," said the lawyer, looking hard at me, "ready to suffer any inconvenience and to run any risk for your mistress's sake?"

"There is nothing I can do, Sir," said I, "that I will not do. I am afraid I am not clever enough to be of much use. But so far as troubles and risks are concerned, I am ready for any thing from this moment."

My mistress took the handkerchief from her face, looked at me with her eyes full of tears, and held out her hand. How I came to do it I don't know, but I stooped down and kissed the hand she offered me; feeling half startled, half ashamed at my own boldness the moment after.

"You will do, my man," said the lawyer, nodding his head. "Don't trouble yourself about the cleverness or the cunning that may be wanted. My clerk has got head enough for two. I have only one word more to say before you go down stairs again. Remember that this investigation and the cause that leads to it must be kept a profound secret. Except us three, and the clergyman here (to whom your mistress has written word of what has happened), nobody knows any thing about it. I will let my clerk into the secret, when he joins us. As soon as you and he are away from the house you may talk about it. Until then, you will close your lips on the subject."

The clerk did not keep us long waiting. He came as fast as the mail from London could bring him. I had expected, from his master's description, to see a serious, sedate man, rather sly in his looks and rather reserved in his manner. To my amazement, this practiced hand at delicate investigations was a brisk, plump, jolly little man, with a comfortable double chin, a pair of very bright black eyes, and a big bottle-nose of the true convivial red color. He wore a suit of black and a limp, dingy white cravat; took snuff perpetually out of a very large box; walked with his hands crossed behind his back; and looked, upon the whole, much more like a parson of free and easy habits than a lawyer's clerk. "How d'ye do?" says he, when I opened the door to him. "I'm the man you expect from the office in London. Just say Mr. Dark, will you? I'll sit down here till you come back; and, I say, young man, if there is such a thing as a glass of ale in the house, I don't mind committing myself so far as to say that I'll drink it."

I got him the ale before I announced him. He winked at me as he put it to his lips. "Your good health," says he. "I like you. Don't forget that the name's Dark; and just leave the jug and glass, will you, in case my master keeps me waiting."

I announced him at once, and was told to show him into the library. When I got back to the hall the jug was empty, and Mr. Dark was comforting himself with a pinch of snuff, snorting over it like a perfect grampus. He had swallowed more than a pint of the strongest old ale in the house; and, for all the effect it seemed to have had on him, he might just as well have been drinking so much water.

As I led him along the passage to the library Josephine, the French maid, passed us. Mr. Dark winked at me again, and made her a low bow. "Lady's maid," I heard him whisper to himself. "A fine woman to look at, but a d——d bad one to deal with." I turned round on him, rather angry at his cool ways, and looked hard at him, just before I opened the library door. Mr. Dark looked hard at me. "All right," says he. "I can show myself in." And he knocks at the door, and opens it, and goes in, with another wicked wink, all in a moment.

Half an hour later the bell rang for me. Mr. Dark was sitting between my mistress (who was looking at him in amazement), and the lawyer (who was looking at him with approval). He had a map open on his knee, and a pen in his hand. Judging by his face, the communication of the secret about my master did not seem to have made the smallest impression on him.

"I've got leave to ask you a question," says he, the moment I appeared. "When you found your master's yacht gone, did you hear which way she had sailed? Was it northward toward Scotland?"

"Yes," I answered. "The boatman told me that, when I made inquiries at the harbor."

"Well, Sir," says Mr. Dark, turning to the lawyer, "if he said he was going to Sweden he seems to have started on the road to it, at all events. I think I have got my instructions now?"

The lawyer nodded and looked at my mistress, who bowed her head to him. He then said, turning to me,

"Pack up your bag for traveling, William, and have a conveyance got ready to go to the nearest post-town."

"And whatever happens in the future," added my mistress, her kind voice trembling a little, "believe, William, that I shall never forget this proof you now show of your devotion to me. It is still some comfort to know that I have your fidelity to depend on in this dreadful trial—your fidelity, and the extraordinary intelligence and experience of Mr. Dark."

Mr. Dark did not seem to hear the compliment. He was busy writing, with his paper upon the map on his knee. A quarter of an hour later, when I had ordered the dog-cart, and had got down into the hall with my bag packed, I found him there waiting for me. He was sitting on the same chair which he had occupied when he first arrived, and he had another jug of the old ale on the table by his side.

"Got any fishing-rods in the house?" says he, when I put my bag down in the hall.

"Yes," I replied, astonished at the question. "What do you want with them?"

"Pack a couple in cases for traveling," says Mr. Dark, "with lines and hooks and fly-hooks all complete. Have a drop of ale before you go—and don't stare, William. I'll let the light in on you as soon as we are out of the house. Off with you for the rods! I want to be on the road in five minutes."

When I came back with the rods and tackle, I found Mr. Dark in the dog-cart. "Money, luggage, fishing-rods, paper of directions, copy of anonymous letter, guide-book, map," says he, running over in his mind the things wanted for the journey. "All right, so far. Drive off." I took the reins and started the horse. As we left the house, I saw my mistress and Josephine looking after us from two of the windows on the second floor. The memory of those two attentive faces—one so sad and so good, the other so smiling and so wicked—haunted my mind perpetually for many days afterward.

"Now, William," says Mr. Dark, when we were clear of the lodge gates, "I'm going to begin by telling you what you are. You are a clerk in a bank; and I'm another. We have got our regular holiday, that comes, like Christmas, once a year; and we are taking a little tour in Scotland, to see the curiosities, and to breathe the sea air, and to get a little fishing whenever we can. I'm the fat cashier who digs holes in a drawerful of gold with a copper shovel. And you're the arithmetical young man who sits on a perch behind me, and keeps the books. Scotland's a beautiful country, William. Can you make whisky-toddy? I can; and what's more, unlikely as the thing may seem to you, I can actually drink it into the bargain."

"Scotland!" says I. "What are we going to Scotland for?"

"Question for question," says Mr. Dark. "What are we starting on a journey for?"

"To find my master," I answered, "and to make sure if the letter about him is true."

"Very good," says he. "How would *you* set about doing that, eh?"

"I should go and ask about him at Stockholm in Sweden, where he said his letters were to be sent."

"Would you indeed?" says Mr. Dark. "If you were a shepherd, William, and had lost a sheep in Cumberland, would you begin looking for it at the Land's End, or would you try a little nearer home?"

"You're attempting to make a fool of me now," says I.

"No," says Mr. Dark, "I'm only letting the light in on you, as I said I would. Now listen to reason, William, and profit by it as much as you can. Mr. James Smith says he is going on a cruise to Sweden, and makes his word good, at the beginning, by starting northward toward the coast of Scotland. What does he go in? A yacht. Do yachts carry live beasts and a butcher on board? No. Will joints of meat keep fresh all the way from Cumberland to Sweden? No. Do gentlemen like living on salt provisions? No. What follows from these three Noes? That Mr. James Smith must have stopped somewhere, on the way to Sweden, to supply his sea-larder with fresh provisions.

64

Where in that case must he stop? Somewhere in Scotland, supposing he did not alter his course when he was out of sight of your sea-port. Where in Scotland? Northward on the main land, or westward at one of the islands? Most likely on the main land, where the sea-side places are largest and where he is surest of getting all the stores he wants. Next, what is our business? Not to risk losing a link in the chain of evidence by missing any place where he has put his foot on shore. Not to overshoot the mark when we want to hit it in the bull's-eye. Not to waste money and time by taking a long trip to Sweden, till we know that we must absolutely go there. Where is our journey of discovery to take us to first, then? Clearly to the north of Scotland. What do you say to that, Mr. William? Is my catechism all correct, or has your strong ale muddled my head?"

It was evident, by this time, that no ale could do that—and I told him so. He chuckled, winked at me, and, taking another pinch of snuff, said he would now turn the whole case over in his mind again, and make sure that he had got all the bearings of it quite clear. By the time we reached the post-town he had accomplished this mental effort to his own perfect satisfaction, and was quite ready to compare the ale at the inn with the ale at Darrock Hall. The dog-cart was left to be taken back the next morning by the hostler. A post-chaise and horses were ordered out. A loaf of bread, a Bologna sausage, and two bottles of sherry were put into the pockets of the carriage; we took our seats and started briskly on our doubtful journey.

"One word more of friendly advice," said Mr.

Dark, settling himself comfortably in his corner of the carriage. "Take your sleep, William, whenever you feel that you can get it. You won't find yourself in bed again till we get to Glasgow."

Chapter II

Although the events that I am now relating happened many years ago, and although the persons principally affected by them are dead, with the exception of myself and another, I shall still, for caution's sake, avoid mentioning by name the various places visited by Mr. Dark and myself for the purpose of making inquiries. It will be enough if I describe generally what we did, and if I mention in substance only the result at which we ultimately arrived.

On reaching Glasgow, Mr. Dark altered his original intentions of going straight to the north of Scotland, considering it safer to make sure, if possible, of the course the yacht had taken in her cruise along the western coast. The carrying out of this new resolution involved the necessity of delaying our onward journey by perpetually diverging from the direct route. Three times we were sent uselessly to wild places in the Hebrides by false reports. Twice we wandered away inland, following gentlemen who answered generally to the description of Mr. James Smith, but who turned out to be the wrong men as soon as we set eyes on them. These vain excursions—especially the three to the western islands—consumed time terribly. It was more than two months from the day when he had left Darrock Hall before we found ourselves up at the very top of Scotland at last, driving into a considerable sea-side town, with a harbor attached to it. Thus far our journey had led to no results, and I began to despair of our making any discoveries. As for Mr. Dark, he never got to the end of his temper and his patience. "You don't know how to wait, William," was his constant remark whenever he heard me complaining. "I do."

We drove into the town toward evening in a modest little gig, and put up, according to our usual custom, at one of the inferior inns. "We must begin at the bottom," Mr. Dark used to say. "High company in a coffee-room won't be familiar with us. Low company in a tap-room will." And he certainly proved the truth of his own words. The like of him for making intimate friends of total strangers at the shortest notice I have never met with before or since. Cautious as the Scotch are, Mr. Dark seemed to have the knack of twisting them round his finger just as he pleased. He varied his way artfully with different men; but there were three standing opinions of his which he made a point of expressing in all varieties of company while we were in Scotland. In the first place, he thought the view of Edinburgh from Arthur's Seat the finest view in the world. In the second place, he considered whisky to be the most wholesome spirit in the world. In the third place, he believed his late beloved mother to have been the best woman in the world. It may be worthy of note that, whenever he expressed this last opinion, he invariably added that her maiden name had been Macleod.

Well, we put up at a modest little inn near the harbor. I was dead tired with the journey, and lay down on my bed to get some rest. Mr. Dark, whom nothing ever fatigued, left me to take his toddy and pipe among the company in the tap-room.

I don't know how long I had been asleep, when I was roused by a shake on my shoulder. The room was pitch dark, and I felt a hand suddenly clapped over my mouth. Then a strong smell of whisky and tobacco saluted my nostrils, and a whisper stole into my ear:

"William! we have got to the end of our journey."

"Mr. Dark," I stammered out, "is that you? What in Heaven's name do you mean?"

"The yacht put in here," was the answer, still in a whisper, "and your blackguard of a master came ashore—"

"Oh, Mr. Dark," I broke in, "don't tell me that the letter is true!"

"Every word of it," says he. "He was married here, and he was off again to the Mediterranean with Number Two a good three weeks before we left your mistress's house. Hush! don't say a word. Go to sleep again, or strike a light and read, if you like it better. Do any thing but come down stairs with me. I'm going to find out all the particulars without seeming to want to know one of them. Yours is a very good-looking face, William, but it's so infernally honest that I can't trust it in the tap-room. I'm making friends with the Scotchmen already. They know my opinion of Arthur's Seat; they *see* what I think of whisky; and I rather think it won't be long before they hear that my mother's maiden name was Macleod."

With these words he slipped out of the room, and left me, as he had found me, in the dark.

I was far too much agitated by what I had heard to think of going to sleep again; so I struck a light, and tried to amuse myself as well as I could with an old newspaper that had been stuffed into my carpet-bag. It was then nearly ten o'clock. Two hours later, when the house shut up, Mr. Dark came back to me again in high spirits. "I have got the whole case here," says he, tapping his forehead—"the whole case, as neat and clear as if it was drawn in a brief. That master of yours doesn't stick at a trifle, William. It's my opinion that your mistress and you have not seen the last of him yet."

We were sleeping, that night, in a double-bedded room. As soon as Mr. Dark had secured the door and disposed himself comfortably in his bed, he entered on a detailed narrative of the particulars communicated to him in the tap-room. The substance of what he told me may be related as follows:

The yacht had had a wonderful run all the way to Cape Wrath. On rounding that headland she had met the wind nearly dead against her, and had beaten every inch of the way to the sea-port town, where she had put in to get a supply of provisions, and to wait for a change in the wind. Mr. James Smith had gone ashore to look about him, and to see whether the principal hotel was the sort of house at which he would like to stop for a few days. In the course of his wanderings about the town, his attention had been attracted to a decent house, where lodgings were to be let, by the sight of a very pretty girl sitting at work at the parlor-window. He was so struck by her face that he came back twice to look at it, determining, the second time, to try if he could not make acquaintance with her by asking to see the lodgings. He was shown the rooms by the girl's mother, a very respectable woman, whom he discovered to be the wife of the master and part-owner of a small coasting-vessel, then away at sea. With a little maneuvering he managed to get into the parlor where the daughter was at work, and to exchange a few words with her. Her voice and manner equaled and completed the attraction of her face. Mr. James Smith decided, in his headlong way, that he was violently in love with her; and, without hesitating another instant, he took the lodgings on the spot for a month certain.

It is unnecessary to say that his designs on the girl were of the most dishonorable kind, and that he represented himself to the mother and daughter as a single man. Aided by his advantages of money, position, and personal appearance, he had anticipated that the ruin of the girl might be effected with very little difficulty; but he soon found that he had undertaken no easy conquest. The mother's vigilance never relaxed, and the daughter's self-possession never deserted her. She admired Mr. James Smith's tall figure and magnificent whiskers; she showed the most flattering partiality for his society; she listened tenderly to his compliments, and blushed encouragingly under his looks of admiration; but, whether it was cunning calculation, or whether it was pure innocence, she seemed absolutely incapable of understanding that his advances toward her were of any other than an honorable kind. At the slightest approach to undue familiarity she drew back with a kind of contemptuous amazement in her face, which utterly daunted and perplexed Mr. James Smith. He had not calculated on that sort of resistance, and he was perfectly incapable of overcoming it. The weeks passed; the month for which he had taken the lodgings expired. Time had strengthened the girl's hold on him till his admiration for her amounted to absolute infatuation; and he had not advanced one step yet toward the execution of the vicious purpose with which he had entered the house.

At this time he must have made some fresh attempt on the girl's virtue, which produced a coolness between them; for, instead of taking the lodgings on for another term, he removed to his yacht in the harbor, and slept on board for two nights. The wind was now fair, and the stores were on board; but he gave no orders to the sailing-master to weigh anchor. On the third day the cause of the coolness, whatever it was, appears to have been removed, and he returned to his lodgings on shore. Some of the more curious among the towns-people observed soon afterward, when they met him in the street, that he looked rather anxious and uneasy. The conclusion had probably forced itself upon his mind by this time that he must decide on pursuing one of two courses. Either he must resolve to make the sacrifice of leaving the girl altogether, or to commit the villainy of marrying her.

Unscrupulous as he was, he hesitated at encountering the risk—perhaps, also, at being guilty of the crime—involved in the last alternative. While he was still in doubt, the father's coasting-vessel sailed into the harbor, and the father's presence on the scene decided him at last. How this new influence acted it was impossible to ascertain, from the necessarily imperfect evidence of persons who were not admitted to the family councils. The fact, however, was indisputable, that the date of the father's return and the date of Mr. James Smith's first wicked resolution to marry the girl might both be fixed, as nearly as possible, at one and the same time.

Having once made up his mind to the commission of the crime, he proceeded, with all possible coolness and cunning, to provide against the chances of detection. Returning on board his yacht, he announced that he had given up his intention of cruising to Sweden, and that he intended to amuse himself by a long fishing tour in Scotland. After this brief explanation he ordered the vessel to be laid up in the harbor, gave the sailing-master leave of absence to return to his family at Cowes, and paid off the whole of the crew, from the mate to the cabin-boy. By these means he cleared the scene, at one blow, of the only people in the town who knew of the existence of his unhappy wife. After that, the news of his approaching marriage might be made public without risk of discovery; his own common name being of itself a sufficient protection, in case the event was mentioned in the local newspapers. All his friends, even his wife herself, might read a report of the marriage of Mr. James Smith, without having the slightest suspicion of who the bridegroom really was.

A fortnight after the paying off of the crew he was married to the merchant-captain's daughter. The father of the girl was well known among his fellow-townsmen as a selfish, grasping man, who was too sordidly anxious to secure a rich son-in-law to oppose any proposals for hastening the marriage. He and his wife and a few intimate relations had been present at the ceremony. After it had been performed, the newly-married couple left the town at once for a honeymoon trip to the Highland Lakes. Two days later, however, they unexpectedly returned, announcing a complete change in their plans. The bridegroom (thinking, probably, that he would be safer out of England than in it) had been fascinating the bride by his descriptions of the soft climate and lovely scenery of the South. The new Mrs. James Smith was all curiosity to see the shores of Spain and Italy; and, having often proved herself an excellent sailor on board her father's vessel, was anxious to go to the Mediterranean in the easiest way, by sea. Her attached husband, having now no other object in life than to gratify her wishes, had given up the Highland excursion, and had returned to have his yacht got ready for sea immediately. In this explanation there was nothing to awaken the suspicions of the lady's parents. The mother thought her James Smith a model among bridegrooms. The father lent his assistance to man the yacht at the shortest notice, with as competent a crew as could be picked up about the town. Principally through his exertions, the vessel was got ready for sea with extraordinary dispatch. The sails were bent, the provisions were put on board, and Mr. James Smith sailed for the Mediterranean with the unfortunate woman who believed herself to be his wife, before Mr. Dark and myself set forth to look after him from Darrock Hall.

Such was the true account of my master's infamous conduct in Scotland, as it was related to me. On concluding, Mr. Dark intimated that he had something still left to tell me, but declared that he was too sleepy to talk any more that night. As soon as we were awake the next morning he returned to the subject.

"I didn't finish all I had to say last night, did I?" he began.

"You unfortunately told me enough, and more than enough, to prove the truth of the statement in the anonymous letter," I answered.

"Yes," says Mr. Dark; "but did I tell you who wrote the anonymous letter?"

"You don't mean to say you have found that out!" says I.

"I think I have," was the cool answer. "When I heard about your precious master paying off the regular crew of the yacht, I put the circumstance by in my mind, to be brought out again and sifted a little as soon as the opportunity offered. It offered in about half an hour. Says I to the gauger, who was the principal talker in the room, 'How about those men that Mr. Smith paid off? Did they all go as soon as they got their money, or did they stop here till they had spent every farthing of it in the public-houses?' The gauger laughs. 'No such luck,' says he. 'They all went south, to spend their money among finer people than us. When I say all, though, I must make one exception. We thought the steward of the yacht had gone along with the rest; when, the very day Mr. Smith sailed for the Mediterranean, who should turn up unexpectedly but the steward himself? Where he had been hiding, and why he had been hiding, nobody could tell.' 'Perhaps he had been imitating his master, and looking out for a wife,' says I. 'Likely enough,' says the gauger; 'he gave a very confused account of himself, and he cut all questions short by going away south in a violent hurry.' That was enough for me: I said no more and let the subject drop. Clear as daylight, isn't it, William? The steward suspected something wrong—the steward waited and watched—the steward wrote that anonymous letter to your mistress. We can find him, if we want him, by inquiring at Cowes; and we can send to the church for legal evidence of the marriage as soon as we are instructed to do so. All that we have got to do now is to go back to your mistress, and see what course she means to take under the circumstances. It's a pretty case, William, so far—an uncommonly pretty case, as it stands at present."

We returned to Darrock Hall as fast as coaches and post-horses could carry us. Having from the first believed that the statement in the anonymous letter was true, my mistress received the bad news we brought calmly and resignedly—so far, at

75

least, as outward appearances went. She astonished and disappointed Mr. Dark, by declining to act, in any way, on the information that he had collected for her, and by insisting that the whole affair should still be buried in the profoundest secrecy. For the first time since I had known my traveling companion, he became depressed in spirits on hearing that nothing more was to be done; and although he left the Hall with a handsome present, he left it discontentedly.

"Such a pretty case, William!" says he, quite sorrowfully, as we shook hands in the hall. "Such an uncommonly pretty case! It's a thousand pities to stop it, in this way, before it's half over!"

"You don't know what a proud lady and what a delicate lady my mistress is," I answered. "She would die rather than expose her forlorn situation in a public court, for the sake of punishing her husband."

"Bless your simple heart!" says Mr. Dark, "do you really think, now, that such a case as this can be hushed up?"

"Why not," I asked, "if we all keep the secret?"

"That for the secret!" cries Mr. Dark, snapping his fingers. "Your master will let the cat out of the bag, if nobody else does."

"My master!" I repeated, in amazement.

"Yes, your master!" says Mr. Dark. "I have had some experience in my time, and I say you have not seen the last of him yet. Mark my words, William! Mr. James Smith will come back."

With that startling prophecy Mr. Dark irritably treated himself to a final pinch of snuff, and departed in silence on his journey back to his master in London. His last words hung heavily on my mind for days after he had gone. It was some weeks before I got over a habit of starting whenever the bell was rung at the front door.

Our life at the Hall soon returned to its old, dreary course. The lawyer in London wrote to my mistress to ask her to come and stay for a little while with his wife. But she declined the invitation, being averse to facing company after what had happened to her. Though she tried hard to keep the real state of her mind concealed from all about her, I, for one, could see plainly enough that she was pining and wasting under the bitter injury that had been inflicted on her. What effect continued solitude might have had on her spirits I tremble to think. Fortunately for herself, it occurred to her, before long, to send and invite Mr. Meeke to resume his musical practicing with her at the Hall. She told him—and, as it seemed to me, with perfect truth—that any implied engagement which he had made with Mr. James Smith was now canceled, since the person so named had morally forfeited all his claims as a husband— first, by his desertion of her; and, secondly, by his criminal marriage with another woman. After stating this view of the matter, she left it to Mr. Meeke to decide whether the perfectly innocent connection between them should be resumed or not. The little parson, after hesitating and pondering, in his helpless way, ended by agreeing with my mistress, and by coming back once more to the Hall with his fiddle under his arm. This renewal of their old habits might have been imprudent enough, as tending to weaken the strength of my mistress's case in the eyes of the world; but, for all that, it was the most sensible course she could take for her own sake. The harmless company of Mr. Meeke, and the relief of playing the old tunes again in the old way, saved her, I verily believe, from sinking altogether under the oppression of the shocking situation in which she was now placed.

So with the assistance of Mr. Meeke and his fiddle, my mistress got through the weary time. The winter passed; the spring came; and no fresh tidings reached us of Mr. James Smith. It had been a long, hard winter that year, and the spring was backward and rainy. The first really fine day we had was the day that fell on the fourteenth of March.

I am particular in mentioning this date merely because it is fixed forever in my memory. As long as there is life in me I shall remember that fourteenth of March, and the smallest circumstances connected with it. The day began ill, with what superstitious people would think a bad omen. My mistress remained late in her room in the morning, amusing herself by looking over her clothes, and by setting to rights some drawers in her cabinet which she had not opened for some time past. Just before the luncheon hour we were startled by hearing the drawing-room bell rung violently. I ran up to see what was the matter, and Josephine, the French maid, who had heard the bell in another part of the house, hastened to answer it also. She got into the drawing-room first, and I followed close on her heels. My mistress was standing alone on the hearth-rug, with an appearance of great discomposure in her face and manner.

"I have been robbed!" she said, vehemently. "I don't know when or how. But I miss a pair of bracelets, three rings, and a quantity of old-fashioned lace pocket-handkerchiefs."

"If you have any suspicions, ma'am," said Josephine, in a singularly sharp, sudden way, "say who they point at. My boxes, for once, are quite at your disposition."

"Who asked you about your boxes?" said my mistress, angrily. "Be a little less ready with your answer, if you please, the next time I speak."

She then turned to me, and began explaining the circumstances under which she had discovered her loss. I suggested that the missing things should be well searched for, first; and then, if nothing came of that, that I should go for the constable and place the matter under his direction. My mistress agreed to this plan; and the search was undertaken immediately. It lasted till dinner time, and led to no results. I then proposed going for the constable. But my mistress said it was too late to do any thing that day, and told me to wait at the table as usual, and to go on my errand the first thing the next morning. Mr. Meeke was coming with some new music in the evening; and I suspect she was not willing to be disturbed at her favorite occupation by the arrival of the constable.

Dinner was over; the parson came; and the concert went on as usual through the evening. At ten o'clock I took up the tray, with the wine and soda-water and biscuits. Just as I was opening one of the bottles of soda-water, there was a sound of wheels on the drive outside, and a ring at the bell.

I had unfastened the wires of the cork, and could not put the bottle down to run at once to the door. One of the female servants answered it. I heard a sort of half scream—then a sound of footsteps that were familiar to me.

My mistress turned round from the piano, and looked at me.

"William!" she said. "Do you know that step?"

Before I could answer, the door was pushed open, and Mr. James Smith walked into the room.

He had his hat on. His long hair flowed down under it over the collar of his coat; his bright black eyes, after resting an instant on my mistress, turned to Mr. Meeke. His heavy eyebrows met together, and one of his hands went up to one of his bushy black whiskers, and pulled at it angrily.

"You here again!" he said, advancing a few steps toward the little parson who sat trembling all over, with his fiddle hugged up in his arms as if it had been a child.

Seeing her villainous husband advance, my mistress moved too, so as to face him. He turned round on her at the first step she took, as quick as lightning.

"You shameless woman!" he said. "Can you look me in the face in the presence of that man?" He pointed, as he spoke, to Mr. Meeke.

My mistress never shrank when he turned upon her. Not a sign of fear was in her face when they confronted each other. Not the faintest flush of anger came into her cheeks when he spoke. The sense of the insult and injury that he had inflicted on her, and the consciousness of knowing his guilty secret, gave her all her self-possession at that trying moment. The high spirit that despised him spoke its contempt in every feature of her calm, haughty, unchanging face.

"I say to you again," he repeated, finding that she did not answer him. "How dare you look me in the face in the presence of that man?"

She raised her steady eyes to his hat, which he still kept on his head.

"Who has taught you to come into a room and speak to a lady with your hat on?" she asked, in quietly-contemptuous tones. "Is that a habit which is sanctioned by your new wife?"

My eyes were on him as she said those last words. His complexion, naturally dark and swarthy, changed instantly to a livid yellow white; his hand caught at the chair nearest to him; and he dropped into it heavily.

"I don't understand you," he said, after a moment of silence, looking about the room unsteadily while he spoke.

"You do," said my mistress. "Your tongue lies, but your face speaks the truth."

He called back his courage and audacity by a desperate effort, and started up from the chair again with an oath. The instant before this happened I thought I heard the sound of a rustling dress in the passage outside, as if one of the woman servants was stealing up to listen outside the door. I should have gone at once to see whether this was the case or not, but my master stopped me just after he had risen from the chair.

"Order the bed to be made in the Red Room,

and light a fire there directly," he said, with his fiercest look and in his roughest tones. "When I ring the bell, bring me a kettle of boiling water and a bottle of brandy. As for you," he continued, turning toward Mr. Meeke, who still sat pale and speechless with his fiddle hugged up in his arms, "leave the house, or you won't find your cloth any protection to you."

At this insult the blood flew into my mistress's face. Before she could say any thing Mr. James Smith raised his voice loud enough to drown hers.

"I won't hear another word from you," he cried out, brutally. "You have been talking like a mad woman—you look like a mad woman—you are out of your senses. As sure as you live I'll have you examined by the doctors tomorrow. Why the devil do you stand there, you scoundrel?" he roared, wheeling round on his heel to me. "Why don't you obey my orders?"

I looked at my mistress. If she had directed me to knock Mr. James Smith down, big as he was, I think at that moment I could have done it.

"Do as he tells you, William," she said, squeezing one of her hands firmly over her bosom, as if she was trying to keep down the rising indignation in that way. "This is the last order of his giving that I shall ask you to obey."

"Do you threaten me, you mad—?" He finished the question by a word that I shall not repeat.

"I tell you," she answered, in clear, ringing, resolute tones, "that you have outraged me past all forgiveness and all endurance, and that you shall never insult me again as you have insulted me to-night."

After saying those words, she fixed one steady look on him, then turned away and walked slowly to the door.

A minute previously, Mr. Meeke had summoned courage enough to get up and leave the room quietly. I noticed him walking demurely away, close to the wall, with his fiddle held under one tail of his long frock coat, as if he was afraid that the savage passions of Mr. James Smith might be wreaked on that unoffending instrument. He got to the door before my mistress. As he softly pulled it open, I saw him start, and I heard the rustling of the gown again in the passage outside.

My mistress followed him into the passage, turning, however, in the opposite direction to that taken by the little parson, in order to reach the staircase that led to her own room. I went out next, leaving Mr. James Smith alone.

I overtook Mr. Meeke in the hall, and opened the door for him.

"I beg your pardon, Sir," I said, "but did you come upon any body listening outside the music-room when you left it just now?"

"Yes, William," said Mr. Meeke, in a faint voice. "I think it was the French maid. But I was so dreadfully agitated that I can't be quite certain about it."

Had she surprised our secret? That was the question I asked myself, as I went away to light the fire in the Red Room. Calling to mind the exact time at which I had first detected the rustling outside the door, I came to the conclusion that she had only heard the last part of the quarrel between my mistress and her rascal of a husband. Those bold words about the "new wife" had been assuredly spoken before I heard Josephine stealing up to the door.

As soon as the fire was alight and the bed made, I went back to the music-room to announce that my orders had been obeyed. Mr. James Smith was walking up and down, in a perturbed way, still keeping his hat on. He followed me to the Red Room without saying a word. Ten minutes later, he rang for the kettle and the bottle of brandy. When I took them in, I found him unpacking a small carpet-bag which was the only luggage he had brought with him. He still kept silence, and did not appear to take any notice of me. I left him for the night without our having exchanged so much as a single word.

So far as I could tell the night passed quietly.

The next morning I heard that my mistress was suffering so severely from a nervous attack that she was unable to rise from her bed. It was no surprise to me to be told that, knowing, as I did, what she had gone through the night before.

About nine o'clock I went with the hot water to the Red Room. After knocking twice, I tried the door, and, finding it not locked, went in with the jug in my hand.

I looked at the bed; I looked all round the room. Not a sign of Mr. James Smith was to be seen any where.

Judging by appearances the bed had certainly been occupied. Thrown across the counterpane lay the night-gown he had worn. I took it up and saw some spots on it. I looked at them a little closer. They were spots of blood.

Chapter III

The first amazement and alarm produced by this discovery deprived me of my presence of mind. Without stopping to think what I ought to do first, I ran back to the servants' hall, calling out that something had happened to my master. All the household hurried directly into the Red Room, Josephine among the rest. I was first brought to my senses, as it were, by observing the strange expression of her countenance when she saw the bed-gown and the empty room. All the other servants were bewildered and frightened. She alone, after giving a little start, recovered herself directly. A look of devilish satisfaction broke out on her face; and she left the room quickly and quietly, without exchanging a word with any of us. I saw this, and it aroused my suspicions. There is no need to mention what they were, for, as events soon showed, they were entirely wide of the mark.

Having come to myself a little, I sent them all out of the room, except the coachman. We two then examined the place. The Red Room was usually occupied by visitors. It was on the ground floor, and looked out into the garden. We found the window-shutters, which I had barred over night, open, but the window itself was down. The fire had been out long enough for the grate to be quite cold. Half the bottle of brandy had been drunk. The carpet-bag was gone. There were no marks of violence or struggling any where about the bed or the room. We examined every corner carefully, but made no other discoveries than these.

When I returned to the servants' hall, bad news of my mistress was awaiting me there. The unusual noise and confusion in the house had reached her ears, and she had been told what had happened without sufficient caution being exercised in preparing her to hear it. In her weak, nervous state, the shock of the intelligence had quite prostrated her. She had fallen into a swoon, and had been brought back to her senses with the greatest difficulty. As to giving me or any body else directions what to do, under the embarrassing circumstances which had now occurred, she was totally incapable of the effort.

I waited till the middle of the day, in the hope that she might get strong enough to give her orders; but no message came from her. At last I resolved to send and ask her what she thought it best to do. Josephine was the proper person to go on this errand; but when I asked for Josephine, she was nowhere to be found. The housemaid, who had searched for her ineffectually, brought word that her bonnet and shawl were not hanging in their usual places. The parlor-maid, who had been in attendance in my mistress's room, came down while we were all aghast at this new disappearance. She could only tell us that Josephine had begged her to do lady's maid's duty that morning as she was not well. Not well! And the first result of her illness appeared to be that she had left the house!

I cautioned the servants on no account to mention this circumstance to my mistress, and then went up stairs myself to knock at her door, and ask if I might count on her approval if I wrote, in her name, to her relation the lawyer in London, and if I afterward went and gave information of what had occurred to the nearest justice of the peace. I might have sent to make this inquiry through one of the female servants; but by this time, though not naturally suspicious, I had got to distrust every body in the house, whether they deserved it or not.

So I asked the question myself, standing outside the door. My mistress thanked me in a faint voice, and begged me to do what I had proposed immediately.

I went into my own bedroom and wrote to the lawyer, merely telling him that Mr. James Smith had appeared unexpectedly at the Hall, and that events had occurred in consequence which required his immediate presence. I made the letter up like a parcel, and sent the coachman with it to catch the mail on its way through to London.

The next thing was to go to the justice of the peace. The nearest lived about five miles off, and was well acquainted with my mistress. He was an old bachelor, and he kept house with his brother who was a widower. The two were much respected and beloved in the county, being kind, unaffected gentlemen who did a great deal of good among the poor. The justice was Mr. Robert Nicholson, and his brother, the widower, was Mr. Philip.

I had got my hat on, and was asking the groom which horse I had better take, when an open carriage drove up to the house. It contained Mr. Philip Nicholson and two persons in plain clothes, not exactly servants and not exactly gentlemen, as far as I could judge.

Mr. Philip looked at me, when I touched my hat to him, in a very grave, downcast way, and asked for my mistress. I told him she was ill in bed. He shook his head at hearing that, and said he wished to speak to me in private. I showed him into the library. One of the men in plain clothes followed us, and sat in the hall. The other waited with the carriage.

"I was just going out, Sir," I said, as I set a chair for him, "to speak to Mr. Robert Nicholson about a very extraordinary circumstance—"

"I know what you refer to," said Mr. Philip, cutting me short rather abruptly, "and I must beg, for reasons which will presently appear, that you will make no statement of any sort to me until you have first heard what I have to say. I am here on a very serious and a very shocking errand, which deeply concerns your mistress and you."

His face suggested something worse than his words expressed. My heart began to beat fast, and I felt that I was turning pale.

"Your master, Mr. James Smith," he went on, "came here unexpectedly, yesterday evening, and slept in this house last night. Before he retired to rest, he and your mistress had high words together, which ended, I am sorry to hear, in a threat of a serious nature addressed by Mrs. James Smith to her husband. They slept in separate rooms. This morning you went into your master's room

88

and saw no sign of him there. You only found his night-gown on the bed, spotted with blood."

"Yes, Sir," I said, in as steady a voice as I could command. "Quite true."

"I am not examining you," said Mr. Philip. "I am only making a certain statement, the truth of which you can admit or deny before my brother."

"Before your brother, Sir!" I repeated. "Am I suspected of any thing wrong?"

"There is a suspicion that Mr. James Smith has been murdered," was the answer I received to that question.

My flesh began to creep all over from head to foot. I tried to speak again, but the words would not come.

"I am shocked, I am horrified to say," Mr. Philip went on "that the suspicion affects your mistress, in the first place, and you, in the second."

I shall not attempt to describe what I felt when he said that. No words of mine, no words of any body's, could give an idea of it. What other men would have done in my situation I don't know. I stood before Mr. Philip, staring straight at him, without speaking, without moving, almost without breathing. If he, or any other man, had struck me at that moment, I do not believe I should have felt the blow.

"Both my brother and myself," said Mr. Philip, "have such unfeigned respect for your mistress, such sympathy for her under these frightful circumstances, and such an implicit belief in her capability of proving her innocence, that we are desirous of sparing her in this dreadful trial as much as possible. For those reasons, I have undertaken to come here with the persons appointed to execute my brother's warrant—"

"Warrant, Sir!" I said, getting command of my voice as he pronounced that word. "A warrant against my mistress!"

"Against her and against you," said Mr. Philip. "The suspicious circumstances have been sworn to by a competent witness, who has declared on oath that your mistress is guilty, and that you are an accomplice."

"What witness, Sir?"

"Your mistress's French maid, who came to my brother this morning, and who has made her deposition in due form."

"And who is as false as hell," I cried out passionately, "in every word she says against my mistress and against me."

"I hope—no, I will go farther, and say, I believe she is," said Mr. Philip. "But her perjury must be proved, and the necessary examination must take place. My carriage is going back to my brother's, and you will go in it in charge of one of my men, who has the warrant to take you in custody. I shall remain here with the man who is waiting in the hall; and, before any steps are taken to execute the other warrant, I shall send for the doctor to ascertain when your mistress can be removed."

"Oh, my poor mistress!" I said. "This will be the death of her, Sir."

"I will take care that the shock shall strike her as tenderly as possible," said Mr. Philip. "I am here for that express purpose. She has my deepest sympathy and respect, and shall have every help and alleviation that I can afford her."

The hearing him say that, and the seeing how sincerely he meant what he said, was the first gleam of comfort in the dreadful affliction that had befallen us. I felt this; I felt a burning anger against the wretch who had done her best to ruin my mistress's fair name and mine; but in every other respect, I was like a man who had been stunned, and whose faculties had not perfectly recovered from the shock. Mr. Philip was obliged to remind me that time was of importance, and that I had better give myself up immediately on the merciful terms which his kindness offered to me. I acknowledged that, and wished him good-morning. But a mist seemed to come over my eyes as I turned round to go away; a mist that prevented me from finding my way to the door. Mr. Philip opened it for me, and said a friendly word or two which I could hardly hear. The man waiting outside took me to his companion in the carriage at the door, and I was driven away—a prisoner for the first time in my life.

On our way to the Justice's, what little thinking faculty I had left in me was all occupied in the attempt to trace a motive for the inconceivable treachery and falsehood of which the French woman had been guilty. Her words, her looks, and her manner, on that unfortunate day when my mistress so far forgot herself as to strike her, came back dimly to my memory, and led to the inference that part of the motive, at least, of which I was in search might be referred to what had happened on that occasion. But was this the only reason for her devilish vengeance against my mistress? And, even if it were so, what fancied injuries had I done her? Why should I be included in the false accusation? In the dazed state of my faculties, at that time, I was quite incapable of seeking the answer to these questions. My mind was clouded all over, and I gave up the attempt to clear it in despair.

I was brought before Mr. Robert Nicholson that day, and the fiend of a French woman was examined in my presence. The first sight of her face—with its wicked self-possession, with its smooth, leering triumph—so sickened and horrified me that I turned my head away and never looked at her a second time throughout the proceedings. The answers she gave amounted to a mere repetition of the deposition to which she had already sworn. I listened to them with the most breathless attention, and was thunder-struck at the inconceivable artfulness with which she had mixed up truth and falsehood in her charge against my mistress and me.

This was, in substance, what she now stated in my presence:

After describing the manner of Mr. James Smith's arrival at the Hall, the witness, Josephine Durand, confessed that she had been led to listen at the music-room door by hearing angry voices inside; and she then described, truly enough, the latter part of the altercation between husband and wife. Fearing, after this, that something serious might happen, she had kept watch in her room, which was on the same floor as her mistress's. She had heard her mistress's door open softly, between one and two in the morning—had followed her mistress, who carried a small lamp, along the passage and down the stairs into the hall—had hidden herself in the porter's chair—had seen her mistress pass on the way that led to the Red Room, with the dagger in the green sheath in her hand —had followed her again, and seen her softly enter the Red Room—had heard the heavy breathing of Mr. James Smith, which gave token that he was asleep—had slipped into an empty room, next door to the Red Room, and had waited there about a quarter of an hour, when her mistress came out again with the dagger in her hand—had followed her mistress again into the hall, where she had put the dagger back in its place—had seen her mistress turn into a side passage that led to my room— had heard her knock at my door, and heard me answer and open it—had hidden again in the porter's chair—had, after a while, seen me and my mistress pass together into the passage that led to the Red Room—had watched us both into the Red Room—and had then, through fear of being discovered and murdered herself, if she risked detection any longer, stolen back to her own room for the rest of the night.

After deposing on oath, to the truth of these atrocious falsehoods, and declaring, in conclusion, that Mr. James Smith had been murdered by my mistress, and that I was an accomplice, the French woman had further asserted, in order to show a motive for the crime, that Mr. Meeke was my mistress's lover, that he had been forbidden the house by her husband, and that he was found in the house, and alone with her, on the evening of

Mr. James Smith's return. Here again there were some grains of truth cunningly mixed up with a revolting lie, and they had their effect in giving to the falsehood a look of probability.

I was cautioned in the usual manner, and asked if I had any thing to say. I replied that I was innocent, but that I would wait for legal assistance before I defended myself. The Justice remanded me; and the examination was over. Three days later my unhappy mistress was subjected to the same trial. I was not allowed to communicate with her. All I knew was that the lawyer had arrived from London to help her. Toward the evening he was admitted to see me. He shook his head sorrowfully when I asked after my mistress.

"I am afraid," he said, "that the horror of the situation in which that vile woman has placed her has affected her brain. Weakened by her previous agitation, she seems to have sunk altogether under this last shock, tenderly and carefully as Mr. Philip Nicholson broke the bad news to her. All her feelings appeared to be strangely blunted at the examination to-day. She answered the questions put to her quite correctly, but at the same time quite mechanically, with no change in her complexion, or in her tone of voice, or in her manner, from beginning to end. It is a sad thing, William, when women can not get their natural vent of weeping, and your mistress has not shed a tear since she left Darrock Hall."

"But surely, Sir," I said, "if my examination has not proved the French woman's perjury, my mistress's examination must have exposed it?"

"Nothing will expose it," answered the lawyer,

"but producing Mr. James Smith, or, at least, legally proving that he is alive. Morally speaking, I have no doubt that the Justice before whom you have been examined is as firmly convinced as we can be that the French woman has perjured herself. Morally speaking, he believes that those threats which your mistress unfortunately used, referred (as she said they did, to-day) to her intention of leaving the Hall early in the morning, with you for her attendant, and coming to me, if she had been well enough to travel, to seek effectual legal protection from her husband for the future. Mr. Nicholson believes that; and I, who know more of the circumstances than he does, believe also that Mr. James Smith stole away from Darrock Hall in the night under fear of being indicted for bigamy. But if I can't find him; if I can't prove him to be alive; if I can't account for those spots of blood on the night-gown, the accidental circumstances of the case remain unexplained—your mistress's rash language, the bad terms on which she has lived with her husband, and her unlucky disregard of appearances in keeping up her intercourse with Mr. Meeke, all tell dead against us—and the Justice has no alternative, in a legal point of view, but to remand you both, as he has now done, for the production of further evidence."

"But how, then, in Heaven's name, is our innocence to be proved, Sir?" I asked.

"In the first place," said the lawyer, "by finding Mr. James Smith; and, in the second place, by persuading him, when he is found, to come forward and declare himself."

"Do you really believe, Sir," said I, "that he would hesitate to do that, when he knows the horrible charge to which his disappearance has exposed his wife? He is a heartless villain, I know; but sure—"

"I don't suppose," said the lawyer, cutting me short, "that he is quite scoundrel enough to decline coming forward, supposing he ran no risk by doing so. But remember that he has placed himself in a position to be tried for bigamy, and that he believes your mistress will put the law in force against him."

I had forgotten that circumstance. My heart sank within me when it was recalled to my memory, and I could say nothing more.

"It is a very serious thing," the lawyer went on; "it is a downright offense against the law of the land to make any private offer of a compromise to this man. Knowing what we know, our duty as good citizens, is to give such information as may bring him to trial. I tell you plainly that, if I did not stand toward your mistress in the position of a relation, as well as a legal adviser, I should think twice about running the risk—the very serious risk—on which I am now about to venture for her sake. As it is, I have taken the right measures to assure Mr. James Smith that he will not be treated according to his deserts. When he knows what the circumstances are, he will trust us—supposing always that we can find him. The search about this neighborhood has been quite useless. I have sent private instructions by to-day's post to Mr. Dark in London, and with them a carefully-worded form of advertisement for the public newspapers. You may rest assured that every human means of tracing him will be tried forthwith. In the mean time, I have an important question to put to you about the French woman. She may know more than we think she does; she may have surprised the secret of the second marriage, and may be keeping it in reserve to use against us. If this should turn out to be the case, I shall want some other chance against her besides the chance of indicting her for perjury. As to her motive, now, for making this horrible accusation, what can you tell me about that, William?"

"Her motive against me, Sir?"

"No, no! not against you. I can see plainly enough that she accuses you because it is necessary to do so to add to the probability of her story—which, of course, assumes that you helped your mistress to dispose of the dead body. You are coolly sacrificed to some devilish vengeance against your mistress. Let us get at that first. Has there ever been a quarrel between them?"

I told him of the quarrel, and of how Josephine had looked and talked when she showed me her cheek.

"Yes," he said, "that is a strong motive for revenge, with a naturally pitiless, vindictive woman. But is that all? Had your mistress any hold over her? Is there any self-interest mixed up along with this motive of vengeance? Think a little, William. Has any thing ever happened in the house to compromise this woman, or to make her fancy herself compromised?"

The remembrance of my mistress's lost trinkets and handkerchiefs, which later and greater troubles had put out of my mind, flashed back into my memory while he spoke. I told him immediately of the alarm in the house when the loss was discovered.

"Did your mistress suspect Josephine and question her?" he asked, eagerly.

"No, Sir," I replied. "Before she could say a word Josephine impudently asked who she suspected, and boldly offered her own boxes to be searched."

The lawyer's face turned red as scarlet. He jumped out of his chair, and hit me such a smack on the shoulder that I thought he had gone mad.

"By Jupiter, William!" he cried out, "we have got the whip hand of that she-devil at last!"

I looked at him in astonishment.

"Why, man alive!" he said, "don't you see how it is? Josephine's the thief! I am as sure of it as that you and I are talking together. This vile accusation against your mistress answers another purpose besides the vindictive one—it is the very best screen that the wretch could possibly set up to hide herself from detection. It has stopped your mistress and you from moving in the matter; it exhibits her in the false character of an honest witness against a couple of criminals; it gives her time to dispose of the goods, or to hide them, or to do any thing she likes with them. Stop! let me be quite sure that I know what the lost things are. A pair of bracelets, three rings, and a lot of lace pocket-handkerchiefs—is that what you said?"

"Yes, Sir."

"Your mistress will describe them particularly, and I will take the right steps the first thing tomorrow morning. Good-evening, William, and keep up your spirits. It shan't be my fault if you don't soon see the French woman in the right place for her—at the prisoner's bar."

With that farewell he went out. The days passed, and I did not see him again until the period of my remand had expired. On this occasion, when I once more appeared before the Justice, my mistress appeared with me. The first sight of her absolutely startled me—she was so sadly altered. Her face looked so pinched and thin that it was like the face of an old woman. The dull vacant resignation of her expression was something shocking to see. It changed a little when her eyes first turned heavily toward me; and she whispered, with a faint smile, "I am sorry for *you*, William: I am very, very sorry for *you*." But as soon as she had said those words the blank look returned, and she sat with her head drooping forward, quiet and inattentive, and hopeless, so changed a being that her oldest friends would hardly have known her.

Our examination was a mere formality. There was no additional evidence, either for or against us, and we were remanded again for another week.

I asked the lawyer, privately, if any chance had offered itself of tracing Mr. James Smith. He looked mysterious, and only said in answer, "Hope for the best." I inquired next, if any progress had been made toward fixing the guilt of the robbery on the French woman.

"I never boast," he replied. "But, cunning as she is, I should not be surprised if Mr. Dark and

I, together, turned out to be more than a match for her."

Mr. Dark! There was something in the mere mention of his name that gave me confidence. If I could only have got my poor mistress's sad dazed face out of my mind, I should not have had much depression of spirits to complain of during the interval of time that elapsed between the second examination and the third.

On the third appearance of my mistress and myself before the Justice, I noticed some faces in the room which I had not seen there before. Greatly to my astonishment—for the previous examinations had been conducted as privately as possible—I remarked the presence of two of the servants from the Hall, and of three or four of the tenants on the Darrock estate, who lived nearest to the house. They all sat together on one side of the justice-room. Opposite to them, and close at the side of a door, stood my old acquaintance Mr. Dark, with his big snuff-box, his jolly face, and his winking eye. He nodded to me, when I looked at him, as jauntily as if we were meeting at a party of pleasure. The French woman, who had been summoned to the examination, had a chair placed opposite to the witness-box, and in a line with the seat occupied by my poor mistress, whose looks, as I was grieved to see, were not altered for the better. The lawyer from London was with her, and I stood behind her chair. We were all quietly disposed in the room in this way, when the Justice, Mr. Robert Nicholson, came in with his brother. It might have been only fancy, but I thought I could see in both their faces that something remarkable had happened since we had met at the last examination.

The deposition of Josephine Durand was read over by the clerk, and she was asked if she had any thing to add to it. She replied in the negative. The Justice then appealed to my mistress's relation, the lawyer, to know if he could produce any evidence relating to the charge against his clients.

"I have evidence," answered the lawyer, getting briskly on his legs, "which, I believe, Sir, will justify me in asking for their discharge."

"Where are your witnesses?" inquired the Justice, looking hard at the French woman while he spoke.

"One of them is in waiting, your worship," said Mr. Dark, opening the door near which he was standing.

He went out of the room, remained away about a minute, and returned with his witness at his heels. My heart gave a bound as if it would jump out of my body. There, with his long hair cut short, and his busy whiskers shaved off—there, in his own proper person, safe and sound as ever, was Mr. James Smith!

The French woman's iron nature resisted the shock of his unexpected presence on the scene with a steadiness that was nothing short of marvelous. Her thin lips closed together convulsively, and there was a slight movement in the muscles of her throat. But not a word, not a sign betrayed her. Even the yellow tinge of her complexion remained absolutely unchanged.

"It is not necessary, Sir, that I should waste time and words in referring to the wicked and

101

preposterous charge against my clients," said the lawyer, addressing Mr. Robert Nicholson. "The one sufficient justification for discharging them immediately is before you at this moment, in the person of that gentleman. There, Sir, stands the murdered Mr. James Smith, of Darrock Hall, alive and well, to answer for himself."

"That is not the man!" cried the French woman, her shrill voice just as high, clear, and steady as ever. "I denounce that man as an impostor! Of my own knowledge I deny that he is Mr. James Smith!"

"No doubt you do," said the lawyer; "but we will prove his identity for all that."

The first witness called was Mr. Philip Nicholson. He could swear that he had seen Mr. James Smith, and spoken to him, at least a dozen times. The person now before him was Mr. James Smith, altered as to personal appearance by having his hair cut short, and his whiskers shaved off, but still, unmistakably, the man he assumed to be.

"Conspiracy!" said the French woman, hissing the word out viciously between her teeth.

"If you are not silent," said Mr. Robert Nicholson, "you will be removed from the room. It will sooner meet the ends of justice," he went on, addressing the lawyer, "if you prove the question of identity by witnesses who have been in habits of daily communication with Mr. James Smith."

Upon this, one of the servants from the Hall was placed in the box. The alteration in his master's appearance evidently puzzled the man. Besides the perplexing change already adverted to, there was also a change in Mr. James Smith's expression and manner. Rascal as he was, I must do him the justice to say that he looked startled and ashamed when he first caught sight of his unfortunate wife. The servant, who was used to be eyed tyrannically by him, and ordered about roughly, stammered and hesitated on being asked to swear to his identity.

"I can hardly say for certain, Sir," said the man, addressing the Justice in a bewildered manner. "He is like my master, and yet he isn't. If he wore whiskers and had his hair long, and if he was, saving your presence, Sir, a little more rough and ready in his way, I could swear to him any where with a safe conscience."

Fortunately for us, at this moment Mr. James Smith's feeling of uneasiness at the situation in which he was placed changed to a feeling of irritation at being coolly surveyed, and then stupidly doubted in the matter of his identity, by one of his own servants.

"Can't you say in plain words, you idiot, whether you know me, or whether you don't?" he called out, angrily.

"That's his voice!" cried the servant, starting in the box. "Whiskers or no whiskers, that's him!"

"If there is any difficulty, your worship, about the gentleman's hair," said Mr. Dark, coming forward with a grin, "here's a small parcel which, I may make so bold as to say, will remove it." Saying that, he opened the parcel, took some locks of hair out of it, and held them up close to Mr. James Smith's head. "A pretty good match, your worship!" continued Mr. Dark. "I have no doubt the gentleman's head feels cooler now it's off. We can't put the whiskers on, I'm afraid, but they match the hair; and there they are in the paper (if one may say such a thing of whiskers) to speak for themselves."

"A lie! a fraud!" cried the French woman. "A lie of lies! a fraud of frauds!"

The Justice made a sign to two of the constables present, as she burst out with those exclamations, and the men removed her to an adjoining room.

The second servant from the Hall was then put in the box, and was followed by one of the tenants. After what they had heard and seen, neither of these men had any hesitation in swearing positively to their master's identity.

"It is quite unnecessary," said the Justice, as soon as the box was empty again, "to examine any more witnesses as to the question of identity. All the legal formalities are accomplished, and the charge against the prisoners falls to the ground. I have great pleasure in ordering the immediate discharge of both the accused persons, and in declaring from this place that they leave the court without the slightest stain on their characters." He bowed low to my mistress as he said that, paused a moment, and then looked inquiringly at Mr. James Smith. "I have hitherto abstained from making any remark unconnected with the immediate matter in hand," he went on. "But now that my duty is done, I can not leave this chair without expressing my strong sense of disapprobation of the conduct of Mr. James Smith—conduct which, whatever may be the motives that occasioned it, has given a false color of probability to a most horrible charge against a lady of unspotted reputation, and against a person in a lower rank in life whose good character ought not to have been imperiled, even for a moment. Mr. Smith may, or may not, choose to explain his mysterious disappearance from Darrock Hall, and the equally unaccountable change which he has chosen to make in his personal appearance. There is no legal charge against him; but, speaking morally, I should be unworthy of the place I hold, if I hesitated to declare my present conviction that his conduct has been deceitful, inconsiderate, and unfeeling in the highest degree."

To this sharp reprimand, Mr. James Smith (evidently tutored beforehand as to what he was to say) replied that, in attending before the Justice, he wished to perform a plain duty, and to keep himself strictly within the letter of the law. He apprehended that the only legal obligation laid on him was to attend in that court to declare himself, and to enable competent witnesses to prove his identity. This duty accomplished, he had only to add that he preferred submitting to a reprimand from the Bench to entering into explanations which would involve the disclosure of domestic circumstances of a very unhappy nature. After that brief reply he had nothing to add, but that he would respectfully request the Justice's permission to withdraw.

The permission was accorded. As he crossed the room he stopped near his wife, and said confusedly, in a very low tone, "I have done you many injuries, but I never intended this. I am sorry for it. Have you any thing to say to me before I go?"

My mistress shuddered and hid her face. He waited a moment, and, finding that she did not answer him, bowed his head politely, and went out. I did not know it then, but I had seen him for the last time.

After he had gone, the lawyer, addressing Mr. Robert Nicholson, said that he had an application to make, in reference to the woman Josephine Durand.

At the mention of that name my mistress hurriedly whispered a few words into her relation's ear. He looked toward Mr. Philip Nicholson, who immediately advanced, offered his arm to my mistress, and led her out. I was about to follow, when Mr. Dark stopped me, and begged that I would wait a few minutes longer, in order to give myself the pleasure of seeing "the end of the case."

In the mean time the Justice had pronounced the necessary order to have the French woman brought back. She came in, as bold and confident as ever. Mr. Robert Nicholson looked away from her in disgust, and said to the lawyer:

"Your application is to have her committed for perjury, of course?"

"For perjury?" said Josephine, with her wicked smile. "Ah, well! well! I shall explain some little things then that I have not explained before. You think I am quite at your mercy now? Bah! I shall make myself a thorn in your sides, yet."

"She has got scent of the second marriage," whispered Mr. Dark to me.

There could be no doubt of it. She had evidently been listening at the door, on the night when my master came back, longer than I had supposed.

She must have heard those words about "the new wife"—she might even have seen the effect of them on Mr. James Smith.

"We do not, at present, propose to charge Josephine Durand with perjury," said the lawyer, "but with another offense, for which it is important to try her immediately, in order to effect the restoration of property that has been stolen. I charge her with stealing from her mistress, while in service at Darrock Hall, a pair of bracelets, three rings, and a dozen and a half of lace pocket-handkerchiefs. The articles in question were taken this morning from between the mattresses of her bed; and a letter was found in the same place which clearly proves that she had represented the property as belonging to herself, and that she had tried to dispose of it to a purchaser in London." While he was speaking Mr. Dark produced the jewelry, the handkerchiefs, and the letter, and laid them before the Justice.

Even the French woman's extraordinary powers of self-control now gave way at last. At the first words of the unexpected charge against her she struck her hands together violently, gnashed her sharp white teeth, and burst out with a torrent of fierce-sounding words in her own language, the meaning of which I did not understand then, and can not explain now.

"I think that's check-mate for Marmzelle," whispered Mr. Dark, with his invariable wink. "Suppose you go back to the Hall, now, William, and draw a jug of that heavenly old ale of yours? I'll be after you in five minutes, as soon as the charge is made out."

I could hardly realize it, when I found myself walking back to Darrock a free man again. In a quarter of an hour's time Mr. Dark joined me, and drank to my health, happiness, and prosperity, in three separate tumblers. After performing this ceremony, he wagged his head and chuckled with an appearance of such excessive enjoyment that I could not avoid remarking on his high spirits.

"It's the Case, William: it's the beautiful neatness of the Case that quite upsets me. Oh, Lord, what a privilege it is to be concerned in such a job as this!" cries Mr. Dark, slapping his stumpy hands on his fat knees in a sort of ecstasy.

I had a very different opinion of the case, for my own part, but I did not venture on expressing it. I was too anxious to know how Mr. James Smith had been discovered and produced at the examination, to enter into any arguments. Mr. Dark guessed what was passing in my mind, and telling me to sit down and make myself comfortable, volunteered, of his own accord, to inform me of all that I wanted to know.

"When I got my instructions and my statement of particulars," he began, "I was not at all surprised to hear that Mr. James Smith had come back. (I prophesied that, if you remember, William, the last time we met?) But I was a good deal astonished, nevertheless, at the turn things had taken; and I can't say I felt very hopeful about finding our man. However, I followed my master's directions, and put the advertisement in the papers. It addressed Mr. James Smith, by name; but it was very carefully worded as to what was wanted of him. Two days after it appeared, a letter came to our office in a woman's handwriting. It was my business to open the letters, and I opened that. The writer was short and mysterious; she requested that somebody would call from our office, at a certain address, between the hours of two and four that afternoon, in reference to the advertisement which we had inserted in the newspapers. Of course, I was the somebody who went. I kept myself from building up hopes by the way, knowing what a lot of Mrs. James Smiths there were in London. On getting to the house, I was shown into the drawing-room; and there, dressed in a wrapper and lying on a sofa, was an uncommonly pretty woman, who looked as if she was just recovering from an illness. She had a newspaper by her side, and came to the point at once: 'My husband's name is James Smith,' she says, 'and I have my reasons for wanting to know if he is the person you are in search of.' I described our man as Mr. James Smith of Darrock Hall, Cumberland. 'I know no such person,' says she—"

"What! was it not the second wife, after all?" I broke out.

"Wait a bit," says Mr. Dark. "I mentioned the name of the yacht next, and she started up on the sofa as if she had been shot. 'I think you were married in Scotland, ma'am?' says I. She turns as pale as ashes, and drops back on the sofa, and says, faintly, 'It *is* my husband. Oh, Sir, what has happened? what do you want with him? Is he in debt?' I take a minute to think, and then make up my mind to tell her every thing—feeling that she would keep her husband (as she called him) out of the way, if I frightened her by making any mysteries. A nice job I had, William, as you may suppose, when she knew about the bigamy business. What with screaming, fainting, crying, and blowing me up (as if I was to blame!), she kept me by that sofa of hers the best part of an hour —kept me there, in short, till Mr. James Smith himself came back. I leave you to judge if that mended matters! He found me mopping the poor woman's temples with scent and water; and he would have pitched me out of the window, as sure as I sit here, if I had not met him and staggered him at once with the charge of murder against his wife. That stopped him, when he was in full cry, I promise you. 'Go and wait in the next room,' says he, 'and I'll come in and speak to you directly.' I knew he couldn't get out by the drawing-room windows, and I knew I could watch the door; so away I went, leaving him alone with the lady, who didn't spare him by any manner of means, as I could hear easily enough in the next room. However, all rows in this world come to an end sooner or later; and a man with any brains in his head may do what he pleases with a woman who is fond of him. Before long I heard her crying and kissing him. 'I can't go home,' she says, 'after this. You have behaved like a villain and a monster to me—but oh, Jemmy, I can't give you up to any body! Don't go back to your wife! oh don't, don't go back to your wife!' 'No fear of that,' says he. 'My wife wouldn't have me if I did go back to her.' After that, I heard the door open, and went out to meet him on the landing. He began swearing the moment he saw me, as if that was any good!

'Business first, if you please, Sir,' says I, 'and any pleasure you like, in the way of swearing, afterward.' With that beginning, I mentioned our terms to him, and asked the pleasure of his company to Cumberland in return. He was uncommonly suspicious at first, but I promised to draw out a legal document (mere waste paper, of no earthly use except to pacify him), engaging to hold him harmless throughout the proceedings; and what with that, and telling him of the frightful danger his wife was in, I managed, at last, to carry my point."

"But did the second wife make no objection to his going away with you?" I inquired.

"Not she," said Mr. Dark. "I stated the case to her, just as it stood; and soon satisfied her that there was no danger of Mr. James Smith's first wife laying any claim to him. After hearing that, she joined me in persuading him to do his duty, and said she pitied your mistress from the bottom of her heart. With her to back me, I had no great fear of our man changing his mind. I had the door watched that night, however, so as to make quite sure of him. The next morning he was ready to time when I called; and a quarter of an hour after that, we were off together for the north road. We made the journey with post-horses, being afraid of chance passengers, you know, in public conveyances. On the way down Mr. James Smith and I got on as comfortably together as if we had been a pair of old friends. I told the story of our tracing him to the north of Scotland; and he gave me the particulars, in return, of his bolting from Darrock

111

Hall. They are rather amusing, William—would you like to hear them?"

I told Mr. Dark that he had anticipated the very question I was about to ask him.

"Well," he said, "this is how it was: To begin at the beginning, our man really took Number Two to the Mediterranean as we heard. He sailed up the Spanish coast, and, after short trips ashore, stopped at a sea-side place in France called Cannes. There he saw a house and grounds to be sold, which took his fancy as a nice retired place to keep Number Two in. Nothing particular was wanted but the money to buy it; and, not having the little amount in his own possession, Mr. James Smith makes a virtue of necessity, and goes back overland to his wife with private designs on her purse-strings. Number Two, who objects to be left behind, goes with him as far as London. There he trumps up the first story that comes into his head, about rents in the country, and a house in Lincolnshire that is too damp for her to trust herself in; and so, leaving her for a few days in London, starts boldly for Darrock Hall. His notion was to wheedle your mistress out of the money by good behavior; but it seems he started badly by quarreling with her about a fiddle-playing parson who—"

"Yes, yes, I know all about that part of the story," I broke in, seeing by Mr. Dark's manner that he was likely to speak both ignorantly and impertinently of my mistress's unlucky friendship for Mr. Meeke. "Go on to the time when I left my master alone in the Red Room, and tell me what he did between midnight and nine the next morning."

"Did?" said Mr. Dark. "Why he went to bed with the unpleasant conviction on his mind that your mistress had found him out, and with no comfort to speak of, except what he could get out of the brandy-bottle. He couldn't sleep; and the more he tossed and tumbled the more certain he felt that his wife intended to have him tried for bigamy. At last, toward the gray of the morning, he could stand it no longer, and he made up his mind to give the law the slip while he had the chance. As soon as he was dressed it struck him that there might be a reward offered for catching him, and he determined to make that slight change in his personal appearance which puzzled the witnesses so much before the magistrate to-day. So he opens his dressing-case and crops his hair in no time, and takes off his whiskers next. The fire was out, and he had to shave in cold water. What with that, and what with the flurry of his mind, naturally enough he cut himself—"

"And dried the blood with his night-gown!" said I.

"With his night-gown," repeated Mr. Dark. "It was the first thing that lay handy, and he snatched it up. Wait a bit, though, the cream of the thing is to come. When he had done being his own barber, he couldn't for the life of him hit on a way of getting rid of the loose hair. The fire was out, and he had no matches, so he couldn't burn it. As for throwing it away, he didn't dare do that in the house, or about the house, for fear of its being found, and betraying what he had done. So he wraps it all up in paper, crams it into his pocket to be disposed of when he is at a safe distance from the Hall, takes his bag, gets out at the window, shuts it softly after him, and makes for the road as fast as his long legs will carry him. There he walks on till a coach overtakes him; and so travels back to London to find himself in a fresh scrape as soon as he gets there. An interesting situation, William, and hard traveling from one end of France to the other had not agreed together in the case of Number Two. Mr. James Smith found her in bed, with doctor's orders that she was not to be moved. There was nothing for it after that but to lie by in London till the lady got better. Luckily for us she didn't hurry herself; so that, after all, William, your mistress has to thank the very woman who supplanted her for clearing her character by helping us to find Mr. James Smith!"

"And pray how did you come by that loose hair of his which you showed before the Justice to-day?" I asked.

"Thank Number Two again," says Mr. Dark. "I was put up to asking after it by what she told me. While we were talking about the advertisement, I made so bold as to inquire what first set her thinking that her husband and the Mr. James Smith whom we wanted might be one and the same man. 'Nothing,' says she, 'but seeing him come home with his hair cut short and his whiskers shaved off, and finding that he could not give me any good reason for disfiguring himself in that way. I had my suspicions that something was wrong, and the sight of your advertisement strengthened them directly.' The hearing her say that suggested to my mind that there might be a difficulty in identifying him after the change in his looks; and I asked him what he had done with the loose hair before we left London. It was found in the pocket of his traveling coat just as he had huddled it up there on leaving the Hall, worry and fright and vexation having caused him to forget all about it. Of course I took charge of the parcel; and you know what good it did as well as I do. So to speak, William, it just completed this beautifully neat case. Looking at the matter in a professional point of view, I don't hesitate to say that we have managed our business with Mr. James Smith to perfection. We have produced him at the right time, and we are going to get rid of him at the right time. By to-night he will be on his way to foreign parts with Number Two, and he won't show his nose in England again if he lives to the age of Methuselah."

It was a relief to hear that; and it was almost as great a comfort to find, from what Mr. Dark said next, that my mistress need fear nothing that the French woman could do for the future. The threat that had fallen from her on her reappearance before the Justice, he assured me, had not at all surprised him. He had suspected from the first that she must have known of the second marriage, because he believed it to be impossible that she would risk bringing her infamous charge against my mistress and myself without being acquainted with the nature of the circumstance which made it Mr. James Smith's interest to keep out of the way. This information, he said, she might well have gained by listening at the door; but he felt convinced at the same time that it did not include a knowledge of the means by which evidence of the second marriage might be procured. If she had possessed this dangerous information, she would long since have turned it to good account; for the threat of making the evidence public would have given her exactly that hold over her mistress which it was her interest to gain. As matters had turned out, however, there was no reason to fear her, let her know as much as she might. The charge of theft, on which she was about to be tried, did not afford the shadow of an excuse, in law any more than in logic, for alluding to the crime which her master had committed. If she meant to talk about it she might do so at Botany Bay; but she would not have the slightest chance of being listened to previously in a court of law.

"In short," said Mr. Dark, rising to take his leave, "as I have told you already, William, it's check-mate for Marmzelle. She didn't manage the business of the robbery half as sharply as I should have expected. She certainly began well enough by staying modestly at a lodging in the village to give her attendance at the examinations, as it might be required. Nothing could look more innocent and respectable so far. But her hiding the property between the mattresses of her bed—the very first place that any experienced man would think of looking in—was such an amazingly stupid thing to do, that I really can't account for it, unless her mind had more weighing on it than it was able to bear, which, considering the heavy stakes she played for, is likely enough. Any how, her hands are tied now, and her tongue too, for the matter of that. Give my respects to your mistress, and tell her that her runaway husband and her lying maid will never either of them harm her again as long as they live. She has nothing to do now but to pluck up her spirits and live happy. Here's long life to her and to you, William, in the last glass of ale; and here's the same toast to myself in the bottom of the jug." With those words, Mr. Dark pocketed his large snuff-box, gave a last wink with his bright eye, and walked away, whistling, to meet the London coach.

I, who knew my poor mistress far better than he did—I, who had noticed, that very day, that the sad, dull, vacant look in her face never brightened when the Justice spoke the few welcome words which told her that her innocence was made clear, and that she was a free woman again—I, in short, who looked at her and at her future prospects with very different eyes from the eyes of a stranger, felt mournful misgivings at my heart when I thought over Mr. Dark's parting toast after he had left me. Other people—her relation, the lawyer, among them—thought she would get over the shock that had been inflicted on her, with time and care. I alone felt doubts about her recovery from the first. As soon as possible after the occurrence of the events that I have just been relating she was removed to London for change of scene and for the best medical advice. From London she was sent to the sea-side; and her next removal was to the country house on the estate in Yorkshire. I attended her wherever she went, and saw but too plainly the utter uselessness of all the efforts that were made to preserve her life. She drooped and faded slowly, without a look of impatience or a word of complaint, considerate, and kind, and thankful for small services to the last. Long years have passed since those melancholy days, but the sorrowful remembrance of them is still so strong in my memory that I can not be sure of preserving my composure, even now, if I dwell too long on the details of my mistress's last illness. It will be better, on all accounts, to pass over them, and to come quickly to the sad end. In little more than a year from the time of that last examination before the Justice I made one of the mourners who followed her to the grave. The day before she departed I was called to her bedside. All through her illness she had never spoken of the trouble and the terror of the past time. But when she took leave of me forever in this world, she reverted, for a moment, to the old days of sorrow. "We bore the burden of that heavy trial together," she said, "and when I am gone, William, you will find that I have not forgotten you." Those words referred to the legacy which, in her great generosity and gratitude, she left me out of the savings of her income, which were hers to dispose of. It was a large sum—too large a sum for a person like me. I do not underrate the value of that money—I am deeply sensible of the great advantage and security of worldly position, which it has been the means of procuring for me—but I can say, honestly, from the bottom of my heart, that I would have given it all, and more, to have saved my mistress's life, and to have purchased me the privilege of living and dying in her service.

My long story is almost done. A few last words relating to the persons chiefly concerned in the events of this narrative will conclude all that it is now necessary for me to say.

The French woman was found guilty of the robbery, and was transported for seven years. She did not live to serve out her time. After two years' submission to punishment, she and another woman joined some male convicts in an attempt to escape. They succeeded in getting away, but perished fearfully in the interior of the country. The bodies were discovered by the help of the natives; and certain appearances were observed which led to horrible suspicions of cannibalism on the part of the men, who probably survived starvation longest. The circumstances are all detailed, I believe, in the Parliamentary Blue Books. But it is needless for my purpose to say more about them than I have said already.

Mr. Meeke must not be forgotten, although he has dropped out of the latter part of my story. The truth is that he had nothing to do with the serious events which followed the French woman's perjury. I remember hearing that he came to the Hall, after I had been removed to the Justice's, and asked, helplessly, if he could be of any use. In the confusion and wretchedness of the time he was treated with very little ceremony, and went back to his parsonage in despair. There can be no question, I think, that the poor little man was, in his weak way, warmly attached to my mistress. The news of her death quite broke him down. He said he should never forget, to his dying day, that he had been the innocent first cause of all the trouble at Darrock Hall; and he declared that he would devote the rest of his life to a great and good object, as some atonement for the mischief that he had unconsciously produced. When I next heard of him he had carried out his idea by volunteering to join the missionary expedition to the Cape of Good Hope—an object which he was about as fit to forward as my cat there lying asleep on the rug. However, his strength gave way—fortunately, perhaps, for himself—before responsibilities of any sort were fairly laid on his shoulders. On the voyage out he suffered so severely from sea-sickness that they were obliged to put him ashore at Madeira. He had broken a blood-vessel, and was given over by the ship's surgeon; but he languished, rather than lived, for some time, in the fine climate in which they left him. When the last weak remains of life were exhausted, Death took him very quietly. He departed with my mistress's name on his lips, and he is now laid in the English burial-ground at Madeira.

As for Mr. James Smith, he was spared for many years, and lived quietly abroad with his Scotch wife. I hope, for his own sake, that he took advantage of the opportunity for repentance which was mercifully granted to him. It may seem unjust, to our earthly eyes, that he should have offended so grievously, and have escaped suffering for his wickedness in this world; but our punishments, as well as our rewards, wait for us beyond our mortal time. He has gone to answer for his sins before a Judge who can never err. I heard nothing of his last moments; and I can say no more of him, now I have spoken the words that record his death.

Hardly six months have passed since I heard of his widow. She has married again, and is settled in London. She, and I, and Mr. Dark—who is now a feeble old man, the eldest of a brotherhood occupying a charitable asylum—are the only survivors of the troubles at Darrock Hall. I take Mr. Dark a present of snuff once a year. The last time I saw him his faculties were thought to be decaying. He knew who I was, however; for he winked feebly, and muttered and mumbled several words together. I could not make out one half of them; but I heard enough to convince me that he was still given to talking about the Tour in Scotland, and the "beautifully neat case" in which it ended.

I have perhaps wearied you, Sir, by a very long story. But I hope I have not occupied your time without convincing you that I had some little cause for speaking as I did when I said that there was no sight in the country I would not sooner take you to see than the empty house which is known by the name of Darrock Hall.

Robert Barr
(1850–1912)

LORD CHIZELRIGG'S
MISSING FORTUNE

from *The Triumphs of Eugène Valmont*

Robert Barr's Valmont, the first humorous detective, felt by many observers to be the model for Agatha Christie's later Hercule Poirot, is remembered today because of the much-admired "Absent-Minded Coterie" from the same collection. But there are other "Triumphs" worth review, including this one about a will and a hidden fortune—stock elements in most nineteenth-century melodrama.

Today, of course, people have so little to leave that relatives barely notice whether Uncle made a will or not. (Not too many heirs are willing to commit murder for a pair of false teeth, a truss, and a copy of The Royal Wedding in Pictures.)

Intriguingly, Barr introduces a real-life figure (American inventor Thomas Alva Edison) into his fictional account, a literary device that was to gain greater favour with later writers. The Scottish-born Barr spent his early years as a reporter in Canada and the United States.

Chapter I

The name of the late Lord Chizelrigg never comes to my mind without instantly suggesting that of Mr. T. A. Edison. I never saw the late Lord Chizelrigg, and I have met Mr. Edison only twice in my life, yet the two men are linked in my memory, and it was a remark the latter once made that in great measure enabled me to solve the mystery which the former had wrapped round his actions.

There is no memorandum at hand to tell me the year in which those two meetings with Edison took place. I received a note from the Italian Ambassador in Paris requesting me to wait upon him in the Embassy. I learned that on the next day a deputation was to set out from the Embassy to one of the chief hotels, there to make a call in state upon the great American inventor, and formally present to him various insignia accompanying certain honours which the King of Italy had conferred upon him. As many Italian nobles of high rank had been invited, and as these dignitaries would not only be robed in the costumes pertaining to their orders, but in many cases would wear jewels of almost inestimable value, my presence was desired in the belief that I might perhaps be able to ward off any attempt on the part of the deft-handed gentry who might possibly make an effort to gain these treasures, and I may add, with perhaps some little self-gratification, no *contre-temps* occurred.

Mr. Edison, of course, had long before received notification of the hour at which the deputation would wait upon him, but when we entered the large parlour assigned to the inventor, it was evident to me at a glance that the celebrated man had forgotten all about the function. He stood by a bare table, from which the cloth had been jerked and flung into a corner, and upon that table were placed several bits of black and greasy machinery—cog wheels, pulleys, bolts, etc. These seemingly belonged to a French workman who stood on the other side of the table, with one of the parts in his grimy hand. Edison's own hands were not too clean, for he had palpably been examining the material, and conversing with the workman, who wore the ordinary long blouse of an iron craftsman in a small way. I judged him to be a man with a little shop of his own in some back street, who did odd jobs of engineering, assisted perhaps by a skilled helper or two, and a few apprentices. Edison looked sternly towards the door as the solemn procession filed in, and there was a trace of annoyance on his face at the interruption, mixed with a shade of perplexity as to what this gorgeous display all meant. The Italian is as ceremonious as the Spaniard where a function is concerned, and the official who held the ornate box which contained the jewellery resting on a velvet cushion, stepped slowly forward, and came to a stand in front of the bewildered American. Then the Ambassador, in sonorous voice, spoke some gracious words regarding the friendship existing between the United States and Italy, expressed a wish that their rivalry should ever take the form of benefits conferred upon the human race, and instanced the honoured recipient as the most notable example the world had yet produced of a man bestowing blessings upon all nations in the arts of peace. The eloquent Ambassador concluded by saying that, at the command of his Royal master, it was both his duty and his pleasure to present, and so forth and so forth.

Mr. Edison, visibly ill at ease, nevertheless made a suitable reply in the fewest possible words, and the *étalage* being thus at an end, the noblemen, headed by their Ambassador, slowly retired, myself forming the tail of the procession. Inwardly I deeply sympathised with the French workman who thus unexpectedly found himself confronted by so much magnificence. He cast one wild look about him, but saw that his retreat was cut off unless he displaced some of these gorgeous grandees. He tried then to shrink into himself, and finally stood helpless like one paralysed. In spite of Republican institutions, there is deep down in every Frenchman's heart a respect and awe for official pageants, sumptuously staged and costumed as this one was. But he likes to view it from afar, and supported by his fellows, not thrust incongruously into the midst of things, as was the case with this panic-stricken engineer. As I passed out, I cast a glance over my shoulder at the humble artisan content with a profit of a few francs a day, and at the millionaire inventor opposite him. Edison's face, which during the address had been cold and impassive, reminding me vividly of a bust of Napoleon, was now all aglow with enthusiasm as he turned to his humble visitor. He cried joyfully to the workman:—

"A minute's demonstration is worth an hour's

explanation. I'll call round tomorrow at your shop, about ten o'clock, and show you how to make the thing work."

I lingered in the hall until the Frenchman came out, then, introducing myself to him, asked the privilege of visiting his shop next day at ten. This was accorded with that courtesy which you will always find among the industrial classes of France, and next day I had the pleasure of meeting Mr. Edison. During our conversation I complimented him on his invention of the incandescent electric light, and this was the reply that has ever remained in my memory:—

"It was not an invention, but a discovery. We knew what we wanted; a carbonised tissue, which would withstand the electric current in a vacuum for, say, a thousand hours. If no such tissue existed, then the incandescent light, as we know it, was not possible. My assistants started out to find this tissue, and we simply carbonised everything we could lay our hands on, and ran the current through it in a vacuum. At last we struck the right thing, as we were bound to do if we kept on long enough, and if the thing existed. Patience and hard work will overcome any obstacle."

This belief has been of great assistance to me in my profession. I know the idea is prevalent that a detective arrives at his solutions in a dramatic way through following clues invisible to the ordinary man. This doubtless frequently happens, but, as a general thing, the patience and hard work which Mr. Edison commends is a much safer guide. Very often the following of excellent clues had led me to disaster, as was the case with my unfortunate attempt to solve the mystery of the five hundred diamonds.

As I was saying, I never think of the late Lord Chizelrigg without remembering Mr. Edison at the same time, and yet the two were very dissimilar. I suppose Lord Chizelrigg was the most useless man that ever lived, while Edison is the opposite.

One day my servant brought in to me a card on which was engraved "Lord Chizelrigg."

"Show his lordship in," I said, and there appeared a young man of perhaps twenty-four or twenty-five, well dressed, and of most charming manners, who, nevertheless, began his interview by asking a question such as had never before been addressed to me, and which, if put to a solicitor, or other professional man, would have been answered with some indignation. Indeed, I believe it is a written or unwritten law of the legal profession that the acceptance of such a proposal as Lord Chizelrigg made to me, would, if proved, result in the disgrace and ruin of the lawyer.

"Monsieur Valmont," began Lord Chizelrigg, "do you ever take up cases on speculation?"

"On speculation, sir? I do not think I understand you."

His lordship blushed like a girl, and stammered slightly as he attempted an explanation.

"What I mean is, do you accept a case on a contingent fee? That is to say, monsieur—er—well, not to put too fine a point upon it, no results, no pay."

I replied somewhat severely:—

"Such an offer has never been made to me, and

128

I may say at once that I should be compelled to decline it were I favoured with the opportunity. In the cases submitted to me, I devote my time and attention to their solution. I try to deserve success, but I cannot command it, and as in the interim I must live, I am reluctantly compelled to make a charge for my time, at least. I believe the doctor sends in his bill, though the patient dies."

The young man laughed uneasily, and seemed almost too embarrassed to proceed, but finally he said:—

"Your illustration strikes home with greater accuracy than probably you imagined when you uttered it. I have just paid my last penny to the physician who attended my late uncle, Lord Chizelrigg, who died six months ago. I am fully aware that the suggestion I made may seem like a reflection upon your skill, or rather, as implying a doubt regarding it. But I should be grieved, monsieur, if you fell into such an error. I could have come here and commissioned you to undertake some elucidation of the strange situation in which I find myself, and I make no doubt you would have accepted the task if your numerous engagements had permitted. Then, if you failed, I should have been unable to pay you, for I am practically bankrupt. My whole desire, therefore, was to make an honest beginning, and to let you know exactly how I stand. If you succeed, I shall be a rich man; if you do not succeed, I shall be what I am now, penniless. Have I made it plain now why I began with a question which you had every right to resent?"

129

"Perfectly plain, my lord, and your candour does you credit."

I was very much taken with the unassuming manners of the young man, and his evident desire to accept no service under false pretences. When I had finished my sentence the pauper nobleman rose to his feet, and bowed.

"I am very much your debtor, monsieur, for your courtesy in receiving me, and can only beg pardon for occupying your time on a futile quest. I wish you good-morning, monsieur."

"One moment, my lord," I rejoined, waving him to his chair again. "Although I am unprepared to accept a commission on the terms you suggest, I may, nevertheless, be able to offer a hint or two that will prove of service to you. I think I remember the announcement of Lord Chizelrigg's death. He was somewhat eccentric, was he not?"

"Eccentric?" said the young man, with a slight laugh, seating himself again— "well, *rather!*"

"I vaguely remember that he was accredited with the possession of something like twenty thousand acres of land?"

"Twenty-seven thousand, as a matter of fact," replied my visitor.

"Have you fallen heir to the lands as well as to the title?"

"Oh, yes; the estate was entailed. The old gentleman could not divert it from me if he would, and I rather suspect that fact must have been the cause of some worry to him."

"But surely, my lord, a man who owns, as one might say, a principality in this wealthy realm of England, cannot be penniless?"

130

Again the young man laughed.

"Well, no," he replied, thrusting his hand in his pocket and bringing to light a few brown coppers, and a white silver piece. "I possess enough money to buy some food to-night, but not enough to dine at the Hotel Cecil. You see, it is like this. I belong to a somewhat ancient family, various members of whom went the pace, and mortgaged their acres up to the hilt. I could not raise a further penny on my estates were I to try my hardest, because at the time the money was lent, land was much more valuable than it is to-day. Agricultural depression, and all that sort of thing, have, if I may put it so, left me a good many thousands worse off than if I had no land at all. Besides this, during my late uncle's life, Parliament, on his behalf, intervened once or twice, allowing him in the first place to cut valuable timber, and in the second place to sell the pictures of Chizelrigg Chase at Christie's for figures which make one's mouth water."

"And what became of the money?" I asked, whereupon once more this genial nobleman laughed.

"That is exactly what I came up in the lift to learn if Monsieur Valmont could discover."

"My lord, you interest me," I said, quite truly, with an uneasy apprehension that I should take up his case after all, for I liked the young man already. His lack of pretence appealed to me, and that sympathy which is so universal among my countrymen enveloped him, as I may say, quite independent of my own will.

"My uncle," went on Lord Chizelrigg, "was

somewhat of an anomaly in our family. He must have been a reversal to a very, very ancient type; a type of which we have no record. He was as miserly as his forefathers were prodigal. When he came into the title and estate some twenty years ago, he dismissed the whole retinue of servants, and, indeed, was defendant in several cases at law where retainers of our family brought suit against him for wrongful dismissal, or dismissal without a penny compensation in lieu of notice. I am pleased to say he lost all his cases, and when he pleaded poverty, got permission to sell a certain number of heirlooms, enabling him to make compensation, and giving him something on which to live. These heirlooms at auction sold so unexpectedly well, that my uncle acquired a taste, as it were, of what might be done. He could always prove that the rents went to the mortgagees, and that he had nothing on which to exist, so on several occasions he obtained permission from the courts to cut timber and sell pictures, until he denuded the estate and made an empty barn of the old manor house. He lived like any labourer, occupying himself sometimes as a carpenter, sometimes as a blacksmith; indeed, he made a blacksmith's shop of the library, one of the most noble rooms in Britain, containing thousands of valuable books which again and again he applied for permission to sell, but this privilege was never granted to him. I find on coming into the property that my uncle quite persistently evaded the law, and depleted this superb collection, book by book, surreptitiously through dealers in London. This, of course, would have got him into deep trouble if it had been discovered before his death, but now the valuable volumes are gone, and there is no redress. Many of them are doubtless in America, or in museums and collections of Europe."

"You wish me to trace them, perhaps?" I interpolated.

"Oh, no; they are past praying for. The old man made tens of thousands by the sale of the timber, and other of thousands by disposing of the pictures. The house is denuded of its fine old furniture, which was immensely valuable, and then the books, as I have said, must have brought in the revenue of a prince, if he got anything like their value, and you may be sure he was shrewd enough to know their worth. Since the last refusal of the courts to allow him further relief, as he termed it, which was some seven years ago, he had quite evidently been disposing of books and furniture by a private sale, in defiance of the law. At that time I was under age, but my guardians opposed his application to the courts, and demanded an account of the moneys already in his hands. The judges upheld the opposition of my guardians, and refused to allow a further spoliation of the estate, but they did not grant the accounting my guardians asked, because the proceeds of the former sales were entirely at the disposal of my uncle, and were sanctioned by the law to permit him to live as befitted his station. If he lived meagerly instead of lavishly, as my guardians contended, that, the judges said, was his affair, and there the matter ended.

"My uncle took a violent dislike to me on account of this opposition to his last application, although, of course, I had nothing whatever to do with the matter. He lived like a hermit, mostly in the library, and was waited upon by an old man and his wife, and these three were the only inhabitants of a mansion that could comfortably house a hundred. He visited nobody, and would allow no one to approach Chizelrigg Chase. In order that all who had the misfortune to have dealing with him should continue to endure trouble after his death, he left what might be called a will, but which rather may be termed a letter to me. Here is a copy of it."

My dear Tom,—You will find your fortune between a couple of sheets of paper in the library.

Your affectionate uncle,
Reginald Moran, Earl of Chizelrigg.

"I should doubt if that were a legal will," said I.

"It doesn't need to be," replied the young man with a smile. "I am next-of-kin, and heir to everything he possessed, although, of course, he might have given his money elsewhere if he had chosen to do so. Why he did not bequeath it to some institution, I do not know. He knew no man personally except his own servants, whom he misused and starved, but, as he told them, he misused and starved himself, so they had no cause to grumble. He said he was treating them like one of the family. I suppose he thought it would cause me more worry and anxiety if he concealed the money, and put me on the wrong scent, which I am convinced he has done, than to leave it openly to any person or charity."

"I need not ask if you have searched the library?"

"Searched it? Why, there never was such a search since the world began!"

"Possibly you put the task into incompetent hands?"

"You are hinting, Monsieur Valmont, that I engaged others until my money was gone, then came to you with a speculative proposal. Let me assure you such is not the case. Incompetent hands, I grant you, but the hands were my own. For the past six months I have lived practically as my uncle lived. I have rummaged that library from floor to ceiling. It was left in a frightful state, littered with old newspapers, accounts, and what-not. Then, of course, there were the books remaining in the library, still a formidable collection."

"Was your uncle a religious man?"

"I could not say. I surmise not. You see, I was unacquainted with him, and never saw him until after his death. I fancy he was not religious, otherwise he could not have acted as he did. Still, he proved himself a man of such twisted mentality that anything is possible."

"I knew a case once where an heir who expected a large sum of money was bequeathed a family Bible, which he threw into the fire, learning afterwards, to his dismay, that it contained many thousands of pounds in Bank of England notes, the object of the devisor being to induce the legatee to read the good Book or suffer through the neglect of it."

"I have searched the Scriptures," said the youthful Earl with a laugh, "but the benefit has been moral rather than material."

"Is there any chance that your uncle has deposited his wealth in a bank, and has written a cheque for the amount, leaving it between two leaves of a book?"

"Anything is possible, monsieur, but I think that highly improbable. I have gone through every tome, page by page, and I suspect very few of the volumes have been opened for the last twenty years."

"How much money do you estimate he accumulated?"

"He must have cleared more than a hundred thousand pounds, but speaking of banking it, I would like to say that my uncle evinced a deep distrust of banks, and never drew a cheque in his life so far as I am aware. All accounts were paid in gold by this old steward, who first brought the receipted bill in to my uncle, and then received the exact amount, after having left the room, and waited until he was rung for, so that he might not learn the repository from which my uncle drew his store. I believe if the money is ever found it will be in gold, and I am very sure that this will was written, if we may call it a will, to put us on the wrong scent."

"Have you had the library cleared out?"

"Oh, no, it is practically as my uncle left it. I realised that if I were to call in help, it would be well that the new-comer found it undisturbed."

"You were quite right, my lord. You say you examined all the papers?"

"Yes; so far as that is concerned, the room has been very fairly gone over, but nothing that was in it the day my uncle died has been removed, not even his anvil."

"His anvil?"

"Yes; I told you he made a blacksmith's shop, as well as bedroom, of the library. It is a huge room, with a great fire-place at one end which formed an excellent forge. He and the steward built the forge in the eastern fire-place of brick and clay, with their own hands, and erected there a second-hand blacksmith's bellows."

"What work did he do at his forge?"

"Oh, anything that was required about the place. He seems to have been a very expert iron-worker. He would never buy a new implement for the garden or the house so long as he could get one second-hand, and he never bought anything second-hand while at his forge he might repair what was already in use. He kept an old cob, on which he used to ride through the park, and he always put the shoes on this cob himself, the steward informs me, so he must have understood the use of blacksmith's tools. He made a carpenter's shop of the chief drawing-room and erected a bench there. I think a very useful mechanic was spoiled when my uncle became an earl."

"You have been living at the Chase since your uncle died?"

"If you call it living, yes. The old steward and his wife have been looking after me, as they looked after my uncle, and, seeing me day after day, coatless, and covered with dust, I imagine they think me a second edition of the old man."

"Does the steward know the money is missing?"

"No; no one knows it but myself. This will was left on the anvil, in an envelope addressed to me."

"Your statement is exceedingly clear, Lord Chizelrigg, but I confess I don't see much daylight through it. Is there a pleasant country around Chizelrigg Chase?"

"Very; especially at this season of the year. In autumn and winter the house is a little draughty. It needs several thousand pounds to put it in repair."

"Draughts do not matter in the summer. I have been long enough in England not to share the fear of my countrymen for a *courant d'air*. Is there a spare bed in the manor house, or shall I take down a cot with me, or let us say a hammock?"

"Really," stammered the earl, blushing again, "you must not think I detailed all these circumstances in order to influence you to take up what may be a hopeless case. I, of course, am deeply interested, and, therefore, somewhat prone to be carried away when I begin a recital of my uncle's eccentricities. If I receive your permission, I will call on you again in a month or two. To tell you the truth, I borrowed a little money from the old steward, and visited London to see my legal advisers, hoping that in the circumstances I may get permission to sell something that will keep me from starvation. When I spoke of the house being denuded, I meant relatively, of course. There are still a good many antiquities which would doubtless bring me in a comfortable sum of money. I have been borne up by the belief that I should find my uncle's gold. Lately, I have been beset by a suspicion that the old gentleman thought the library the only valuable asset left, and for this reason wrote his note, thinking I would be afraid to sell anything from that room. The old rascal must have made a pot of money out of those shelves. The catalogue shows that there was a copy of the first book printed in England by Caxton, and several priceless Shakespeares, as well as many other volumes that a collector would give a small fortune for. All these are gone. I think when I show this to be the case, the authorities cannot refuse me the right to sell something, and, if I get this permission, I shall at once call upon you."

"Nonsense, Lord Chizelrigg. Put your application in motion, if you like. Meanwhile I beg of you to look upon me as a more substantial banker than your old steward. Let us enjoy a good dinner together at the Cecil to-night, if you will do me the honour to be my guest. To-morrow we can leave for Chizelrigg Chase. How far is it?"

"About three hours," replied the young man, becoming as red as a new Queen Anne villa. "Really, Monsieur Valmont, you overwhelm me with your kindness, but nevertheless I accept your generous offer."

"Then that's settled. What's the name of the old steward?"

"Higgins."

"You are certain he has no knowledge of the hiding-place of this treasure?"

"Oh, quite sure. My uncle was not a man to make a confidant of any one, least of all an old babbler like Higgins."

"Well, I should like to be introduced to Higgins as a benighted foreigner. That will make him despise me and treat me like a child."

"Oh, I say," protested the earl, "I should have thought you'd lived long enough in England to have got out of the notion that we do not appreciate the foreigner. Indeed, we are the only nation in the world that extends a cordial welcome to him, rich or poor."

"*Certainement,* my lord, I should be deeply disappointed did you not take me at my proper valuation, but I cherish no delusions regarding the contempt with which Higgins will regard me. He will look upon me as a sort of simpleton to whom the Lord had been unkind by not making England my native land. Now, Higgins must be led to believe that I am in his own class; that is, a servant of yours. Higgins and I will gossip over the fire together, should these spring evenings prove chilly, and before two or three weeks are past I shall have learned a great deal about your uncle that you never dreamed of. Higgins will talk more freely with a fellow-servant than with his master, however much he may respect that master, and then, as I am a foreigner, he will babble down to my comprehension, and I shall get details that he never would think of giving to a fellow-countryman."

Chapter II

The young earl's modesty in such description of his home as he had given me, left me totally unprepared for the grandeur of the mansion, one corner of which he inhabited. It is such a place as you read of in romances of the Middle Ages; not a pinnacled or turreted French château of that period, but a beautiful and substantial stone manor house of a ruddy colour, whose warm hue seemed to add a softness to the severity of its architecture. It is built round an outer and an inner courtyard and could house a thousand, rather than the hundred with which its owner had accredited it. There are many stone-mullioned windows, and one at the end of the library might well have graced a cathedral. This superb residence occupies the centre of a heavily timbered park, and from the lodge at the gates we drove at least a mile and a half under the grandest avenue of old oaks I have ever seen. It seemed incredible that the owner of all this should actually lack the ready money to pay his fare to town!

Old Higgins met us at the station with a somewhat rickety cart, to which was attached the ancient cob that the late earl used to shoe. We entered a noble hall, which probably looked the larger because of the entire absence of any kind of furniture, unless two complete suits of venerable armour which stood on either hand might be considered as furnishing. I laughed aloud when the door was shut, and the sound echoed like the merriment of ghosts from the dim timbered roof above me.

"What are you laughing at?" asked the earl.

"I am laughing to see you put your modern tall hat on that mediaeval helmet."

"Oh, that's it! Well, put yours on the other. I mean no disrespect to the ancestor who wore this suit, but we are short of the harmless, necessary hatrack, so I put my topper on the antique helmet, and thrust the umbrella (if I have one) in behind here, and down one of his legs. Since I came in possession, a very crafty-looking dealer from London visited me, and attempted to sound me regarding the sale of these suits of armour. I gathered he would give enough money to keep me in new suits, London made, for the rest of my life, but when I endeavoured to find out if he had had commercial dealings with my prophetic uncle, he became frightened and bolted. I imagine that if I had possessed presence of mind enough to have lured him into one of our most uncomfortable dungeons, I might have learned where some of the family treasures went to. Come up these stairs, Monsieur Valmont, and I will show you your room."

We had lunched on the train coming down, so after a wash in my own room I proceeded at once to inspect the library. It proved, indeed, a most noble apartment, and it had been scandalously used by the old reprobate, its late tenant. There were two huge fire-places, one in the middle of the north wall and the other at the eastern end. In the latter had been erected a rude brick forge, and beside the forge hung a great black bellows, smoky with usage. On a wooden block lay the anvil, and around it rested and rusted several ham-

142

mers, large and small. At the western end was a glorious window filled with ancient stained glass, which, as I have said, might have adorned a cathedral. Extensive as the collection of books was, the great size of this chamber made it necessary that only the outside wall should be covered with bookcases, and even these were divided by tall windows. The opposite wall was blank, with the exception of a picture here and there, and these pictures offered a further insult to the room, for they were cheap prints, mostly coloured lithographs that had appeared in Christmas numbers of London weekly journals, encased in poverty-stricken frames, hanging from nails ruthlessly driven in above them. The floor was covered with a litter of papers, in some places knee-deep, and in the corner farthest from the forge still stood the bed on which the ancient miser had died.

"Looks like a stable, doesn't it?" commented the earl, when I had finished my inspection. "I am sure the old boy simply filled it up with this rubbish to give me the trouble of examining it. Higgins tells me that up to within a month before he died the room was reasonably clear of all this muck. Of course it had to be, or the place would have caught fire from the sparks of the forge. The old man made Higgins gather all the papers he could find anywhere about the place, ancient accounts, newspapers, and what not, even to the brown wrapping paper you see, in which parcels came, and commanded him to strew the floor with this litter, because, as he complained, Higgins's boots on the boards made too much noise, and Higgins, who is not in the least of an inquiring mind, accepted this explanation as entirely meeting the case."

Higgins proved to be a garrulous old fellow, who needed no urging to talk about the late earl; indeed, it was almost impossible to deflect his conversation into any other channel. Twenty years' intimacy with the eccentric nobleman had largely obliterated that sense of deference with which an English servant usually approaches his master. An English underling's idea of nobility is the man who never by any possibility works with his hands. The fact that Lord Chizelrigg had toiled at the carpenter's bench; had mixed cement in the drawing-room; had caused the anvil to ring out till midnight, aroused no admiration in Higgins's mind. In addition to this, the ancient nobleman had been penuriously strict in his examination of accounts, exacting the uttermost farthing, so the humble servitor regarded his memory with supreme contempt. I realised before the drive was finished from the station to Chizelrigg Chase that there was little use of introducing me to Higgins as a foreigner and a fellow-servant. I found myself completely unable to understand what the old fellow said. His dialect was as unknown to me as the Choctaw language would have been, and the young earl was compelled to act as interpreter on the occasions when we set this garrulous talking-machine going.

The new Earl of Chizelrigg, with the enthusiasm of a boy, proclaimed himself my pupil and assistant, and said he would do whatever he was told. His thorough and fruitless search of the library had convinced him that the old man was merely chaffing him, as he put it, by leaving such a letter as he had written. His lordship was certain that the money had been hidden somewhere else; probably buried under one of the trees in the park. Of course this was possible, and represented the usual method by which a stupid person conceals treasure, yet I did not think it probable. All conversations with Higgins showed the earl to have been an extremely suspicious man; suspicious of banks, suspicious even of Bank of England notes, suspicious of every person on earth, not omitting Higgins himself. Therefore, as I told his nephew, the miser would never allow the fortune out of his sight and immediate reach.

From the first the oddity of the forge and anvil being placed in his bedroom struck me as peculiar, and I said to the young man,—

"I'll stake my reputation that forge or anvil, or both, contain the secret. You see, the old gentleman worked sometimes till midnight, for Higgins could hear his hammering. If he used hard coal on the forge the fire would last through the night, and being in continual terror of thieves, as Higgins says, barricading the castle every evening before dark as if it were a fortress, he was bound to place the treasure in the most unlikely spot for a thief to get at it. Now, the coal fire smouldered all night long, and if the gold was in the forge underneath the embers, it would be extremely difficult to get at. A robber rummaging in the dark would burn his fingers in more senses than one. Then, as his lordship kept no less than four loaded revolvers under his pillow, all he had to do, if a thief entered his room, was to allow the search to go on until the thief started at the forge, then doubtless, as he had the range with reasonable accuracy night or day, he might sit up in bed and blaze away with revolver after revolver. There were twenty-eight shots that could be fired in about double as many seconds, so you see the robber stood little chance in the face of such a fusillade. I propose that we dismantle the forge."

Lord Chizelrigg was much taken by my reasoning, and one morning early we cut down the big bellows, tore it open, found it empty, then took brick after brick from the forge with a crowbar, for the old man had builded better than he knew with Portland cement. In fact, when we cleared away the rubbish between the bricks and the core of the furnace we came upon one cube of cement which was as hard as granite. With the aid of Higgins, and a set of rollers and levers, we managed to get this block out into the park, and attempted to crush it with the sledge hammers belonging to the forge, in which we were entirely unsuccessful. The more it resisted our efforts, the more certain we became that the coins would be found within it. As this would not be treasure-trove in the sense that the Government might make a claim upon it, there was no particular necessity for secrecy, so we had up a man from the mines near by with drills and dynamite, who speedily shattered the block into a million pieces, more or less. Alas! there was no trace in its debris of "pay dirt," as the western miner puts it. While the dynamite expert was on the spot, we induced him to shatter the anvil as well as the block of cement, and then the workman, doubtless thinking the new earl was as insane as the old one had been, shouldered his tools, and went back to his mine.

The earl reverted to his former opinion that the gold was concealed in the park, while I held even more firmly to my own belief that the fortune rested in the library.

"It is obvious," I said to him, "that if the treasure is buried outside, some one must have dug the hole. A man so timorous and so reticent as your uncle would allow no one to do this but himself. Higgins maintained the other evening that all picks and spades were safely locked up by himself each night in the tool-house. The mansion itself was barricaded with such exceeding care that it would have been difficult for your uncle to get outside even if he wished to do so. Then such a man as your uncle is described to have been would continually desire ocular demonstration that his savings were intact, which would be practically impossible if the gold had found a grave in the park. I propose now that we abandon violence and dynamite, and proceed to an intellectual search of the library."

"Very well," replied the young earl, "but as I have already searched the library very thoroughly, your use of the word 'intellectual,' Monsieur Valmont, is not in accord with your customary politeness. However, I am with you. 'Tis for you to command, and me to obey."

"Pardon me, my lord," I said, "I used the word 'intellectual' in contradistinction to the word 'dynamite.' It had no reference to your former search. I merely propose that we now abandon the use of chemical reaction, and employ the much greater force of mental activity. Did you notice any writing on the margins of the newspapers you examined?"

"No, I did not."

"It is possible that there may have been some communication on the white border of a newspaper?"

"It is, of course, possible."

"Then will you set yourself to the task of glancing over the margin of every newspaper, piling them away in another room when your scrutiny of each is complete? Do not destroy anything, but we must clear out the library completely. I am interested in the accounts, and will examine them."

It was exasperatingly tedious work, but after several days my assistant reported every margin scanned without result, while I had collected each bill and memorandum, classifying them according to date. I could not get rid of a suspicion that the contrary old beast had written instructions for the finding of the treasure on the back of some account, or on the fly-leaf of a book, and as I looked at the thousands of volumes still left in the library, the prospect of such a patient and minute search appalled me. But I remembered Edison's words to the effect that if a thing exists, search, exhaustive enough, will find it. From the mass of accounts I selected several; the rest I placed in another room, alongside the heap of the earl's newspapers.

"Now," said I to my helper, "if it please you,

we will have Higgins in, as I wish some explanation of these accounts."

"Perhaps I can assist you," suggested his lordship, drawing up a chair opposite the table on which I had spread the statements. "I have lived here for six months, and know as much about things as Higgins does. He is so difficult to stop when once he begins to talk. What is the first account you wish further light upon?"

"To go back thirteen years I find that your uncle bought a second-hand safe in Sheffield. Here is the bill. I consider it necessary to find that safe."

"Pray forgive me, Monsieur Valmont," cried the young man, springing to his feet and laughing; "so heavy an article as a safe should not slip readily from a man's memory, but it did from mine. The safe is empty, and I gave no more thought to it."

Saying this the earl went to one of the bookcases that stood against the wall, pulled it round as if it were a door, books and all, and displayed the front of an iron safe, the door of which he also drew open, exhibiting the usual empty interior of such a receptacle.

"I came on this," he said, "when I took down all these volumes. It appears that there was once a secret door leading from the library into an outside room, which has long since disappeared; the walls are very thick. My uncle doubtless caused this door to be taken off its hinges, and the safe placed in the aperture, the rest of which he then bricked up."

"Quite so," said I, endeavouring to conceal my disappointment. "As this strong box was bought

149

second-hand and not made to order, I suppose there can be no secret crannies in it?"

"It looks like a common or garden safe," reported my assistant, "but we'll have it out if you say so."

"Not just now," I replied; "we've had enough of dynamiting to make us feel like housebreakers already."

"I agree with you. What's the next item on the programme?"

"Your uncle's mania for buying things at second-hand was broken in three instances so far as I have been able to learn from a scrutiny of these accounts. About four years ago he purchased a new book from Denny and Co., the well-known booksellers of the Strand. Denny and Co. deal only in new books. Is there any comparatively new volume in the library?"

"Not one."

"Are you sure of that?"

"Oh, quite; I searched all the literature in the house. What is the name of the volume he bought?"

"That I cannot decipher. The initial letter looks like 'M,' but the rest is a mere wavy line. I see, however, that it cost twelve-and-sixpence, while the cost of carriage by parcel post was sixpence, which shows it weighed something under four pounds. This, with the price of the book, induces me to think that it was a scientific work, printed on heavy paper and illustrated."

"I know nothing of it," said the earl.

"The third account is for wall paper; twenty-seven rolls of an expensive wall paper, and twenty-seven rolls of a cheap paper, the latter being just half the price of the former. The wall paper seems to have been supplied by a tradesman in the station road in the village of Chizelrigg."

"There's your wall paper," cried the youth, waving his hand; "he was going to paper the whole house, Higgins told me, but got tired after he had finished the library, which took him nearly a year to accomplish, for he worked at it very intermittently, mixing the paste in the boudoir, a pailful at a time as he needed it. It was a scandalous thing to do, for underneath the paper is the most exquisite oak panelling, very plain, but very rich in colour."

I rose and examined the paper on the wall. It was dark brown, and answered the description of the expensive paper on the bill.

"What became of the cheap paper?" I asked.

"I don't know."

"I think," said I, "we are on the track of the mystery. I believe that paper covers a sliding panel or concealed door."

"It is very likely," replied the earl. "I intended to have the paper off, but I had no money to pay a workman, and I am not so industrious as was my uncle. What is your remaining account?"

"The last also pertains to paper, but comes from a firm in Budge Row, London, E.C. He has had, it seems, a thousand sheets of it, and it appears to have been frightfully expensive. This bill is also illegible, but I take it a thousand sheets were supplied, although of course it may have been a thousand quires, which would be a little more reasonable for the price charged, or a thousand reams, which would be exceedingly cheap."

"I don't know anything about that. Let's turn on Higgins."

Higgins knew nothing of this last order of paper either. The wall paper mystery he at once cleared up. Apparently the old earl had discovered by experiment that the heavy, expensive wall paper would not stick to the glossy panelling, so he had purchased a cheaper paper, and had pasted that on first. Higgins said he had gone all over the panelling with a yellowish-white paper, and after that was dry, he pasted over it the more expensive rolls.

"But," I objected, "the two papers were bought and delivered at the same time; therefore, he could not have found by experiment that the heavy paper would not stick."

"I don't think there is much in that," commented the earl; "the heavy paper may have been bought first, and found to be unsuitable, and then the coarse, cheap paper bought afterwards. The bill merely shows that the account was sent in on that date. Indeed, as the village of Chizelrigg is but a few miles away, it would have been quite possible for my uncle to have bought the heavy paper in the morning, tried it, and in the afternoon sent for the commoner lot; but in any case, the bill would not have been presented until months after the order, and the two purchases were thus lumped together."

I was forced to confess that this seemed reasonable.

Now, about the book ordered from Denny's.

Did Higgins remember anything regarding it? It came four years ago.

Ah, yes, Higgins did; he remembered it very well indeed. He had come in one morning with the earl's tea, and the old man was sitting up in bed reading his volume with such interest that he was unaware of Higgins's knock, and Higgins himself, being a little hard of hearing, took for granted the command to enter. The earl hastily thrust the book under the pillow, alongside the revolvers, and rated Higgins in a most cruel way for entering the room before getting permission to do so. He had never seen the earl so angry before, and he laid it all to this book. It was after the book had come that the forge had been erected and the anvil bought. Higgins never saw the book again, but one morning, six months before the earl died, Higgins, in raking out the cinders of the forge, found what he supposed was a portion of the book's cover. He believed his master had burnt the volume.

Having dismissed Higgins, I said to the earl,—

"The first thing to be done is to enclose this bill to Denny and Co., booksellers, Strand. Tell them you have lost the volume, and ask them to send another. There is likely some one in the shop who can decipher the illegible writing. I am certain the book will give us a clue. Now, I shall write to Braun and Sons, Budge Row. This is evidently a French company; in fact, the name as connected with paper-making runs in my mind, although I cannot at this moment place it. I shall ask them the use of this paper that they furnished to the late earl."

This was done accordingly, and now, as we thought, until the answers came, we were two men out of work. Yet the next morning, I am pleased to say, and I have always rather plumed myself on the fact, I solved the mystery before replies were received from London. Of course, both the book and the answer of the paper agents, by putting two and two together, would have given us the key.

After breakfast, I strolled somewhat aimlessly into the library, whose floor was now strewn merely with brown wrapping paper, bits of string, and all that. As I shuffled among this with my feet, as if tossing aside dead autumn leaves in a forest path, my attention was suddenly drawn to several squares of paper, unwrinkled, and never used for wrapping. These sheets seemed to me strangely familiar. I picked one of them up, and at once the significance of the name Braun and Sons occurred to me. They are paper makers in France, who produce a smooth, very tough sheet, which, dear as it is, proves infinitely cheap compared with the fine vellum it deposed in a certain branch of industry. In Paris, years before, these sheets had given me the knowledge of how a gang of thieves disposed of their gold without melting it. The paper was used instead of vellum in the rougher processes of manufacturing gold-leaf. It stood the constant beating of the hammer nearly as well as the vellum, and here at once there flashed on me the secret of the old man's midnight anvil work. He was transforming his sovereigns into gold-leaf, which must have been of a rude, thick kind, because to produce the gold-leaf of

154

commerce he still needed the vellum as well as a "cutch" and other machinery, of which we had found no trace.

"My lord," I called to my assistant; he was at the other end of the room; "I wish to test a theory on the anvil of your own fresh common sense."

"Hammer away," replied the earl, approaching me with his usual good-natured, jocular expression.

"I eliminate the safe from our investigations because it was purchased thirteen years ago, but the buying of the book, of wall covering, of this tough paper from France, all group themselves into a set of incidents occurring within the same month as the purchase of the anvil and the building of the forge; therefore, I think they are related to one another. Here are some sheets of paper he got from Budge Row. Have you ever seen anything like it? Try to tear this sample."

"It's reasonably tough," admitted his lordship, fruitlessly endeavouring to rip it apart.

"Yes. It was made in France, and is used in gold beating. Your uncle beat his sovereigns into gold-leaf. You will find that the book from Denny's is a volume on gold beating, and now as I remember that scribbled word which I could not make out, I think the title of the volume is 'Metallurgy.' It contains, no doubt, a chapter on the manufacture of gold-leaf."

"I believe you," said the earl; "but I don't see that the discovery sets us any further forward. We're now looking for gold-leaf instead of sovereigns."

155

"Let's examine this wall paper," said I.

I placed my knife under a corner of it at the floor, and quite easily ripped off a large section. As Higgins had said, the brown paper was on top, and the coarse, light-coloured paper underneath. But even that came away from the oak panelling as easily as though it hung there from habit, and not because of paste.

"Feel the weight of that," I cried, handing him the sheet I had torn from the wall.

"By Jove!" said the earl, in a voice almost of awe.

I took it from him, and laid it, face downwards, on the wooden table, threw a little water on the back, and with a knife scraped away the porous white paper. Instantly there gleamed up at us the baleful yellow of the gold. I shrugged my shoulders and spread out my hands. The Earl of Chizelrigg laughed aloud and very heartily.

"You see how it is," I cried. "The old man first covered the entire wall with this whitish paper. He heated his sovereigns at the forge and beat them out on the anvil, then completed the process rudely between the sheets of this paper from France. Probably he pasted the gold to the wall as soon as he shut himself in for the night, and covered it over with the more expensive paper before Higgins entered in the morning."

We found afterwards, however, that he had actually fastened the thick sheets of gold to the wall with carpet tacks.

His lordship netted a trifle over a hundred and twenty-three thousand pounds through my discovery, and I am pleased to pay tribute to the

156

young man's generosity by saying that his voluntary settlement made my bank account swell stout as a City alderman.

Emmuska, Baroness Orczy
(1865–1947)

THE FORDWYCH CASTLE MYSTERY

from *Lady Molly of Scotland Yard*

Baroness Orczy, the daughter of a Hungarian musi-cian, later settled in Britain and created the Scarlet Pimpernel as well as three important early detectives: the Old Man in the Corner (the prototypic armchair detective who leaves the legwork to others), Skin O' My Tooth (a lawyer of shady methods which nonethe-less serve the ends of justice), and Lady Molly of Scot-land Yard, the first female detective with official status. In the last chapter of the book, "our Lady" saves a man falsely accused of murder by marrying him secretly and leading the real perpetrator into a trap.

Lady Molly is one of the great female rivals of Sherlock Holmes, a formidable figure who never fails her reader.

The ornate descriptions and perfumed Victorian sentiment are a reminder of popular Romantic liter-ature, while the feminist spirit of the Lady herself looks ahead across several generations.

Can you wonder that, when some of the ablest of our fellows at the Yard were at their wits' ends to know what to do, the chief instinctively turned to Lady Molly?

Surely the Fordwych Castle Mystery, as it was universally called, was a case which more than any other required feminine tact, intuition, and all those qualities of which my dear lady possessed more than her usual share.

With the exception of Mr. McKinley, the lawyer, and young Jack d'Alboukirk, there were only women connected with the case.

If you have studied Debrett at all, you know as well as I do that the peerage is one of those old English ones which date back some six hundred years, and that the present Lady d'Alboukirk is a baroness in her own right, the title and estates descending to heirs-general. If you have perused that same interesting volume carefully, you will also have discovered that the late Lord d'Alboukirk had two daughters, the eldest, Clementina Cecilia—the present Baroness, who succeeded him—the other, Margaret Florence, who married in 1884 Jean Laurent Duplessis, a Frenchman whom Debrett vaguely describes as "of Pondicherry, India," and of whom she had issue two daughters, Henriette Marie, heir now to the ancient barony of d'Alboukirk of Fordwych, and Joan, born two years later.

There seems to have been some mystery or romance attached to this marriage of the Honourable Margaret Florence d'Alboukirk to the dashing young officer of the Foreign Legion. Old Lord d'Alboukirk at the time was British Ambassador in Paris, and he seems to have had grave objections to the union, but Miss Margaret, openly flouting her father's displeasure, and throwing prudence to the winds, ran away from home one fine day with Captain Duplessis, and from Pondicherry wrote a curt letter to her relatives telling them of her marriage with the man she loved best in all the world. Old Lord d'Alboukirk never got over his daughter's wilfulness. She had been his favourite, it appears, and her secret marriage and deceit practically broke his heart. He was kind to her, however, to the end, and when the first baby girl was born and the young pair seemed to be in straitened circumstances, he made them an allowance until the day of his daughter's death, which occurred three years after her elopement, on the birth of her second child.

When, on the death of her father, the Honourable Clementina Cecilia came into the title and fortune, she seemed to have thought it her duty to take some interest in her late sister's eldest child, who, failing her own marriage, and issue, was heir to the barony of d'Alboukirk. Thus it was that Miss Henriette Marie Duplessis came, with her father's consent, to live with her aunt at Fordwych Castle. Debrett will tell you, moreover, that in 1901 she assumed the name of d'Alboukirk, in lieu of her own, by royal licence. Failing her, the title and estate would devolve firstly on her sister Joan, and subsequently on a fairly distant cousin, Captain John d'Alboukirk, at present a young officer in the Guards.

According to her servants, the present Baroness d'Alboukirk is very self-willed, but otherwise neither more nor less eccentric than any north-country old maid would be who had such an exceptional position to keep up in the social world. The one soft trait in her otherwise not very lovable character is her great affection for her late sister's child. Miss Henriette Duplessis d'Alboukirk has inherited from her French father dark eyes and hair and a somewhat swarthy complexion, but no doubt it is from her English ancestry that she has derived a somewhat masculine frame and a very great fondness for all outdoor pursuits. She is very athletic, knows how to fence and to box, rides to hounds, and is a remarkably good shot.

From all accounts, the first hint of trouble in that gorgeous home was coincident with the arrival at Fordwych of a young, very pretty girl visitor, who was attended by her maid, a half-caste woman, dark-complexioned and surly of temper, but obviously of doglike devotion towards her young mistress. This visit seems to have come as a surprise to the entire household at Fordwych Castle, her ladyship having said nothing about it until the very morning that the guests were expected. She then briefly ordered one of the housemaids to get a bedroom ready for a young lady, and to put up a small camp bedstead in an adjoining dressing room. Even Miss Henriette seems to have been taken by surprise at the announcement of this visit, for, according to Jane Taylor, the housemaid in question, there was a violent word-passage between the old lady and her niece, the latter winding up an excited speech with the words:

"At any rate, aunt, there won't be room for both of us in this house!" After which she flounced out of the room, banging the door behind her.

Very soon the household was made to understand that the newcomer was none other than Miss Joan Duplessis, Miss Henriette's younger sister. It appears that Captain Duplessis had recently died in Pondicherry, and that the young girl then wrote to her aunt, Lady d'Alboukirk, claiming her help and protection, which the old lady naturally considered it her duty to extend to her.

It appears that Miss Joan was very unlike her sister, as she was petite and fair, more English-looking than foreign, and had pretty, dainty ways which soon endeared her to the household. The devotion existing between her and the half-caste woman she had brought from India was, moreover, unique.

It seems, however, that from the moment these newcomers came into the house, dissensions, often degenerating into violent quarrels, became the order of the day. Henriette seemed to have taken a strong dislike to her younger sister, and most particularly to the latter's dark attendant, who was vaguely known in the house as Roonah.

That some events of serious import were looming ahead, the servants at Fordwych were pretty sure. The butler and footmen at dinner heard scraps of conversation which sounded very ominous. There was talk of "lawyers," of "proofs," of "marriage and birth certificates," quickly suppressed when the servants happened to be about. Her ladyship looked terribly anxious and worried, and she and Miss Henriette spent long hours closeted together in a small boudoir, whence proceeded ominous sounds of heart-rending weeping on her ladyship's part, and angry and violent words from Miss Henriette.

Mr. McKinley, the eminent lawyer from London, came down two or three times to Fordwych, and held long conversations with her ladyship, after which the latter's eyes were very swollen and red. The household thought it more than strange that Roonah, the Indian servant, was almost invariably present at these interviews between Mr. McKinley, her ladyship, and Miss Joan. Otherwise the woman kept herself very much aloof; she spoke very little, hardly took any notice of anyone save of her ladyship and of her young mistress, and the outbursts of Miss Henriette's temper seemed to leave her quite unmoved. A strange fact was that she had taken a sudden and great fancy for frequenting a small Roman Catholic convent chapel which was distant about half a mile from the Castle, and presently it was understood that Roonah, who had been a Parsee, had been converted by the attendant priest to the Roman Catholic faith.

All this happened, mind you, within the last two or three months; in fact, Miss Joan had been in the Castle exactly twelve weeks when Captain Jack d'Alboukirk came to pay his cousin one of his periodical visits. From the first he seems to have taken a great fancy to his cousin Joan, and soon everyone noticed that this fancy was rapidly ripening into love. It was equally certain that from that moment dissensions between the two sisters became more frequent and more violent; the generally accepted opinion being that Miss Henriette was jealous of Joan, whilst Lady d'Alboukirk herself, for some unexplainable reason, seems to have regarded this love-making with marked disfavour.

Then came the tragedy.

One morning Joan ran downstairs, pale, and trembling from head to foot, moaning and sobbing as she ran:

"Roonah!—my poor old Roonah!—I knew it —I knew it!"

Captain Jack happened to meet her at the foot of the stairs. He pressed her with questions, but the girl was unable to speak. She merely pointed mutely to the floor above. The young man, genuinely alarmed, ran quickly upstairs; he threw open the door leading to Roonah's room, and there, to his horror, he saw the unfortunate woman lying across the small camp bedstead, with a handkerchief over her nose and mouth, and her throat cut.

The sight was horrible.

Poor Roonah was obviously dead.

Without losing his presence of mind, Captain Jack quietly shut the door again, after urgently begging Joan to compose herself, and to try to keep up, at any rate until the local doctor could be sent for and the terrible news gently broken to Lady d'Alboukirk.

The doctor, hastily summoned, arrived some twenty minutes later. He could but confirm Joan's and Captain Jack's fears. Roonah was indeed dead —in fact, she had been dead some hours.

From the very first, mind you, the public took a more than usually keen interest in this mysterious occurrence. The evening papers on the very day of the murder were ablaze with flaming headlines such as:

THE TRAGEDY AT FORDWYCH CASTLE

Mysterious Murder of an Important Witness
Grave Charges Against Persons in High Life

and so forth.

As time went on, the mystery deepened more and more, and I suppose Lady Molly must have had an inkling that sooner or later the chief would have to rely on her help and advice, for she sent me down to attend the inquest, and gave me strict orders to keep eyes and ears open for every detail in connection with the crime—however trivial it might seem. She herself remained in town, awaiting a summons from the chief.

The inquest was held in the dining room of Fordwych Castle, and the noble hall was crowded to its utmost when the coroner and jury finally took their seats, after having viewed the body of the poor murdered woman upstairs.

The scene was dramatic enough to please any novelist, and an awed hush descended over the crowd when, just before the proceedings began, a door was thrown open, and in walked—stiff and erect—the Baroness d'Alboukirk, escorted by her niece, Miss Henriette, and closely followed by her cousin, Captain Jack, of the Guards.

The old lady's face was as indifferent and haughty as usual, and so was that of her athletic niece. Captain Jack, on the other hand, looked troubled and flushed. Everyone noted that, directly he entered the room, his eyes sought a small, dark figure that sat silent and immovable beside the portly figure of the great lawyer, Mr. Hubert McKinley. This was Miss Joan Duplessis, in a plain black stuff gown, her young face pale and tear-stained.

Dr. Walker, the local practitioner, was, of course, the first witness called. His evidence was purely medical. He deposed to having made an examination of the body, and stated that he found that a handkerchief saturated with chloroform had been pressed to the woman's nostrils, probably while she was asleep, her throat having subsequently been cut with a sharp knife; death must have been instantaneous, as the poor thing did not appear to have struggled at all.

In answer to a question from the coroner, the doctor said that no great force or violence would be required for the gruesome deed, since the victim was undeniably unconscious when it was done. At the same time it argued unusual coolness and determination.

The handkerchief was produced, also the knife. The former was a bright-coloured one, stated to be the property of the deceased. The latter was a foreign, old-fashioned hunting knife, one of a panoply of small arms and other weapons which adorned a corner of the hall. It had been found by Detective Elliott in a clump of gorse on the adjoining golf links. There could be no question that it had been used by the murderer for his fell purpose, since at the time it was found it still bore traces of blood.

Captain Jack was the next witness called. He

had very little to say, as he merely saw the body from across the room, and immediately closed the door again and, having begged his cousin to compose herself, called his own valet and sent him off for the doctor.

Some of the staff of Fordwych Castle were called, all of whom testified to the Indian woman's curious taciturnity, which left her quite isolated among her fellow servants. Miss Henriette's maid, however, Jane Partlett, had one or two more interesting facts to record. She seems to have been more intimate with the deceased woman than anyone else, and on one occasion, at least, had quite a confidential talk with her.

"She talked chiefly about her mistress," said Jane, in answer to a question from the coroner, "to whom she was most devoted. She told me that she loved her so, she would readily die for her. Of course, I thought that silly-like, and just mad, foreign talk, but Roonah was very angry when I laughed at her, and then she undid her dress in front, and showed me some papers which were sewn in the lining of her dress. 'All these papers my little missee's fortune,' she said to me. 'Roonah guard these with her life. Someone must kill Roonah before taking them from her!'

"This was about six weeks ago," continued Jane, whilst a strange feeling of awe seemed to descend upon all those present whilst the girl spoke. "Lately she became much more silent, and, on my once referring to the papers, she turned on me savage-like and told me to hold my tongue."

Asked if she had mentioned the incident of the papers to anyone, Jane replied in the negative.

"Except to Miss Henriette, of course," she added, after a slight moment of hesitation.

Throughout all these preliminary examinations Lady d'Alboukirk, sitting between her cousin Captain Jack and her niece Henriette, had remained quite silent in an erect attitude expressive of haughty indifference. Henriette, on the other hand, looked distinctly bored. Once or twice she had yawned audibly, which caused quite a feeling of anger against her among the spectators. Such callousness in the midst of so mysterious a tragedy, and when her own sister was obviously in such deep sorrow, impressed everyone very unfavourably. It was well known that the young lady had had a fencing lesson just before the inquest in the room immediately below that where Roonah lay dead, and that within an hour of the discovery of the tragedy she was calmly playing golf.

Then Miss Joan Duplessis was called.

When the young girl stepped forward there was that awed hush in the room which usually falls upon an attentive audience when the curtain is about to rise on the crucial act of a dramatic play. But she was calm and self-possessed, and wonderfully pathetic-looking in her deep black and with the obvious lines of sorrow which the sad death of a faithful friend had traced on her young face.

In answer to the coroner, she gave her name as Joan Clarissa Duplessis, and briefly stated that until the day of her servant's death she had been a resident at Fordwych Castle, but that since then she had left that temporary home, and had taken

169

up her abode at the d'Alboukirk Arms, a quiet little hostelry on the outskirts of the town.

There was a distinct feeling of astonishment on the part of those who were not aware of this fact, and then the coroner said kindly:

"You were born, I think, in Pondicherry, in India, and are the younger daughter of Captain and Mrs. Duplessis, who was own sister to her ladyship?"

"I was born in Pondicherry," replied the young girl, quietly, "and I am the only legitimate child of the late Captain and Mrs. Duplessis, own sister to her ladyship."

A wave of sensation, quickly suppressed by the coroner, went through the crowd at these words. The emphasis which the witness had put on the word "legitimate" could not be mistaken, and everyone felt that here must lie the clue to the so far impenetrable mystery of the Indian woman's death.

All eyes were now turned on old Lady d'Alboukirk and on her niece Henriette, but the two ladies were carrying on a whispered conversation together, and had apparently ceased to take any further interest in the proceedings.

"The deceased was your confidential maid, was she not?" asked the coroner, after a slight pause.

"Yes."

"She came over to England with you recently?"

"Yes; she had to accompany me in order to help me to make good my claim to being my late mother's only legitimate child, and therefore the heir to the barony of d'Alboukirk."

Her voice had trembled a little as she said this,

but now, as breathless silence reigned in the room, she seemed to make a visible effort to control herself, and, replying to the coroner's question, she gave a clear and satisfactory account of her terrible discovery of her faithful servant's death. Her evidence had lasted about a quarter of an hour or so, when suddenly the coroner put the momentous question to her:

"Do you know anything about the papers which the deceased woman carried about her person, and reference to which has already been made?"

"Yes," she replied quietly; "they were the proofs relating to my claim. My father, Captain Duplessis, had in early youth, and before he met my mother, contracted a secret union with a half-caste woman, who was Roonah's own sister. Being tired of her, he chose to repudiate her—she had no children—but the legality of the marriage was never for a moment in question. After that, he married my mother, and his first wife subsequently died, chiefly of a broken heart; but her death only occurred two months *after* the birth of my sister Henriette. My father, I think, had been led to believe that his wife had died some two years previously, and he was no doubt very much shocked when he realised what a grievous wrong he had done our mother. In order to mend matters somewhat, he and she went through a new form of marriage—a legal one this time—and my father paid a lot of money to Roonah's relatives to have the matter hushed up. Less than a year after this second—and only legal—marriage, I was born and my mother died."

"Then the papers of which so much has been said—what did they consist of?"

"There were the marriage certificates of my father's first wife—and two sworn statements as to her death, two months *after* the birth of my sister Henriette; one by Dr. Rénaud, who was at the time a well-known medical man in Pondicherry, and the other by Roonah herself, who had held her dying sister in her arms. Dr. Rénaud is dead, and now Roonah has been murdered, and all the proofs have gone with her—"

Her voice broke in a passion of sobs, which, with manifest self-control, she quickly suppressed. In that crowded court you could have heard a pin drop, so great was the tension of intense excitement and attention.

"Then those papers remained in your maid's possession? Why was that?" asked the coroner.

"I did not dare to carry the papers about with me," said the witness, while a curious look of terror crept into her young face as she looked across at her aunt and sister. "Roonah would not part with them. She carried them in the lining of her dress, and at night they were all under the pillow. After her—her death, and when Dr. Walker had left, I thought it my duty to take possession of the papers which meant my whole future to me, and which I desired then to place in Mr. McKinley's charge. But, though I carefully searched the bed and all the clothing by my poor Roonah's side, I did not find the papers. They were gone."

I won't attempt to describe to you the sensation caused by the deposition of this witness. All eyes

172

wandered from her pale young face to that of her sister, who sat almost opposite to her, shrugging her athletic shoulders and gazing at the pathetic young figure before her with callous and haughty indifference.

"Now, putting aside the question of the papers for the moment," said the coroner, after a pause, "do you happen to know anything of your late servant's private life? Had she an enemy, or perhaps a lover?"

"No," replied the girl; "Roonah's whole life was centred in me and in my claim. I had often begged her to place our papers in Mr. McKinley's charge, but she would trust no one. I wish she had obeyed me," here moaned the poor girl involuntarily, "and I should not have lost what means my whole future to me, and the being who loved me best in all the world would not have been so foully murdered."

Of course, it was terrible to see this young girl thus instinctively, and surely unintentionally, proffering so awful an accusation against those who stood so near to her. That the whole case had become hopelessly involved and mysterious, nobody could deny. Can you imagine the mental picture formed in the mind of all present by the story, so pathetically told, of this girl who had come over to England in order to make good her claim which she felt to be just, and who, in one fell swoop, saw that claim rendered very difficult to prove through the dastardly murder of her principal witness?

That the claim was seriously jeopardised by the death of Roonah and the disappearance of the papers, was made very clear, mind you, through the statements of Mr. McKinley, the lawyer. He could not say very much, of course, and his statements could never have been taken as actual proof, because Roonah and Joan had never fully trusted him and had never actually placed the proofs of the claim in his hands. He certainly had seen the marriage certificate of Captain Duplessis's first wife, and a copy of this, as he very properly stated, could easily be obtained. The woman seems to have died during the great cholera epidemic of 1881, when, owing to the great number of deaths which occurred, the deceit and concealment practised by the natives at Pondicherry, and the supineness of the French Government, death certificates were very casually and often incorrectly made out.

Roonah had come over to England ready to swear that her sister had died in her arms two months after the birth of Captain Duplessis's eldest child, and there was the sworn testimony of Dr. Rénaud, since dead. These affidavits Mr. McKinley had seen and read.

Against that, the only proof which now remained of the justice of Joan Duplessis's claim was the fact that her mother and father went through a second form of marriage sometime *after* the birth of their first child, Henriette. This fact was not denied, and, of course, it could be easily proved, if necessary, but even then it would in no way be conclusive. It implied the presence of a doubt in Captain Duplessis's mind, a doubt which the second marriage ceremony may have served to set at rest; but it in no way established the illegitimacy of his eldest daughter.

In fact, the more Mr. McKinley spoke, the more convinced did everyone become that the theft of the papers had everything to do with the murder of the unfortunate Roonah. She would not part with the proofs which meant her mistress's fortune, and she paid for her devotion with her life.

Several more witnesses were called after that. The servants were closely questioned, the doctor was recalled, but, in spite of long and arduous efforts, the coroner and jury could not bring a single real fact to light beyond those already stated.

The Indian woman had been murdered!

The papers which she always carried about her body had disappeared.

Beyond that, nothing! An impenetrable wall of silence and mystery!

The butler at Fordwych Castle had certainly missed the knife with which Roonah had been killed from its accustomed place on the morning after the murder had been committed, but not before, and the mystery further gained in intensity from the fact that the only purchase of chloroform in the district had been traced to the murdered woman herself.

She had gone down to the local chemist one day some two or three weeks previously, and shown him a prescription for cleansing the hair which required some chloroform in it. He gave her a very small quantity in a tiny bottle, which was subsequently found empty on her own dressing table. No one at Fordwych Castle could swear to having heard any unaccustomed noise during that memorable night. Even Joan, who slept in the room adjoining that where the unfortunate Roonah lay, said she had heard nothing unusual. But then, the door of communication between the two rooms was shut, and the murderer had been quick and silent.

Thus this extraordinary inquest drew to a close, leaving in its train an air of dark suspicion and of unexplainable horror.

The jury returned a verdict of "Wilful murder against some person or persons unknown," and the next moment Lady d'Alboukirk rose, and leaning on her niece's arm, quietly walked out of the room.

Two of our best men from the Yard, Pegram and Elliott, were left in charge of the case. They remained at Fordwych (the little town close by), as did Miss Joan, who had taken up her permanent abode at the d'Alboukirk Arms, whilst I returned to town immediately after the inquest. Captain Jack had rejoined his regiment, and apparently the ladies of the Castle had resumed their quiet, luxurious life just the same as heretofore. The old lady led her own somewhat isolated, semi-regal life; Miss Henriette fenced and boxed, played hockey and golf, and over the fine Castle and its haughty inmates there hovered like an ugly bird of prey the threatening presence of a nameless suspicion.

The two ladies might choose to flout public opinion, but public opinion was dead against them. No one dared formulate a charge, but everyone remembered that Miss Henriette had, on the very morning of the murder, been playing golf in the field where the knife was discovered, and that if Miss Joan Duplessis ever failed to make good her claim to the barony of d'Alboukirk, Miss Henriette would remain in undisputed possession. So now, when the ladies drove past in the village street, no one doffed a cap to salute them, and when at church the parson read out the Sixth Commandment, "Thou shalt do no murder," all eyes gazed with fearsome awe at the old Baroness and her niece.

Splendid isolation reigned at Fordwych Castle. The daily papers grew more and more sarcastic at the expense of the Scotland Yard authorities, and the public more and more impatient.

Then it was that the chief grew desperate and sent for Lady Molly, the result of the interview being that I once more made the journey down to Fordwych, but this time in the company of my dear lady, who had received carte blanche from headquarters to do whatever she thought right in the investigation of the mysterious crime.

She and I arrived at Fordwych at 8:00 P.M., after the usual long wait at Newcastle. We put up at the d'Alboukirk Arms, and, over a hasty and very bad supper, Lady Molly allowed me a brief insight into her plans.

"I can see every detail of that murder, Mary," she said earnestly, "just as if I had lived at the Castle all the time. I know exactly where our fellows are wrong, and why they cannot get on. But, although the chief has given me a free hand, what

I am going to do is so irregular that if I fail I shall probably get my immediate *congé*, whilst some of the disgrace is bound to stick to you. It is not too late—you may yet draw back, and leave me to act alone."

I looked her straight in the face. Her dark eyes were gleaming; there was the power of second sight in them, or of marvellous intuition of "men and things."

"I'll follow your lead, my Lady Molly," I said quietly.

"Then go to bed now," she replied, with that strange transition of manner which to me was so attractive and to everyone else so unaccountable.

In spite of my protest, she refused to listen to any more talk or to answer any more questions, and, perforce, I had to go to my room. The next morning I saw her graceful figure, immaculately dressed in a perfect tailor-made gown, standing beside my bed at a very early hour.

"Why, what is the time?" I ejaculated, suddenly wide awake.

"Too early for you to get up," she replied quietly. "I am going to early Mass at the Roman Catholic convent close by."

"To Mass at the Roman Catholic convent?"

"Yes. Don't repeat all my words, Mary; it is silly, and wastes time. I have introduced myself in the neighbourhood as the American, Mrs. Silas A. Ogden, whose motor has broken down and is being repaired at Newcastle, while I, its owner, amuse myself by viewing the beauties of the neighbourhood. Being a Roman Catholic, I go to Mass first, and, having met Lady d'Alboukirk once in

London, I go to pay her a respectful visit afterwards. When I come back we will have breakfast together. You might try in the meantime to scrape up an acquaintance with Miss Joan Duplessis, who is still staying here, and ask her to join us at breakfast."

She was gone before I could make another remark, and I could but obey her instantly to the letter.

An hour later I saw Miss Joan Duplessis strolling in the hotel garden. It was not difficult to pass the time of day with the young girl, who seemed quite to brighten up at having someone to talk to. We spoke of the weather and so forth, and I steadily avoided the topic of the Fordwych Castle tragedy until the return of Lady Molly at about ten o'clock. She came back looking just as smart, just as self-possessed, as when she had started three hours earlier. Only I, who knew her so well, noted the glitter of triumph in her eyes, and knew that she had not failed. She was accompanied by Pegram, who, however, immediately left her side and went straight into the hotel, whilst she joined us in the garden and, after a few graceful words, introduced herself to Miss Joan Duplessis and asked her to join us in the coffee room upstairs.

The room was empty and we sat down to table, I quivering with excitement and awaiting events. Through the open window I saw Elliott walking rapidly down the village street. Presently the waitress went off, and I being too excited to eat or to speak, Lady Molly carried on a running conversation with Miss Joan, asking her about her life in India and her father, Captain Duplessis. Joan admitted that she had always been her father's favourite.

"He never liked Henriette, somehow," she explained.

Lady Molly asked her when she had first known Roonah.

"She came to the house when my mother died," replied Joan, "and she had charge of me as a baby." At Pondicherry no one had thought it strange that she came as a servant into an officer's house where her own sister had reigned as mistress. Pondicherry is a French settlement, and manners and customs there are often very peculiar.

I ventured to ask her what were her future plans.

"Well," she said, with a great touch of sadness, "I can, of course, do nothing whilst my aunt is alive. I cannot force her to let me live at Fordwych or to acknowledge me as her heir. After her death, if my sister does assume the title and fortune of d'Alboukirk," she added, whilst suddenly a strange look of vengefulness—almost of hatred and cruelty—marred the childlike expression of her face, "then I shall revive the story of the tragedy of Roonah's death, and I hope that public opinion—"

She paused here in her speech, and I, who had been gazing out of the window, turned my eyes on her. She was ashy-pale, staring straight before her; her hands dropped the knife and fork which she had held. Then I saw that Pegram had come into the room, that he had come up to the table and placed a packet of papers in Lady Molly's hand.

I saw it all as in a flash!

There was a loud cry of despair like an animal at bay, a shrill cry, followed by a deep one from Pegram of "No, you don't," and before anyone could prevent her, Joan's graceful young figure stood outlined for a short moment at the open window.

The next morning she had disappeared into the depth below, and we heard a dull thud which nearly froze the blood in my veins.

Pegram ran out of the room, but Lady Molly sat quite still.

"I have succeeded in clearing the innocent," she said quietly; "but the guilty has meted out to herself her own punishment."

"Then it was she?" I murmured, horror-struck.

"Yes. I suspected it from the first," replied Lady Molly calmly. "It was this conversion of Roonah to Roman Catholicism and her consequent change of manner which gave me the first clue."

"But why—why?" I muttered.

"A simple reason, Mary," she rejoined, tapping the packet of papers with her delicate hand; and, breaking open the string that held the letters, she laid them out upon the table. "The whole thing was a fraud from beginning to end. The woman's marriage certificate was all right, of course, but I mistrusted the genuineness of the other papers from the moment that I heard that Roonah would not part with them and would not allow Mr. McKinley to have charge of them. I am sure that the idea at first was merely one of blackmail. The papers were only to be the means of extorting money from the old lady, and there was no thought of taking them into court.

"Roonah's part was, of course, the important thing in the whole case, since she was here prepared to swear to the actual date of the first Madame Duplessis's death. The initiative, of course, may have come either from Joan or from Captain Duplessis himself, out of hatred for the family who would have nothing to do with him and his favourite younger daughter. That, of course, we shall never know. At first Roonah was a Parsee, with a doglike devotion to the girl whom she had nursed as a baby, and who no doubt had drilled her well into the part she was to play. But presently she became a Roman Catholic—an ardent convert, remember, with all a Roman Catholic's fear of hell-fire. I went to the convent this morning. I heard the priest's sermon there, and I realised what an influence his eloquence must have had over poor, ignorant, superstitious Roonah. She was still ready to die for her young mistress, but she was no longer prepared to swear to a lie for her sake. After Mass I called at Fordwych Castle. I explained my position to old Lady d'Alboukirk, who took me into the room where Roonah had slept and died. There I found two things," continued Lady Molly, as she opened the elegant reticule which still hung upon her arm, and placed the big key and a prayer book before me.

"The key I found in a drawer of an old cupboard in the dressing room where Roonah slept, with all sorts of odds and ends belonging to the unfortunate woman, and going to the door which led into what had been Joan's bedroom, I found that it was locked, and that this key fitted into the lock. Roonah had locked the door herself on her own side—*she was afraid of her mistress*. I knew now that I was right in my surmise. The prayer book is a Roman Catholic one. It is heavily thumb-marked there, where false oaths and lying are denounced as being deadly sins for which hell-fire would be the punishment. Roonah, terrorised by fear of the supernatural, a new convert to the faith, was afraid of committing a deadly sin.

"Who knows what passed between the two women, both of whom have come to so violent and terrible an end? Who can tell what prayers, tears, persuasions Joan Duplessis employed from the time she realised that Roonah did not mean to swear to the lie which would have brought her mistress wealth and glamour until the awful day when she finally understood that Roonah would no longer even hold her tongue, and devised a terrible means of silencing her for ever?

"With this certainty before me, I ventured on my big coup. I was so sure, you see. I kept Joan talking in here whilst I sent Pegram to her room with orders to break open the locks of her handbag and dressing case. There!—I told you that if I was wrong I would probably be dismissed from the force for irregularity, as of course I had no right to do that; but if Pegram found the papers there where I felt sure they would be, we could bring the murderer to justice. I know my own sex pretty well, don't I, Mary? I knew that Joan Duplessis had not destroyed—never would destroy—those papers."

Even as Lady Molly spoke we could hear heavy tramping outside the passage. I ran to the door, and there was met by Pegram.

"She is quite dead, miss," he said. "It was a drop of forty feet, and a stone pavement down below."

The guilty had indeed meted out her own punishment to herself!

Lady d'Alboukirk sent Lady Molly a cheque for £5,000 the day the whole affair was made known to the public.

I think you will say that it had been well earned. With her own dainty hands my dear lady had lifted the veil which hung over the tragedy of Fordwych Castle, and with the finding of the papers in Joan Duplessis's dressing bag, and the unfortunate girl's suicide, the murder of the Indian woman was no longer a mystery.

R. Austin Freeman
(1862–1943)
THE BLUE SCARAB

*R. Austin Freeman was, like Conan Doyle, a physician-writer. Unlike him, he made his series detective Dr. Thorndyke a medical detective. His stories are sober and painstaking, more concerned with the artifacts in the case and their interrelationship than with personalities and emotions expressed. Not surprisingly, this man of scientific method introduced the inverted tale—where the perpetrator is known and the method of discovery occupies the reader (*The Singing Bone, *1912).*

The meticulous Thorndyke first appeared in 1907 and remained active into the World War II years, seeing real-life forensic investigation become the science he had anticipated.

Medico-legal practice is largely concerned with crimes against the person, the details of which are often sordid, gruesome and unpleasant. Hence the curious and romantic case of the Blue Scarab (though really outside our specialty) came as somewhat of a relief. But to me it is of interest principally as illustrating two of those remarkable gifts which made my friend, Thorndyke, unique as an investigator: his uncanny power of picking out the one essential fact at a glance, and his capacity to produce, when required, inexhaustible stores of unexpected knowledge of the most out-of-the-way subjects.

It was late in the afternoon when Mr. James Blowgrave arrived, by appointment, at our chambers, accompanied by his daughter, a rather strikingly pretty girl of about twenty-two; and when we had mutually introduced ourselves, the consultation began without preamble.

"I didn't give any details in my letter to you," said Mr. Blowgrave. "I thought it better not to, for fear you might decline the case. It is really a matter of a robbery, but not quite an ordinary robbery. There are some unusual and rather mysterious features in the case. And as the police hold out very little hope, I have come to ask if you will give me your opinion on the case and perhaps look into it for me. But first I had better tell you how the affair happened.

"The robbery occurred just a fortnight ago, about half-past nine o'clock in the evening. I was sitting in my study with my daughter, looking over some things that I had taken from a small deed-box, when a servant rushed in to tell us that one of the outbuildings was on fire. Now my study opens by a French window on the garden at the back, and, as the outbuilding was in a meadow at the side of the garden, I went out that way, leaving the French window open; but before going I hastily put the things back in the deed-box and locked it.

"The building—which I used partly as a lumber store and partly as a workshop—was well alight and the whole household was already on the spot, the boy working the pump and the two maids carrying the buckets and throwing water on the fire. My daughter and I joined the party and helped to carry the buckets and take out what goods we could reach from the burning building. But it was nearly half an hour before we got the fire completely extinguished, and then my daughter and I went to our rooms to wash and tidy ourselves up. We returned to the study together, and when I had shut the French window my daughter proposed that we should resume our interrupted occupation. Thereupon I took out of my pocket the key of the deed-box and turned to the cabinet on which the box always stood.

"But there was no deed-box there!

"For a moment I thought I must have moved it, and cast my eyes round the room in search of it. But it was nowhere to be seen, and a moment's reflection reminded me that I had left it in its usual place. The only possible conclusion was that during our absence at the fire, somebody must have come in by the window and taken it. And it looked as if that somebody had deliberately set fire to the outbuilding for the express purpose of luring us all out of the house."

"That is what the appearances suggest," Thorndyke agreed. "Is the study window furnished with a blind or curtains?"

"Curtains," replied Mr. Blowgrave. "But they were not drawn. Any one in the garden could have seen into the room; and the garden is easily accessible to an active person who could climb over a low wall."

"So far, then," said Thorndyke, "the robbery might be the work of a casual prowler who had got into the garden and watched you through the window, and assuming that the things you had taken from the box were of value, seized an easy opportunity to make off with them. Were the things of any considerable value?"

"To a thief they were of no value at all. There were a number of share certificates, a lease, one or two agreements, some family photographs and a small box containing an old letter and a scarab. Nothing worth stealing, you see, for the certificates were made out in my name and were therefore unnegotiable."

"And the scarab?"

"That may have been lapis lazuli, but more probably it was a blue glass imitation. In any case it was of no considerable value. It was about an inch and a half long. But before you come to any conclusion, I had better finish the story. The robbery was on Tuesday, the 7th of June. I gave information to the police, with a description of the missing property, but nothing happened until Wednesday, the 15th, when I received a registered parcel bearing the Southampton postmark. On opening it I found, to my astonishment, the entire contents of the deed-box, with the exception of the scarab, and this rather mysterious communication."

He took from his pocket-book and handed to Thorndyke an ordinary envelope addressed in typewritten characters, and sealed with a large, elliptical seal, the face of which was covered with minute hieroglyphics.

"This," said Thorndyke, "I take to be an impression of the scarab; and an excellent impression it is."

"Yes," replied Mr. Blowgrave, "I have no doubt that it is the scarab. It is about the same size."

Thorndyke looked quickly at our client with an expression of surprise. "But," he asked, "don't you recognize the hieroglyphics on it?"

Mr. Blowgrave smiled deprecatingly. "The fact is," said he, "I don't know anything about hieroglyphics, but I should say, as far as I can judge, these look the same. What do you think, Nellie?"

Miss Blowgrave looked at the seal—rather vaguely—and replied, "I am in the same position. Hieroglyphics are to me just funny-looking things that don't mean anything. But these look the same to me as those on our scarab, though I expect any other hieroglyphics would, for that matter."

Thorndyke made no comment on this statement, but examined the seal attentively through his lens. Then he drew out the contents of the envelope, consisting of two letters, one typewritten and the other in a faded brown handwriting. The former he read through and then inspected the paper closely, holding it up to the light to observe the watermark.

"The paper appears to be of Belgian manufacture," he remarked, passing it to me. I confirmed this observation and then read the letter, which was headed "Southampton" and ran thus:—

Dear old pal,

I am sending you back some trifles removed in error. The ancient document is enclosed with this, but the curio is at present in the custody of my respected uncle. Hope its temporary loss will not inconvenience you, and that I may be able to return it to you later. Meanwhile, believe me,

Your ever affectionate,
Rudolpho.

"Who is Rudolpho?" I asked.

"The Lord knows," replied Mr. Blowgrave. "A pseudonym of our absent friend, I presume. He seems to be a facetious sort of person."

"He does," agreed Thorndyke. "This letter and the seal appear to be what the schoolboys would call a leg-pull. But still, this is all quite normal. He has returned you the worthless things and has kept the one thing that has any sort of negotiable value. Are you quite clear that the scarab is not more valuable than you have assumed?"

"Well," said Mr. Blowgrave, "I have had an expert opinion on it. I showed it to M. Fouquet, the Egyptologist, when he was over here from Brussels a few months ago, and his opinion was that it was a worthless imitation. Not only was it not a genuine scarab, but the inscription was a sham, too; just a collection of hieroglyphic characters jumbled together without sense or meaning."

"Then," said Thorndyke, taking another look at the seal through his lens, "it would seem that Rudolpho, or Rudolpho's uncle, has got a bad bargain. Which doesn't throw much light on the affair."

At this point Miss Blowgrave intervened. "I think, father," said she, "you have not given Dr. Thorndyke quite all the facts about the scarab. He ought to be told about its connection with Uncle Reuben."

As the girl spoke Thorndyke looked at her with a curious expression of suddenly awakened interest. Later I understood the meaning of that look, but at the time there seemed to me nothing particularly arresting in her words.

"It is just a family tradition," Mr. Blowgrave said deprecatingly. "Probably it is all nonsense."

"Well, let us have it, at any rate," said Thorndyke. "We may get some light from it."

Thus urged, Mr. Blowgrave hemmed a little shyly and began:

"The story concerns my great-grandfather, Silas Blowgrave, and his doings during the war with France. It seems that he commanded a privateer, of which he and his brother Reuben were the joint owners, and that in the course of their last cruise, they acquired a very remarkable and valuable collection of jewels. Goodness knows how they got them; not very honestly, I suspect, for they appear to have been a pair of precious rascals. Something has been said about the loot from a South American church or cathedral, but there is really nothing known about the affair. There are no documents. It is mere oral tradition and very vague and sketchy. The story goes that when they had sold off the ship, they came down to live at Shawstead in Hertfordshire, Silas occupying the

191

manor house—in which I live at present—and Reuben a farm-house adjoining. The bulk of the loot they shared out at the end of the cruise, but the jewels were kept apart to be dealt with later —perhaps when the circumstances under which they had been acquired had been forgotten. However, both men were inveterate gamblers, and it seems—according to the testimony of a servant of Reuben's who overheard them—that on a certain night when they had been playing heavily, they decided to finish up by playing for the whole collection of jewels as a single stake. Silas, who had the jewels in his custody, was seen to go to the manor house and return to Reuben's house carrying a small, iron-bound chest.

"Apparently they played late into the night, after every one else but the servant had gone to bed, and the luck was with Reuben, though it seems probable that he gave luck some assistance. At any rate, when the play was finished and the chest handed over, Silas roundly accused him of cheating, and we may assume that a pretty serious quarrel took place. Exactly what happened is not clear, for when the quarrel began Reuben dismissed the servant, who retired to her bedroom in a distant part of the house. But in the morning it was discovered that Reuben and the chest of jewels had both disappeared, and there were distinct traces of blood in the room in which the two men had been playing. Silas professed to know nothing about the disappearance; but a strong— and probably just—suspicion arose that he had murdered his brother and made away with the jewels. The result was that Silas also disappeared, and for a long time his whereabouts was not known even by his wife. Later it transpired that he had taken up his abode, under an assumed name, in Egypt, and that he had developed an enthusiastic interest in the then new science of Egyptology—the Rosetta Stone had been deciphered only a few years previously. After a time he resumed communication with his wife, but never made any statement as to the mystery of his brother's disappearance. A few months before his death he visited his home in disguise and he then handed to his wife a little sealed packet which was to be delivered to his only son, William, on his attaining the age of twenty-one. That packet contained the scarab and the letter which you have taken from the envelope."

"Am I to read it?" asked Thorndyke.

"Certainly, if you think it worth while," was the reply.

Thorndyke opened the yellow sheet of paper and, glancing through the brown and faded writing, read aloud:

"Cairo, 4th March, 1833
"My dear Son,
    "I am sending you, as my last gift, a valuable scarab, and a few words of counsel on which I would bid you meditate. Believe me, there is much wisdom in the lore of Old Egypt. Make it your own. Treasure the scarab as a precious inheritance. Handle it often but show it to none. Give your Uncle Reuben Christian burial. It is your duty, and you will have your

193

*reward. He robbed your father, but he shall
make restitution.*

> *"Farewell!*
> *"Your affectionate father,*
> *"Silas Blowgrave."*

As Thorndyke laid down the letter he looked inquiringly at our client.

"Well," he said, "here are some plain instructions. How have they been carried out?"

"They haven't been carried out at all," replied Mr. Blowgrave. "As to his son William, my grandfather, he was not disposed to meddle in the matter. This seemed to be a frank admission that Silas killed his brother and concealed the body, and William didn't choose to reopen the scandal. Besides, the instructions are not so very plain. It is all very well to say, 'Give your Uncle Reuben Christian burial,' but where the deuce is Uncle Reuben?"

"It is plainly hinted," said Thorndyke, "that whoever gives the body Christian burial will stand to benefit, and the word 'restitution' seems to suggest a clue to the whereabouts of the jewels. Has no one thought it worth while to find out where the body is deposited?"

"But how could they?" demanded Blowgrave. "He doesn't give the faintest clue. He talks as if his son knew where the body was. And then, you know, even supposing Silas did not take the jewels with him, there was the question, whose property were they? To begin with, they were pretty certainly stolen property, though no one knows where they came from. Then Reuben apparently

194

got them from Silas by fraud, and Silas got them back by robbery and murder. If William had discovered them he would have had to give them up to Reuben's sons, and yet they weren't strictly Reuben's property. No one had an undeniable claim to them, even if they could have found them."

"But that is not the case now," said Miss Blowgrave.

"No," said Mr. Blowgrave, in answer to Thorndyke's look of inquiry. "The position is quite clear now. Reuben's grandson, my cousin Arthur, has died recently, and as he had no children, he has dispersed his property. The old farm-house and the bulk of his estate he has left to a nephew, but he made a small bequest to my daughter and named her as the residuary legatee. So that whatever rights Reuben had to the jewels are now vested in her, and on my death she will be Silas's heir, too. As a matter of fact," Mr. Blowgrave continued, "we were discussing this very question on the night of the robbery. I may as well tell you that my girl will be left pretty poorly off when I go, for there is a heavy mortgage on our property and mighty little capital. Uncle Reuben's jewels would have made the old home secure for her if we could have laid our hands on them. However, I mustn't take up your time with our domestic affairs."

"Your domestic affairs are not entirely irrelevant," said Thorndyke. "But what is it that you want me to do in the matter?"

"Well," said Blowgrave, "my house has been robbed and my premises set fire to. The police

195

can apparently do nothing. They say there is no clue at all unless the robbery was committed by somebody in the house, which is absurd, seeing that the servants were all engaged in putting out the fire. But I want the robber traced and punished, and I want to get the scarab back. It may be intrinsically valueless, as M. Fouquet said, but Silas's testamentary letter seems to indicate that it had some value. At any rate, it is an heirloom, and I am loath to lose it. It seems a presumptuous thing to ask you to investigate a trumpery robbery, but I should take it as a great kindness if you would look into the matter."

"Cases of robbery pure and simple," replied Thorndyke, "are rather alien to my ordinary practice, but in this one there are certain curious features that seem to make an investigation worth while. Yes, Mr. Blowgrave, I will look into the case, and I have some hope that we may be able to lay our hands on the robber, in spite of the apparent absence of clues. I will ask you to leave both these letters for me to examine more minutely, and I shall probably want to make an inspection of the premises—perhaps tomorrow."

"Whenever you like," said Blowgrave. "I am delighted that you are willing to undertake the inquiry. I have heard so much about you from my friend Stalker, of the Griffin Life Assurance Company, for whom you have acted on several occasions."

"Before you go," said Thorndyke, "there is one point that we must clear up. Who is there besides yourselves that knows of the existence of the scarab and this letter and the history attaching to them?"

"I really can't say," replied Blowgrave. "No one has seen them but my cousin Arthur. I once showed them to him, and he may have talked about them in the family. I didn't treat the matter as a secret."

When our visitors had gone we discussed the bearings of the case.

"It is quite a romantic story," said I, "and the robbery has its points of interest, but I am rather inclined to agree with the police—there is mighty little to go on."

"There would have been less," said Thorndyke, "if our sporting friend hadn't been so pleased with himself. That typewritten letter was a piece of gratuitous impudence. Our gentleman overrated his security and crowed too loud."

"I don't see that there is much to be gleaned from the letter, all the same," said I.

"I am sorry to hear you say that, Jervis," he exclaimed, "because I was proposing to hand the letter over to you to examine and report on."

"I was only referring to the superficial appearances," I said hastily. "No doubt a detailed examination will bring something more distinctive into view."

"I have no doubt it will," he said, "and as there are reasons for pushing on the investigation as quickly as possible, I suggest that you get to work at once. I shall occupy myself with the old letter and the envelope."

On this I began my examination without delay,

and as a preliminary I proceeded to take a facsimile photograph of the letter by putting it in a large printing-frame with a sensitive plate and a plate of clear glass. The resulting negative showed not only the typewritten lettering, but also the watermark and wire lines of the paper, and a faint grease spot. Next I turned my attention to the lettering itself, and here I soon began to accumulate quite a number of identifiable peculiarities. The machine was apparently a Corona, fitted with the small "Elite" type, and the alignment was markedly defective. The "lower case"—or small—"a" was well below the line, although the capital "A" appeared to be correctly placed; the "u" was slightly above the line, and the small "m" was partly clogged with dirt.

Up to this point I had been careful to manipulate the letter with forceps (although it had been handled by at least three persons, to my knowledge), and I now proceeded to examine it for fingerprints. As I could detect none by mere inspection, I dusted the back of the paper with finely powdered fuchsin, and distributed the powder by tapping the paper lightly. This brought into view quite a number of finger-prints, especially round the edges of the letter, and though most of them were very faint and shadowy, it was possible to make out the ridge pattern well enough for our purpose. Having blown off the excess of powder, I took the letter to the room where the large copying camera was set up, to photograph it before developing the finger-prints on the front. But here I found our laboratory assistant, Polton, in possession, with the sealed envelope fixed to the copying easel.

"I shan't be a minute, sir," said he. "The doctor wants an enlarged photograph of this seal. I've got the plate in."

I waited while he made his exposure and then proceeded to take the photograph of the letter, or rather of the finger-prints on the back of it. When I had developed the negative I powdered the front of the letter and brought out several more finger-prints—mostly thumbs this time. They were a little difficult to see where they were imposed on the lettering, but, as the latter was bright blue and the fuchsin powder was red, this confusion disappeared in the photograph, in which the lettering was almost invisible while the finger-prints were more distinct than they had appeared to the eye. This completed my examination, and when I had verified the make of typewriter by reference to our album of specimens of typewriting, I left the negatives for Polton to dry and print and went down to the sitting-room to draw up my little report. I had just finished this and was speculating on what had become of Thorndyke, when I heard his quick step on the stair and a few moments later he entered with a roll of paper in his hand. This he unrolled on the table, fixing it open with one or two lead paper-weights, and I came round to inspect it, when I found it to be a sheet of the Ordnance map on the scale of twenty-five inches to the mile.

"Here is the Blowgraves' place," said Thorndyke, "nearly in the middle of the sheet. This is his house—Shawstead Manor—and that will probably be the outbuilding that was on fire. I take it that the house marked Dingle Farm is the one that Uncle Reuben occupied."

"Probably," I agreed. "But I don't see why you wanted this map if you are going down to the place itself to-morrow."

"The advantage of a map," said Thorndyke, "is that you can see all over it at once and get the lie of the land well into your mind; and you can measure all distances accurately and quickly with a scale and a pair of dividers. When we go down to-morrow, we shall know our way about as well as Blowgrave himself."

"And what use will that be?" I asked. "Where does the topography come into the case?"

"Well, Jervis," he replied, "there is the robber, for instance; he came from somewhere and he went somewhere. A study of the map may give us a hint as to his movements. But here comes Polton 'with the documents,' as poor Miss Flite would say. What have you got for us, Polton?"

"They aren't quite dry, sir," said Polton, laying four large bromide prints on the table. "There's the enlargement of the seal—ten by eight, mounted—and three unmounted prints of Dr. Jervis's."

Thorndyke looked at my photographs critically. "They're excellent, Jervis," said he. "The fingerprints are perfectly legible, though faint. I only hope some of them are the right ones. That is my left thumb. I don't see yours. The small one is presumable Miss Blowgrave's. We must take her fingerprints to-morrow, and her father's, too. Then we shall know if we have got any of the

Thorndyke's tracing of the impression of the scarab.

robber's." He ran his eye over my report and nodded approvingly. "There is plenty there to enable us to identify the typewriter if we can get hold of it, and the paper is very distinctive. What do you think of the seal?" he added, laying the enlarged photograph before me.

"It is magnificent," I replied, with a grin. "Perfectly monumental."

"What are you grinning at?" he demanded.

"I was thinking that you seem to be counting your chickens in pretty good time," said I.

"You are making elaborate preparations to identify the scarab, but you are rather disregarding the classical advice of the prudent Mrs. Glasse."

"I have a presentiment that we shall get that scarab," said he. "At any rate we ought to be in a position to identify it instantly and certainly if we are able to get a sight of it."

"We are not likely to," said I. "Still, there is no harm in providing for the improbable."

This was evidently Thorndyke's view, and he certainly made ample provision for this most improbable contingency; for, having furnished himself with a drawing-board and a sheet of tracing-paper, he pinned the latter over the photograph on the board and proceeded, with a fine pen and hectograph ink, to make a careful and minute tracing of the intricate and bewildering hieroglyphic inscription on the seal. When he had finished it he transferred it to a clay duplicator and took off half a dozen copies, one of which he handed to me. I looked at it dubiously and remarked: "You have said that the medical jurist must make all knowledge his province. Has he got to be an Egyptologist, too?"

"He will be the better medical jurist if he is," was the reply, of which I made a mental note for my future guidance. But meanwhile Thorndyke's proceedings were, to me, perfectly incomprehensible. What was his object in making this minute tracing? The seal itself was sufficient for identification. I lingered awhile hoping that some fresh development might throw a light on the mystery. But his next proceeding was like to have reduced me to stupefaction. I saw him go to the book-shelves and take down a book. As he laid it on the table I glanced at the title, and when I saw that it was Raper's "Navigation Tables" I stole softly out into the lobby, put on my hat and went for a walk.

When I returned the investigation was apparently concluded, for Thorndyke was seated in his easy chair, placidly reading "The Compleat Angler." On the table lay a large circular protractor, a straight-edge, an architect's scale and a sheet of tracing-paper on which was a tracing in hectograph ink of Shawstead Manor.

"Why did you make this tracing?" I asked. "Why not take the map itself?"

"We don't want the whole of it," he replied, "and I dislike cutting up maps."

By taking an informal lunch in the train, we arrived at Shawstead Manor by half-past two. Our approach up the drive had evidently been observed, for Blowgrave and his daughter were waiting at the porch to receive us. The former came forward with outstretched hand, but a distinctly woebegone expression, and exclaimed: "It is most kind of you to come down; but alas! you are too late."

"Too late for what?" demanded Thorndyke.

"I will show you," replied Blowgrave, and seizing my colleague by the arm, he strode off excitedly to a little wicket at the side of the house, and, passing through it, hurried along a narrow alley that skirted the garden wall and ended in a large meadow, at one end of which stood a dilapidated windmill. Across this meadow he bustled, dragging my colleague with him, until he reached a heap of freshly-turned earth, where he halted and pointed tragically to a spot where the turf had evidently been raised and untidily replaced.

"There!" he exclaimed, stooping to pull up the loose turfs and thereby exposing what was evidently a large hole, recently and hastily filled in. "That was done last night or early this morning, for I walked over this meadow only yesterday evening and there was no sign of disturbed ground then."

Thorndyke stood looking down at the hole with a faint smile. "And what do you infer from that?" he asked.

"Infer!" shrieked Blowgrave. "Why, I infer that whoever dug this hole was searching for Uncle Reuben and the lost jewels!"

"I am inclined to agree with you," Thorndyke said calmly. "He happened to search in the wrong place, but that is his affair."

"The wrong place!" Blowgrave and his daughter exclaimed in unison. "How do you know it is the wrong place?"

"Because," replied Thorndyke, "I believe I know the right place, and this is not it. But we can put the matter to the test, and we had better do so. Can you get a couple of men with picks and shovels? Or shall we handle the tools ourselves?"

"I think that would be better," said Blowgrave, who was quivering with excitement. "We don't want to take any one into our confidence if we can help it."

"No," Thorndyke agreed. "Then I suggest that you fetch the tools while I locate the spot."

Blowgrave assented eagerly and went off at a brisk trot, while the young lady remained with us and watched Thorndyke with intense curiosity.

"I mustn't interrupt you with questions," said she, "but I can't imagine how you found out where Uncle Reuben was buried."

"We will go into that later," he replied; "but first we have got to find Uncle Reuben." He laid his research-case down on the ground, and opening it, took out three sheets of paper, each bearing a duplicate of his tracing of the map; and on each was marked a spot on this meadow from which a number of lines radiated like the spokes of a wheel.

"You see, Jervis," he said, exhibiting them to me, "the advantage of a map. I have been able to rule off these sets of bearings regardless of obstructions, such as those young trees, which have arisen since Silas's day, and mark the spot in its correct place. If the recent obstructions prevent us from taking the bearings, we can still find the spot by measurements with the land-chain or tape."

"Why have you got three plans?" I asked.

"Because there are three imaginable places. No. 1 is the most likely; No. 2 less likely, but possible; No. 3 is impossible. That is the one that our friend tried last night. No. 1 is among those young trees, and we will now see if we can pick up the bearings in spite of them."

We moved on to the clump of young trees, where Thorndyke took from the research-case a tall, folding camera-tripod and a large prismatic compass with an aluminium dial. With the latter he took one or two trial bearings and then, setting up the tripod, fixed the compass on it. For some minutes Miss Blowgrave and I watched him as he shifted the tripod from spot to spot, peering through the sight-vane of the compass and glancing occasionally at the map. At length he turned to us and said:

"We are in luck. None of these trees interferes with our bearings." He took from the research-case a surveyor's arrow, and sticking it in the ground under the tripod, added: "That is the spot. But we may have to dig a good way round it, for a compass is only a rough instrument."

At this moment Mr. Blowgrave staggered up, breathing hard, and flung down on the ground three picks, two shovels and a spade. "I won't hinder you, doctor, by asking for explanations," said he, "but I am utterly mystified. You must tell us what it all means when we have finished our work."

This Thorndyke promised to do, but meanwhile he took off his coat, and rolling up his shirt sleeves, seized the spade and began cutting out a large square of turf. As the soil was uncovered, Blowgrave and I attacked it with picks and Miss Blowgrave shovelled away the loose earth.

"Do you know how far down we have to go?" I asked.

"The body lies six feet below the surface," Thorndyke replied; and as he spoke he laid down his spade, and taking a telescope from the research-case, swept it round the margin of the meadow and finally pointed it at a farm-house some six hundred yards distant, of which he made a somewhat prolonged inspection, after which he took the remaining pick and fell to work on the opposite corner of the exposed square of earth.

For nearly half an hour we worked on steadily, gradually eating our way downwards, plying pick and shovel alternately, while Miss Blowgrave cleared the loose earth away from the edges of the deepening pit. Then a halt was called and we came to the surface, wiping our faces.

"I think, Nellie," said Blowgrave, divesting himself of his waistcoat, "a jug of lemonade and four tumblers would be useful, unless our visitors would prefer beer."

We both gave our votes for lemonade, and Miss Nellie tripped away towards the house, while Thorndyke, taking up his telescope, once more inspected the farm-house.

"You seem greatly interested in that house," I remarked.

"I am," he replied, handing me the telescope. "Just take a look at the window in the right hand gable, but keep under the tree."

I pointed the telescope at the gable and there observed an open window at which a man was seated. He held a binocular glass to his eyes and the instrument appeared to be directed at us.

"We are being spied on, I fancy," said I, passing the telescope to Blowgrave, "but I suppose it doesn't matter. This is your land, isn't it?"

"Yes," replied Blowgrave, "but still, we didn't

want any spectators. That is Harold Bowker," he added, steadying the telescope against a tree, "my cousin Arthur's nephew, whom I told you about as having inherited the farm-house. He seems mighty interested in us; but small things interest one in the country."

Here the appearance of Miss Nellie, advancing across the meadow with an inviting-looking basket, diverted our attention from our inquisitive watcher. Six thirsty eyes were riveted on that basket until it drew near and presently disgorged a great glass jug and four tumblers, when we each took off a long and delicious draught and then jumped down into the pit to resume our labours.

Another half-hour passed. We had excavated in some places to nearly the full depth and were just discussing the advisability of another short rest when Blowgrave, who was working in one corner, uttered a loud cry and stood up suddenly, holding something in his fingers. A glance at the object showed it to be a bone, brown and earth-stained, but evidently a bone. Evidently, too, a human bone, as Thorndyke decided when Blowgrave handed it to him triumphantly.

"We have been very fortunate," said he, "to get so near at the first trial. This is from the right great toe, so we may assume that the skeleton lies just outside this pit, but we had better excavate carefully in your corner and see exactly how the bones lie." This he proceeded to do himself, probing cautiously with the spade and clearing the earth away from the corner. Very soon the remaining bones of the right foot came into view and then the ends of the two leg-bones and a portion of the left foot.

"We can see now," said he, "how the skeleton lies, and all we have to do is to extend the excavation in that direction. But there is only room for one to work down here. I think you and Mr. Blowgrave had better dig down from the surface."

On this, I climbed out of the pit, followed reluctantly by Blowgrave, who still held the little brown bone in his hand and was in a state of wild excitement and exultation that somewhat scandalized his daughter.

"It seems rather ghoulish," she remarked, "to be gloating over poor Uncle Reuben's body in this way."

"I know," said Blowgrave, "it isn't reverent. But I didn't kill Uncle Reuben, you know, whereas— well it was a long time ago." With this rather in consequent conclusion he took a draught of lemonade, seized his pick and fell to work with a will. I, too, indulged in a draught and passed a full tumbler down to Thorndyke. But before resuming my labours I picked up the telescope and once more inspected the farm-house. The window was still open, but the watcher had apparently become bored with the not very thrilling spectacle. At any rate he had disappeared.

From this time onward every few minutes brought some discovery. First, a pair of deeply rusted steel shoe buckles; then one or two buttons, and presently a fine gold watch with a fob-chain and a bunch of seals, looking uncannily new and fresh and seeming more fraught with tragedy than even the bones themselves. In his cautious digging, Thorndyke was careful not to disturb the skeleton; and looking down into the narrow trench that was growing from the corner of the pit, I could see both legs, with only the right foot missing, projecting from the miniature cliff. Meanwhile our part of the trench was deepening rapidly, so that Thorndyke presently warned us to stop digging and bade us come down and shovel away the earth as he disengaged it.

At length the whole skeleton, excepting the head, was uncovered, though it lay undisturbed as it might have lain in its coffin. And now, as Thorndyke picked away the earth around the head, we could see that the skull was propped forward as if it rested on a high pillow. A little more careful probing with the pick-point served to explain this appearance. For as the earth fell away and disclosed the grinning skull, there came into view the edge and iron-bound corners of a small chest.

It was an impressive spectacle; weird, solemn and rather dreadful. There for over a century the ill-fated gambler had lain, his mouldering head pillowed on the booty of unrecorded villainy, booty that had been won by fraud, retrieved by violence, and hidden at last by the final winner with the witness of his crime.

"Here is a fine text for a moralist who would preach on the vanity of riches," said Thorndyke.

We all stood silent for a while, gazing, not without awe, at the stark figure that lay guarding the ill-gotten treasure. Miss Blowgrave—who had been helped down when we descended—crept closer to her father and murmured that it was "rather awful"; while Blowgrave himself displayed a queer mixture of exultation and shuddering distaste.

Suddenly the silence was broken by a voice from above, and we all looked up with a start. A youngish man was standing on the brink of the pit, looking down on us with very evident disapproval.

"It seems that I have come just in the nick of time," observed the newcomer. "I shall have to take possession of that chest, you know, and of the remains, too, I suppose. That is my ancestor, Reuben Blowgrave."

"Well, Harold," said Blowgrave, "you can have Uncle Reuben if you want him. But the chest belongs to Nellie."

Here Mr. Harold Bowker—I recognized him now as the watcher from the window—dropped down into the pit and advanced with something of a swagger.

"I am Reuben's heir," said he, "through my Uncle Arthur, and I take possession of this property and the remains."

"Pardon me, Harold," said Blowgrave, "but Nellie is Arthur's residuary legatee, and this is the residue of the estate."

"Rubbish!" exclaimed Bowker. "By the way, how did you find out where he was buried?"

"Oh, that was quite simple," replied Thorndyke with unexpected geniality. "I'll show you the plan." He climbed up to the surface and returned in a few moments with the three tracings and his letter-case. "This is how we located the spot." He handed the plan marked No. 3 to

Bowker, who took it from him and stood looking at it with a puzzled frown.

"But this isn't the place," he said at length.

"Isn't it?" queried Thorndyke. "No, of course; I've given you the wrong one. This is the plan." He handed Bowker the plan marked No. 1, and took the other from him, laying it down on a heap of earth. Then, as Bowker pored gloomily over No. 1, he took a knife and a pencil from his pocket, and with his back to our visitor, scraped the lead of the pencil, letting the black powder fall on the plan that he had just laid down. I watched him with some curiosity; and when I observed that the black scrapings fell on two spots near the edges of the paper, a sudden suspicion flashed into my mind, which was confirmed when I saw him tap the paper lightly with his pencil, gently blow away the powder, and quickly producing my photograph of the typewritten letter from his case, hold it for a moment beside the plan.

"This is all very well," said Bowker, looking up from the plan, "but how did you find out about these bearings?"

Thorndyke swiftly replaced the letter in his case, and turning round, replied, "I am afraid I can't give you any further information."

"Can't you, indeed!" Bowker exclaimed insolently. "Perhaps I shall compel you to. But, at any rate, I forbid any of you to lay hands on my property."

Thorndyke looked at him steadily and said in an ominously quiet tone:

"Now, listen to me, Mr. Bowker. Let us have

an end of this nonsense. You have played a risky game and you have lost. How much you have lost I can't say until I know whether Mr. Blowgrave intends to prosecute."

"To prosecute!" shouted Bowker. "What the deuce do you mean by prosecute?"

"I mean," said Thorndyke, "that on the 7th of June, after nine o'clock at night, you entered the dwelling-house of Mr. Blowgrave and stole and carried away certain of his goods and chattels. A part of them you have restored, but you are still in possession of some of the stolen property, to wit, a scarab and a deed-box."

As Thorndyke made his statement in his calm, level tones, Bowker's face blanched to a tallowy white, and he stood staring at my colleague, the very picture of astonishment and dismay. But he fired a last shot.

"This is sheer midsummer madness," he exclaimed huskily; "and you know it."

Thorndyke turned to our host. "It is for you to settle, Mr. Blowgrave," said he. "I hold conclusive evidence that Mr. Bowker stole your deed-box. If you decide to prosecute I shall produce that evidence in court and he will certainly be convicted."

Blowgrave and his daughter looked at the accused man with an embarrassment almost equal to his own.

"I am astounded," the former said at length; "but I don't want to be vindictive. Look here, Harold, hand over the scarab and we'll say no more about it."

"You can't do that," said Thorndyke. "The law

doesn't allow you to compound a robbery. He can return the property if he pleases and you can do as you think best about prosecuting. But you can't make conditions."

There was silence for some seconds; then, without another word, the crestfallen adventurer turned, and scrambling up out of the pit, took a hasty departure.

It was nearly a couple of hours later that, after a leisurely wash and a hasty, nondescript meal, we carried the little chest from the dining-room to the study. Here, when he had closed the French window and drawn the curtains, Mr. Blowgrave produced a set of tools and we fell to work on the iron fastenings of the chest. It was no light task, though a century's rust had thinned the stout bands, but at length the lid yielded to the thrust of a long case-opener and rose with a protesting creak. The chest was lined with a double thickness of canvas, apparently part of a sail, and contained a number of small leathern bags, which, as we lifted them out, one by one, felt as if they were filled with pebbles. But when we untied the thongs of one and emptied its contents into a wooden bowl, Blowgrave heaved a sigh of ecstasy and Miss Nellie uttered a little scream of delight. They were all cut stones, and most of them of exceptional size; rubies, emeralds, sapphires, and a few diamonds. As to their value, we could form but the vaguest guess; but Thorndyke, who was a fair judge of gemstones, gave it as his opinion that they were fine specimens of their kind, though roughly cut, and that they had probably formed the enrichment of some shrine.

"The question is," said Blowgrave, gazing gloatingly on the bowl of sparkling gems, "what are we to do with them?"

"I suggest," said Thorndyke, "that Dr. Jervis stays here to-night to help you guard them and that in the morning you take them up to London and deposit them at your bank."

Blowgrave fell in eagerly with this suggestion, which I seconded. "But," said he, "that chest is a queer-looking package to be carrying abroad. Now, if we only had that confounded deed-box—"

"There's a deed-box on the cabinet behind you," said Thorndyke.

Blowgrave turned round sharply. "God bless us!" he exclaimed. "It has come back the way it went. Harold must have slipped in at the window while we were at tea. Well, I'm glad he has made restitution. When I look at that bowl and think what he must have narrowly missed, I don't feel inclined to be hard on him. I suppose the scarab is inside—not that it matters much now."

The scarab was inside in an envelope; and as Thorndyke turned it over in his hand and examined the hieroglyphics on it through his lens, Miss Blowgrave asked: "Is it of any value, Dr. Thorndyke? It can't have any connection with the secret of the hiding-place, because you found the jewels without it.

"By the way, doctor, I don't know whether it is permissible for me to ask, but how on earth *did* you find out where the jewels were hidden? To me it looks like black magic."

Thorndyke laughed in a quiet, inward fashion. "There is nothing magical about it," said he. "It was a perfectly simple, straightforward problem. But Miss Nellie is wrong. We had the scarab; that is to say we had the wax impression of it, which is the same thing. And the scarab was the key to the riddle. You see," he continued, "Silas's letter and the scarab formed together a sort of intelligence test."

"Did they?" said Blowgrave. "Then he drew a blank every time."

Thorndyke chuckled. "His descendants were certainly a little lacking in enterprise," he admitted. "Silas's instructions were perfectly plain and explicit. Whoever would find the treasure must first acquire some knowledge of Egyptian lore and must study the scarab attentively. It was the broadest of hints, but no one—excepting Harold Bowker, who must have heard about the scarab from his Uncle Arthur—seems to have paid any attention to it.

"Now it happens that I have just enough elementary knowledge of the hieroglyphic characters to enable me to spell them out when they are used alphabetically; and as soon as I saw the seal, I could see that these hieroglyphics formed English words. My attention was first attracted by the second group of signs, which spelled the word 'Reuben,' and then I saw that the first group spelled 'Uncle.' Of course, the instant I heard Miss Nellie speak of the connection between the scarab and Uncle Reuben, the murder was out. I saw at a glance that the scarab contained all the required information. Last night I made a careful tracing of the hieroglyphics and then rendered them into our own alphabet. This is the result."

He took from his letter-case and spread out on the table a duplicate of the tracing which I had seen him make, and of which he had given me a copy. But since I had last seen it, it had received an addition; under each group of signs the equivalents in modern Roman lettering had been written, and these made the following words:

UNKL RUBN IS IN TH MILL FIELD SKS FT DOWN CHURCH SPIR NORTH TEN THIRTY EAST DINGL SOUTH GABL NORTH ATY FORTY FIF WST GOD SAF KING JORJ.

Our two friends gazed at Thorndyke's transliteration in blank astonishment. At length Blowgrave remarked: "But this translation must have demanded a very profound knowledge of the Egyptian writing."

"Not at all," replied Thorndyke. "Any intelligent person could master the Egyptian alphabet in an hour. The language, of course, is quite another matter. The spelling of this is a little crude, but it is quite intelligible and does Silas great credit, considering how little was known in his time."

"How do you suppose M. Fouquet came to overlook this?" Blowgrave asked.

"Naturally enough," was the reply. "He was looking for an Egyptian inscription. But this is

217

UNKL RUBN IS IN TH MILL
FIELD SKS FT DOWN
CHURCH SPIR NORTH TEN THIRTY
EAST DINGL SOUTH GABL NORTH
ATY FORTY FIF WST GOD SAF
KING JORJ

The transliteration of the hieroglyphics.

not an Egyptian inscription. Does he speak English?"

"Very little. Practically not at all."

"Then, as the words are English words and imperfectly spelt, the hieroglyphics must have appeared to him mere nonsense. And he was right as to the scarab being an imitation."

"There is another point," said Blowgrave. "How was it that Harold made that extraordinary mistake about the place? The directions are clear enough. All you had to do was to go out there with a compass and take the bearings just as they were given."

"But," said Thorndyke, "that is exactly what he did, and hence the mistake. He was apparently unaware of the phenomenon known as the Secular Variation of the Compass. As you know, the compass does not—usually—point to true north, but to the Magnetic North; and the Magnetic North is continually changing its position. When Reuben was buried—about 1810—it was twenty-four degrees, twenty-six minutes west of true north; at the present time it is fourteen degrees, forty-eight minutes west of true north. So Harold's bearings would be no less than ten degrees out, which, of course, gave him a totally wrong position. But Silas was a ship-master, a navigator, and of course, knew all about the vagaries of the compass; and, as his directions were intended for use at some date unknown to him, I assumed that the bearings that he gave were true bearings—that when he said 'north' he meant true north, which is always the same; and this turned out to be the case. But I also prepared a plan with magnetic bearings corrected up to date. Here are the three plans: No. 1—the one we used—showing true bearings; No. 2, showing corrected magnetic bearings which might have given us the correct spot; and No. 3, with uncorrected magnetic bearings, giving us the spot where Harold dug, and which could not possible have been the right spot."

On the following morning I escorted the deed-box, filled with the booty and tied up and sealed with the scarab, to Mr. Blowgrave's bank. And that ended our connection with the case; excepting that, a month or two later, we attended by request the unveiling in Shawstead churchyard of a fine monument to Reuben Blowgrave. This took the slighty inappropriate form of an obelisk, on which were cut the name and approximate dates, with the added inscription: "Cast thy bread upon the waters and it shall return after many days"; concerning which Thorndyke remarked dryly that he supposed the exhortation applied equally even if the bread happened to belong to some one else.

G. K. Chesterton
(1874–1936)
THE DOOM OF THE
DARNAWAYS

*The exact counterpart to the impersonal, clinical Free-
man was the humanist and social observer Gilbert
Keith Chesterton. Where Thorndyke concentrated on
scientific procedure, Father Brown triumphs through
knowledge of human nature and foible. Though Father Brown's rhapsodies on human nature can wear
on the ear, his good-heartedness makes for a warmer
and more memorable detective.*

*Whereas Freeman looks ahead to a cleaner, more
modern style of contemporary mystery fiction, Chesterton, especially in this tale from* The Incredulity
of Father Brown, *with its curses, old paintings, heirs,
and Brontë-esque female character looks back to Victorian models.*

*Chesterton was a commanding figure of his time,
the first president of London's celebrated Detection
Club, founded in 1932, which set the standards of
the Art of Classy Mystery Writing.*

Two landscape-painters stood looking at one landscape, which was also a sea-scape, and both were
curiously impressed by it, though their impres-

sions were not exactly the same. To one of them, who was a rising artist from London, it was new as well as strange. To the other, who was a local artist, but with something more than a local celebrity, it was better known; but perhaps all the more strange for what he knew of it.

In terms of tone and form, as these men saw it, it was a stretch of sands against a stretch of sunset, the whole scene lying in strips of sombre colour, dead green and bronze and brown and a drab that was not merely dull but in that gloaming in some way more mysterious than gold. All that broke these level lines was a long building which ran out from the fields into the sands of the sea, so that its fringe of dreary weeds and rushes seemed almost to meet the seaweed. But its most singular feature was that the upper part of it had the ragged outlines of a ruin, pierced by so many wide windows and large rents as to be a mere dark skeleton against the dying light; while the lower bulk of the building had hardly any windows at all, most of them being blind and bricked up and their outlines faintly traceable in the twilight. But one window at least was still a window; and it seemed strangest of all that it showed a light.

"Who on earth can live in that old shell?" exclaimed the Londoner, who was a big, bohemian-looking man, young but with a shaggy red beard that made him look older; Chelsea knew him familiarly as Harry Payne.

"Ghosts, you might suppose," replied his friend Martin Wood. "Well, the people who live there really are rather like ghosts."

It was perhaps rather a paradox that the London

222

artist seemed almost bucolic in his boisterous freshness and wonder, while the local artist seemed a more shrewd and experienced person, regarding him with mature and amiable amusement; indeed, the latter was altogether a quieter and more conventional figure, wearing darker clothes and with his square and stolid face clean-shaven.

"It is only a sign of the times, of course," he went on, "or of the passing of old times and old families with them. The last of the great Darnaways live in that house; and not many of the new poor are as poor as they are. They can't even afford to make their own top story habitable; but have to live in the lower rooms of a ruin, like bats and owls. Yet they have family portraits that go back to the Wars of the Roses and the first portrait-painting in England, and very fine some of them are; I happen to know, because they asked for my professional advice in overhauling them. There's one of them especially, and one of the earliest, but it's so good that it gives you the creeps."

"The whole place gives you the creeps, I should think by the look of it," replied Payne.

"Well," said his friend, "to tell you the truth it does."

The silence that followed was stirred by a faint rustle among the rushes by the moat; and it gave them, rationally enough, a slight nervous start when a dark figure brushed along the bank, moving rapidly and almost like a startled bird. But it was only a man walking briskly with a black bag in his hand; a man with a long sallow face and sharp eyes that glanced at the London stranger in a slightly darkling and suspicious manner.

"It's only Dr. Barnet," said Wood with a sort of relief. "Good evening, Doctor. Are you going up to the house? I hope nobody's ill."

"Everybody's always ill in a place like that," growled the doctor, "only sometimes they're too ill to know it. The very air of the place is a blight and a pestilence. I don't envy the young man from Australia."

"And who," asked Payne abruptly and rather absently, "may the young man from Australia be?"

"Ah!" snorted the doctor, "hasn't your friend told you about him? As a matter of fact I believe he is arriving today. Quite a romance in the old style of melodrama; the heir coming back from the Colonies to his ruined castle, all complete even down to an old family compact for his marrying the lady watching in the ivied tower. Queer old stuff, isn't it; but it really happens sometimes. He's even got a little money, which is the only bright spot there ever was in this business."

"What does Miss Darnaway herself, in her ivied tower, think of the business?" asked Martin Wood dryly.

"What she thinks of everything else by this time," replied the doctor. "They don't think in this weedy old den of superstitions; they only dream and drift. I think she accepts the family contract and the colonial husband as part of the Doom of the Darnaways, don't you know. I really think that if he turned out to be a humpbacked Negro with one eye and a homicidal maniac, she would only think it added a finishing touch and fitted in with the twilight scenery."

"You're not giving my friend from London a very lively picture of my friends in the country," said Wood, laughing. "I had intended taking him there to call; no artist ought to miss those Darnaway portraits if he gets the chance. But perhaps I'd better postpone it if they're in the middle of the Australian invasion."

"Oh, do go in and see them, for the Lord's sake," said Dr. Barnet warmly. "Anything that will brighten their blighted lives will make my task easier. It will need a good many colonial cousins to cheer things up, I should think; and the more the merrier. Come, I'll take you in myself."

As they drew nearer to the house it was seen to be isolated like an island in a moat of brackish water which they crossed by a bridge. On the other side spread a fairly wide stony floor or embankment with great cracks across it, in which little tufts of weed and thorn sprouted here and there. This rock platform looked large and bare in the grey twilight; and Payne could hardly have believed that such a corner of space could have contained so much of the soul of a wilderness. This platform only jutted out on one side, like a giant doorstep, and beyond it was the door; a very low-browed Tudor archway standing open but dark, like a cave.

When the brisk doctor led them inside without ceremony, Payne had, as it were, another shock of depression. He could have expected to find himself mounting to a very ruinous tower, by very narrow winding staircases; but in this case the first steps into the house were actually steps down-wards. They went down several short and broken stairways into large twilit rooms which, but for their lines of dark pictures and dusty book-shelves, might have been the traditional dungeons beneath the castle moat. Here and there a candle in an old candlestick lit up some dusty accidental detail of a dead elegance; but the visitor was not so much impressed, or depressed, by this artificial light as by the one pale gleam of natural light. As he passed down the long room he saw the only window in that wall, a curious low oval window of a late-seventeenth century fashion. But the strange thing about it was that it did not look out directly on any space of sky but only on a reflection of sky; a pale strip of daylight merely mirrored in the moat, under the hanging shadow of the bank. Payne had a memory of the Lady of Shalott who never saw the world outside except in a mirror. The lady of this Shalott not only in some sense saw the world in a mirror, but even saw the world upside-down.

"It's as if the house of Darnaway were falling literally as well as metaphorically," said Wood in a low voice, "as if it were sinking slowly into a swamp or a quicksand; until the sea goes over it like a green roof."

Even the sturdy Dr. Barnet started a little at the silent approach of the figure that came to re-ceive them. Indeed, the room was so silent that they were all startled to realize that it was not empty. There were three people in it when they entered; three dim figures motionless in the dim room; all three dressed in black and looking like dark shadows. As the foremost figure drew nearer the grey light from the window, he showed a face that looked almost as grey as its frame of hair. This was old Vine, the steward, long left *in loco parentis* since the death of that eccentric parent, the last Lord Darnaway. He would have been a handsome old man if he had had no teeth. As it was he had one, which showed every now and then and gave him a rather sinister appearance. He received the doctor and his friends with a fine courtesy and escorted them to where the other two figures in black were seated. One of them seemed to Payne to give another appropriate touch of gloomy antiquity to the castle by the mere fact of being a Roman Catholic priest, who might have come out of a priest's hole in the dark old days. Payne could imagine him muttering prayers or telling beads or doing a number of indistinct and melancholy things in that melancholy place. Just then he might be supposed to have been giving religious consolation to the lady; but it could hardly be supposed that the consolation was very consoling, or at any rate that it was very cheering. For the rest, the priest was personally insignificant enough, with plain and rather expressionless features; but the lady was a very different matter. Her face was very far from being plain or insignificant; it stood out from the darkness of her dress and hair and background with a pallor that was almost awful, but a beauty that was almost awfully alive. Payne looked at it as long as he dared; and he was to look at it a good deal longer before he died.

Wood merely exchanged with his friends such

pleasant and polite phrases as would lead up to his purpose of revisiting the portraits. He apologized for calling on the day which he heard was to be one of family welcome; but he was soon convinced that the family was rather mildly relieved to have visitors to distract them or break the shock. He did not hesitate, therefore, to lead Payne through the central reception-room into the library beyond, where hung the portrait, for there was one which he was especially bent on showing, not only as a picture but almost as a puzzle. The little priest trudged along with them; he seemed to know something about old pictures as well as about old prayers.

"I'm rather proud of having spotted this," said Wood. "I believe it's a Holbein. If it isn't, there was somebody living in Holbein's time who was as great as Holbein."

It was a portrait in the hard but sincere and living fashion of the period, representing a man clad in black trimmed with gold and fur, with a heavy, full, rather pale face but watchful eyes.

"What a pity art couldn't have stopped for ever at just that transition stage," cried Wood, "and never transitioned any more. Don't you see it's just realistic enough to be real? Don't you see the face speaks all the more because it stands out from a rather stiffer framework of less essential things? And the eyes are even more real than the face. On my soul, I think the eyes are too real for the face! It's just as if those sly, quick eyeballs were protruding out of a great pale mask."

"The stiffness extends to the figure a little, I think," said Payne. "They hadn't quite mastered anatomy when mediaevalism ended, at least in the north. That left leg looks to me a good deal out of drawing."

"I'm not so sure," replied Wood quietly. "Those fellows who painted just when realism began to be done, and before it began to be overdone, were often more realistic than we think. They put real details of portraiture into things that are thought merely conventional. You might say this fellow's eyebrows or eye-sockets are a little lopsided; but I bet if you knew him you'd find that one of his eyebrows did really stick up more than the other. And I shouldn't wonder if he was lame or something, and that black leg was meant to be crooked."

"What an old devil he looks!" burst out Payne suddenly. "I trust his reverence will excuse my language."

"I believe in the devil, thank you," said the priest with an inscrutable face. "Curiously enough there was a legend that the devil was lame."

"I say," protested Payne, "you can't really mean that he was the devil; but who the devil was he?"

"He was the Lord Darnaway under Henry VII and Henry VIII," replied his companion. "But there are curious legends about him too; one of them is referred to in that inscription round the frame, and further developed in some notes left by somebody in a book I found here. They are both rather curious reading."

Payne leaned forward, craning his head so as to follow the archaic inscription round the frame. Leaving out the antiquated lettering and spelling, it seemed to be a sort of rhyme running somewhat thus:

> *In the seventh heir I shall return,*
> *In the seventh hour I shall depart,*
> *None in that hour shall hold my hand,*
> *And woe to her that holds my heart.*

"It sounds creepy somehow," said Payne, "but that may be partly because I don't understand a word of it."

"It's pretty creepy even when you do," said Wood in a low voice. "The record made at a later date, in the old book I found, is all about how this beauty deliberately killed himself in such a way that his wife was executed for his murder. Another note commemorates a later tragedy, seven successions later under the Georges, in which another Darnaway committed suicide, having first thoughtfully left poison in his wife's wine. It's said that both suicides took place at seven in the evening. I suppose the inference is that he does really return with every seventh inheritor and makes things pleasant, as the rhyme suggests, for any lady unwise enough to marry him."

"On that argument," replied Payne, "it would be a trifle uncomfortable for the next seventh gentleman."

Wood's voice was lower still as he said:

"The new heir will be the seventh."

Harry Payne suddenly heaved up his great chest and shoulders like a man flinging off a burden.

"What crazy stuff are we all talking?" he cried. "We're all educated men in an enlightened age, I

230

suppose. Before I came into this damned dank atmosphere I'd never have believed I should be talking of such things, except to laugh at them."

"You are right," said Wood. "If you lived long enough in this underground palace you'd begin to feel differently about things. I've begun to feel very curiously about that picture, having had so much to do with handling and hanging it. It sometimes seems to me that the painted face is more alive than the dead faces of the people living here; that it is a sort of talisman or magnet: that it commands the elements and draws out the destinies of men and things. I suppose you would call it very fanciful."

"What is that noise?" cried Payne suddenly.

They all listened, and there seemed to be no noise except the dull boom of the distant sea; then they began to have the sense of something mingling with it; something like a voice calling through the sound of the surf, dulled by it at first, but coming nearer and nearer. The next moment they were certain; someone was shouting outside in the dusk.

Payne turned to the low window behind him and bent to look out. It was the window from which nothing could be seen except the moat with its reflection of bank and sky. But that inverted vision was not the same that he had seen before. From the hanging shadow of the bank in the water depended two dark shadows reflected from the feet and legs of a figure standing above upon the bank. Through that limited aperture they could see nothing but the two legs black against the reflection of a pale and livid sunset. But somehow

231

the very fact of the head being invisible, as if in the clouds, gave something dreadful to the sound that followed; the voice of a man crying aloud what they could not properly hear or understand. Payne especially was peering out of the little window with an altered face, and he spoke with an altered voice.

"How queerly he's standing!"

"No, no," said Wood, in a sort of soothing whisper. "Things often look like that in reflection. It's the wavering of the water that makes you think that."

"Think what?" asked the priest shortly.

"That his left leg is crooked," said Wood.

Payne had thought of the oval window as a sort of mystical mirror; and it seemed to him that there were in it other inscrutable images of doom. There was something else beside the figure that he did not understand; three thinner legs showing in dark lines against the light, as if some monstrous three-legged spider or bird were standing beside the stranger. Then he had the less crazy thought of a tripod like that of the heathen oracles; and the next moment the thing had vanished and the legs of the human figure passed out of the picture.

He turned to meet the pale face of old Vine, the steward, with his mouth open, eager to speak, and his single tooth showing.

"He has come," he said. "The boat arrived from Australia this morning."

Even as they went back out of the library into the central salon, they heard the footsteps of the newcomer clattering down the entrance steps, with various items of light luggage trailed behind them. When Payne saw one of them, he laughed with a reaction of relief. His tripod was nothing but the telescopic legs of a portable camera, easily packed and unpacked; and the man who was carrying it seemed so far to take on equally solid and normal qualities. He was dressed in dark clothes, but of a careless and holiday sort, his shirt was of grey flannel, and his boots echoed uncompromisingly enough in those still chambers; as he strode forward to greet his new circle his stride had scarcely more than the suggestion of a limp. But Payne and his companions were looking at his face, and could scarcely take their eyes from it.

He evidently felt there was something curious and uncomfortable about his reception; but they could have sworn that he did not himself know the cause of it. The lady supposed to be in some sense already betrothed to him was certainly beautiful enough to attract him; but she evidently also frightened him. The old steward brought him a sort of feudal homage, yet treated him as if he were the family ghost. The priest still looked at him with a face which was quite undecipherable, and therefore perhaps all the more unnerving. A new sort of irony, more like the Greek irony, began to pass over Payne's mind. He had dreamed of the stranger as a devil, but it seemed almost worse that he was an unconscious destiny. He seemed to march towards crime with the monstrous innocence of Oedipus. He had approached the family mansion in so blindly buoyant a spirit as to have set up his camera to photograph his first sight of it; and even the camera had taken on the semblance of the tripod of a tragic pythoness.

Payne was surprised, when taking his leave a

little while after, at something which showed that the Australian was already less unconscious of his surroundings. He said in a low voice:

"Don't go . . . or come again soon. You look like a human being. This place fairly gives me the jumps."

When Payne emerged out of those almost subterranean halls and came into the night air and the smell of the sea, he felt as if he had come out of that underworld of dreams in which events tumble on top of each other in a way at once unrestful and unreal. The arrival of the strange relative had been somehow unsatisfying and as it were unconvincing. The doubling of the same face in the old portrait and the new arrival troubled him like a two-headed monster. And yet it was not altogether a nightmare; nor was it that face, perhaps, that he saw most vividly.

"Did you say," he asked of the doctor, as they strode together across the striped dark sands by the darkening sea, "did you say that young man was betrothed to Miss Darnaway by a family compact or something? Sounds rather like a novel."

"But an historical novel," answered Dr. Barnet. "The Darnaways all went to sleep a few centuries ago, when things were really done that we only read of in romances. Yes, I believe there's some family tradition by which second or third cousins always marry when they stand in a certain relation of age, in order to unite the property. A damned silly tradition, I should say; and if they often married in-and-in in that fashion, it may account on principles of heredity for their having gone so rotten."

"I should hardly say," answered Payne a little stiffly, "that they had all gone rotten."

"Well," replied the doctor, "the young man doesn't *look* rotten, of course, though he's certainly lame."

"The young man!" cried Payne, who was suddenly and unreasonably angry. "Well, if you think the young lady looks rotten, I think it's you who have rotten taste."

The doctor's face grew dark and bitter. "I fancy I know more about it than you do," he snapped.

They completed the walk in silence, each feeling that he had been irrationally rude and had suffered equally irrational rudeness, and Payne was left to brood alone on the matter, for his friend Wood had remained behind to attend to some of his business in connexion with the pictures.

Payne took very full advantage of the invitation extended by the colonial cousin, who wanted somebody to cheer him up. During the next few weeks he saw a good deal of the dark interior of the Darnaway home; though it might be said that he did not confine himself entirely to cheering the colonial cousin up. The lady's melancholy was of longer standing and perhaps needed more lifting; anyhow, he showed a laborious readiness to lift it. He was not without a conscience however, and the situation made him doubtful and uncomfortable. Weeks went by and nobody could discover from the demeanour of the new Darnaway whether he considered himself engaged according to the old compact or no. He went mooning about the dark galleries and stood staring vacantly at the dark and sinister picture. The shades of that prison house were certainly beginning to close on him, and there was little of his Australian assurance left. But Payne could discover nothing upon the point that concerned him most. Once he attempted to confide in his friend Martin Wood, as he was pottering about in his capacity of picture-hanger; but even out of him he got very little satisfaction.

"It seems to me you can't butt in," said Wood shortly, "because of the engagement."

"Of course I shan't butt in if there is an engagement," retorted his friend, "but is there? I haven't said a word to her, of course; but I've seen enough of her to be pretty certain she doesn't think there is, even if she thinks there may be. He doesn't say there is, or even hint that there ought to be. It seems to me this shilly shallying is rather unfair on everybody."

"Especially on you I suppose," said Wood a little harshly, "but if you ask me, I'll tell you what I think. I think he's afraid."

"Afraid of being refused?" asked Payne.

"No, afraid of being accepted," answered the other. "Don't bite my head off—I don't mean afraid of the lady. I mean afraid of the picture."

"Afraid of the picture!" repeated Payne.

"I mean afraid of the curse," said Wood. "Don't you remember the rhyme about the Darnaway doom falling on him and her?"

"Yes, but look here," cried Payne. "Even the Darnaway doom can't have it both ways. You tell me first I mustn't have my own way because of the compact, and then that the compact mustn't have its own way because of the curse. But if the

236

curse can destroy the compact, why should she be tied to the compact? If they're frightened of marrying each other, they're free to marry anybody else, and there's an end of it. Why should I suffer for the observance of something they don't propose to observe? It seems to me your position is very unreasonable."

"Of course it's all a tangle," said Wood rather crossly, and went on hammering at the frame of a canvas.

Suddenly, one morning, the new heir broke his long and baffling silence. He did it in a curious fashion, a little crude, as was his way, but with an obvious anxiety to do the right thing. He asked frankly for advice, not of this or that individual as Payne had done, but collectively as of a crowd. When he did speak, he threw himself on the whole company, like a statesman going to the country. He called it "a show-down." Fortunately the lady was not included in this large gesture; and Payne shuddered when he thought of her feelings. But the Australian was quite honest; he thought the natural thing was to ask for help and for information; calling a sort of family council at which he put his cards on the table. It might be said that he flung down his cards on the table. For he did it with a rather desperate air, like one who had been harassed for days and nights by the increasing pressure of a problem. In that short time the shadows of that place of low windows and sinking pavements had curiously changed him and increased a certain resemblance that crept through all their memories.

The five men, including the doctor, were sitting

round a table; and Payne was idly reflecting that his own light tweeds and red hair must be the only colours in the room; for the priest and the steward were in black and Wood and Darnaway habitually wore dark grey suits that looked almost like black. Perhaps this incongruity had been what the young man had meant by calling him a human being. At that moment the young man himself turned abruptly in his chair and began to talk. A moment after the dazed artist knew that he was talking about the most tremendous thing in the world.

"Is there anything in it?" he was saying. "That is what I've come to asking myself till I'm nearly crazy. I'd never have believed I should come to thinking of such things; but I think of the portrait and the rhyme and the coincidences or whatever you call them, and I go cold. Is there anything in it? Have I got a right to marry, or shall I bring something big and black out of the sky, that I know nothing about, on myself and somebody else?"

His rolling eye had roamed round the table and rested on the plain face of the priest, to whom he now seemed to be speaking. Payne's submerged practicality rose in protest against the problem of superstition being brought before that supremely superstitious tribunal. He was sitting next to Darnaway and struck in before the priest could answer.

"Well, the coincidences are curious, I admit," he said, rather forcing a note of cheerfulness; "but surely we——" and then he stopped as if he had been struck by lightning. For Darnaway had turned his head sharply over his shoulder at the interruption, and with the movement his left eye-brow jerked up far above its fellow and for an instant the face of the portrait glared at him with a ghastly exaggeration of exactitude. The rest saw it; and all had the air of having been dazzled by an instant of light. The old steward gave a hollow groan.

"It is no good," he said hoarsely, "we are dealing with something too terrible."

"Yes," assented the priest in a low voice, "we are dealing with something terrible; with the most terrible thing I know; and the name of it is nonsense."

"What did you say?" said Darnaway, still looking towards him.

"I said nonsense," repeated the priest. "I have not said anything in particular up to now; for it was none of my business; I was only taking temporary duty in the neighbourhood and Miss Darnaway wanted to see me. But since you're asking me personally and pointblank, why, it's easy enough to answer. Of course there's no Doom of the Darnaways to prevent your marrying anybody you have any decent reason for marrying. A man isn't fated to fall into the smallest venial sin, let alone into crimes like suicide and murder. You can't be made to do wicked things against your will because your name is Darnaway, any more than I can because my name is Brown. The Doom of the Browns," he added with relish—"the Weird of the Browns would sound even better."

"And you of all people," repeated the Australian staring, "tell me to think like that about it."

"I tell you to think about something else," replied the priest cheerfully. "What has become of the rising art of photography? How is the camera getting on? I know it's rather dark downstairs, but those hollow arches on the floor above could easily be turned into a first-rate photographic studio. A few workmen could fit it out with a glass roof in no time."

"Really," protested Martin Wood, "I do think you should be the last man in the world to tinker about with those beautiful Gothic arches, which are about the best work your own religion has ever done in the world. I should have thought you'd have had some feeling for that sort of art; but I can't see why you should be so uncommonly keen on photography."

"I'm uncommonly keen on daylight," answered Father Brown, "especially in this dingy business; and photography has the virtue of depending on daylight. And if you don't know that I would grind all the Gothic arches in the world to powder to save the sanity of a single human soul, you don't know so much about my religion as you think you do."

The young Australian had sprung to his feet like a man rejuvenated. "By George, that's the talk," he cried, "though I never thought to hear it from that quarter. I'll tell you what, reverend sir, I'll do something that will show I haven't lost my courage after all."

The old steward was still looking at him with quaking watchfulness, as if he felt something *fey* about the young man's defiance. "Oh," he cried, "what are you going to do now?"

"I am going to photograph the portrait," replied Darnaway.

Yet it was barely a week afterwards that the storm of the catastrophe seemed to swoop out of the sky, darkening that sun of sanity to which the priest had appealed in vain, and plunging the mansion once more in the darkness of the Darnaway doom. It had been easy enough to fit up the new studio; and seen from inside it looked very like any other such studio, empty except for the fullness of the white light. A man coming from the gloomy rooms below had more than normally the sense of stepping into a more than modern brilliancy, as blank as the future. At the suggestion of Wood, who knew the castle well and had got over his first aesthetic grumblings, a small room remaining intact in the upper ruins was easily turned into a dark room, into which Darnaway went out of the white daylight to grope by the crimson gleams of a red lamp. Wood said, laughing, that the red lamp had reconciled him to the vandalism; as that bloodshot darkness was as romantic as an alchemist's cave.

Darnaway had risen at daybreak on the day that he meant to photograph the mysterious portrait; and had it carried up from the library by the single corkscrew staircase that connected the two floors. There he had set it up in the wide white daylight on a sort of easel and planted his photographic tripod in front of it. He said he was anxious to send a reproduction of it to a great antiquary who had written on the antiquities of the house; but the others knew that this was an excuse covering much deeper things. It was, if not exactly a spir-

241

itual duel between Darnaway and the demoniac picture, at least a duel between Darnaway and his own doubts. He wanted to bring the daylight of photography face to face with that dark masterpiece of painting; and to see whether the sunshine of the new art would not drive out the shadows of the old.

Perhaps this was why he preferred to do it by himself; even if some of the details seemed to take longer and involve more than normal delay. Anyhow, he rather discouraged the few who visited his studio during the day of the experiment, and who found him focussing and fussing about in a very isolated and impenetrable fashion. The steward had left a meal for him as he refused to come down; the old gentleman also returned some hours afterwards and found the meal more or less normally disposed of; but when he brought it he got no more gratitude than a grunt. Payne went up once to see how he was getting on, but finding the photographer disinclined for conversation came down again. Father Brown had wandered that way in an unobtrusive style, to take Darnaway a letter from the expert to whom the photograph was to be sent. But he left the letter in a tray, and whatever he thought of that great glass-house full of daylight and devotion to a hobby, a world he had himself in some sense created, he kept it to himself and came down. He had reason to remember very soon that he was the last to come down the solitary staircase connecting the floors, leaving a lonely man and an empty room behind him. The others were standing in the salon that led into the library; just under the great black ebony clock that looked like a titanic coffin.

"How was Darnaway getting on," asked Payne, a little later, "when you last went up?"

The priest passed a hand over his forehead. "Don't tell me I'm getting psychic," he said with a sad smile. "I believe I'm quite dazzled with daylight up in that room and couldn't see things straight. Honestly, I felt for a flash as if there were something uncanny about Darnaway's figure standing before that portrait."

"Oh, that's the lame leg," said Barnet promptly. "We know all about that."

"Do you know," said Payne abruptly, but lowering his voice, "I don't think we do know all about it or anything about it. What's the matter with his leg? What was the matter with his ancestor's leg?"

"Oh, there's something about that in the book I was reading, in there, in the family archives," said Wood. "I'll fetch it for you"; and he stepped into the library just beyond.

"I think," said Father Brown quietly, "Mr. Payne must have some particular reason for asking that."

"I may as well blurt it out once and for all," said Payne, but in a yet lower voice. "After all, there is a rational explanation. A man from anywhere might have made up to look like the portrait. What do we know about Darnaway? He is behaving rather oddly—"

The others were staring at him in a rather startled fashion; but the priest seemed to take it very calmly.

"I don't think the old portrait's ever been photographed," he said. "That's why he wants to do it. I don't think there's anything odd about that."

"Quite an ordinary state of things, in fact," said Wood with a smile; he had just returned with the book in his hand. And even as he spoke there was a stir in the clockwork of the great dark clock behind him and successive strokes thrilled through the room up to the number of seven. With the last stroke there came a crash from the door above that shook the house like a thunderbolt, and Father Brown was already two steps up the winding staircase before the sound had ceased.

"My God!" cried Payne involuntarily, "he is alone up there."

"Yes," said Father Brown without turning as he vanished up the stairway. "We shall find him alone."

When the rest recovered from their first paralysis and ran helter-skelter up the stone steps and found their way to the new studio, it was true in that sense that they found him alone. They found him lying in a wreck of his tall camera, with its long splintered legs standing out grotesquely at three different angles; and Darnaway had fallen on top of it with one black crooked leg lying at a fourth angle along the floor. For the moment the dark heap looked as if he were entangled with some huge and horrible spider. Little more than a glance and a touch were needed to tell them that he was dead. Only the portrait stood untouched upon the easel, and one could fancy the smiling eyes shone.

An hour afterwards Father Brown, in helping

to calm the confusion of the stricken household, came upon the old steward muttering almost as mechanically as the clock had ticked and struck the terrible hour. Almost without hearing them, he knew what the muttered words must be.

> *In the seventh heir I shall return,*
> *In the seventh hour I shall depart.*

As he was about to say something soothing, the old man seemed suddenly to start awake and stiffen into anger; his mutterings changed to a fierce cry.

"You!" he cried, "you and your daylight! Even you won't say now there is no doom for the Darnaways."

"My opinion about that is unchanged," said Father Brown mildly.

Then after a pause he added, "I hope you will observe poor Darnaway's last wish; and see the photograph is sent off."

"The photograph!" cried the doctor sharply. "What's the good of that? As a matter of fact, it's rather curious; but there isn't any photograph. It seems he never took it after all, after pottering about all day."

Father Brown swung round sharply. "Then take it yourselves," he said. "Poor Darnaway was perfectly right. It's most important that the photograph should be taken."

As all the visitors, the doctor, the priest and the two artists trailed away in a black and dismal procession across the brown and yellow sands, they were at first more or less silent, rather as if

245

they had been stunned. And certainly there had been something like a crack of thunder in a clear sky about the fulfilment of that forgotten superstition at the very time when they had most forgotten it; when the doctor and the priest had both filled their minds with rationalism as the photographer had filled his rooms with daylight. They might be as rationalistic as they liked; but in broad daylight, the seventh heir had returned and in broad daylight, at the seventh hour he had perished.

"I'm afraid everybody will always believe in the Darnaway superstition now," said Martin Wood.

"I know one who won't," said the doctor sharply. "Why should I indulge in superstition because somebody indulges in suicide?"

"You think poor Mr. Darnaway committed suicide?" asked the priest.

"I am sure he committed suicide," replied the doctor.

"It is possible," agreed the other.

"He was quite alone up there, and he had a whole drug-store of poisons in the dark room. Besides, it's just the sort of thing that Darnaways do."

"You don't think there's anything in the fulfilment of the family curse?"

"Yes," said the doctor, "I believe in one family curse and that is the family constitution. I told you it was the heredity and they are all half mad. If you stagnate and breed in and brood in your own swamp like that, you're bound to degenerate whether you like it or not. The laws of heredity can't be dodged; the truths of science can't be denied. The minds of the Darnaways are falling to pieces as their blighted old sticks and stones are falling to pieces, eaten away by the sea and the salt air. Suicide—of course he committed suicide; I daresay all the rest will commit suicide. Perhaps the best thing they could do."

As the man of science spoke there sprang suddenly and with startling clearness into Payne's memory the face of the daughter of the Darnaways, a tragic mask pale against an unfathomable blackness, but itself of a blinding and more than mortal beauty. He opened his mouth to speak and found himself speechless.

"I see," said Father Brown to the doctor, "so you do believe in the superstition after all."

"What do you mean—believe in the superstition? I believe in the suicide as a matter of scientific necessity."

"Well," replied the priest, "I don't see a pin to choose between your scientific superstition and the other magical superstition. They both seem to end in turning people into paralytics, who can't move their own legs or arms or save their own lives or souls. The rhyme said it was the doom of the Darnaways to be killed and the scientific textbook says it is the doom of the Darnaways to kill themselves. Both ways they seem to be slaves."

"But I thought you said you believed in rational views of these things," said Dr. Barnet. "Don't you believe in heredity?"

"I said I believed in daylight," replied the priest in a loud and clear voice, "and I won't choose between two tunnels of subterranean superstition that both end in the dark. And the proof of it is this; that you are all entirely in the dark about what really happened in that house."

"Do you mean about the suicide?" asked Payne.

"I mean about the murder," said Father Brown, and his voice, though only slightly lifted to a louder note seemed somehow to resound over the whole shore. "It was murder: but murder is of the will, which God made free."

What the others said at the moment in answer to it Payne never knew. For the word had a rather curious effect on him; stirring him like the blast of a trumpet and yet bringing him to a halt. He stood still in the middle of the sandy waste and let the others go on in front of him; he felt the blood crawling through all his veins and the sensation that is called the hair standing on end; and yet he felt a new and unnatural happiness. A psychological process too quick and too complicated for himself to follow had already reached a conclusion that he could not analyze; but the conclusion was one of relief. After standing still for a moment he turned and went back slowly across the sands to the house of the Darnaways.

He crossed the moat with a stride that shook the bridge, descended the stairs and traversed the long rooms with a resounding tread, till he came to the place where Adelaide Darnaway sat haloed with the low light of the oval window, almost like some forgotten saint left behind in the land of death. She looked up, and an expression of wonder made her face yet more wonderful.

"What is it?" she said. "Why have you come back?"

"I have come for the Sleeping Beauty," he said

248

in a tone that had the resonance of a laugh. "This old house went to sleep long ago, as the doctor said; but it is silly for you to pretend to be old. Come up into the daylight and hear the truth. I have brought you a word; it is a terrible word; but it breaks the spell of your captivity."

She did not understand a word he said; but something made her rise and let him lead her down the long hall and up the stairs and out under the evening sky. The ruins of a dead garden stretched towards the sea; and an old fountain with the figure of a triton, green with rust, remained poised there, pouring nothing out of a dried horn into an empty basin. He had often seen that desolate outline against the evening sky as he passed, and it had seemed to him a type of fallen fortunes in more ways than one. Before long, doubtless, those hollow fonts would be filled, but it would be with the pale green bitter waters of the sea and the flowers would be drowned and strangled in seaweed. So, he had told himself, the daughter of the Darnaways might indeed be wedded, but she would be wedded to death and a doom as deaf and ruthless as the sea. But now he laid a hand on the bronze triton that was like the hand of a giant, and shook it as if he meant to hurl it over like an idol or an evil god of the garden.

"What do you mean?" she asked steadily. "What is this word that will set us free?"

"The word is murder," he said, "and the freedom it brings is as fresh as the flowers of spring. No; I do not mean I have murdered anybody. But the fact that anybody can be murdered is itself good news, after the evil dreams you have been living in. Don't you understand? In that dream of yours everything that happened to you came from inside you; the doom of the Darnaways was stored up in the Darnaways; it unfolded itself like a horrible flower. There was no escape even by happy accident; it was all inevitable; whether it was Vine and his old wives' tales or Barnet and his new-fangled heredity. But this man who died was not the victim of a magic curse or inherited madness. He was murdered; and for us that murder is simply an accident; yes, *requiescat in pace*, but a happy accident. It is a ray of daylight; because it comes from outside."

She suddenly smiled. "Yes, I believe I understand. I suppose you are talking like a lunatic; but I understand. But who murdered him?"

"I do not know," he answered calmly, "but Father Brown knows. And as Father Brown says, murder is at least done by the will, free as that wind from the sea."

"Father Brown is a wonderful person," she said after a pause. "He was the only person who ever brightened my existence in any way at all until—"

"Until what?" asked Payne, and made a movement almost impetuous, leaning towards her and thrusting away the bronze monster so that it seemed to rock on its pedestal.

"Well, until you did," she said and smiled again.

So was the sleeping palace awakened, and it is no part of this story to describe the stages of its awakening, though much of it had come to pass before the dark of the evening had fallen upon the shore. As Harry Payne strode homewards once more across those dark sands that he had crossed in so many moods, he was at the highest turn of happiness that is given in this mortal life, and the whole red sea within him was at the top of its tide. He would have had no difficulty in picturing all that place again in flower and the bronze triton bright as a golden god and the fountain flowing with water or wine. But all this brightness and blossoming had been unfolded for him by the one word "murder," and it was still a word that he did not understand. He had taken it on trust, and he was not unwise; for he was one of those who have a sense of the sound of truth.

It was more than a month later that Payne returned to his London house to keep an appointment with Father Brown, taking the required photograph with him. His personal romance had prospered as well as was fitting under the shadow of such a tragedy, and the shadow itself therefore lay rather more lightly on him; but it was hard to view it as anything but the shadow of a family fatality. In many ways he had been much occupied and it was not until the Darnaway household had resumed its somewhat stern routine and the portrait had long been restored to its place in the library that he had managed to photograph it with a magnesium flare. Before sending it to the antiquary as originally arranged, he brought it to the priest who had so pressingly demanded it.

"I can't understand your attitude about all this, Father Brown," he said. "You act as if you had already solved the problem in some way of your own."

The priest shook his head mournfully. "Not a

251

bit of it," he answered. "I must be very stupid but I'm quite stuck; stuck about the most practical point of all. It's a queer business; so simple up to a point, and then—Let me have a look at that photograph, will you?"

He held it close to his screwed, short-sighted eyes for a moment, and then said, "Have you got a magnifying glass?"

Payne produced one, and the priest looked through it intently for some time and then said, "Look at the title of that book at the edge of the bookshelf beside the frame: it's *The History of Pope Joan*. Now, I wonder. . . yes, by George; and the one above is something or other of Iceland. Lord! what a queer way to find it out! What a dolt and donkey I was not to notice it when I was there!"

"But what have you found out?" asked Payne impatiently.

"The last link," said Father Brown, "and I'm not stuck any longer. Yes, I think I know how that unhappy story went from first to last now."

"But why?" insisted the other.

"Why, because," said the priest with a smile, "the Darnaway library contained books about Pope Joan and Iceland, not to mention another I see with the title beginning *The Religion of Frederick*, which is not so very hard to fill up." Then, seeing the other's annoyance, his smile faded and he said more earnestly:

"As a matter of fact, this last point, though it is the last link, is not the main business. There were much more curious things in the case than that. One of them is rather a curiosity of evidence. Let me begin by saying something that may surprise you. Darnaway did not die at seven o'clock that evening. He had been already dead for a whole day."

"Surprise is rather a mild word," said Payne grimly, "since you and I both saw him walking about afterwards."

"No, we did not," replied Father Brown. "I think we both saw him, or thought we saw him, fussing about with the focussing of his camera. Wasn't his head under that black cloak when you passed through the room? It was when I did. And that's why I felt there was something queer about the room and the figure. It wasn't that the leg was crooked; but rather that it wasn't crooked. It was dressed in the same sort of dark clothes; but if you see what you believe to be one man standing in the way that another man stands, you will think he's in a strange and strained attitude."

"Do you really mean," cried Payne with something like a shudder, "that it was some unknown man?"

"It was the murderer," said Father Brown. "He had already killed Darnaway at daybreak and hid the corpse and himself in the dark room—an excellent hiding-place, because nobody normally goes into it or can see much if he does. But he let it fall out on the floor at seven o'clock, of course, that the whole thing might be explained by the curse."

"But I don't understand," observed Payne. "Why didn't he kill him at seven o'clock then, instead of loading himself with a corpse for fourteen hours?"

"Let me ask you another question," said the

priest. "Why was there no photograph taken? Because the murderer made sure of killing him when he first got up, and before he could take it. It was essential to the murderer to prevent that photograph reaching the expert on the Darnaway antiquities."

There was a sudden silence for a moment, and then the priest went on in a lower tone:

"Don't you see how simple it is? Why, you yourself saw one side of the possibility; but it's simpler even than you thought. You said a man might be faked to resemble an old picture. Surely it's simpler that a picture should be faked to resemble a man. In plain words, it's true in a rather special way that there was no doom of the Darnaways. There was no old picture; there was no old rhyme; there was no legend of a man who caused his wife's death. But there was a very wicked and a very clever man who was willing to cause another man's death in order to rob him of his promised wife."

The priest suddenly gave Payne a sad smile, as if in reassurance. "For the moment I believe you thought I meant you," he said, "but you were not the only person who haunted that house for sentimental reasons. You know the man, or rather you think you do. But there were depths in the man called Martin Wood, artist and antiquary, which none of his mere artistic acquaintances were likely to guess. Remember that he was called in to criticize and catalogue the pictures; in an aristocratic dust-bin of that sort that practically meant simply to tell the Darnaways what art treasures they had got. They would not be surprised at

254

things turning up they had never noticed before. It had to be done well, and it was; perhaps he was right when he said that if it wasn't Holbein it was somebody of the same genius."

"I feel rather stunned," said Payne, "and there are twenty things I don't see yet. How did he know what Darnaway looked like? How did he actually kill him; the doctors seem rather puzzled at present."

"I saw a photograph the lady had which the Australian sent on before him," said the priest, "and there are several ways in which he could have learned things when the new heir was once recognized. We may not know these details; but they are not difficulties. You remember he used to help in the dark room; it seems to me an ideal place, say, to prick a man with a poisoned pin; with the poisons all handy. No, I say these were not difficulties. The difficulty that stumped me was how Wood could be in two places at once. How could he take the corpse from the darkroom and prop it against the camera so that it would fall in a few seconds, without coming downstairs, when he was in the library looking out a book? And I was such a fool that I never looked at the books in the library; and it was only in this photograph, by very undeserved good luck, that I saw the simple fact of a book about Pope Joan."

"You've kept your best riddle for the end," said Payne grimly. "What on earth can Pope Joan have to do with it?"

"Don't forget the book about the Something of Iceland," advised the priest, "or the religion of somebody called Frederick. It only remains to ask what sort of a man was the late Lord Darnaway."

"Oh, does it?" observed Payne heavily.

"He was a cultivated, humorous sort of eccentric, I believe," went on Father Brown. "Being cultivated, he knew there was no such person as Pope Joan. Being humorous, he was very likely to have thought of the title of 'The Snakes of Iceland' or something else that didn't exist. I venture to reconstruct the third title as *The Religion of Frederick the Great*—which also didn't exist. Now, doesn't it strike you that those could be just the titles to put on the backs of books, that didn't exist; or in other words on a book-case that wasn't a bookcase?"

"Ah," cried Payne, "I see what you mean now. There was some hidden staircase—"

"Up to the room Wood himself selected as a dark room," said the priest nodding. "I'm sorry. It couldn't be helped. It's dreadfully banal and stupid, as stupid as I have been on this pretty banal case. But we were mixed up in a real musty old romance of decayed gentility and a fallen family mansion; and it was too much to hope that we could escape having a secret passage. It was a priest's hole and I deserve to be put in it."

Dame Agatha Christie
(1890–1976)

THE SHADOW ON THE GLASS

from *The Mysterious Mr. Quin*

Talk about Agatha Christie and you are speaking about the most successful writer of English literature ever. She created not one but two of the most celebrated detectives of fiction: the eccentric Belgian Hercule Poirot and the endearing, enduring Miss Jane Marple of St. Mary's Mead. She also created Mr. Parker Pyne, amateur psychologist and Mr. Fixit; Tuppence and Tommy Beresford, a pair vaguely suggestive of Nick and Nora Charles as imagined by Noel Coward; and Mr. Harley Quin, the shadowy hero of the story that follows.

Christie's mastery of the English Country House setting is so sure as to suggest she devised it herself. Her command of the mystery plot is so complete as to make one wonder why anyone has dared to write in the form since. Hers was a pen dipped in gold. A collection of her old shopping lists would probably sell out a first edition.

"Listen to this, " said Lady Cynthia Drage.

She read aloud from the journal she held in her hand.

" 'Mr. and Mrs. Unkerton are entertaining a party at Greenways House this week. Among the guests are Lady Cynthia Drage, Mr. and Mrs. Richard Scott, Major Porter, D.S.O., Mrs. Staverton, Captain Allenson and Mr. Satterthwaite.' "

"It's as well, " remarked Lady Cynthia, casting away the paper, "to know what we're in for. But they *have* made a mess of things!"

Her companion, that same Mr. Satterthwaite whose name figured at the end of the list of guests, looked at her interrogatively. It had been said that if Mr. Satterthwaite was found at the houses of those rich who had newly arrived, it was a sign either that the cooking was unusually good, or that a drama of human life was to be enacted there. Mr. Satterthwaite was abnormally interested in the comedies and tragedies of his fellow men.

Lady Cynthia, who was a middle-aged woman, with a hard face and a liberal allowance of make-up, tapped him smartly with the newest thing in parasols which lay rakishly across her knee.

"Don't pretend you don't understand me. You do perfectly. What's more I believe you're here on purpose to see the fur fly!"

Mr. Satterthwaite protested vigorously. He didn't know what she was talking about.

"I'm talking about Richard Scott. Do you pretend you've never heard of him?"

"No, of course not. He's the Big Game man, isn't he?"

"That's it—'Great big bears and tigers, etc.,'

258

as the song says. Of course, he's a great lion himself just now—the Unkertons would naturally be
mad to get hold of him—and the bride! A charming child—oh! quite a charming child—but so
naïve, only twenty, you know, and he must be at
least forty-five."

"Mrs. Scott seems to me very charming," said
Mr. Satterthwaite sedately.

"Yes, poor child."

"Why poor child?"

Lady Cynthia cast him a look of reproach, and
went on approaching the point at issue in her own
manner.

"Porter's all right—a dull dog, though—another of these African hunters, all sunburn and
silence. Second fiddle to Richard Scott and always
has been—lifelong friends and all that sort of
thing. When I come to think of it, I believe they
were together on that trip—"

"Which trip?"

"*The* trip. The Mrs. Staverton trip. You'll be
saying next you've never heard of Mrs. Staverton."

"I *have* heard of Mrs. Staverton," said Mr. Satterthwaite, almost with unwillingness.

And he and Lady Cynthia exchanged glances.

"It's so exactly like the Unkertons," wailed the
latter; "they are absolutely hopeless—socially, I
mean. The idea of asking those two together! Of
course they'd heard that Mrs. Staverton was a
sportswoman and a traveller and all that, and
about her book. People like the Unkertons don't
even begin to realise what pitfalls there are! I've
been running them, myself, for the last year, and

what I've gone through nobody knows. One has to be constantly at their elbow. 'Don't do that! You can't do this!' Thank goodness, I'm through with it now. Not that we've quarrelled—oh! no, I never quarrel—but somebody else can take on the job. As I've always said, I can put up with vulgarity, but I can't stand meanness!"

After this somewhat cryptic utterance, Lady Cynthia was silent for a moment, ruminating on the Unkertons' meanness as displayed to herself.

"If I'd still been running the show for them," she went on presently, "I should have said quite firmly and plainly: 'You can't ask Mrs. Staverton with the Richard Scotts. She and he were once—'"

She stopped eloquently.

"But were they once?" asked Mr. Satterthwaite.

"My dear man! It's well known. That trip into the Interior! I'm surprised the woman had the face to accept the invitation."

"Perhaps she didn't know the others were coming," suggested Mr. Satterthwaite.

"Perhaps she did. That's far more likely."

"You think—"

"She's what I call a dangerous woman—the sort of woman who'd stick at nothing. I wouldn't be in Richard Scott's shoes this week-end."

"And his wife knows nothing, you think?"

"I'm certain of it. But I suppose some kind friend will enlighten her sooner or later. Here's Jimmy Allenson. Such a nice boy. He saved my life in Egypt last winter—I was so bored, you know. Hullo, Jimmy, come here at once."

Captain Allenson obeyed, dropping down on the turf beside her. He was a handsome young fellow of thirty, with white teeth and an infectious smile.

"I'm glad somebody wants me," he observed. "The Scotts are doing the turtle dove stunt, two required, not three, Porter's devouring the Field, and I've been in mortal danger of being entertained by my hostess."

He laughed. Lady Cynthia laughed with him. Mr. Satterthwaite, who was in some ways a little old-fashioned, so much so that he seldom made fun of his host and hostess until after he had left their house, remained grave.

"Poor Jimmy," said Lady Cynthia.

"Mine not to reason why, mine but to swiftly fly. I had a narrow escape of being told the family ghost story."

"An Unkerton ghost," cried Lady Cynthia. "How screaming."

"Not an Unkerton ghost," said Mr. Satterthwaite. "A Greenways ghost. They bought it with the house."

"Of course," said Lady Cynthia. "I remember now. But it doesn't clank chains, does it? It's only something to do with a window."

Jimmy Allenson looked up quickly.

"A window?"

But for the moment Mr. Satterthwaite did not answer. He was looking over Jimmy's head at three figures approaching from the direction of the house—a slim girl between two men. There was a superficial resemblance between the men, both were tall and dark with bronzed faces and quick eyes, but looked at more closely the resemblance vanished.

261

Richard Scott, hunter and explorer, was a man of extraordinarily vivid personality. He had a manner that radiated magnetism. John Porter, his friend and fellow hunter, was a man of squarer build with an impassive, rather wooden face, and very thoughtful grey eyes. He was a quiet man, content always to play second fiddle to his friend.

And between these two walked Moira Scott who, until three months ago, had been Moira O'Connell, a slender figure, big wistful brown eyes, and golden red hair that stood out round her small face like a saint's halo.

"That child mustn't be hurt," said Mr. Satterthwaite to himself. "It would be abominable that a child like that should be hurt."

Lady Cynthia greeted the newcomers with a wave of the latest thing in parasols.

"Sit down, and don't interrupt," she said. "Mr. Satterthwaite is telling us a ghost story."

"I love ghost stories," said Moira Scott. She dropped down on the grass.

"The ghost of Greenways House?" asked Richard Scott.

"Yes, you know about it?"

Scott nodded.

"I used to stay here in the old days," he explained. "Before the Elliots had to sell up. The Watching Cavalier, that's it, isn't it?"

"The Watching Cavalier," said his wife softly. "I like that. It sounds interesting. Please go on."

But Mr. Satterthwaite seemed somewhat loath to do so. He assured her that it was not really interesting at all.

"Now you've done it, Satterthwaite," said

Richard Scott sardonically. "That hint of reluctance clinches it."

In response to popular clamour, Mr. Satterthwaite was forced to speak.

"It's really very uninteresting," he said apologetically. "I believe the original story centres round a Cavalier ancestor of the Elliot family. His wife had a Roundhead lover. The husband was killed by the lover in an upstairs room, and the guilty pair fled; but, as they fled, they looked back at the house, and saw the face of the dead husband at the window, watching them. That is the legend, but the ghost story is only concerned with a pane of glass in the window of that particular room, on which is an irregular stain, almost imperceptible from near at hand, but which from far away certainly gives the effect of a man's face looking out."

"Which window is it?" asked Mrs. Scott, looking up at the house.

"You can't see it from here," said Mr. Satterthwaite. "It is round the other side, but was boarded up from the inside some years ago—forty years ago, I think, to be accurate."

"What did they do that for? I thought you said the ghost didn't walk."

"It doesn't," Mr. Satterthwaite assured her. "I suppose—well, I suppose there grew to be a superstitious feeling about it, that's all."

Then, deftly enough, he succeeded in turning the conversation. Jimmy Allenson was perfectly ready to hold forth upon Egyptian sand diviners.

"Frauds, most of them. Ready enough to tell you vague things about the past, but won't commit themselves as to the future."

263

"I should have thought it was usually the other way about," remarked John Porter.

"It's illegal to tell the future in this country, isn't it?" said Richard Scott. "Moira persuaded a gypsy into telling her fortune, but the woman gave her her shilling back, and said there was nothing doing, or words to that effect."

"Perhaps she saw something so frightful that she didn't like to tell it me," said Moira.

"Don't pile on the agony, Mrs. Scott," said Allenson lightly. "I, for one, refuse to believe that an unlucky fate is hanging over you."

"I wonder," thought Mr. Satterthwaite to himself. "I wonder."

Then he looked up sharply. Two women were coming from the house, a short stout woman, with black hair, inappropriately dressed in jade green, and a tall slim figure in creamy white. The first woman was his hostess, Mrs. Unkerton; the second was a woman he had often heard of, but never met.

"Here's Mrs. Staverton," announced Mrs. Unkerton, in a tone of great satisfaction. "All friends here, I think."

"These people have an uncanny gift for saying just the most awful things they can," murmured Lady Cynthia, but Mr. Satterthwaite was not listening. He was watching Mrs. Staverton.

Very easy—very natural. Her careless "Hullo! Richard, ages since we met. Sorry I couldn't come to the wedding. Is this your wife? You must be tired of meeting all your husband's weather-beaten old friends." Moira's response—suitable, rather

264

shy. The elder woman's swift appraising glance that went on lightly to another old friend.

"Hullo, John!" The same easy tone, but with a subtle difference in it—a warming quality that had been absent before.

And then that sudden smile. It transformed her. Lady Cynthia had been quite right. A dangerous woman! Very fair—deep blue eyes—not the traditional colouring of the siren—a face almost haggard in repose. A woman with a slow dragging voice and a sudden dazzling smile.

Iris Staverton sat down. She became naturally and inevitably the centre of the group. So, you felt, it would always be.

Mr. Satterthwaite was recalled from his thoughts by Major Porter's suggesting a stroll. Mr. Satterthwaite, who was not, as a general rule, much given to strolling, acquiesced. The two men sauntered off together across the lawn.

"Very interesting story of yours just now," said the Major.

"I will show you the window," said Mr. Satterthwaite.

He led the way round to the west side of the house. Here there was a small formal garden—the Privy Garden, it was always called, and there was some point in the name, for it was surrounded by high holly hedges, and even the entrance to it ran zigzag between the same high prickly hedges.

Once inside, it was very charming with an old world charm of formal flower beds, flagged paths and a low stone seat, exquisitely carved. When they had reached the centre of the garden, Mr. Satterthwaite turned and pointed up at the house.

The length of Greenways House ran north and south. In this narrow west wall there was only one window, a window on the first floor, almost over-grown by ivy, with grimy panes, and which you could just see was boarded up on the inside.

"There you are," said Mr. Satterthwaite.

Craning his neck a little, Porter looked up.

"H'm, I can see a kind of discolouration on one of the panes, nothing more."

"We're too near," said Mr. Satterthwaite. "There's a clearing higher up in the woods where you get a really good view."

He led the way out of the Privy Garden, and, turning sharply to the left, struck into the woods. A certain enthusiasm of showmanship possessed him, and he hardly noticed that the man at his side was absent and inattentive.

"They had, of course, to make another window, when they boarded up this one," he explained. "The new one faces south, overlooking the lawn where we were sitting just now. I rather fancy the Scotts have the room in question. That is why I didn't want to pursue the subject. Mrs. Scott might have felt nervous if she had realised that she was sleeping in what might be called the haunted room."

"Yes. I see," said Porter.

Mr. Satterthwaite looked at him sharply, and realised that the other had not heard a word of what he was saying.

"Very interesting," said Porter. He slashed with his stick at some tall foxgloves, and, frowning, he said: "She ought not to have come. She ought never to have come."

People often spoke after this fashion to Mr. Satterthwaite. He seemed to matter so little, to have so negative a personality. He was merely a glorified listener.

"No," said Porter, "she ought never to have come."

Mr. Satterthwaite knew instinctively that it was not of Mrs. Scott he spoke.

"You think not?" he asked.

Porter shook his head as though in foreboding.

"I was on that trip," he said abruptly. "The three of us went. Scott and I and Iris. She's a wonderful woman—and a damned fine shot." He paused. "What made them ask her?" he finished abruptly.

Mr. Satterthwaite shrugged his shoulders.

"Ignorance," he said.

"There's going to be trouble," said the other. "We must stand by—and do what we can."

"But surely Mrs. Staverton—"

"I'm talking of Scott." He paused. "You see— there's Mrs. Scott to consider."

Mr. Satterthwaite had been considering her all along, but he did not think it necessary to say so, since the other man had so clearly forgotten her until this minute.

"How did Scott meet his wife?" he asked.

"Last winter, in Cairo. A quick business. They were engaged in three weeks, and married in six."

"She seems to me very charming."

"She is; no doubt about it. And he adores her —but that will make no difference." And again Major Porter repeated to himself, using the pronoun that meant to him one person only: "Hang it all, she shouldn't have come."

Just then they stepped out upon a high grassy knoll at some little distance from the house. With again something of the pride of the showman, Mr. Satterthwaite stretched out his arm.

"Look," he said.

It was fast growing dusk. The window could still be plainly descried, and apparently pressed against one of the panes was a man's face surmounted by a plumed cavalier's hat.

"Very curious," said Porter. "Really very curious. What will happen when that pane of glass gets smashed some day?"

Mr. Satterthwaite smiled.

"That is one of the most interesting parts of the story. That pane of glass has been replaced to my certain knowledge at least eleven times, perhaps oftener. The last time was twelve years ago when the then owner of the house determined to destroy the myth. But it's always the same. *The stain reappears*—not all at once, the discolouration spreads gradually. It takes a month or two as a rule."

For the first time, Porter showed signs of real interest. He gave a sudden quick shiver.

"Damned odd, these things. No accounting for them. What's the real reason of having the room boarded up inside?"

"Well, an idea got about that the room was—unlucky. The Eveshams were in it just before the divorce. Then Stanley and his wife were staying here, and had that room when he ran off with his chorus girl."

Porter raised his eyebrows.

"I see. Danger, not to life, but to morals."

"And now," thought Mr. Satterthwaite to himself, "the Scotts have it. I wonder—"

They retraced their steps in silence to the house. Walking almost noiselessly on the soft turf, each absorbed in his own thoughts, they became unwittingly eavesdroppers. They were rounding the corner of the holly hedge when they heard Iris Staverton's voice, raised fierce and clear from the depths of the Privy Garden:

"You shall be sorry—sorry—for this!"

Scott's voice answered, low and uncertain, so that the words could not be distinguished; and then the woman's voice rose again, speaking words that they were to remember later.

"Jealousy—it drives one to the Devil—it *is* the Devil! It can drive one to black murder. Be careful, Richard; for God's sake, be careful."

And then, on that, she had come out of the Privy Garden, ahead of them, and on round the corner of the house without seeing them, walking swiftly, almost running, like a woman hagridden and pursued.

Mr. Satterthwaite thought again of Lady Cynthia's words. A dangerous woman. For the first time, he had a premonition of tragedy, coming swift and inexorable, not to be gainsaid.

Yet that evening he felt ashamed of his fears. Everything seemed normal and pleasant. Mrs. Staverton, with her easy insouciance, showed no sign of strain. Moira Scott was her charming unaffected self. The two women appeared to be getting on very well. Richard Scott himself seemed to be in boisterous spirits.

The most worried-looking person was stout Mrs. Unkerton. She confided at length in Mr. Satterthwaite.

"Think it silly or not, as you like, there's something giving me the creeps. And I'll tell you frankly, I've sent for the glazier, unbeknown to Ned."

"The glazier?"

"To put a new pane of glass in that window. It's all very well. Ned's proud of it—says it gives the house a tone. I don't like it. I tell you flat. We'll have a nice, plain, modern pane of glass, with no nasty stories attached to it."

"You forget," said Mr. Satterthwaite. "Or perhaps you don't know. The stain comes back."

"That's as it may be," said Mrs. Unkerton. "All I can say is, if it does, it's against nature!"

Mr. Satterthwaite raised his eyebrows, but did not reply.

"And what if it does?" pursued Mrs. Unkerton defiantly. "We're not so bankrupt, Ned and I, that we can't afford a new pane of glass every month—or every week if need be for the matter of that."

Mr. Satterthwaite did not meet the challenge. He had seen too many things crumple and fall before the power of money to believe that even a Cavalier ghost could put up a successful fight. Nevertheless, he was interested by Mrs. Unkerton's manifest uneasiness. Even she was not exempt from the tension in the atmosphere—only

270

she attributed it to an attenuated ghost story, not to the clash of personalities among her guests.

Mr. Satterthwaite was fated to hear yet another scrap of conversation which threw light upon the situation. He was going up the wide staircase to bed. John Porter and Mrs. Staverton were sitting together in an alcove of the big hall. She was speaking with a faint irritation in her golden voice.

"I hadn't the least idea the Scotts were going to be here. I daresay, if I had known, I shouldn't have come; but I can assure you, my dear John, that now I am here, I'm not going to run away."

Mr. Satterthwaite passed on up the staircase out of earshot. He thought to himself: "I wonder now. How much of that is true? Did she know? I wonder. What's going to come of it?"

He shook his head.

In the clear light of the morning he felt that he had perhaps been a little melodramatic in his imaginings of the evening before. A moment of strain—yes, certainly—inevitable under the circumstances—but nothing more. People adjusted themselves. His fancy that some great catastrophe was pending was nerves—pure nerves—or possibly liver. Yes, that was it, liver. He was due at Carlsbad in another fortnight.

On his own account he proposed a little stroll that evening just as it was growing dusk. He suggested to Major Porter that they should go up to the clearing and see if Mrs. Unkerton had been as good as her word, and had a new pane of glass put in. To himself, he said: "Exercise, that's what I need. Exercise."

The two men walked slowly through the woods. Porter, as usual, was taciturn.

"I can't help feeling," said Mr. Satterthwaite, loquaciously, "that we were a little foolish in our imaginings yesterday. Expecting—er—trouble, you know. After all, people have to behave themselves—swallow their feelings and that sort of thing."

"Perhaps," said Porter. After a minute or two he added: "Civilised people."

"You mean?"

"People who've lived outside civilisation a good deal sometimes go back. Revert. Whatever you call it."

They emerged on to the grassy knoll. Mr. Satterthwaite was breathing rather fast. He never enjoyed going up hill.

He looked toward the window. The face was still there, more lifelike than ever.

"Our hostess has repented, I see."

Porter threw it only a cursory glance.

"Unkerton cut up rough, I expect," he said indifferently. "He's the sort of man who is willing to be proud of another family's ghost, and who isn't going to run the risk of having it driven away when he's paid spot cash for it."

He was silent a minute or two, staring, not at the house, but at the thick undergrowth by which they were surrounded.

"Has it ever struck you," he said, "that civilisation's damned dangerous?"

"Dangerous?" Such a revolutionary remark shocked Mr. Satterthwaite to the core.

"Yes. There are no safety valves, you see."

272

He turned abruptly, and they descended the path by which they had come.

"I really am quite at a loss to understand you," said Mr. Satterthwaite, pattering along with nimble steps to keep up with the other's strides. "Reasonable people—"

Porter laughed. A short disconcerting laugh. Then he looked at the correct little gentleman by his side.

"You think it's all bunkum on my part, Mr. Satterthwaite? But there are people, you know, who can tell you when a storm's coming. They feel it beforehand in the air. And other people can foretell trouble. There's trouble coming now, Mr. Satterthwaite, big trouble. It may come any minute. It may—"

He stopped dead, clutching Mr. Satterthwaite's arm. And in that tense minute of silence it came —the sound of two shots and, following them, a cry—a cry in a woman's voice.

"My God!" cried Porter, "it's come."

He raced down the path, Mr. Satterthwaite panting behind him. In a minute they came out onto the lawn, close by the hedge of the Privy Garden. At the same time, Richard Scott and Mr. Unkerton came round the opposite corner of the house. They halted, facing each other, to the left and right of the entrance to the Privy Garden.

"It—it came from in there," said Unkerton, pointing with a flabby hand.

"We must see," said Porter. He led the way into the enclosure. As he rounded the last bend of the holly hedge, he stopped dead. Mr. Satterth-

273

waite peered over his shoulder. A loud cry burst from Richard Scott.

There were three people in the Privy Garden. Two of them lay on the grass near the stone seat, a man and a woman. The third was Mrs. Staverton. She was standing quite close to them by the holly hedge, gazing with horror-stricken eyes, and holding something in her right hand.

"Iris," cried Porter. "Iris. For God's sake! What's that you've got in your hand?"

She looked down at it then—with a kind of wonder, an unbelievable indifference.

"It's a pistol," she said wonderingly. And then—after what seemed an interminable time, but was in reality only a few seconds, "I—picked it up."

Mr. Satterthwaite had gone forward to where Unkerton and Scott were kneeling on the turf.

"A doctor," the latter was murmuring. "We must have a doctor."

But it was too late for any doctor. Jimmy Allenson, who had complained that the sand diviners hedged about the future, and Moira Scott, to whom a gypsy had returned a shilling, lay there in the last great stillness.

It was Richard Scott who completed a brief examination. The iron nerve of the man showed in this crisis. After the first cry of agony, he was himself again.

He laid his wife gently down again.

"Shot from behind," he said briefly. "The bullet has passed right through her."

Then he handled Jimmy Allenson. The wound

here was in the breast and the bullet was lodged in the body.

John Porter came toward them.

"Nothing should be touched," he said sternly. "The police must see it all exactly as it is now."

"The police," said Richard Scott. His eyes lit up with a sudden flame as he looked at the woman standing by the holly hedge. He made a step in that direction, but at the same time John Porter also moved, so as to bar his way. For a moment it seemed as though there was a duel of eyes between the two friends.

Porter very quietly shook his head.

"No, Richard," he said. "It looks like it—but you're wrong."

Richard Scott spoke with difficulty, moistening his dry lips.

"Then why—has she got that in her hand?"

And again Iris Staverton said in the same lifeless tone, "I—picked it up."

"The police," said Unkerton, rising. "We must send for the police—at once. You will telephone perhaps, Scott? Someone should stay here—yes, I am sure someone should stay here."

In his quiet gentlemanly manner, Mr. Satterthwaite offered to do so. His host accepted the offer with manifest relief.

"The ladies," he explained. "I must break the news to the ladies, Lady Cynthia and my dear wife."

Mr. Satterthwaite stayed in the Privy Garden looking down on the body of that which had once been Moira Scott.

"Poor child," he said to himself. "Poor child."

He quoted to himself the tag about the evil men do living after them. For was not Richard Scott in a way responsible for his innocent wife's death? They would hang Iris Staverton, he supposed, not that he liked to think of it, but was not it at least a part of the blame he laid at the man's door? The evil that men do—

And the girl, the innocent girl, had paid.

He looked down at her with a very deep pity. Her small face, so white and wistful, a half smile on the lips still. The ruffled golden hair, the delicate ear. There was a spot of blood on the lobe of it. With an inner feeling of being something of a detective, Mr. Satterthwaite deduced an earring, torn away in her fall. He craned his neck forward. Yes, he was right, there was a small pearl drop hanging from the other ear.

Poor child, poor child.

"And now, sir," said Inspector Winkfield.

They were in the library. The Inspector, a shrewd-looking forceful man of forty-odd, was concluding his investigations. He had questioned most of the guests, and had by now pretty well made up his mind on the case. He was listening to what Major Porter and Mr. Satterthwaite had to say. Mr. Unkerton sat heavily in a chair, staring with protruding eyes at the opposite wall.

"As I understand it, gentlemen," said the Inspector, "you'd been for a walk. You were returning to the house by a path that winds round the left side of what they call the Privy Garden. Is that correct?"

"Quite correct, Inspector."

"You heard two shots, and a woman's scream?"

"Yes."

"You then ran as fast as you could, emerged from the woods and made your way to the entrance of the Privy Garden. If anybody had left that garden, they could only do so by the one entrance. The holly hedges are impassable. If anyone had run out of the garden and turned to the right, he would have been met by Mr. Unkerton and Mr. Scott. If he had turned to the left, he could not have done so without being seen by you. Is that right?"

"That is so," said Major Porter. His face was very white.

"That seems to settle it," said the Inspector. "Mr. and Mrs. Unkerton and Lady Cynthia Drage were sitting on the lawn, Mr. Scott was in the billiard room, which opens on to that lawn. At ten minutes past six, Mrs. Staverton came out of the house, spoke a word or two to those sitting there, and went round the corner of the house toward the Privy Garden. Two minutes later the shots were heard. Mr. Scott rushed out of the house and, together with Mr. Unkerton, ran to the Privy Garden. At the same time, you and Mr.—er Satterthwaite arrived from the opposite direction. Mrs. Staverton was in the Privy Garden with a pistol in her hand from which two shots had been fired. As I see it, she shot the lady first from behind, as she was sitting on the bench. Then Captain Allenson sprang up and went for her, and she shot him in the chest as he came toward her. I understand that there had been a—er—previous attachment between her and Mr. Richard Scott—"

"That's a damned lie," said Porter.

His voice rang out hoarse and defiant. The Inspector said nothing, merely shook his head.

"What is her own story?" asked Mr. Satterthwaite.

"She says that she went into the Privy Garden to be quiet for a little. Just before she rounded the last hedge, she heard the shots. She came round the corner, saw the pistol lying at her feet, and picked it up. No one passed her, and she saw no one in the garden but the two victims." The Inspector gave an eloquent pause. "That's what she says—and although I cautioned her, she insisted on making a statement."

"If she said that," said Major Porter, and his face was still deadly white, "she was speaking the truth. I know Iris Staverton."

"Well, sir," said the Inspector, "there'll be plenty of time to go into all that later. In the meantime, I've got my duty to do."

With an abrupt movement, Porter turned to Mr. Satterthwaite.

"You! Can't you help? Can't *you* do something?"

Mr. Satterthwaite could not help feeling immensely flattered. He had been appealed to, he, most insignificant of men, and by a man like John Porter.

He was just about to flutter out a regretful reply, when the butler, Thompson, entered, with a card upon a salver which he took to his master with an apologetic cough. Mr. Unkerton was still sitting huddled up in a chair, taking no part in the proceedings.

"I told the gentleman you would probably not be able to see him, sir," said Thompson, "but he insisted that he had an appointment and that it was most urgent."

Unkerton took the card.

"Mr. Harley Quin," he read. "I remember, he was to see me about a picture. I did make an appointment, but as things are—"

But Mr. Satterthwaite had started forward.

"Mr. Harley Quin, did you say?" he cried. "How extraordinary, how very extraordinary. Major Porter, you asked me if I could help you. I think I can. This Mr. Quin is a friend—or I should say, an acquaintance of mine. He is a most remarkable man."

"One of these amateur solvers of crime, I suppose," remarked the Inspector disparagingly.

"No," said Mr. Satterthwaite. "He is not that kind of man at all. But he has a power—an almost uncanny power—of showing you what you have seen with your own eyes, of making clear to you what you have heard with your own ears. Let us, at any rate, give him an outline of the case, and hear what he has to say."

Mr. Unkerton glanced at the Inspector, who merely snorted and looked at the ceiling. Then the former gave a short nod to Thompson, who left the room and returned ushering in a tall slim stranger.

"Mr. Unkerton?" The stranger shook him by the hand. "I am sorry to intrude upon you at such a time. We must leave our little picture chat until another time. Ah! my friend, Mr. Satterthwaite. Still as fond of the drama as ever?"

279

A faint smile played for a minute round the stranger's lips as he said these last words.

"Mr. Quin," said Mr. Satterthwaite impressively. "We have a drama here; we are in the midst of one. I should like, and my friend Major Porter would like, to have your opinion of it."

Mr. Quin sat down. The red-shaded lamp threw a broad hand of colored light over the checked pattern of his overcoat, and left his face in shadow almost as though he wore a mask.

Succinctly, Mr. Satterthwaite recited the main points of the tragedy. Then he paused, breathlessly awaiting the words of the oracle.

But Mr. Quin merely shook his head.

"A sad story," he said. "A very sad and shocking tragedy. The lack of motive makes it very intriguing."

Unkerton stared at him.

"You don't understand," he said. "Mrs. Staverton was heard to threaten Richard Scott. She was bitterly jealous of his wife. Jealousy—"

"I agree," said Mr. Quin. "Jealousy or Demoniac Possession. It's all the same. But you misunderstand me. I was not referring to the murder of Mrs. Scott, but to that of Captain Allenson."

"You're right," cried Porter, springing forward. "There's a flaw there. If Iris had ever contemplated shooting Mrs. Scott, she'd have got her alone somewhere. No, we're on the wrong tack. And I think I see another solution. Only those three people went into the Privy Garden. That is indisputable, and I don't intend to dispute it. But I reconstruct the tragedy differently. Supposing Jimmy Allenson shoots first Mrs. Scott and then

280

himself. That's possible, isn't it? He flings the pistol from him as he falls—Mrs. Staverton finds it lying on the ground and picks it up just as she said. How's that?"

The Inspector shook his head.

"Won't wash, Major Porter. If Captain Allenson had fired that shot close to his body, the cloth would have been singed."

"He might have held the pistol at arm's length."

"Why should he? No sense in it. Besides, there's no motive."

"Might have gone off his head suddenly," muttered Porter, but without any great conviction. He fell to silence again, suddenly rousing himself to say defiantly: "Well, Mr. Quin?"

The latter shook his head.

"I'm not a magician. I'm not even a criminologist. But I will tell you one thing—I believe in the value of impressions. In any time of crisis, there is always one moment that stands out from all the others, one picture that remains when all else has faded. Mr. Satterthwaite is, I think, likely to have been the most unprejudiced observer of those present. Will you cast your mind back, Mr. Satterthwaite, and tell us the moment that made the strongest impression on you? Was it when you heard the shots? Was it when you first saw the dead bodies? Was it when you first observed the pistol in Mrs. Staverton's hand? Clear your mind of any preconceived standard of values, and tell us."

Mr. Satterthwaite fixed his eyes on Mr. Quin's face, rather as a schoolboy might repeat a lesson of which he was not sure.

"No," he said, slowly. "It was not any of these. The moment that I shall always remember was when I stood alone by the bodies—afterward—looking down on Mrs. Scott. She was lying on her side. Her hair was ruffled. There was a spot of blood on her little ear."

And instantly, as he said it, he felt that he had said a terrific, a significant thing.

"Blood on her ear? Yes, I remember," said Unkerton slowly.

"Her earring must have been torn out when she fell," explained Mr. Satterthwaite.

But it sounded a little improbable as he said it.

"She was lying on her left side," said Porter. "I suppose it was that ear?"

"No," said Mr. Satterthwaite quickly. "It was her right ear."

The Inspector coughed.

"I found this in the grass," he vouchsafed. He held up a loop of gold wire.

"But, my God, man," cried Porter. "The thing can't have been wrenched to pieces by a mere fall. It's more as though it had been shot away by a bullet."

"So it was," cried Mr. Satterthwaite. "It was a bullet. It must have been."

"There were only two shots," said the Inspector. "A shot can't have grazed her ear and shot her in the back as well. And if one shot carried away the earring, and the second shot killed her, it can't have killed Captain Allenson as well—not unless he was standing close in front of her—very close—facing her as it might be. Oh! no, not even then, unless, that is—"

"Unless she was in his arms, you were going to say," said Mr. Quin, with a queer little smile. "Well, why not?"

Everyone stared at each other. The idea was so vitally strange to them—Allenson and Mrs. Scott. Mr. Unkerton voiced the same feeling.

"But they hardly knew each other," he said.

"I don't know," said Mr. Satterthwaite thoughtfully. "They might have known each other better than we thought. Lady Cynthia said he saved her from being bored in Egypt last winter, and you," he turned to Porter, "you told me that Richard Scott met his wife in Cairo last winter. They might have known each other very well indeed out there."

"They didn't seem to be together much," said Unkerton.

"No—they rather avoided each other. It was almost unnatural, now I come to think of it—"

They all looked at Mr. Quin, as if a little startled at the conclusions at which they had arrived so unexpectedly.

Mr. Quin rose to his feet.

"You see," he said, "what Mr. Satterthwaite's impression has done for us." He turned to Unkerton. "It is your turn now."

"Eh? I don't understand you."

"You were very thoughtful when I came into this room. I should like to know exactly what thought it was that obsessed you. Never mind if it has nothing to do with the tragedy. Never mind if it seems to you—superstitious—" Mr. Unkerton started, ever so slightly. "Tell us."

"I don't mind telling you," said Unkerton.

283

"Though it's nothing to do with the business, and you'll probably laugh at me into the bargain. I was wishing that my Missis had left well alone and not replaced that pane of glass in the haunted window. I feel as though doing that has maybe brought a curse upon us."

He was unable to understand why the two men opposite him stared so.

"But she hasn't replaced it yet," said Mr. Satterthwaite at last.

"Yes, she has. Man came first thing this morning."

"My God!" said Porter, "I begin to understand. That room, it's panelled, I suppose, not papered?"

"Yes, but what does that—"

But Porter had swung out of the room. The others followed him. He went straight upstairs to the Scotts' bedroom. It was a charming room, panelled in cream, with two windows facing south. Porter felt with his hands along the panels on the western wall.

"There's a spring somewhere—must be. Ah!" There was a click, and a section of the panelling rolled back. It disclosed the grimy panes of the haunted window. One pane of glass was clean and new. Porter stooped quickly and picked up something. He held it out on the palm of his hand. It was a fragment of ostrich feather. Then he looked at Mr. Quin. Mr. Quin nodded.

He went across to the hat cupboard in the bedroom. There were several hats in it—the dead woman's hats. He took out one with a large brim and curling feathers—an elaborate Ascot hat.

284

Mr. Quin began speaking in a gentle, reflective voice.

"Let us suppose," said Mr. Quin, "a man who is by nature intensely jealous, a man who has stayed here in bygone years and knows the secret of the spring in the panelling. To amuse himself he opens it one day, and looks out over the Privy Garden. There, secure as they think from being overlooked, he sees his wife and another man. There can be no possible doubt in his mind as to the relations between them. He is mad with rage. What shall he do? An idea comes to him. He goes to the cupboard and puts on the hat with the brim and feathers. It is growing dusk, and he remembers the story of the stain on the glass. Anyone looking up at the window will see as they think the Watching Cavalier. Thus secured he watches them, and at the moment they are clasped in each other's arms, he shoots. He is a good shot—a wonderful shot. As they fall, he fires once more —that shot carries away the earring. He flings the pistol out of the window into the Privy Garden, rushes down stairs and out through the billiard room."

Porter took a step toward him.

"But he let her be accused?" he cried. "He stood by and let her be accused? Why? Why?"

"I think you know why," said Mr. Quin. "I should guess—it's only guesswork on my part, mind—that Richard Scott was once madly in love with Iris Staverton—so madly that even meeting her years afterward stirred up the embers of jealousy again. I should say that Iris Staverton once fancied that she might love him, that she went on

285

a hunting trip with him and another—and that she came back in love with the better man."

"The better man," muttered Porter, dazed. "You mean—"

"Yes," said Mr. Quin, with a faint smile. "I mean you." He paused a minute, and then said: "If I were you—I should go to her now."

"I will," said Porter.

He turned and left the room.

Dorothy L. Sayers
(1893–1957)
THE QUEEN'S SQUARE

Lord Peter Wimsey, Dorothy L. Sayers's famed detective, was right at home in the company of Lord and Lady Ferncliffe and others who populated the English Country House in its Golden Age. He was the younger son of the fifteenth Duke of Denver, educated at Eton and Balliol College, Oxford, where he excelled in cricket. His bravery in combat during World War I earned him the Distinguished Service Order. He returned to civilian life as an amateur expert in rare books, history, music, and, of course, criminology.

During the course of the Wimsey saga (1923–42) he marries, has children, and uses his skills as a detective to assist various family members. As in the story at hand, the blue blood flows like wine.

"You Jack o' Di'monds, you Jack o' Di'monds," said Mark Sambourne, shaking a reproachful head, "I know you of old." He rummaged beneath the white satin of his costume, paneled with gigantic oblongs and spotted to represent a set of dominoes. "Hang this fancy rig! Where the blazes has the fellow put my pockets? You rob my pocket, yes, you rob-a my pocket, you rob my

287

pocket of silver and go-ho-hold. How much do you make it?" He extracted a fountain-pen and a check-book.

"Five-seventeen-six," said Lord Peter Wimsey. "That's right, isn't it, partner?" His huge blue-and-scarlet sleeves rustled as he turned to Lady Hermione Creethorpe, who, in her Queen of Clubs costume, looked a very redoubtable virgin, as, indeed, she was.

"Quite right," said the old lady, "and I consider that very cheap."

"We haven't been playing long," said Wimsey apologetically.

"It would have been more, Auntie," observed Mrs. Wrayburn, "if you hadn't been greedy. You shouldn't have doubled those four spades of mine."

Lady Hermione snorted, and Wimsey hastily cut in:

"It's a pity we've got to stop, but Deverill will never forgive us if we're not there to dance Sir Roger. He feels strongly about it. What's the time? Twenty past one. Sir Roger is timed to start sharp at half past. I suppose we'd better tootle back to the ballroom."

"I suppose we had," agreed Mrs. Wrayburn. She stood up, displaying her dress, boldly patterned with the red and black points of a backgammon board. "It's very good of you," she added, as Lady Hermione's voluminous skirts swept through the hall ahead of them, "to chuck your dancing to give Auntie her bridge. She does so hate to miss it."

"Not at all," replied Wimsey. "It's a pleasure.

And in any case I was jolly glad of a rest. These costumes are dashed hot for dancing in."

"You make a splendid Jack of Diamonds, though. Such a good idea of Lady Deverill's, to make everybody come as a game. It cuts out all those wearisome pierrots and columbines." They skirted the south-west angle of the ballroom and emerged into the south corridor, lit by a great hanging lantern in four lurid colors. Under the arcading they paused and stood watching the floor, where Sir Charles Deverill's guests were fox-trotting to a lively tune discoursed by the band in the musicians' gallery at the far end. "Hullo, Giles!" added Mrs. Wrayburn, "you look hot."

"I am hot," said Giles Pomfret. "I wish to goodness I hadn't been so clever about this infernal costume. It's a beautiful billiard-table, but I can't sit down in it." He mopped his heated brow, crowned with an elegant green lamp-shade. "The only rest I can get is to hitch my behind on a radiator, and as they're all in full blast, it's not very cooling. Thank goodness, I can always make these damned sandwich boards an excuse to get out of dancing." He propped himself against the nearest column looking martyred.

"Nina Hartford comes off best," said Mrs. Wrayburn. "Water-polo—so sensible—just a bathing-dress and a ball; though I must say it would look better on a less *Restoration* figure. You playing cards are much the prettiest, and I think the chess-pieces run you close. There goes Gerda Bellingham, dancing with her husband—isn't she *too* marvelous in that red wig? And the bustle and everything—my dear, so attractive. I'm glad they

289

didn't make themselves too Lewis Carroll; Charmian Grayle is the sweetest White Queen—where is she, by the way?"

"I don't like that young woman," said Lady Hermione, "she's fast."

"Dear lady!"

"I've no doubt you think me old-fashioned. Well, I'm glad I am. I say she's fast, and, what's more, heartless. I was watching her before supper, and I'm sorry for Tony Lee. She's been flirting as hard as she can go with Harry Vibart—not to give it a worse name—and she's got Jim Playfair on a string, too. She can't even leave Frank Bellingham alone, though she's staying in his house."

"Oh, I say, Lady H!" protested Sambourne, "you're a bit hard on Miss Grayle. I mean, she's an awfully sporting kid and all that."

"I detest that word 'sporting,'" snapped Lady Hermione. "Nowadays it merely means drunk and disorderly. And she's not such a kid either, young man. In three years' time she'll be a hag, if she goes on at this rate."

"Dear Lady Hermione," said Wimsey, "we can't all be untouched by time, like you."

"You could," retorted the old lady, "if you looked after your stomachs and your morals. Here comes Frank Bellingham—looking for a drink, no doubt. Young people today seem to be positively pickled in gin."

The fox-trot had come to an end, and the Red King was threading his ways towards them through a group of applauding couples.

"Hullo, Bellingham!" said Wimsey. "Your crown's crooked. Allow me." He set wig and head-

PLAN OF THE BALLROOM

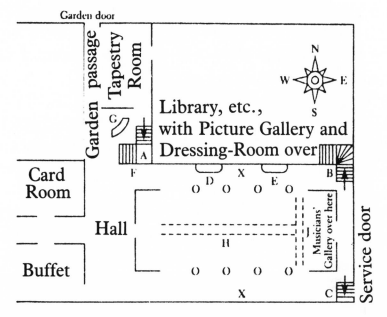

A, Stair to Dressing-room and Gallery; B, Stair to Gallery; C, Stair to Musicians' Gallery only; D, Settee where Joan Carstairs sat; E, Settee where Jim Playfair sat; F, Where Waits stood; G, Where Ephraim Dodd sat; H, Guests' "Sir Roger"; J, Servants' "Sir Roger"; XX, Hanging Lanterns O O O O, Aracading.

dress to rights with skillful fingers. "Not that I blame you. What crown is safe in these Bolshevik days?"

"Thanks," said Bellingham. "I say, I want a drink."

"What did I tell you?" said Lady Hermione.

"Buzz along, then, old man," said Wimsey. "You've got four minutes. Mind you turn up in time for Sir Roger."

"Right you are. Oh, I'm dancing it with Gerda, by the way. If you see her, you might tell her where I've gone to."

291

"We will. Lady Hermione, you're honoring me, of course?"

"Nonsense! You're not expecting me to dance at my age? The Old Maid ought to be a wall-flower."

"Nothing of the sort. If only I'd had the luck to be born earlier, you and I should have appeared side by side, as Matrimony. Of course you're going to dance it with me—unless you mean to throw me over for one of these youngsters."

"I've no use for youngsters," said Lady Hermione. "No guts. Spindleshanks." She darted a swift glance at Wimsey's scarlet hose. "You at least have some suggestion of calves. I can stand up with you without blushing for you."

Wimsey bowed his scarlet cap and curled wig in deep reverence over the gnarled knuckles extended to him.

"You make me the happiest of men. We'll show them all how to do it. Right hand, left hand, both hands across, back to back, round you go and up the middle. There's Deverill going down to tell the band to begin. Punctual old bird, isn't he? Just two minutes to go . . . What's the matter, Miss Carstairs? Lost your partner?"

"Yes—have you seen Tony Lee anywhere?"

"The White King? Not a sign. Nor the White Queen either. I expect they're together somewhere."

"Probably. Poor old Jimmie Playfair is sitting patiently in the north corridor, looking like Casabianca."

"You'd better go along and console him," said Wimsey, laughing.

Joan Carstairs made a face and disappeared in the direction of the buffet, just as Sir Charles Deverill, giver of the party, bustled up to Wimsey and his companions, resplendent in a Chinese costume patterned with red and green dragons, bamboos, circles, and characters, and carrying on his shoulder a stuffed bird with an enormous tail.

"Now, now," he exclaimed, "come along, come along, come along! All ready for Sir Roger. Got your partner, Wimsey? Ah, yes, Lady Hermione—splendid. You must come and stand next to your dear mother and me, Wimsey. Don't be late, don't be late. We want to dance it right through. The waits will begin at two o'clock—I hope they will arrive in good time. Dear me, dear me! Why aren't the servants in yet? I told Watson—I must go and speak to him."

He darted away, and Wimsey, laughing, led his partner up to the top of the room, where his mother, the Dowager Duchess of Denver, stood waiting, magnificent as the Queen of Spades.

"Ah! here you are," said the Duchess placidly. "Dear Sir Charles—he was getting quite flustered. Such a man for punctuality—he ought to have been a Royalty. A delightful party, Hermione, isn't it? Sir Roger and the waits—quite medieval—and a Yule-log in the hall, with the steam radiators and everything—so oppressive!"

"Tumty, tumty, tiddledy, tumty, tumty, tiddledy," sang Lord Peter, as the band broke into the old tune. "I do adore this music. Foot it featly here and there—oh! there's Gerda Bellingham. Just a moment! Mrs. Bellingham—hi! your royal spouse awaits your Red Majesty's pleasure in the

293

buffet. Do hurry him up. He's only got half a minute."

The Red Queen smiled at him, her pale face and black eyes startlingly brilliant beneath her scarlet wig and crown.

"I'll bring him up to scratch all right," she said, and passed on, laughing.

"So she will," said the Dowager. "You'll see that young man in the Cabinet before very long. Such a handsome couple on a public platform, and very sound, I'm told, about pigs, and that's so important, the British breakfast-table being what it is."

Sir Charles Deverill, looking a trifle heated, came hurrying back and took his place at the head of the double line of guests, which now extended three-quarters of the way down the ball-room. At the lower end, just in front of the Musicians' Gallery, the staff had filed in, to form a second Sir Roger, at right angles to the main set. The clock chimed the half-hour. Sir Charles, craning an anxious neck, counted the dancers.

"Eighteen couples. We're two couples short. How vexatious! Who are missing?"

"The Bellinghams?" said Wimsey. "No, they're here. It's the White King and Queen, Badminton and Diabolo."

"There's Badminton!" cried Mrs. Wrayburn, signaling frantically across the room. "Jim! Jim! Bother! He's gone back again. He's waiting for Charmian Grayle."

"Well, we can't wait any longer," said Sir Charles peevishly. "Duchess, will you lead off?"

The Dowager obediently threw her black velvet

train over her arm and skipped away down the center, displaying an uncommonly neat pair of scarlet ankles. The two lines of dancers, breaking into the hop-and-skip step of the country dance, jigged sympathetically. Below them, the cross lines of black and white and livery coats followed their example with respect. Sir Charles Deverill, dancing solemnly down after the Duchess, joined hands with Nina Hartford from the far end of the line. Tumty, tumty, tiddledy, tumty, tumty, tiddledy . . . the first couple turned outward and led the dancers down. Wimsey, catching the hand of Lady Hermione, stooped with her beneath the arch and came triumphantly up to the top of the room, in a magnificent rustle of silk and satin. "My love," sighed Wimsey, "was clad in the black velvet, and I myself in cramoisie." The old lady, well pleased, rapped him over the knuckles with her gilt scepter. Hands clapped merrily.

"Down we go again," said Wimsey, and the Queen of Clubs and Emperor of the great Mahjongg dynasty twirled and capered in the center. The Queen of Spades danced up to meet her Jack of Diamonds. "Bézique," said Wimsey; "double Bézique," as he gave both his hands to the Dowager. Tumty, tumty, tiddledy. He again gave his hand to the Queen of Clubs and led her down. Under their lifted arms the other seventeen couples passed. Then Lady Deverill and her partner followed them down—then five more couples.

"We're working nicely to time," said Sir Charles, with his eye on the clock. "I worked it out at two minutes per couple. Ah! here's one of the missing pairs." He waved an agitated arm. "Come into the center—come along—in here."

A man whose head was decorated with a huge shuttlecock, and Joan Carstairs, dressed as a Diabolo, had emerged from the north corridor. Sir Charles, like a fussy rooster with two frightened hens, guided and pushed them into place between two couples who had not yet done their "hands across," and heaved a sigh of relief. It would have worried him to see them miss their turn. The clock chimed a quarter to two.

"I say, Playfair, have you seen Charmian Grayle or Tony Lee anywhere about?" asked Giles Pomfret of the Badminton costume. "Sir Charles is quite upset because we aren't complete."

"Not a sign of 'em. I was supposed to be dancing this with Charmian, but she vanished upstairs and hasn't come down again. Then Joan came barging along looking for Tony, and we thought we'd better see it through together."

"Here are the waits coming in," broke in Joan Carstairs. "Aren't they sweet? Too-too-truly-rural!"

Between the columns on the north side of the ballroom the waits could be seen filing into place in the corridor, under the command of the Vicar. Sir Roger jigged on his exhausting way. Hands across. Down the center and up again. Giles Pomfret, groaning, scrambled in his sandwich boards beneath the lengthening arch of hands for the fifteenth time. Tumty, tiddledy. The nineteenth couple wove their way through the dance. Once again, Sir Charles and the Dowager Duchess, both as fresh as paint, stood at the top of the room.

296

The clapping was loudly renewed; the orchestra fell silent; the guests broke up into groups; the servants arranged themselves in a neat line at the lower end of the room; the clock struck two; and the Vicar, receiving a signal from Sir Charles, held his tuning-fork to his ear and gave forth a sonorous A. The waits burst shrilly into the opening bars of "Good King Wenceslas."

It was just as the night was growing darker and the wind blowing stronger that a figure came thrusting its way through the ranks of the singers, and hurried across to where Sir Charles stood; Tony Lee, with his face as white as his costume.

"Charmian . . . in the tapestry room . . . dead . . . strangled."

Superintendent Johnson sat in the library, taking down the evidence of the haggard revelers, who were ushered in upon him one by one. First, Tony Lee, his haunted eyes like dark hollows in a mask of gray paper.

"Miss Grayle had promised to dance with me the last dance before Sir Roger; it was a fox-trot. I waited for her in the passage under the Musicians' Gallery. She never came. I did not search for her. I did not see her dancing with anyone else. When the dance was nearly over, I went out into the garden, by way of the service door under the musicians' stair. I stayed in the garden till Sir Roger de Coverley was over—"

"Was anybody with you, sir?"

"No, nobody."

"You stayed alone in the garden from—yes, from 1:20 past 2 o'clock. Rather disagreeable, was it not, sir, with the snow on the ground?" The Superintendent glanced keenly from Tony's stained and sodden white shoes to his strained face.

"I didn't notice. The room was hot—I wanted air. I saw the waits arrive at about 1:40—I daresay they saw me. I came in a little after 2 o'clock—"

"By the service door again, sir?"

"No; by the garden door on the other side of the house, at the end of the passage which runs along beside the tapestry room. I heard singing going on in the ballroom and saw two men sitting in the little recess at the foot of the staircase on the left-hand side of the passage. I think one of them was the gardener. I went into the tapestry room—"

"With any particular purpose in mind, sir?"

"No—except that I wasn't keen on rejoining the party. I wanted to be quiet." He paused; the Superintendent said nothing. "Then I went into the tapestry room. The light was out. I switched it on and saw—Miss Grayle. She was lying close against the radiator. I thought she had fainted. I went over to her and found she was—dead. I only waited long enough to be sure, and then I went into the ballroom and gave the alarm."

"Thank you, sir. Now, may I ask, what were your relations with Miss Grayle?"

"I—I admired her very much."

"Engaged to her, sir?"

"No, not exactly."

"No quarrel—misunderstanding—anything of that sort?"

"Oh, no!"

Superintendent Johnson looked at him again, and again said nothing, but his experienced mind informed him:

"He's lying."

Aloud he only thanked and dismissed Tony. The White King stumbled drearily out, and the Red King took his place.

"Miss Grayle," said Frank Bellingham, "is a friend of my wife and myself; she was staying at our house. Mr. Lee is also our guest. We all came in one party. I believe there was some kind of understanding between Miss Grayle and Mr. Lee—no actual engagement. She was a very bright, lively, popular girl. I have known her for about six years, and my wife has known her since our marriage. I know of no one who could have borne a grudge against Miss Grayle. I danced with her the last dance but two—it was a waltz. After that came a fox-trot and then Sir Roger. She left me at the end of the waltz; I think she said she was going upstairs to tidy. I think she went out by the door at the upper end of the ballroom. I never saw her again. The ladies' dressing-room is on the second floor, next door to the picture-gallery. You reach it by the staircase that goes up from the garden-passage. You have to pass the door of the tapestry room to get there. The only other way to the dressing-room is by the stair at the east end of the ballroom, which goes up to the picture-gallery. You would then have to pass through the picture-gallery to get to the dressing-room. I know the house well; my wife and I have often stayed here."

Next came Lady Hermione, whose evidence, delivered at great length, amounted to this:

"Charmian Grayle was a minx and no loss to anybody. I am not surprised that someone has strangled her. Women like that ought to be strangled. I would cheerfully have strangled her myself. She has been making Tony Lee's life a burden to him for the last six weeks. I saw her flirting with Mr. Vibart tonight on purpose to make Mr. Lee jealous. She made eyes at Mr. Bellingham and Mr. Playfair. She made eyes at everybody. I should think at least half a dozen people had very good reason to wish her dead."

Mr. Vibart, who arrived dressed in a gaudy Polo costume, and still ludicrously clutching a hobby-horse, said that he had danced several times that evening with Miss Grayle. She was a damn sportin' girl, rattlin' good fun. Well, a bit hot, perhaps, but, dash it all, the poor kid was dead. He might have kissed her once or twice, perhaps, but no harm in that. Well, perhaps poor old Lee did take it a bit hard. Miss Grayle liked pulling Tony's leg. He himself had liked Miss Grayle and was dashed cut-up about the whole beastly business.

Mrs. Bellingham confirmed her husband's evidence. Miss Grayle had been their guest, and they were all on the very best of terms. She felt sure that Mr. Lee and Miss Grayle had been very fond of one another. She had not seen Miss Grayle during the last three dances, but had attached no importance to that. If she had thought about it at all, she would have supposed Miss Grayle was sitting out with somebody. She herself had not been up to the dressing-room since about midnight, and had not seen Miss Grayle go upstairs. She had first missed Miss Grayle when they all stood up for Sir Roger.

Mrs. Wrayburn mentioned that she had seen Miss Carstairs in the ballroom looking for Mr. Lee, just as Sir Charles Deverill went down to speak to the band. Miss Carstairs had then mentioned that Mr. Playfair was in the north corridor, waiting for Miss Grayle. She could say for certain that the time was then 1:28. She had seen Mr. Playfair himself at 1:30. He had looked in from the corridor and gone out again. The whole party had then been standing up together, except Miss Grayle, Miss Carstairs, Mr. Lee, and Mr. Playfair. She knew that, because Sir Charles had counted the couples.

Then came Jim Playfair, with a most valuable piece of evidence.

"Miss Grayle was engaged to me for Sir Roger de Coverley. I went to wait for her in the north corridor as soon as the previous dance was over. That was at 1:25. I sat on the settee in the eastern half of the corridor. I saw Sir Charles go down to speak to the band. Almost immediately afterwards, I saw Miss Grayle come out of the passage, under the Musicians' Gallery and go up the stairs at the end of the corridor. I called out: 'Hurry up! they're just going to begin.' I do not think she heard me; she did not reply. I am quite sure I saw her. The staircase has open banisters. There is no light in that corner except from the swinging lantern in the corridor, but that is very powerful. I could not be mistaken in the costume. I waited for Miss Grayle till the dance was half over; then

I gave it up and joined forces with Miss Carstairs, who had also mislaid her partner."

The maid in attendance on the dressing-room was next examined. She and the gardener were the only two servants who had not danced Sir Roger. She had not quitted the dressing-room at any time since supper, except that she might have gone as far as the door. Miss Grayle had certainly not entered the dressing-room during the last hour of the dance.

The Vicar, much worried and distressed, said that his party had arrived by the garden door at 1:40. He had noticed a man in a white costume smoking a cigarette in the garden. The waits had removed their outer clothing in the garden passage and then gone out to take up their position in the north corridor. Nobody had passed them till Mr. Lee had come in with his sad news.

Mr. Ephraim Dodd, the sexton, made an important addition to this evidence. This aged gentleman was, as he confessed, no singer, but was accustomed to go round with the waits to carry the lantern and collecting box. He had taken a seat in the garden passage "to rest me pore feet." He had seen the gentleman come in from the garden "all in white with a crown on 'is 'ead." The choir were then singing "Bring me flesh and bring me wine." The gentleman had looked about a bit, "made a face, like," and gone into the room at the foot of the stairs. He hadn't been absent "more nor a minute," when he "come out faster than he gone in," and had rushed immediately into the ballroom.

In addition to all this, there was, of course,

the evidence of Dr. Pattison. He was a guest at the dance, and had hastened to view the body of Miss Grayle as soon as the alarm was given. He was of opinion that she had been brutally strangled by someone standing in front of her. She was a tall, strong girl, and he thought it would have needed a man's strength to overpower her. When he saw her at five minutes past two he concluded that she must have been killed within the last hour, but not within the last five minutes or so. The body was still quite warm, but, since it had fallen close to the hot radiator, they could not rely very much upon that indication.

Superintendent Johnson rubbed a thoughtful ear and turned to Lord Peter Wimsey, who had been able to confirm much of the previous evidence and, in particular, the exact times at which various incidents had occurred. The Superintendent knew Wimsey well, and made no bones about taking him into his confidence.

"You see how it stands, my lord. If the poor young lady was killed when Dr. Pattison says, it narrows it down a good bit. She was last seen dancing with Mr. Bellingham at—call it 1:20. At 2 o'clock she was dead. That gives us forty minutes. But if we're to believe Mr. Playfair, it narrows it down still further. He says he saw her alive just after Sir Charles went down to speak to the band, which you put at 1:28. That means that there's only five people who could possibly have done it, because all the rest were in the ballroom after that, dancing Sir Roger. There's the maid in the dressing-room; between you and me, sir, I think we can leave her out. She's a little slip of a thing, and it's not clear what motive she could have had. Besides, I've known her from a child, and she isn't the sort to do it. Then there's the gardener; I haven't seen him yet, but there again, he's a man I know well, and I'd as soon suspect myself. Well now, there's this Mr. Tony Lee, Miss Carstairs, and Mr. Playfair himself. The girl's the least probable, for physical reasons, and besides, strangling isn't a woman's crime—not as a rule. But Mr. Lee—that's a queer story, if you like. What was he doing all that time out in the garden by himself?"

"It sounds to me," said Wimsey, "as if Miss Grayle had given him the push and he had gone into the garden to eat worms."

"Exactly, my lord; and that's where his motive might come in."

"So it might," said Wimsey, "but look here. There's a couple of inches of snow on the ground. If you can confirm the time at which he went out, you ought to be able to see, from his tracks, whether he came in again before Ephraim Dodd saw him. Also, where he went in the interval and whether he was alone."

"That's a good idea, my lord. I'll send my sergeant to make inquiries."

"Then there's Mr. Bellingham. Suppose he killed her after the end of his waltz with her. Did anyone see him in the interval between that and the fox-trot?"

"Quite, my lord. I've thought of that. But you see where *that* leads. It means that Mr. Playfair must have been in a conspiracy with him to do it. And from all we hear, that doesn't seem likely."

"No more it does. In fact, I happen to know that Mr. Bellingham and Mr. Playfair were not on the best of terms. You can wash that out."

"I think so, my lord. And that brings us to Mr. Playfair. It's him we're relying on for the time. We haven't found anyone who saw Miss Grayle during the dance before his—that was the fox-trot. What was to prevent him doing it then? Wait a bit. What does he say himself? Says he danced the fox-trot with the Duchess of Denver." The Superintendent's face fell, and he hunted through his notes again. "She confirms that. Says she was with him during the interval and danced the whole dance with him. Well, my lord, I suppose we can take Her Grace's word for it."

"I think you can," said Wimsey, smiling. "I've known my mother practically since my birth, and have always found her very reliable."

"Yes, my lord. Well, that brings us to the end of the fox-trot. After that, Miss Carstairs saw Mr. Playfair waiting in the north corridor. She says she noticed him several times during the interval and spoke to him. And Mrs. Wrayburn saw him there at 1:30 or thereabouts. Then at 1:45 he and Miss Carstairs came and joined the company. Now, is there anyone who can check all these points? That's the next thing we've got to see to."

Within a very few minutes, abundant confirmation was forthcoming. Mervyn Bunter, Lord Peter's personal man, said that he had been helping to take refreshments along to the buffet. Throughout the interval between the waltz and the fox-trot, Mr. Lee had been standing by the service door beneath the musicians' stair, and half-way through the fox-trot he had been seen to go out into the garden by way of the servants' hall. The police-sergeant had examined the tracks in the snow and found that Mr. Lee had not been joined by any other person, and that there was only the one set of his footprints, leaving the house by the servants' hall and returning by the garden door near the tapestry room. Several persons were also found who had seen Mr. Bellingham in the interval between the waltz and the fox-trot, and who were able to say that he had danced the fox-trot through with Mrs. Bellingham. Joan Carstairs had also been seen continuously throughout the waltz and the fox-trot, and during the following interval and the beginning of Sir Roger. More-over, the servants who had danced at the lower end of the room were positive that from 1:29 to 1:45 Mr. Playfair had sat continuously on the set-tee in the north corridor, except for the few seconds during which he had glanced into the ballroom. They were also certain that during that time no one had gone up the staircase at the lower end of the corridor, while Mr. Dodd was equally positive that, after 1:40, nobody except Mr. Lee had entered the garden passage or the tapestry room.

Finally, the circle was closed by William Hog-garty, the gardener. He asserted with the most obvious sincerity that from 1:30 to 1:40 he had been stationed in the garden passage to receive the waits and marshal them to their places. During that time, no one had come down the stair from the picture-gallery or entered the tapestry room. From 1:40 onwards, he had sat beside Mr. Dodd in the passage and nobody had passed him except Mr. Lee.

These points being settled, there was no further reason to doubt Jim Playfair's evidence, since his partners were able to prove his whereabouts during the waltz, the fox-trot, and the intervening interval. At 1:28 or just after, he had seen Charmian Grayle alive. At 2:02 she had been found dead in the tapestry room. During that interval, no one had been seen to enter the room, and every person had been accounted for.

At 6 o'clock, the exhausted guests had been allowed to go to their rooms, accommodation being provided in the house for those who, like the Bellinghams, had come from a distance, since the Superintendent had announced his intention of interrogating them all afresh later in the day.

This new inquiry produced no result. Lord Peter Wimsey did not take part in it. He and Bunter (who was an expert photographer) occupied themselves in photographing the ballroom and adjacent rooms and corridors from every imaginable point of view, for, as Lord Peter said, "You never know what may turn out to be relevant." Late in the afternoon they retired together to the cellar, where with dishes, chemicals, and safe-light hastily procured from the local chemist, they proceeded to develop the plates.

"That's the lot, my lord," observed Bunter at length, sloshing the final plate in the water and tipping it into the hypo. "You can switch the light on now, my lord."

Wimsey did so, blinking in the sudden white glare.

"A very hefty bit of work," said he. "Hullo! What's that plateful of blood you've got there?"

"That's the red backing they put on these plates, my lord, to obviate halation. You may have observed me washing it off before inserting the plate in the developing-dish. Halation, my lord, is a phenomenon—"

Wimsey was not attending.

"But why didn't I notice it before?" he demanded. "That stuff looked to me exactly like clear water."

"So it would, my lord, in the red safe-light. The appearance of whiteness is produced," added Bunter sententiously, "by the reflection of *all* the available light. When all the available light is red, red and white are, naturally, indistinguishable. Similarly, in a green light—"

"Good God!" said Wimsey. "Wait a moment, Bunter, I must think this out . . . Here! Damn those plates—let them be. I want you upstairs."

He led the way at a canter to the ballroom, dark now, with the windows in the south corridor already curtained and only the dimness of the December evening filtering through the high windows of the clerestory above the arcading. He first turned on the three great chandeliers in the ballroom itself. Owing to the heavy oak paneling that rose to the roof at both ends and all four angles of the room, these threw no light at all upon the staircase at the lower end of the north corridor. Next, he turned on the light in the four-sided hanging lantern, which hung in the north corridor above and between the two settees. A vivid shaft of green light immediately flooded the lower half of the corridor and the staircase; the upper half was bathed in strong amber, while the remaining sides of the lantern showed red towards the ballroom and blue towards the corridor wall.

Wimsey shook his head.

"Not much room for error there. Unless—I know! Run, Bunter, and ask Miss Carstairs and Mr. Playfair to come here a moment."

While Bunter was gone, Wimsey borrowed a step-ladder from the kitchen and carefully examined the fixing of the lantern. It was a temporary affair, the lantern being supported by a hook screwed into a beam and lit by means of a flex run from the socket of a permanent fixture at a little distance.

"Now, you two," said Wimsey, when the two guests arrived, "I want to make a little experiment. Will you sit down on this settee, Playfair, as you did last night. And you, Miss Carstairs— I picked you out to help because you're wearing a white dress. Will you go up the stairs at the end of the corridor as Miss Grayle did last night. I want to know whether it looks the same to Playfair as it did then—bar all the other people, of course."

He watched them as they carried out this maneuver. Playfair looked puzzled.

"It doesn't seem quite the same, somehow. I don't know what the difference is, but there is a difference."

Joan, returning, agreed with him.

"I was sitting on that other settee part of the

309

time," she said, "and it looks different to me. I think it's darker."

"Lighter," said Jim.

"Good!" said Wimsey. "That's what I wanted you to say. Now, Bunter, swing that lantern through a quarter-turn to the left."

The moment this was done, Joan gave a little cry.

"That's it! That's it! The blue light! I remember thinking how frosty-faced those poor waits looked as they came in."

"And you, Playfair?"

"That's right," said Jim, satisfied. "The light was red last night. *I* remember thinking how warm and cosy it looked."

Wimsey laughed.

"We're on to it, Bunter. What's the chessboard rule? *The Queen stands on a square of her own color.* Find the maid who looked after the dressing-room, and ask her whether Mrs. Bellingham was there last night between the fox-trot and Sir Roger."

In five minutes Bunter was back with his report.

"The maid says, my lord, that Mrs. Bellingham did not come into the dressing-room at that time. But she saw her come out of the picture-gallery and run downstairs towards the tapestry room just as the band struck up Sir Roger."

"And that," said Wimsey, "was at 1:29."

"Mrs. Bellingham?" said Jim. "But you said you saw her yourself in the ballroom before 1:30. She couldn't have had time to commit the murder."

"No, she couldn't," said Wimsey. "But Charmian Grayle was dead long before that. It was the Red Queen, not the White, you saw upon the staircase. Find out why Mrs. Bellingham lied about her movements, and then we shall know the truth."

"A very sad affair, my lord," said Superintendent Johnson, some hours later. "Mr. Bellingham came across with it like a gentleman as soon as we told him we had evidence against his wife. It appears that Miss Grayle knew certain facts about him which would have been very damaging to his political career. She'd been getting money out of him for years. Earlier in the evening she surprised him by making fresh demands. During the last waltz they had together, they went into the tapestry room and a quarrel took place. He lost his temper and laid hands on her. He says he never meant to hurt her seriously, but she started to scream and he took hold of her throat to silence her and— sort of accidentally—throttled her. When he found what he'd done, he left her there and came away, feeling, as he says, all of a daze. He had the next dance with his wife. He told her what had happened, and then discovered that he'd left the little scepter affair he was carrying in the room with the body. Mrs. Bellingham—she's a brave woman—undertook to fetch it back. She slipped through the dark passage under the Musicians' Gallery—which was empty—and up the stair to the picture-gallery. She did not hear Mr. Playfair speak to her. She ran through the gallery and down the other stair, secured the scepter, and hid it under her own dress. Later, she heard from Mr.

311

Playfair about what he saw, and realized that in the red light he had mistaken her for the White Queen. In the early hours of this morning, she slipped downstairs and managed to get the lantern shifted round. Of course, she's an accessory after the fact, but she's the kind of wife a man would like to have. I hope they let her off light."

"Amen!" said Lord Peter Wimsey.

Dame Ngaio Marsh
(1899–1983)
DEATH ON THE AIR

Edith Ngaio Marsh wrote many novels, but only a handful of short stories. "Death on the Air" is the sole English Country House example, which explains its popularity among anthologists.

Marsh's other great interest was the theater and amateur productions. She took several months each year away from her writing to direct theater groups and become something of an authority on Shakespeare. Not surprisingly, many of her finest works are set in the theater, as is another of her short stories, "I Can Find My Way Out." After her success she divided time between her native New Zealand and England.

On the 25th of December at 7:30 A.M. Mr. Septimus Tonks was found dead beside his wireless set.

It was Emily Parks, an under-housemaid, who discovered him. She butted open the door and entered, carrying mop, duster, and carpet-sweeper. At that precise moment she was greatly startled by a voice that spoke out of the darkness.

"Good morning, everybody," said the voice in

superbly inflected syllables, "and a Merry Christmas!"

Emily yelped, but not loudly, as she immediately realized what had happened. Mr. Tonks had omitted to turn off his wireless before going to bed. She drew back the curtains, revealing a kind of pale murk which was a London Christmas dawn, switched on the light, and saw Septimus.

He was seated in front of the radio. It was a small but expensive set, specially built for him. Septimus sat in an armchair, his back to Emily, his body tilted towards the radio.

His hands, the fingers curiously bunched, were on the ledge of the cabinet under the tuning and volume knobs. His chest rested against the shelf below and his head leaned on the front panel.

He looked rather as though he was listening intently to the interior secrets of the wireless. His head was bent so that Emily could see his bald top with its trail of oiled hairs. He did not move.

"Beg pardon, sir," gasped Emily. She was again greatly startled. Mr. Tonks's enthusiasm for radio had never before induced him to tune in at seven-thirty in the morning.

"Special Christmas service," the cultured voice was saying. Mr. Tonks sat very still. Emily, in common with the other servants, was terrified of her master. She did not know whether to go or to stay. She gazed wildly at Septimus and realized that he wore a dinner-jacket. The room was now filled with the clamor of pealing bells.

Emily opened her mouth as wide as it would go and screamed and screamed and screamed. . . .

Chase, the butler, was the first to arrive. He

314

was a pale, flabby man but authoritative. He said: "What's the meaning of this outrage?" and then saw Septimus. He went to the armchair, bent down, and looked into his master's face.

He did not lose his head, but said in a loud voice: "My Gawd!" And then to Emily: "Shut your face." By this vulgarism he betrayed his agitation. He seized Emily by the shoulders and thrust her towards the door, where they were met by Mr. Hislop, the secretary, in his dressing-gown. Mr. Hislop said: "Good heavens, Chase, what is the meaning—" and then his voice too was drowned in the clamor of bells and renewed screams.

Chase put his fat white hand over Emily's mouth.

"In the study if you please, sir. An accident. Go to your room, will you, and stop that noise or I'll give you something to make you." This to Emily, who bolted down the hall, where she was received by the rest of the staff who had congregated there.

Chase returned to the study with Mr. Hislop and locked the door. They both looked down at the body of Septimus Tonks. The secretary was the first to speak.

"But—but—he's dead," said little Mr. Hislop.

"I suppose there can't be any doubt," whispered Chase.

"Look at the face. Any doubt! My God!"

Mr. Hislop put out a delicate hand towards the bent head and then drew it back. Chase, less fastidious, touched one of the hard wrists, gripped, and then lifted it. The body at once tipped backwards as if it was made of wood. One of the hands knocked against the butler's face. He sprang back with an oath.

There lay Septimus, his knees and his hands in the air, his terrible face turned up to the light. Chase pointed to the right hand. Two fingers and the thumb were slightly blackened.

Ding, dong, dang, ding.

"For God's sake stop those bells," cried Mr. Hislop. Chase turned off the wall switch. Into the sudden silence came the sound of the door-handle being rattled and Guy Tonks's voice on the other side.

"Hislop! Mr. Hislop! Chase! What's the matter?"

"Just a moment, Mr. Guy." Chase looked at the secretary. "You go, sir."

So it was left to Mr. Hislop to break the news to the family. They listened to his stammering revelation in stupefied silence. It was not until Guy, the eldest of the three children, stood in the study that any practical suggestion was made.

"What has killed him?" asked Guy.

"It's extraordinary," burbled Hislop. "Extraordinary. He looks as if he'd been—

"Galvanized," said Guy.

"We ought to send for a doctor," suggested Hislop timidly.

"Of course. Will you, Mr. Hislop? Dr. Meadows."

Hislop went to the telephone and Guy returned to his family. Dr. Meadows lived on the other side of the square and arrived in five minutes. He examined the body without moving it. He questioned Chase and Hislop. Chase was very voluble about the burns on the hand. He uttered the word "electrocution" over and over again.

"I had a cousin, sir, that was struck by lightning. As soon as I saw the hand—"

"Yes, yes," said Dr. Meadows. "So you said. I can see the burns for myself."

"Electrocution," repeated Chase. "There'll have to be an inquest."

Dr. Meadows snapped at him, summoned Emily, and then saw the rest of the family—Guy, Arthur, Phillipa, and their mother. They were clustered round a cold grate in the drawing-room. Phillipa was on her knees, trying to light the fire.

"What was it?" asked Arthur as soon as the doctor came in.

"Looks like electric shock. Guy, I'll have a word with you if you please. Phillipa, look after your mother, there's a good child. Coffee with a dash of brandy. Where are those damn maids? Come on, Guy."

Alone with Guy, he said they'd have to send for the police.

"The police!" Guy's dark face turned very pale. "Why? What's it got to do with them?"

"Nothing, as like as not, but they'll have to be notified. I can't give a certificate as things are. If it's electrocution, how did it happen?"

"But the police!" said Guy. "That's simply ghastly. Dr. Meadows, for God's sake couldn't you—?"

"No," said Dr. Meadows, "I couldn't. Sorry, Guy, but there it is."

"But can't we wait a moment? Look at him again. You haven't examined him properly."

"I don't want to move him, that's why. Pull yourself together, boy. Look here. I've got a pal in the C.I.D.—Alleyn. He's a gentleman and all that. He'll curse me like a fury, but he'll come if he's in London, and he'll make things easier for you. Go back to your mother. I'll ring Alleyn up."

That was how it came about that Chief Detective-Inspector Roderick Alleyn spent his Christmas Day in harness. As a matter of fact he was on duty, and as he pointed out to Dr. Meadows, would have had to turn out and visit his miserable Tonkses in any case. When he did arrive it was with his usual air of remote courtesy. He was accompanied by a tall, thick-set officer—Inspector Fox—and by the divisional police-surgeon. Dr. Meadows took them into the study. Alleyn, in his turn, looked at the horror that had been Septimus.

"Was he like this when he was found?"

"No. I understand he was leaning forward with his hands on the ledge of the cabinet. He must have slumped forward and been propped up by the chair arms and the cabinet."

"Who moved him?"

"Chase, the butler. He said he only meant to raise the arm. *Rigor* is well established."

Alleyn put his hand behind the rigid neck and pushed. The body fell forward into its original position.

"There you are, Curtis," said Alleyn to the divisional surgeon. He turned to Fox. "Get the camera man, will you, Fox?"

The photographer took four shots and departed.

Alleyn marked the position of the hands and feet with chalk, made a careful plan of the room and turned to the doctors.

"Is it electrocution, do you think?"

"Looks like it," said Curtis. "Have to be a p.m. of course."

"Of course. Still, look at the hands. Burns. Thumb and two fingers bunched together and exactly the distance between the two knobs apart. He'd been tuning his hurdy-gurdy."

"By gum," said Inspector Fox, speaking for the first time.

"D'you mean he got a lethal shock from his radio?" asked Dr. Meadows.

"I don't know. I merely conclude he had his hands on the knobs when he died."

"It was still going when the house-maid found him. Chase turned it off and got no shock."

"Yours, partner," said Alleyn, turning to Fox. Fox stooped down to the wall switch.

"Careful," said Alleyn.

"I've got rubber soles," said Fox, and switched it on. The radio hummed, gathered volume, and found itself.

"No-oel, No-o-el," it roared. Fox cut it off and pulled out the wall plug.

"I'd like to have a look inside this set," he said.

"So you shall, old boy, so you shall," rejoined Alleyn. "Before you begin, I think we'd better move the body. Will you see to that, Meadows? Fox, get Bailey, will you? He's out in the car."

Curtis, Hislop, and Meadows carried Septimus Tonks into a spare downstairs room. It was a difficult and horrible business with that contorted

319

body. Dr. Meadows came back alone, mopping his brow, to find Detective-Sergeant Bailey, a fingerprint expert, at work on the wireless cabinet.

"What's all this?" asked Dr. Meadows. "Do you want to find out if he'd been fooling round with the innards?"

"He," said Alleyn, "or—somebody else."

"Umph!" Dr. Meadows looked at the Inspector. "You agree with me, it seems. Do you suspect—?"

"Suspect? I'm the least suspicious man alive. I'm merely being tidy. Well, Bailey?"

"I've got a good one off the chair arm. That'll be the deceased's, won't it, sir?"

"No doubt. We'll check up later. What about the wireless?"

Fox, wearing a glove, pulled off the knob of the volume control.

"Seems to be O.K." said Bailey. "It's a sweet bit of work. Not too bad at all, sir." He turned his torch into the back of the radio, undid a couple of screws underneath the set, lifted out the works.

"What's the little hole for?" asked Alleyn.

"What's that, sir?" said Fox.

"There's a hole bored through the panel above the knob. About an eighth of an inch in diameter. The rim of the knob hides it. One might easily miss it. Move your torch, Bailey. Yes. There, do you see?"

Fox bent down and uttered a bass growl. A fine needle of light came through the front of the radio.

"That's peculiar, sir," said Bailey from the other side. "I don't get the idea at all."

Alleyn pulled out the tuning knob.

320

"There's another one there," he murmured. "Yes. Nice clean little holes. Newly bored. Unusual, I take it?"

"Unusual's the word, sir," said Fox.

"Run away, Meadows," said Alleyn.

"Why the devil?" asked Dr. Meadows indignantly. "What are you driving at? Why shouldn't I be here?"

"You ought to be with the sorrowing relatives. Where's your corpseside manner?"

"I've settled them. What are you up to?"

"Who's being suspicious now?" asked Alleyn mildly. "You may stay for a moment. Tell me about the Tonkses. Who are they? What are they? What sort of a man was Septimus?"

"If you must know, he was a damned unpleasant sort of a man."

"Tell me about him."

Dr. Meadows sat down and lit a cigarette.

"He was a self-made bloke," he said, "as hard as nails and—well, coarse rather than vulgar."

"Like Dr. Johnson perhaps?"

"Not in the least. Don't interrupt. I've known him for twenty-five years. His wife was a neighbor of ours in Dorset. Isabel Foreston. I brought the children into this vale of tears and, by jove, in many ways it's been one for them. It's an extraordinary household. For the last ten years Isabel's condition has been the sort that sends these psycho-jokers dizzy with rapture. I'm only an out-of-date G.P., and I'd just say she is in an advanced stage of hysterical neurosis. Frightened into fits of her husband."

"I can't understand these holes," grumbled Fox to Bailey.

"Go on, Meadows," said Alleyn.

"I tackled Sep about her eighteen months ago. Told him the trouble was in her mind. He eyed me with a sort of grin on his face and said: 'I'm surprised to learn that my wife has enough mentality to—' But look here, Alleyn, I can't talk about my patients like this. What the devil am I thinking about?"

"You know perfectly well it'll go no further unless—"

"Unless what?"

"Unless it has to. Do go on."

But Dr. Meadows hurriedly withdrew behind his professional rectitude. All he would say was that Mr. Tonks had suffered from high blood pressure and a weak heart, that Guy was in his father's city office, that Arthur had wanted to study art and had been told to read for law, and that Phillipa wanted to go on the stage and had been told to do nothing of the sort.

"Bullied his children," commented Alleyn.

"Find out for yourself. I'm off." Dr. Meadows got as far as the door and came back.

"Look here," he said, "I'll tell you one thing. There was a row here last night. I'd asked Hislop, who's a sensible little beggar, to let me know if anything happened to upset Mrs. Sep. Upset her badly, you know. To be indiscreet again, I said he'd better let me know if Sep cut up rough because Isabel and the young had had about as much of that as they could stand. He was drinking pretty heavily. Hislop rang me up at ten-twenty last night

322

to say there'd been a hell of a row; Sep bullying Phips—Phillipa, you know; always call her Phips—in her room. He said Isabel—Mrs. Sep —had gone to bed. I'd had a big day and I didn't want to turn out. I told him to ring again in half an hour if things hadn't quieted down. I told him to keep out of Sep's way and stay in his own room, which is next to Phips's and see if she was all right when Sep cleared out. Hislop was involved. I won't tell you how. The servants were all out. I said that if I didn't hear from him in half an hour I'd ring again and if there was no answer I'd know they were all in bed and quiet. I did ring, got no answer, and went to bed myself. That's all. I'm off. Curtis knows where to find me. You'll want me for the inquest, I suppose. Good-bye."

When he had gone Alleyn embarked on a systematic prowl round the room. Fox and Bailey were still deeply engrossed with the wireless.

"I don't see how the gentleman could have got a bump-off from the instrument," grumbled Fox. "These control knobs are quite in order. Everything's as it should be. Look here, sir."

He turned on the wall switch and tuned in. There was a prolonged humming.

". . . concludes the program of Christmas carols," said the radio.

"A very nice tone," said Fox approvingly.

"Here's something, sir," announced Bailey suddenly.

"Found the sawdust, have you?" said Alleyn.

"Got it in one," said the startled Bailey.

Alleyn peered into the instrument, using the

323

torch. He scooped up two tiny traces of sawdust from under the holes.

" 'Vantage number one," said Alleyn. He bent down to the wall plug. "Hullo! A two-way adapter. Serves the radio and the radiator. Thought they were illegal. This is a rum business. Let's have another look at those knobs."

He had his look. They were the usual wireless fitments, bakelite knobs fitting snugly to the steel shafts that projected from the front panel.

"As you say," he murmured, "quite in order. Wait a bit." He produced a pocket lens and squinted at one of the shafts. "Ye-es. Do they ever wrap blotting-paper round these objects, Fox?"

"Blotting-paper!" ejaculated Fox. "They do not."

Alleyn scraped at both the shafts with his pen-knife, holding an envelope underneath. He rose, groaning, and crossed to the desk. "A corner torn off the bottom bit of blotch," he said presently. "No prints on the wireless, I think you said, Bailey?"

"That's right," agreed Bailey morosely.

"There'll be none, or too many, on the blotter, but try, Bailey, try," said Alleyn. He wandered about the room, his eyes on the floor; got as far as the window and stopped.

"Fox!" he said. "A clue. A very palpable clue."

"What is it?" asked Fox.

"The odd wisp of blotting-paper, no less." Alleyn's gaze traveled up the side of the window curtain. "Can I believe my eyes?"

He got a chair, stood on the seat, and with his

gloved hand pulled the buttons from the ends of the curtainrod.

"Look at this." He turned to the radio, detached the control knobs, and laid them beside the ones he had removed from the curtainrod.

Ten minutes later Inspector Fox knocked on the drawing-room door and was admitted by Guy Tonks. Phillipa had got the fire going and the family was gathered round it. They looked as though they had not moved or spoken to one another for a long time.

It was Phillipa who spoke first to Fox. "Do you want one of us?"

"If you please, miss," said Fox. "Inspector Alleyn would like to see Mr. Guy Tonks for a moment, if convenient."

"I'll come," said Guy, and led the way to the study. At the door he paused. "Is he—my father—still—?"

"No, no, sir," said Fox comfortably. "It's all ship-shape in there again."

With a lift of his chin Guy opened the door and went in, followed by Fox. Alleyn was alone, seated at the desk. He rose to his feet.

"You want to speak to me?" asked Guy.

"Yes, if I may. This has all been a great shock to you, of course. Won't you sit down?"

Guy sat in the chair farthest away from the radio.

"What killed my father? Was it a stroke?"

"The doctors are not quite certain. There will have to be a *post-mortem.*"

"Good God! And an inquest?"

325

"I'm afraid so."

"Horrible!" said Guy violently. "What do you think was the matter? Why the devil do these quacks have to be so mysterious? What killed him?"

"They think an electric shock."

"How did it happen?"

"We don't know. It looks as if he got it from the wireless."

"Surely that's impossible. I thought they were fool-proof."

"I believe they are, if left to themselves."

For a second undoubtedly Guy was startled. Then a look of relief came into his eyes. He seemed to relax all over.

"Of course," he said, "he was always monkeying about with it. What had he done?"

"Nothing."

"But you said—if it killed him he must have done something to it."

"If anyone interfered with the set it was put right afterwards."

Guy's lips parted but he did not speak. He had gone very white.

"So you see," said Alleyn, "your father could not have done anything."

"Then it was not the radio that killed him."

"That we hope will be determined by the *post-mortem*."

"I don't know anything about the wireless," said Guy suddenly. "I don't understand. This doesn't seem to make sense. Nobody ever touched the thing except my father. He was most particular about it. Nobody went near the wireless."

"I see. He was an enthusiast?"

"Yes, it was his only enthusiasm except—except his business."

"One of my men is a bit of an expert," Alleyn said. "He says this is a remarkably good set. You are not an expert you say. Is there anyone in the house who is?"

"My young brother was interested at one time. He's given it up. My father wouldn't allow another radio in the house."

"Perhaps he may be able to suggest something."

"But if the thing's all right now—"

"We've got to explore every possibility."

"You speak as if—as—if—"

"I speak as I am bound to speak before there has been an inquest," said Alleyn. "Had anyone a grudge against your father, Mr. Tonks?"

Up went Guy's chin again. He looked Alleyn squarely in the eyes.

"Almost everyone who knew him," said Guy.

"Is that an exaggeration?"

"No. You think he was murdered, don't you?"

Alleyn suddenly pointed to the desk beside him.

"Have you ever seen those before?" he asked abruptly. Guy stared at two black knobs that lay side by side on an ashtray.

"Those?" he said. "No. What are they?"

"I believe they are the agents of your father's death."

The study door opened and Arthur Tonks came in.

"Guy," he said, "what's happening? We can't stay cooped up together all day. I can't stand it. For God's sake what happened to him?"

"They think those things killed him," said Guy.

"Those?" For a split second Arthur's glance slewed to the curtainrods. Then, with a characteristic flicker of his eyelids, he looked away again.

"What do you mean?" he asked Alleyn.

"Will you try one of those knobs on the shaft of the volume control?"

"But," said Arthur, "they're metal."

"It's disconnected," said Alleyn.

Arthur picked one of the knobs from the tray, turned to the radio, and fitted the knob over one of the exposed shafts.

"It's too loose," he said quickly, "it would fall off."

"Not if it was packed—with blotting-paper, for instance."

"Where did you find these things?" demanded Arthur.

"I think you recognized them, didn't you? I saw you glance at the curtainrod."

"Of course I recognized them. I did a portrait of Phillipa against those curtains when—he—was away last year. I've painted the damn things."

"Look here," interrupted Guy, "exactly what are you driving at, Mr. Alleyn? If you mean to suggest that my brother—"

"I!" cried Arthur. "What's it got to do with me? Why should you suppose—"

"I found traces of blotting-paper on the shafts and inside the metal knobs," said Alleyn. "It suggested a substitution of the metal knobs for the bakelite ones. It is remarkable, don't you think, that they should so closely resemble one another? If you examine them, of course, you find they are not identical. Still, the difference is scarcely perceptible."

Arthur did not answer this. He was still looking at the wireless.

"I've always wanted to have a look at this set," he said surprisingly.

"You are free to do so now," said Alleyn politely. "We have finished with it for the time being."

"Look here," said Arthur suddenly, "suppose metal knobs were substituted for bakelite ones, it couldn't kill him. He wouldn't get a shock at all. Both the controls are grounded."

"Have you noticed those very small holes drilled through the panel?" asked Alleyn. "Should they be there, do you think?"

Arthur peered at the little steel shafts. "By God, he's right, Guy," he said. "That's how it was done."

"Inspector Fox," said Alleyn, "tells me those holes could be used for conducting wires and that a lead could be taken from the—the transformer, is it?—to one of the knobs."

"And the other connected to earth," said Fox. "It's a job for an expert. He could get three hundred volts or so that way."

"That's not good enough," said Arthur quickly; "there wouldn't be enough current to do any damage—only a few hundredths of an amp."

"I'm not an expert," said Alleyn, "but I'm sure you're right. Why were the holes drilled then? Do you imagine someone wanted to play a practical joke on your father?"

"A practical joke? On *him*?" Arthur gave an

329

unpleasant screech of laughter. "Do you hear that, Guy?"

"Shut up," said Guy. "After all, he is dead."

"It seems almost too good to be true, doesn't it?"

"Don't be a bloody fool, Arthur. Pull yourself together. Can't you see what this means? They think he's been murdered."

"Murdered! They're wrong. None of us had the nerve for that, Mr. Inspector. Look at me. My hands are so shaky they told me I'd never be able to paint. That dates from when I was a kid and he shut me up in the cellars for a night. Look at me. Look at Guy. He's not so vulnerable, but he caved in like the rest of us. We were conditioned to surrender. Do you know—"

"Wait a moment," said Alleyn quietly. "Your brother is quite right, you know. You'd better think before you speak. This may be a case of homicide."

"Thank you, sir," said Guy quickly. "That's extraordinarily decent of you. Arthur's a bit above himself. It's a shock."

"The relief, you mean," said Arthur. "Don't be such an ass. I didn't kill him and they'll find it out soon enough. Nobody killed him. There must be some explanation."

"I suggest that you listen to me," said Alleyn. "I'm going to put several questions to both of you. You need not answer them, but it will be more sensible to do so. I understand no one but your father touched this radio. Did any of you ever come into this room while it was in use?"

330

"Not unless he wanted to vary the program with a little bullying," said Arthur.

Alleyn turned to Guy, who was glaring at his brother.

"I want to know exactly what happened in this house last night. As far as the doctors can tell us, your father died not less than three and not more than eight hours before he was found. We must try to fix the time as accurately as possible."

"I saw him at about a quarter to nine," began Guy slowly. "I was going out to a supper-party at the Savoy and had come downstairs. He was crossing the hall from the drawing-room to his room."

"Did you see him after a quarter to nine, Mr. Arthur?"

"No. I heard him, though. He was working in here with Hislop. Hislop had asked to go away for Christmas. Quite enough. My father discovered some urgent correspondence. Really, Guy, you know, he was pathological. I'm sure Dr. Meadows thinks so."

"When did you hear him?" asked Alleyn.

"Some time after Guy had gone. I was working on a drawing in my room upstairs. It's above his. I heard him bawling at little Hislop. It must have been before ten o'clock, because I went out to a studio party at ten. I heard him bawling as I crossed the hall."

"And when," said Alleyn, "did you both return?"

"I came home at about twenty past twelve," said Guy immediately. "I can fix the time because we had gone on to Chez Carlo, and they had a midnight stunt there. We left immediately after-

331

wards. I came home in a taxi. The radio was on full blast."

"You heard no voices?"

"None. Just the wireless."

"And you, Mr. Arthur?"

"Lord knows when I got in. After one. The house was in darkness. Not a sound."

"You had your own key?"

"Yes," said Guy. "Each of us has one. They're always left on a hook in the lobby. When I came in I noticed Arthur's was gone."

"What about the others? How did you know it was his?"

"Mother hasn't got one and Phips lost hers weeks ago. Anyway, I knew they were staying in and that it must be Arthur who was out."

"Thank you," said Arthur ironically.

"You didn't look in the study when you came in," Alleyn asked him.

"Good Lord, no," said Arthur as if the suggestion was fantastic. "I say," he said suddenly, "I suppose he was sitting here—dead. That's a queer thought." He laughed nervously. "Just sitting here, behind the door in the dark."

"How do you know it was in the dark?"

"What d'you mean? Of course it was. There was no light under the door."

"I see. Now do you two mind joining your mother again? Perhaps your sister will be kind enough to come in here for a moment. Fox, ask her, will you?"

Fox returned to the drawing-room with Guy and Arthur and remained there, blandly unconscious of any embarrassment his presence might cause the Tonkses. Bailey was already there, ostensibly examining the electric points.

Phillipa went to the study at once. Her first remark was characteristic. "Can I be of any help?" asked Phillipa.

"It's extremely nice of you to put it like that," said Alleyn. "I don't want to worry you for long. I'm sure this discovery has been a shock to you."

"Probably," said Phillipa. Alleyn glanced quickly at her. "I mean," she explained, "that I suppose I must be shocked but I can't feel anything much. I just want to get it all over as soon as possible. And then think. Please tell me what has happened."

Alleyn told her they believed her father had been electrocuted and that the circumstances were unusual and puzzling. He said nothing to suggest that the police suspected murder.

"I don't think I'll be much help," said Phillipa, "but go ahead."

"I want to try to discover who was the last person to see your father or speak to him."

"I should think very likely I was," said Phillipa composedly. "I had a row with him before I went to bed."

"What about?"

"I don't see that it matters."

Alleyn considered this. When he spoke again it was with deliberation.

"Look here," he said, "I think there is very little doubt that your father was killed by an electric shock from his wireless set. As far as I know the circumstances are unique. Radios are normally incapable of giving a lethal shock to anyone. We

333

have examined the cabinet and are inclined to think that its internal arrangements were disturbed last night. Very radically disturbed. Your father may have experimented with it. If anything happened to interrupt or upset him, it is possible that in the excitement of the moment he made some dangerous readjustment."

"You don't believe that, do you?" asked Phillipa calmly.

"Since you ask me," said Alleyn, "no."

"I see," said Phillipa; "you think he was murdered, but you're not sure." She had gone very white, but she spoke crisply. "Naturally you want to find out about my row."

"About everything that happened last evening," amended Alleyn.

"What happened was this," said Phillipa; "I came into the hall some time after ten. I'd heard Arthur go out and had looked at the clock at five past. I ran into my father's secretary, Richard Hislop. He turned aside, but not before I saw . . . not quickly enough. I blurted out: 'You're crying.' We looked at each other. I asked him why he stood it. None of the other secretaries could. He said he had to. He's a widower with two children. There have been doctor's bills and things. I needn't tell you about his. . . about his damnable servitude to my father nor about the refinements of cruelty he'd had to put up with. I think my father was mad, really mad, I mean. Richard gabbled it all out to me higgledy-piggledy in a sort of horrified whisper. He's been here two years, but I'd never realized until that moment that we . . . that . . ." A faint flush came into her cheeks. "He's such a funny little man. Not at all the sort I've always thought . . . not good-looking or exciting or anything."

She stopped, looking bewildered.

"Yes?" said Alleyn.

"Well, you see—I suddenly realized I was in love with him. He realized it too. He said: 'Of course, it's quite hopeless, you know. Us, I mean. Laughable, almost.' Then I put my arms round his neck and kissed him. It was very odd, but it seemed quite natural. The point is my father came out of his room into the hall and saw us."

"That was bad luck," said Alleyn.

"Yes, it was. My father really seemed delighted. He almost licked his lips. Richard's efficiency had irritated my father for a long time. It was difficult to find excuses for being beastly to him. Now, of course. . . He ordered Richard to the study and me to my room. He followed me upstairs. Richard tried to come too, but I asked him not to. My father. . . I needn't tell you what he said. He put the worst possible construction on what he'd seen. He was absolutely foul, screaming at me like a madman. He was insane. Perhaps it was D.T.'s. He drank terribly, you know. I dare say it's silly of me to tell you all this."

"No," said Alleyn.

"I can't feel anything at all. Not even relief. The boys are frankly relieved. I can't feel afraid either." She stared meditatively at Alleyn. "Innocent people needn't feel afraid, need they?"

"It's an axiom of police investigation," said Alleyn and wondered if indeed she was innocent.

"It just *can't* be murder," said Phillipa. "We

335

were all too much afraid to kill him. I believe he'd win even if you murdered him. He'd hit back somehow." She put her hands to her eyes. "I'm all muddled."

"I think you are more upset than you realize. I'll be as quick as I can. Your father made this scene in your room. You say he screamed. Did any one hear him?"

"Yes. Mummy did. She came in."

"What happened?"

"I said: 'Go away, darling, it's all right.' I didn't want her to be involved. He nearly killed her with the things he did. Sometimes he'd . . . we never knew what happened between them. It was all secret, like a door shutting quietly as you walk along a passage."

"Did she go away?"

"Not at once. He told her he'd found out that Richard and I were lovers. He said. . . it doesn't matter. I don't want to tell you. She was terrified. He was stabbing at her in some way I couldn't understand. Then, quite suddenly, he told her to go to her own room. She went at once and he followed her. He locked me in. That's the last I saw of him, but I heard him go downstairs later."

"Were you locked in all night?"

"No. Richard Hislop's room is next to mine. He came up and spoke through the wall to me. He wanted to unlock the door, but I said better not in case—he—came back. Then, much later, Guy came home. As he passed my door I tapped on it. The key was in the lock and he turned it."

"Did you tell him what had happened?"

336

"Just that there'd been a row. He only stayed a moment."

"Can you hear the radio from your room?"

She seemed surprised.

"The wireless? Why, yes. Faintly."

"Did you hear it after your father returned to the study?"

"I don't remember."

"Think. While you lay awake all that long time until your brother came home?"

"I'll try. When he came out and found Richard and me, it was not going. They had been working, you see. No, I can't remember hearing it at all unless—wait a moment. Yes. After he had gone back to the study from mother's room I remember there was a loud crash of static. Very loud. Then I think it was quiet for some time. I fancy I heard it again later. Oh, I've remembered something else. After the static my bedside radiator went out. I suppose there was something wrong with the electric supply. That would account for both, wouldn't it? The heater went on again about ten minutes later."

"And did the radio begin again then, do you think?"

"I don't know. I'm very vague about that. It started again sometime before I went to sleep."

"Thank you very much indeed. I won't bother you any longer now."

"All right," said Phillipa calmly, and went away.

Alleyn sent for Chase and questioned him about the rest of the staff and about the discovery of the body. Emily was summoned and dealt with. When

337

she departed, awestruck but complacent, Alleyn turned to the butler.

"Chase," he said, "had your master any peculiar habits?"

"Yes, sir."

"In regard to the wireless?"

"I beg pardon, sir. I thought you meant generally speaking."

"Well, then, generally speaking."

"If I may so, sir, he was a mass of them."

"How long have you been with him?"

"Two months, sir, and due to leave at the end of this week."

"Oh. Why are you leaving?"

Chase produced the classic remark of his kind.

"There are some things," he said, "that flesh and blood will not stand, sir. One of them's being spoke to like Mr. Tonks spoke to his staff."

"Ah. His peculiar habits, in fact?"

"It's my opinion, sir, he was mad. Stark, staring."

"With regard to the radio. Did he tinker with it?"

"I can't say I've ever noticed, sir. I believe he knew quite a lot about wireless."

"When he tuned the thing, had he any particular method? Any characteristic attitude or gesture?"

"I don't think so, sir. I never noticed, and yet I've often come into the room when he was at it. I can seem to see him now, sir."

"Yes, yes," said Alleyn swiftly. "That's what we want. A clear mental picture. How was it now? Like this?"

In a moment he was across the room and seated in Septimus's chair. He swung round to the cabinet and raised his right hand to the tuning control.

"Like this?"

"No, sir," said Chase promptly, "that's not him at all. Both hands it should be."

"Ah." Up went Alleyn's left hand to the volume control. "More like this?"

"Yes, sir," said Chase slowly. "But there's something else and I can't recollect what it was. Something he was always doing. It's in the back of my head. You know, sir. Just on the edge of my memory, as you might say."

"I know."

"It's a kind—something—to do with irritation," said Chase slowly.

"Irritation? His?"

"No. It's no good, sir. I can't get it."

"Perhaps later. Now look here, Chase, what happened to all of you last night? All the servants, I mean."

"We were all out, sir. It being Christmas Eve. The mistress sent for me yesterday morning. She said we could take the evening off as soon as I had taken in Mr. Tonks's grog-tray at nine o'clock. So we went," ended Chase simply.

"When?"

"The rest of the staff got away about nine. I left at ten past, sir, and returned about eleven-twenty. The others were back then, and all in bed. I went straight to bed myself, sir."

"You came in by a back door, I suppose?"

"Yes, sir. We've been talking it over. None of us noticed anything unusual."

"Can you hear the wireless in your part of the house?"

"No, sir."

"Well," said Alleyn, looking up from his notes, "that'll do, thank you."

Before Chase reached the door Fox came in.

"Beg pardon, sir," said Fox, "I just want to take a look at the *Radio Times* on the desk."

He bent over the paper, wetted a gigantic thumb, and turned a page.

"That's it, sir," shouted Chase suddenly. "That's what I tried to think of. That's what he was always doing."

"But what?"

"Licking his fingers, sir. It was a habit," said Chase. "That's what he always did when he sat down to the radio. I heard Mr. Hislop tell the doctor it nearly drove him demented, the way the master couldn't touch a thing without first licking his fingers."

"Quite so," said Alleyn. "In about ten minutes, ask Mr. Hislop if he will be good enough to come in for a moment. That will be all, thank you, Chase."

"Well, sir," remarked Fox when Chase had gone, "if that's the case and what I think's right, it'd certainly make matters worse."

"Good heavens, Fox, what an elaborate remark. What does it mean?"

"If metal knobs were substituted for bakelite ones and fine wires brought through those holes to make contact, then he'd get a bigger bump if he tuned in with *damp* fingers."

"Yes. And he always used both hands. Fox!"

"Sir."

"Approach the Tonkses again. You haven't left them alone, of course?"

"Bailey's in there making out he's interested in the light switches. He's found the main switchboard under the stairs. There's signs of a blown fuse having been fixed recently. In a cupboard underneath there are odd lengths of flex and so on. Same brand as this on the wireless and the heater."

"Ah, yes. Could the cord from the adapter to the radiator be brought into play?"

"By gum," said Fox, "you're right! That's how it was done, Chief. The heavier flex was cut away from the radiator and shoved through. There was a fire, so he wouldn't want the radiator and wouldn't notice."

"It might have been done that way, certainly, but there's little to prove it. Return to the bereaved Tonkses, my Fox, and ask prettily if any of them remember Septimus's peculiarities when tuning his wireless."

Fox met little Mr. Hislop at the door and left him alone with Alleyn. Phillipa had been right, reflected the Inspector, when she said Richard Hislop was not a noticeable man. He was nondescript. Grey eyes, drab hair; rather pale, rather short, rather insignificant; and yet last night there had flashed up between those two the realization of love. Romantic but rum, thought Alleyn.

"Do sit down," he said. "I want you, if you will, to tell me what happened between you and Mr. Tonks last evening."

"What happened?"

341

"Yes. You all dined at eight, I understand. Then you and Mr. Tonks came in here?"

"Yes."

"What did you do?"

"He dictated several letters."

"Anything unusual take place?"

"Oh, no."

"Why did you quarrel?"

"Quarrel!" The quiet voice jumped a tone. "We did not quarrel, Mr. Alleyn."

"Perhaps that was the wrong word. What upset you?"

"Phillipa has told you?"

"Yes. She was wise to do so. What was the matter, Mr. Hislop?"

"Apart from the . . . what she told you . . . Mr. Tonks was a difficult man to please. I often irritated him. I did so last night."

"In what way?"

"In almost every way. He shouted at me. I was startled and nervous, clumsy with papers, and making mistakes. I wasn't well. I blundered and then . . . I . . . I broke down. I have always irritated him. My very mannerisms—"

"Had he no irritating mannerisms, himself?"

"He! My God!"

"What were they?"

"I can't think of anything in particular. It doesn't matter, does it?"

"Anything to do with the wireless, for instance?"

There was a short silence.

"No," said Hislop.

"Was the radio on in here last night, after dinner?"

"For a little while. Not after—after the incident in the hall. At least, I don't think so. I don't remember."

"What did you do after Miss Phillipa and her father had gone upstairs?"

"I followed and listened outside the door for a moment." He had gone very white and had backed away from the desk.

"And then?"

"I heard someone coming. I remembered Dr. Meadows had told me to ring him up if there was one of the scenes. I returned here and rang him up. He told me to go to my room and listen. If things got any worse I was to telephone again. Otherwise I was to stay in my room. It is next to hers."

"And you did this?" He nodded. "Could you hear what Mr. Tonks said to her?"

"A—a good deal of it."

"What did you hear?"

"He insulted her. Mrs. Tonks was there. I was just thinking of ringing Dr. Meadows up again when she and Mr. Tonks came out and went along the passage. I stayed in my room."

"You did not try to speak to Miss Phillipa?"

"We spoke through the wall. She asked me not to ring Dr. Meadows, but to stay in my room. In a little while, perhaps it was as much as twenty minutes—I really don't know—I heard him come back and go downstairs. I again spoke to Phillipa. She implored me not to do anything and said that she herself would speak to Dr. Meadows in the morning. So I waited a little longer and then went to bed."

"And to sleep?"

"My God, no!"

"Did you hear the wireless again?"

"Yes. At least I heard static."

"Are you an expert on wireless?"

"No. I know the ordinary things. Nothing much."

"How did you come to take this job, Mr. Hislop?"

"I answered an advertisement."

"You are sure you don't remember any particular mannerism of Mr. Tonks's in connection with the radio?"

"No."

"And you can tell me no more about your interview in the study that led to the scene in the hall?"

"No."

"Will you please ask Mrs. Tonks if she will be kind enough to speak to me for a moment?"

"Certainly," said Hislop, and went away.

Septimus's wife came in looking like death. Alleyn got her to sit down and asked her about her movements on the preceding evening. She said she was feeling unwell and dined in her room. She went to bed immediately afterwards. She heard Septimus yelling at Phillipa and went to Phillipa's room. Septimus accused Mr. Hislop and her daughter of "terrible things." She got as far as this and then broke down quietly. Alleyn was very gentle with her. After a little while he learned that

Septimus had gone to her room with her and had continued to speak of "terrible things."

"What sort of things?" asked Alleyn.

"He was not responsible," said Isabel. "He did not know what he was saying. I think he had been drinking."

She thought he had remained with her for perhaps a quarter of an hour. Possibly longer. He left her abruptly and she heard him go along the passage, past Phillipa's door, and presumably downstairs. She had stayed awake for a long time. The wireless could not be heard from her room. Alleyn showed her the curtain knobs, but she seemed quite unable to take in their significance. He let her go, summoned Fox, and went over the whole case.

"What's your idea on the show?" he asked when he had finished.

"Well, sir," said Fox, in his stolid way, "on the face of it the young gentlemen have got alibis. We'll have to check them up, of course, and I don't see we can go much further until we have done so."

"For the moment," said Alleyn, "let us suppose Masters Guy and Arthur to be safely established behind cast-iron alibis. What then?"

"Then we've got the young lady, the old lady, the secretary, and the servants."

"Let us parade them. But first let us go over the wireless game. You'll have to watch me here. I gather that the only way in which the radio could be fixed to give Mr. Tonks his quietus is like this: Control knobs removed. Holes bored in front panel with fine drill. Metal knobs substituted and

345

packed with blotting-paper to insulate them from metal shafts and make them stay put. Heavier flex from adapter to radiator cut and the ends of the wires pushed through the drilled holes to make contact with the new knobs. Thus we have a positive and negative pole. Mr. Tonks bridges the gap, gets a mighty wallop as the current passes through him to the earth. The switchboard fuse is blown almost immediately. All this is rigged by murderer while Sep was upstairs bullying wife and daughter. Sep revisited study some time after ten-twenty. Whole thing was made ready between ten, when Arthur went out, and the time Sep returned—say, about ten-forty-five. The murderer reappeared, connected radiator with flex, removed wires, changed back knobs, and left the thing tuned in. Now I take it that the burst of static described by Phillipa and Hislop would be caused by the short-circuit that killed our Septimus?"

"That's right."

"It also affected all the heaters in the house. *Vide* Miss Tonks's radiator."

"Yes. He put all that right again. It would be a simple enough matter for anyone who knew how. He'd just have to fix the fuse on the main switchboard. How long do you say it would take to— what's the horrible word?—to recondition the whole show?"

"M'm," said Fox deeply. "At a guess, sir, fifteen minutes. He'd have to be nippy."

"Yes," agreed Alleyn. "He or she."

"I don't see a female making a success of it," grunted Fox. "Look here, Chief, you know what

346

I'm thinking. Why did Mr. Hislop lie about deceased's habit of licking his thumbs? You say Hislop told you he remembered nothing and Chase says he overheard him saying the trick nearly drove him dippy."

"Exactly," said Alleyn. He was silent for so long that Fox felt moved to utter a discreet cough.

"Eh?" said Alleyn. "Yes, Fox, yes. It'll have to be done." He consulted the telephone directory and dialed a number.

"May I speak to Dr. Meadows? Oh, it's you, is it? Do you remember Mr. Hislop telling you that Septimus Tonks's trick of wetting his fingers nearly drove Hislop demented? Are you there? You don't? Sure? All right. All right. Hislop rang up at ten-twenty, you said? And you telephoned him? At eleven. Sure of the times? I see. I'd be glad if you'd come round. Can you? Well, do if you can."

He hung up the receiver.

"Get Chase again, will you, Fox?"

Chase, recalled, was most insistent that Mr. Hislop had spoken about it to Dr. Meadows.

"It was when Mr. Hislop had flu, sir. I went up with the doctor. Mr. Hislop had a high temperature and was talking very excited. He kept on and on, saying the master had guessed his ways had driven him crazy and that the master kept on purposely to aggravate. He said if it went on much longer he'd. . . he didn't know what he was talking about, sir, really."

"What did he say he'd do?"

"Well, sir, he said he'd—he'd do something desperate to the master. But it was only his ram-

347

bling, sir. I daresay he wouldn't remember anything about it."

"No," said Alleyn, "I daresay he wouldn't." When Chase had gone he said to Fox: "Go and find out about those boys and their alibis. See if they can put you on to a quick means of checking up. Get Master Guy to corroborate Miss Phillipa's statement that she was locked in her room."

Fox had been gone for some time and Alleyn was still busy with his notes when the study door burst open and in came Dr. Meadows.

"Look here, my giddy sleuth-hound," he shouted, "what's all this about Hislop? Who says he disliked Sep's abominable habits?"

"Chase does. And don't bawl at me like that. I'm worried."

"So am I, blast you. What are you driving at? You can't imagine that . . . that poor little broken-down hack is capable of electrocuting anybody, let alone Sep?"

"I have no imagination," said Alleyn wearily.

"I wish to God I hadn't called you in. If the wireless killed Sep, it was because he'd monkeyed with it."

"And put it right after it had killed him?"

Dr. Meadows stared at Alleyn in silence.

"Now," said Alleyn, "you've got to give me a straight answer, Meadows. Did Hislop, while he was semi-delirious, say that this habit of Tonks's made him feel like murdering him?"

"I'd forgotten Chase was there," said Dr. Meadows.

"Yes, you'd forgotton that."

"But even if he did talk wildly, Alleyn, what

348

of it? Damn it, you can't arrest a man on the strength of a remark made in delirium."

"I don't propose to do so. Another motive has come to light."

"You mean—Phips—last night?"

"Did he tell you about that?"

"She whispered something to me this morning. I'm very fond of Phips. My God, are you sure of your grounds?"

"Yes," said Alleyn. "I'm sorry. I think you'd better go, Meadows."

"Are you going to arrest him?"

"I have to do my job."

There was a long silence.

"Yes," said Dr. Meadows at last. "You have to do your job. Good-bye, Alleyn."

Fox returned to say that Guy and Arthur had never left their parties. He had got hold of two of their friends. Guy and Mrs. Tonks confirmed the story of the locked door.

"It's a process of elimination," said Fox. "It must be the secretary. He fixed the radio while deceased was upstairs. He must have dodged back to whisper through the door to Miss Tonks. I suppose he waited somewhere down here until he heard deceased blow himself to blazes and then put everything straight again, leaving the radio turned on."

Alleyn was silent.

"What do we do now, sir?" asked Fox.

"I want to see the hook inside the front-door where they hang their keys."

Fox, looking dazed, followed his superior to the little entrance hall.

"Yes, there they are," said Alleyn. He pointed to a hook with two latch-keys hanging from it. "You could scarcely miss them. Come on, Fox."

Back in the study they found Hislop with Bailey in attendance.

Hislop looked from one Yard man to another. "I want to know if it's murder."

"We think so," said Alleyn.

"I want you to realize that Phillipa—Miss Tonks—was locked in her room all last night."

"Until her brother came home and unlocked the door," said Alleyn.

"That was too late. He was dead by then."

"How do you know when he died?"

"It must have been when there was that crash of static."

"Mr. Hislop," said Alleyn, "why would you not tell me how much that trick of licking his fingers exasperated you?"

"But—how do you know! I never told anyone."

"You told Dr. Meadows when you were ill."

"I don't remember." He stopped short. His lips trembled. Then, suddenly he began to speak.

"Very well. It's true. For two years he's tortured me. You see, he knew something about me. Two years ago when my wife was dying, I took money from the cash-box in that desk. I paid it back and thought he hadn't noticed. He knew all the time. From then on he had me where he wanted me. He used to sit there like a spider. I'd hand him a paper. He'd wet his thumbs with a clicking noise and a sort of complacent grimace. Click, click. Then he'd thumb the papers. He knew it drove me crazy. He'd look at me and

350

then. . . click, click. And then he'd say something about the cash. He'd never quite accused me, just hinted. And I was impotent. You think I'm insane. I'm not. I could have murdered him. Often and often I've thought how I'd do it. Now you think I've done it. I haven't. There's the joke of it. I hadn't the pluck. And last night when Phillipa showed me she cared, it was like Heaven—unbelievable. For the first time since I've been here I *didn't* feel like killing him. And last night someone else *did!*"

He stood there trembling and vehement. Fox and Bailey, who had watched him with bewildered concern, turned to Alleyn. He was about to speak when Chase came in. "A note for you, sir," he said to Alleyn. "It came by hand."

Alleyn opened it and glanced at the first few words. He looked up.

"You may go, Mr. Hislop. Now I've got what I expected—what I fished for."

When Hislop had gone they read the letter.

Dear Alleyn,

Don't arrest Hislop. I did it. Let him go at once if you've arrested him and don't tell Phips you ever suspected him. I was in love with Isabel before she met Sep. I've tried to get her to divorce him, but she wouldn't because of the kids. Damned nonsense, but there's no time to discuss it now. I've got to be quick. He suspected us. He reduced her to a nervous wreck. I was afraid she'd go under altogether. I thought it all out. Some weeks ago I took Phips's key from the hook inside the front door. I had the tools and

351

the flex and wire all ready. I knew where the main switchboard was and the cupboard. I meant to wait until they all went away at the New Year, but last night when Hislop rang me I made up my mind at once. He said the boys and servants were out and Phips locked in her room. I told him to stay in his room and to ring me up in half an hour if things hadn't quieted down. He didn't ring up. I did. No answer, so I knew Sep wasn't in his study.

I came round, let myself in, and listened. All quiet upstairs but the lamp still on in the study, so I knew he would come down again. He'd said he wanted to get the midnight broadcast from somewhere.

I locked myself in and got to work. When Sep was away last year, Arthur did one of his modern monstrosities of painting in the study. He talked about the knobs making a good pattern. I noticed then that they were very like the ones on the radio and later on I tried one and saw that it would fit if I packed it up a bit. Well, I did the job just as you worked it out, and it only took twelve minutes. Then I went into the drawing-room and waited.

He came down from Isabel's room and evidently went straight to the radio. I hadn't thought it would make such a row, and half expected someone would come down. No one came. I went back, switched off the wireless, mended the fuse in the main switchboard, using my torch. Then I put everything right in the study.

There was no particular hurry. No one would

*come in while he was there and I got the radio
going as soon as possible to suggest he was at it.
I knew I'd be called in when they found him.
My idea was to tell them he had died of a
stroke. I'd been warning Isabel it might happen
at any time. As soon as I saw the burned hand I
knew that cat wouldn't jump. I'd have tried to
get away with it if Chase hadn't gone round
bleating about electrocution and burned fingers.
Hislop saw the hand. I daren't do anything but
report the case to the police, but I thought you'd
never twig the knobs. One up to you.*

*I might have bluffed through if you hadn't
suspected Hislop. Can't let you hang the blighter.
I'm enclosing a note to Isabel, who won't forgive
me, and an official one for you to use. You'll
find me in my bedroom upstairs. I'm using cya-
nide. It's quick.*

*I'm sorry, Alleyn. I think you knew, didn't
you? I've bungled the whole game, but if you
will be a supersleuth . . . Good-bye.*

Henry Meadows

Margery Allingham
(1904–1966)
THE SAME TO US

*Margery Allingham, the last of our quartet of Golden Age Mistresses, came from a family of authors and settled upon a career in writing at the age of seven. Her first mystery appeared in 1924—*The White Cottage Mystery*—and her first book featuring series detective Albert Campion five years later—*The Crime at Black Dudley.

Unlike Christie, Marsh, and Sayers, Allingham grew restless within the conventions of the English Country House Mystery form. During World War II she practically banished Campion from her work and turned from mystery to social history. Gradually Campion returned, at first as a minor character, somewhat changed. He does not appear in this story, which shows Allingham's intelligence and impatience with the style. A more classic account, including Campion, can be found in the collection Murder for Christmas.

It was particularly unfortunate for Mrs. Christopher Molesworth that she should have had burglars on the Sunday night of what was, perhaps, the crowningly triumphant week-end of her career as a hostess.

As a hostess Mrs. Molesworth was a connoisseur. She chose her guests with a nice discrimination, disdaining everything but the most rare. Mere notoriety was no passport to Molesworth Court.

Nor did mere friendship obtain many crumbs from the Molesworth table, though the ability to please and do one's piece might possibly earn one a bed when the lion of the hour promised to be dull, uncomfortable and liable to be bored.

That was how young Petterboy came to be there at the great week-end. He was diplomatic, presentable, near enough a teetotaller to be absolutely trustworthy, even at the end of the evening, and he spoke a little Chinese.

This last accomplishment had done him but little good before, save with very young girls at parties, who relieved their discomfort at having no conversation by persuading him to tell them how to ask for their baggage to be taken ashore at Hong Kong, or to ascertain the way to the bathroom at a Peking hotel.

However, now the accomplishment was really useful, for it obtained for him an invitation to Mrs. Molesworth's greatest week-end party.

This party was so select that it numbered but six all told. There were the Molesworths themselves—Christopher Molesworth was an M.P., rode to hounds, and backed up his wife in much the same way as a decent black frame backs up a coloured print.

Then there was Petterboy himself, the Feison brothers, who looked so restful and talked only if necessary, and finally the guest of all time, the gem of a magnificent collection, the catch of a

356

lifetime, Dr. Koo Fin, the Chinese scientist himself—Dr. Koo Fin, the Einstein of the East, the man with the Theory. After quitting his native Peking he had only left his house in New England on one memorable occasion when he delivered a lecture in Washington to an audience which was unable to comprehend a word. His works were translated but since they were largely concerned with higher mathematics the task was comparatively simple.

Mrs. Molesworth had every reason to congratulate herself on her capture. "The Chinese Einstein," as the newspapers had nicknamed him, was hardly a social bird. His shyness was proverbial, as was also his dislike and mistrust of women. It was this last foible which accounted for the absence of femininity at Mrs. Molesworth's party. Her own presence was unavoidable, of course, but she wore her severest gowns, and took a mental vow to speak as little as necessary. It is quite conceivable that had Mrs. Molesworth been able to change her sex she would have done so nobly for that week-end alone.

She had met the sage at a very select supper party after his only lecture in London. It was the same lecture which had thrown Washington into a state of bewilderment. Since Dr. Koo Fin arrived he had been photographed more often than any film star. His name and his round Chinese face were better known than those of the principals in the latest *cause célèbre*, and already television comedians referred to his great objectivity theory in their patter.

Apart from that one lecture, however, and the

supper party after it, he had been seen nowhere else save in his own closely guarded suite in his hotel.

How Mrs. Molesworth got herself invited to the supper party, and how, once there, she persuaded the sage to consent to visit Molesworth Court, is one of those minor miracles which do sometimes occur. Her enemies made many unworthy conjectures, but, since the university professors in charge of the proceedings on that occasion were not likely to have been corrupted by money or love, it is probable that Mrs. Molesworth moved the mountain by faith in herself alone.

The guest chamber prepared for Dr. Koo Fin was the third room in the west wing. This architectural monstrosity contained four bedrooms, each furnished with french windows leading on to the same balcony.

Young Petterboy occupied the room at the end of the row. It was one of the best in the house, as a matter of fact, but had no bathroom attached, since this had been converted by Mrs. Molesworth, who had the second chamber, into a gigantic clothes press. After all, as she said, it was her own house.

Dr. Koo Fin arrived on the Saturday by train, like a lesser person. He shook hands with Mrs. Molesworth and Christopher and young Petterboy and the Feisons as if he actually shared their own intelligence, and smiled at them all in his bland, utterly-too Chinese way.

From the first he was a tremendous success. He ate little, drank less, spoke not at all, but he nodded appreciatively at young Petterboy's halting

Chinese, and grunted once or twice most charmingly when someone inadvertently addressed him in English. Altogether he was Mrs. Molesworth's conception of a perfect guest.

On the Sunday morning Mrs. Molesworth actually received a compliment from him, and saw herself in a giddy flash the most talked-of woman in the cocktail parties of the coming week.

The charming incident occurred just before lunch. The sage rose abruptly from his chair on the lawn, and as the whole house party watched him with awe, anxious not to miss a single recountable incident, he stalked boldly across the nearest flower bed, trampling violas and London Pride with the true dreamer's magnificent disregard for physical obstacles, and, plucking the head off a huge rose from Christopher's favourite standard, trampled back with it in triumph and laid it in Mrs. Molesworth's lap.

Then, as she sat in ecstasy, he returned quietly to his seat and considered her affably. For the first time in her life Mrs. Molesworth was really thrilled. She told a number of people so afterwards.

However, on the Sunday night there were burglars. It was sickeningly awkward. Mrs. Molesworth had a diamond star, two sets of ear-rings, a bracelet and five rings, all set in platinum, and she kept them in a wall safe under a picture in her bedroom. On the Sunday night, after the rose incident, she gave up the self-effacement programme and came down to dinner in full war paint. The Molesworths always dressed on Sunday and she certainly looked devastatingly feminine, all blue mist and diamonds.

It was the more successful evening of the two. The sage revealed an engaging talent for making card houses, and he also played five-finger exercises on the piano. The great simplicity of the man was never better displayed. Finally, dazed, honoured and happy, the house party went to bed.

Mrs. Molesworth removed her jewellery and placed it in the safe, but unfortunately did not lock it at once. Instead, she discovered that she had dropped an ear-ring, and went down to look for it in the drawing-room. When at last she returned without it the safe was empty. It really was devastatingly awkward, and the resourceful Christopher, hastily summoned from his room in the main wing, confessed himself in a quandary.

The servants, discreetly roused, whispered that they had heard nothing and gave unimpeachable alibis. There remained the guests. Mrs. Molesworth wept. For such a thing to happen at any time was terrible enough, but for it to occur on such an occasion was more than she could bear. One thing she and Christopher agreed: the sage must never guess . . . must never dream . . .

There remained the Feisons and the unfortunate young Petterboy. The Feisons were ruled out almost at once. From the fact that the window catch in Mrs. Molesworth's room was burst, it was fairly obvious that the thief had entered from the balcony; therefore, had either of the Feisons passed that way from their rooms they would have had to pass the sage, who slept with his window wide. So there was only young Petterboy. It seemed fairly obvious.

Finally, after a great deal of consultation, Christopher went to speak to him as man to man, and came back fifteen minutes later hot and uncommunicative.

Mrs. Molesworth dried her eyes, put on her newest negligée, and, sweeping aside her fears and her husband's objections, went in to speak to young Petterboy like a mother. Poor young Petterboy gave up laughing at her after ten minutes, suddenly got angry, and demanded that the sage too should be asked if he had "heard anything." Then he forgot himself completely, and vulgarly suggested sending for the police.

Mrs. Molesworth nearly lost her head, recovered herself in time, apologised by innuendo, and crept back disconsolately to Christopher and bed.

The night passed most wretchedly.

In the morning poor young Petterboy cornered his hostess and repeated his requests of the night before. But the sage was departing by the 11:12 and Mrs. Molesworth was driving with him to the station. In that moment of her triumph the diamonds seemed relatively unimportant to Elvira Molesworth, who had inherited the Cribbage fortune a year before. Indeed, she kissed poor young Petterboy and said it really didn't matter, and hadn't they had a wonderful, wonderful weekend? And that he must come down again some time soon.

The Feisons said good-bye to the sage, and as Mrs. Molesworth was going with him, made their adieux to her as well. As the formalities had been accomplished there seemed no point in staying, and Christopher saw them off in their car, with poor young Petterboy leading the way in his.

As he was standing on the lawn waving somewhat perfunctorily to the departing cars, the post arrived. One letter for his wife bore the crest of the Doctor's hotel, and Christopher, with one of those intuitions which made him such a successful husband, tore it open.

It was quite short, but in the circumstances, wonderfully enlightening:

Dear Madam,

In going through Dr. Koo Fin's memoranda, I find to my horror that he promised to visit you this week-end. I know you will forgive Dr. Koo Fin when you hear that he never takes part in social occasions. As you know, his arduous work occupies his entire time. I know it is inexcusable of me not to have let you know before now, but it is only a moment since I discovered that the Doctor had made the engagement.

I do hope his absence has not put you to any inconvenience, and that you will pardon this atrocious slip.

I have the honour to remain, Madam,

Yours most apologetically,
Lo Pei Fu
Secretary.

P.S. The Doctor should have written himself, but, as you know, his English is not good. He

362

begs to be reminded to you and hopes for your forgiveness.

As Christopher raised his eyes from the note his wife returned. She stopped the car in the drive and came running across the lawn towards him.

"Darling, wasn't it wonderful?" she said, throwing herself into his arms with an abandonment she did not often display to him.

"What's in the post?" she went on, disengaging herself.

Christopher slipped the letter he had been reading into his pocket with unobtrusive skill.

"Nothing, my dear," he said gallantly. "Nothing at all." He was amazingly fond of his wife.

Mrs. Molesworth wrinkled her white forehead.

"Darling," she said, "now about my jewellery. Wasn't it too odious for such a thing to happen when that dear, sweet old man was here: what shall we do?"

Christopher drew her arm through his own. "I think, my dear," he said firmly, "you'd better leave all that to me. We mustn't have a scandal."

"Oh, no," said Mrs. Molesworth, her eyes growing round with alarm. "Oh, no; that would spoil everything."

In a first class compartment on the London train the elderly Chinese turned over the miscellaneous collection of jewellery which lay in a large silk handkerchief on his knee. His smile was childlike, bland and faintly wondering. After a while he folded the handkerchief over its treasure and placed the package in his breast pocket.

Then he leaned back against the upholstery and

looked out of the window. The green undulating landscape was pleasant. The fields were neat and well tilled. The sky was blue, the sunlight beautiful. It was a lovely land.

He sighed and marvelled in his heart that it could be the home of a race of cultivated barbarians to whom, providing that height, weight and age were relatively the same, all Chinese actually did look alike.

Freeman Wills Crofts
(1879–1952)
THE HUNT BALL

Variant: *The Inverted Country House Mystery*

The inverted mystery, since R. Austin Freeman, has attracted many practitioners. By describing the perpetrator and his crime at the outset, it allows the reader to concentrate completely on the means of deduction. One of the most successful recent examples was the American Columbo *television program where in each episode, a celebrity murderer would commit the perfect crime only to be methodically undone by the rumpled, dogged police lieutenant.*

Freeman Wills Crofts, the Anglo-Irish creator of Inspector French, contributed many fine English mysteries in conventional form, but "The Hunt Ball" is perhaps the best of all the inverted stories in the tradition.

(N.B.: To all you purists out there who will observe that this is strictly an English Country House Mystery without an English Country House and seize upon this as a reason to be distressed, I offer the following suggestion: Imagine Town Hall, the site of the Hunt Ball, to be the residence of Lord and Lady Town. All else will fall into place.)

Howard Skeffington had reached the end of his tether. He sat, hunched forward and staring unseeingly into the fire, as he faced the terrible conclusion to which inexorably he was being impelled: that his only escape from ruin lay in the death of his former friend, Justin Holt.

He, Howard Skeffington, must murder Holt! If he didn't, this pleasant life he was living, this fortune which seemed almost within his grasp, would be irretrievably lost. He would have to leave the country and everything he valued and look somewhere abroad for a job. And what job could he get?

To a certain extent Skeffington was an adventurer. Possessed of a good appearance, charming manners and an admirable seat on a horse, he had made friends at Cambridge with some of the young men from this Seldon Sorby country, this centre of the hunting life of England. At their homes he had spent vacations, riding their horses with skill, if not distinction. Alone in the world and not drawn to any career which involved hard work, he had conceived the idea of settling down at Seldon Sorby, and if possible marrying money.

The first part of this scheme he had carried out successfully. He had taken rooms in the district and been accepted as a member of the hunt. He had joined an associated and very select club and his social prospects seemed flourishing.

But he was up against one difficulty—money. His capital, he had estimated, would last him for four years, and on these four years he had staked his all. If before the end of that period he was unable to bring off the second part of his programme, he would be finished: down and out.

His chances in this respect, however, he considered rosy. Elaine Goff-Powell, Sir Richard Goff-Powell's only daughter, would have enough for any husband. Moreover he was sure she admired him, and he had made himself very agreeable to her father. Elaine was neither a beauty nor a wit: in fact, in moments of depression he realized she was, as he put it, damned plain and damned dull, too. But this gave him all the more hope. It wiped out the most dangerous of his potential competitors. As yet he had not risked a proposal, but he felt the time would soon be ripe and he had little fear of the result.

Unhappily, while the affair was moving, it was not moving quickly enough. Unless an engagement could be achieved soon, his resources would not stand the strain. Another five or six hundred would undoubtedly enable him to pull it off. As it was, the thing would be touch and go.

He had done what he could to borrow, but with indifferent success. Professional money-lenders would not touch him. Friends who might with luck be good for a tenner, certainly would not stretch to anything more: and it would take a good many tenners to be of use to Skeffington.

In this difficulty he had embarked on a course which normally he would have avoided like the plague. He had taken to cheating at cards. He realized very fully the risk he ran, but he did not see that any other way was open to him.

For some weeks he had managed successfully and he had determined to put his fortunes to the test at the Christmas Hunt Ball, which was to take place in a few days. With reasonable luck he would be accepted, and then this dreadfully wearing period of his life would be over.

But now, five days before the ball, disaster had overtaken him. His cheating had been discovered.

And yet not wholly discovered. What had happened was this.

During a game at the club one of the men, this Justin Holt, suddenly ceased playing. His face took on an expression of agony, and after swaying about for a moment, his head pitched forward on the table, the cards dropping from his nerveless fingers. The others jumped to their feet, but before they could do anything Holt raised himself. He was covered with confusion and apologized profusely. He had, he explained, got a severe pain and giddiness. It had come so suddenly that for the moment it had bowled him over, but already it was better. Infinitely he regretted breaking up the party, but with the others' consent he would go home and lie down. When they wanted to help he hesitated, then asked Skeffington, who lived in his direction, if he would mind seeing him to his quarters.

The affair puzzled Skeffington, who had never before seen such a seizure. But for him the mystery was soon cleared up. When they were alone Holt suddenly found himself able to walk normally and the expression of pain vanished from his face.

He remained, however, looking extremely worried. "I did that little bit of play-acting for a reason, Skeffington," he said. "The truth is, I saw what you were doing. I've been suspicious for some time, and so, I may tell you, have been a number of the others. But to-night I watched you, and I saw the whole thing. Skeffington, you're finished at Seldon Sorby."

To Skeffington it sounded like a sentence of death, but he quickly pulled himself together. Staring at Holt as coolly as he could, he said: "Perhaps you'll kindly explain what you're talking about?"

Holt shook his head irritably. "Don't be a complete fool," he begged. "I tell you I saw it. There's no use in your pretending. I know."

"You can't know anything," Skeffington returned doggedly. "If you had seen anything at that table, you'd have said so at the time. You didn't."

"I didn't," Holt explained, "for an obvious reason. I have some thought for the hunt, if you haven't. I didn't want to make a scandal. If we had been by ourselves I would have spoken. But with outsiders present naturally I didn't."

"Very thoughtful," Skeffington sneered. "It hasn't occurred to you that your consideration has rendered your story useless? Even if you had seen anything, which I deny, you can't prove it."

"I can tell what I saw."

"That's not proof. I shall deny it and then where will you be? You will have made a libelous statement which you can't prove. I think, my dear Holt, you, and not I, will be the one to retire."

Again Holt shook his head. "That sounds all right, Skeffington, but you know as well as I do that I would be believed. You know, or you ought to, that several of the men suspect you as it is. If

369

I describe what I saw you do, they will believe me."

"You just try it on," Skeffington said as contemptuously as he could. "It doesn't matter what anybody believes or doesn't believe privately. You can prove nothing, and you'll be the one who will suffer."

"That may be," Holt admitted, "but I'll tell you what I shall do. I'll give you three days to think it over. If by then you have sent in your resignation from the hunt, I will never refer to the matter again. If you have not resigned, I shall tell the committee. You do what you like."

Though Skeffington had attempted a mild bluff, he knew that Holt had the whip hand. It was true what the man had said: he would be believed rather than Skeffington. Holt's transparent honesty was universally recognized, whereas Skeffington was aware that his own reputation was by no means too secure. His phenomenal luck had been remarked on jokingly—or was it jokingly? —by several members, and the somewhat spectacular wins which had produced these remarks would be remembered—if Holt told what he had seen.

Skeffington rapidly considered the matter. He must somehow get Holt to keep silence. There must be no scandal, for scandal would mean complete ruin. The least breath and all chance of marrying Elaine Goff-Powell would be at an end. Indeed, if he didn't pull off an engagement at the ball next Tuesday, this last hope would be gone. He could not propose again for some weeks, and his money would not stretch to that.

But what could he do to restrain Holt? Nothing! Holt was one of those men who believed in doing what they considered was their duty. No, he could not hope to influence Holt.

Then first occurred to Skeffington the terrible idea that there was a way in which he could silence his enemy. One way: and only one.

Skeffington felt that he was at the most dreadful crisis of his life. To give up his present position, and practically penniless, to begin looking for a job—for which he had no training—would mean destitution, misery and death. And he could look forward to nothing else—if Holt were to live. But could he face the alternative; if Holt were to die? . . . Drops of sweat formed on his forehead.

He realized of course that his future did not depend solely on Holt. If Elaine turned him down he would equally be ruined. Therefore if Elaine turned him down there was no need to consider Holt any more. He was down and out in any case.

But if Elaine accepted him? Then Holt's actions would become vital. In this case . . .

All Skeffington's instincts were now prompting him to gain time. At all costs he must close Holt's mouth till after the ball. Then he, Skeffington, would either disappear and go under, or he would somehow deal with Holt. He turned to the man and spoke quietly and with more hesitation.

"Don't be in a hurry, Holt, I must think this over. Without admitting anything, I see you can do me a lot of harm. You have given me an ultimatum; resign or take the consequences. I want you to compromise."

"Compromise?" Holt was shocked. "How can

371

I compromise on a thing of that sort? Why, it's fundamental! You're not a fool, Skeffington: you must see that."

Skeffington shrugged. "I suppose you're right," he admitted presently. "Well, I'll tell you. I'll agree to your conditions provided you give me six days instead of three to make my arrangements. And what's more: during these six days I promise not to enter the card room. At the end of the six days, if I haven't resigned, you can go to the committee. Hang it all, Holt, that's not too much to ask. I must fix up some reason for the resignation. I'll have an uncle die in America and leave me money, or something of that kind. Then I'll go abroad and that will be the end of me so far as you're concerned."

Holt hesitated.

"Look here," went on Skeffington, "I'll not ask six days. Give me till the ball. We'll meet there and I'll let you have every satisfaction."

"But damn it, Skeffington, you mustn't come to the ball."

This was what Skeffington had feared. He shrugged, then turned away. "Oh well," he said coldly, "if you're going to be unreasonable I withdraw my offer. You tell the committee now, and when I am approached I shall deny everything and ask for your proof. And if you don't give it I shall press for your expulsion, and if you don't leave I shall start proceedings against you for defamation of character. A worse scandal that than my going to the ball!" He paused, then continued in a pleasanter tone. "But I don't want to do that. If you will wait till the ball it'll give me a chance to

372

explain my departure. That's all I ask." He suddenly changed his tone. "I'm not attempting any extenuation, Holt, but try and imagine the ruin this means for me. It's not like you to kick a man when he's down."

There had been some further argument and Skeffington had triumphed. Holt had agreed to say nothing provided that at or before the ball Skeffington resigned.

Left alone, Skeffington hardened his heart and began to work out the solution of his terrible problem. First, if Elaine refused him. By borrowing from his friends and selling some of his stuff he could raise, he thought, a couple of hundred pounds. He had better do this at once and buy tickets to the Argentine, where he thought his knowledge of horses might stand him in good stead. No doubt before leaving he could borrow a little more. Enough to get past the immigration laws at all events. It would be hell after what he was accustomed to: but it would be at least a chance for life.

But if Elaine accepted him?

Then he was set up for life with all the money he could want: his future absolutely assured—if only Holt were dealt with.

Skeffington took care to speak to various members of the committee and others to whom Holt might have told his story, and in every case he was satisfied from their manner that they had heard nothing. Holt therefore was the only danger. If he were silenced, Skeffington would be safe.

For three days Skeffington thought over the

problem and then at last he saw how the man might be eliminated, and with absolute secrecy. Admittedly there would be a little risk at one point, but that point once passed, no further hitch could arise. Carefully Skeffington made his preparations. He avoided the club on the excuse of private business and kept rigorously out of Holt's way.

At last the fateful night arrived, a dark and bitter evening with the ground like iron and a frosty fog in the air. The Christmas Hunt Ball was *the* social event of the year, when the local four hundred thronged the Seldon Sorby Town Hall and everyone who was anyone felt he must be present. The somewhat drab building was transformed out of all recognition with bunting and greenery, and the hunt colors made the gathering what the local paper invariably called a spectacle of sparkling brilliance.

The first two essentials of Skeffington's plan were to drive some people to the ball and to park his car in a secluded place near the back entrance of the hall. The former he managed by inviting a young married couple called Hatherley and a bachelor friend named Scarlett to accompany him, the second by a careful timing of his arrival, coupled with his knowledge of how the park filled. The market at the back of the hall was used as a park, and there he succeeded in placing the car in the corner he desired. He knew that before long it would be completely surrounded and that no one was likely to remain near it.

In the car, hooked up under the dash, was a heavy spanner round which he had wrapped a soft cloth. It was so fixed that he could lift it out by simply opening the door and putting in his hand.

He had taken just enough whisky to steady his nerves, and in spite of the terrible deed which was in front of him, he felt confident and in his best form.

To his delight Elaine had greeted him with more than her usual warmth. For half the evening he had danced exclusively with her, and now he led her to a deserted corner and with trepidation put the vital question. A thrill of overwhelming satisfaction shot through him when he heard the answer. Elaine would marry him, and further would agree to the engagement being announced at once.

But that thrill was accompanied by a pang of something not far removed from actual horror. To preserve what he had won he must now pass through the most hideous ten minutes of his life. Now also he realized that there would be more danger in the affair than he had anticipated. However, there was no alternative. The thing must be faced.

When he judged the time propitious—when the chauffeurs were at supper—he told Elaine that he wished to ask her father's blessing on the engagement. She suggested accompanying him, and he had to use all his tact to prevent her. However, by assuring her that he could speak more movingly of her goodness and charm if she were not present, he was able to leave her dancing with Scarlett.

Instead of seeking out Sir Richard Goff-Powell, Skeffington found Holt. Waiting till he had handed on his partner, he passed him, and without stopping, murmured: "Come to the cloak room. I've something to show you."

Skeffington hung about the passage till Holt hove in sight. "I've decided to resign," he said in a low voice, "but I've got a strange letter which I wish to show you. We can't talk here in private. Come out to my car and let me explain what has arisen."

Holt was unwilling, but Skeffington persuaded him by the argument that if they were seen discussing confidential matters, it might connect him with the resignation.

Skeffington passed out to the park, followed by his victim. Though the tops of the cars were faintly illuminated by distant lights, the spaces between them were dark as pitch. As they walked Skeffington removed his immaculate gloves, fearing tell-tale stains or even smears of blood. He was satisfied that they reached the car unobserved.

"Here's the letter," he said, opening the forward door and taking a paper from a cubby hole. "My inside light has failed, but the letter's very short and you can read it by the side light. I'll switch it on. Then we can get in out of the cold and discuss it."

Holt, grumbling about being brought out of the warm hall, moved forward to the front of the wing to bring the paper to the lamp. In doing so he momentarily turned his back to Skeffington.

To produce this movement had been Skeffington's aim. Instead of switching on the light, his fingers grasped the spanner, and as Holt made that slight turn he brought the heavy tool down with all his force on the man's head. Holt dropped like a log.

With a tiny pocket-torch Skeffington glanced at his victim's head. It was all right. There was no blood, but there was deformation of the bone. There could be no doubt that Holt was dead.

Hastily Skeffington completed his programme. Opening the rear door of his car, he tried to lift the body in. This he found more difficult than he had expected. He had to leave it sitting on the floor propped up against the seat and go to the other side of the car and draw it in after him, returning to lift in the feet, one by one. He left it on the floor covered with a rug, then hastened back to the hall. This time also he was sure he was unobserved. A wash, a brush and a stiff glass of whisky, and he was once more in the ballroom.

He would have given anything to have slipped off to his rooms, but he daren't do so. Instead he found Sir Richard, and taking his courage in both hands, he went up to him.

"I have something to tell you, sir," he began, "and I most sincerely hope you will be pleased. Elaine has done me the honour to say she will marry me," and he expatiated on his news.

Sir Richard did not appear particularly pleased, but neither did he raise any objection. He shrugged and said the matter was one for Elaine. As soon as Skeffington could, he returned to the young woman.

How he endured to the end of the proceedings Skeffington scarcely knew. But at long last Elaine departed with her family and he went in search of his friends.

"I'll bring the car to the steps," he told the Hatherleys, then adding to Scarlett: "You might come and help me if you don't mind. It's a job to get out of such a jam."

Reaching the car, Skeffington opened the near forward door for Scarlett, then went round to the driver's side and got in himself. He thus had a witness of all his proceedings, while Scarlett had not seen the body.

As Skeffington pulled in to the steps a commissionaire opened the rear door for Mrs. Hatherley. He lifted away the rug, then swore hoarsely while Mrs. Hatherley gave a shrill scream.

What happened then seemed a confused muddle to Skeffington. He got out and tried to edge round to the door through the dense crowd which had instantly formed.

"What is it?" he heard himself shouting. "What's wrong?"

He heard murmurs all about him. "A man!" "Seems to be dead!" "There in the back of the car!"—then an authoritative voice which he recognized as that of the chief constable of the county: "Keep back everyone, please, and let Dr. Hackett pass. Doctor, will you please have a look here."

Everyone but Skeffington and Scarlett moved back. Someone provided a torch. For a moment time seemed to stand still, then the doctor said slowly: "It's Holt and I'm afraid he's dead. A blow on the head. Must have been instantaneous."

Time began to move once more, in fact it now raced so quickly that Skeffington could hardly keep up with it.

As if by magic police appeared. The guests were

politely herded back into the ballrooms. Skeffington was asked by a sharp-looking young inspector if he could give any explanation of the affair, and when he replied that he could not, he was told not so politely to wait where he was for further interrogation.

The whole place buzzed as if a swarm of colossal bees had invaded it. Then gradually people began to leave, their names and addresses taken and a few questions put and answered. At long last the police returned to Skeffington.

He had taken a little more whisky, enough to subdue his fear and steady his hands, but not enough to make him stupid.

"Will you tell me what you know of this affair, Mr. Skeffington?" asked the local superintendent, who had now arrived and taken charge of the proceedings.

Skeffington replied without hesitation. He had driven Mr. and Mrs. Hatherly and Mr. Scarlett to the ball. He had parked in the corner of the market. All had then got out and gone into the ball. When Mrs. Hatherley was ready to go home he and Scarlett had gone for the car. He had driven it to the steps and when the rear door had been opened the body had been found. The affair was just as great a mystery to him as to the super.

It was a simple story and Skeffington told it well. Superintendent Redfern asked many questions, but he could not in any way shake the tale, and at last he thanked Skeffington and said that would be all.

Rather shakily Skeffington drove home.

During the next couple of days events moved quickly at police headquarters at Seldon Sorby. The place had been shaken to the core. Such a murder, taking place at the most fashionable event in the town's year, and involving the death of a relative of Lord Bonniton, master of the most famous hunt in the country, seemed almost a national disaster. The chief constable was frantic and without delay had wired to Scotland Yard for help. A couple of hours later Chief Inspector French and Sergeant Carter had arrived to assist in the inquiry. French had heard all that had been done, had studied the various statements made, and had examined the Town Hall and market. As he had not thereupon laid his hand on the guilty party, the chief constable had asked querulous and suggestive questions.

"Silly fool," French grumbled to Carter that night at their hotel. "Does he think we're thought readers? If he was in all that hurry, why didn't he do the job himself?"

Later that evening French sat smoking over the lounge fire and imbibing cup after cup of strong coffee, as he puzzled his brains in the attempt to find some line of investigation which would give him his solution. He had put in train all the obvious inquiries: about Holt's career and recent activities, who had seen him at the ball, who had been in the market while the cars were parked, and such like, but he wanted to find some short-cut, some royal road almost, to the criminal. Sir Mortimer Ellison, the Assistant Commissioner at the Yard, had given him a hint before he started.

"It's a society place," he had said, "and the big bugs are society people. You'll find them touchy down there because this case will get them on the raw. Hence the quicker you pull it off, the better for all concerned." And now he had been down for two days and he was no further on than when he arrived.

For three hours he considered the matter and then a point struck him, a very simple point. It might not lead to anything, but, on the other hand, it might. The following day he would try a reconstruction.

Accordingly next morning he demanded a man of the approximate build of the deceased and a car like Skeffington's. These he took to a secluded corner of the police yard.

The dummy was a young constable named Arthurs. He grinned when French explained that he wanted to smash in his head.

"Right sir," he agreed. "I hope you'll remember the wife and kiddies when I'm gone."

"No one, I'm afraid, will know how it was done," French assured him. "Now, Arthurs, just where you're standing I hit you a bat on the head and stove in your skull. See?"

"Yes, sir."

"Well, go ahead. You don't want me to do it in reality, I suppose?"

"I'm afraid, sir, if my skull. . ."

French jerked round. "Good heavens, man, use your brains! Collapse!"

With a sudden look of comprehension Arthurs sank quietly on to the ground beside the car, while French adjured him to relax completely.

"Now, Carter, lift him into the position the dead man occupied."

Carter opened the rear door, and lifting the grinning Arthurs beneath the arms, tried to get him into the car. But like Skeffington he found he couldn't do it from where he was standing. He also had to go round to the other side and draw him in.

"Can't you pull in the legs?" French prompted.

Carter tried. "No, sir," he returned, "I'll have to go back and lift them in."

French watched him, a smile of satisfaction playing on his lips. "I rather thought that might happen," he declared. "Come along to the mortuary." He looked into the car. "Thank you, Arthurs, we've done with you. You made a good corpse."

On reaching the room where Holt's clothes lay, French took out his powdering apparatus and dusted the deceased's patent leather shoes. Several fingerprints showed up. French blew away the surplus, then photographed the prints.

"Now the deceased's fingers," he went on.

Soon the ten impressions were taken and photographed in their turn. A proper comparison would require enlargements and detailed observation, but a certain amount could be learned from mere casual inspection. French quickly satisfied himself. Most of the prints belonged to the deceased himself, but certain others were not his. From their position they might well have been caused by lifting the feet into a car.

Two hours later the club started a new waiter in the bar. Gradually a row of used glasses accumulated, each neatly labelled with the name of the drinker. At intervals French tested and compared the fingerprints. Suddenly the affair clicked. Skeffington had lifted Holt's shoes.

The correct line of investigation was now indicated. Judicious enquiries brought to light Skeffington's financial position and mysterious luck at cards, Holt's strange illness, and the fact that Holt had asked Skeffington to accompany him to his rooms. The fact of the latter's engagement also became known. Here, French saw, was the motive.

"He thought putting the corpse in his own car would absolve him from suspicion, but the prints on the shoes are proof positive that he did it," he concluded to the chief constable. "We're ready for an arrest, I think?"

"To-night," nodded the chief constable.

John Dickson Carr
(1905 – 1977)

THE INCAUTIOUS BURGLAR

Carr, a master of the puzzle mystery, became one of the pillars of the Detection Club and the only one, it is safe to say, born and raised in Uniontown, Pennsylvania. His writing was greatly influenced by G. K. Chesterton, the inspiration for his celebrated detective Dr. Fell (". . . vast and beaming, wearing a box-pleated cape as big as a tent . . . his [pince-nez] eyeglasses . . . set precariously on a pink nose, the black ribbon [blowing] wide with each vast puff of breath . . .").

In 1932 he married an Englishwoman and settled in England for the next twenty-six years, a dedicated Anglophile and proponent of the Grand Tradition. Carr's fondness for locked-room puzzles marries well with the Country House style he grew to master.

Two guests, who were not staying the night at Cranleigh Court, left at shortly past eleven o'clock. Marcus Hunt saw them to the front door. Then he returned to the dining-room, where the poker-chips were now stacked into neat piles of white, red, and blue.

"Another game?" suggested Rolfe.

"No good," said Derek Henderson. His tone,

as usual, was weary. "Not with just the three of us."

Their host stood by the sideboard and watched them. The long, low house, overlooking the Weald of Kent, was so quiet that their voices rose with startling loudness. The dining-room, large and panelled, was softly lighted by electric wall-candles which brought out the sombre colours of the paintings. It is not often that anybody sees, in one room of an otherwise commonplace country house, two Rembrandts and a Van Dyck. There was a kind of defiance about those paintings.

To Arthur Rolfe—the art dealer—they represented enough money to make him shiver. To Derek Henderson—the art critic—they represented a problem. What they represented to Marcus Hunt was not apparent.

Hunt stood by the sideboard, his fists on his hips, smiling. He was a middle-sized, stocky man, with a full face and a high complexion. Equip him with a tuft of chin-whisker, and he would have looked like a Dutch burgher or a Dutch brush. His shirt-front bulged out untidily. He watched with ironical amusement while Henderson picked up a pack of cards in long fingers, cut them into two piles, and shuffled with a sharp flick of each thumb which made the cards melt together like a conjuring trick.

Henderson yawned.

"My boy," said Hunt, "you surprise me."

"That's what I try to do," answered Henderson, still wearily. He looked up. "But why do you say so, particularly?"

Henderson was young, he was long, he was lean,

he was immaculate; and he wore a beard. It was a reddish beard, which moved some people to hilarity. But he wore it with an air of complete naturalness.

"I'm surprised," said Hunt, "that you enjoy anything so bourgeois—so plebeian—as poker."

"I enjoy reading people's characters," said Henderson. "Poker's the best way to do it, you know."

Hunt's eyes narrowed. "Oh? Can you read my character, for instance?"

"With pleasure," said Henderson. Absently he dealt himself a poker-hand, face up. It contained a pair of fives, and the last card was the ace of spades. Henderson remained staring at it for a few seconds before he glanced up again.

"And I can tell you," he went on, "that *you* surprise *me*. Do you mind if I'm frank? I had always thought of you as the Colossus of Business; the smasher; the plunger; the fellow who took the long chances. Now, you're not like that at all."

Marcus Hunt laughed. But Henderson was undisturbed.

"You're tricky, but you're cautious. I doubt if you ever took a long chance in your life. Another surprise"—he dealt himself a new hand—"is Mr. Rolfe here. He's the man who, given the proper circumstances, would take the long chances."

Arthur Rolfe considered this. He looked startled, but rather flattered. Though in height and build not unlike Hunt, there was nothing untidy about him. He had a square, dark face, with thin shells of eyeglasses, and a worried forehead.

"I doubt that," he declared, very serious about this. Then he smiled. "A person who took long chances in my business would find himself in the soup." He glanced round the room. "Anyhow, I'd be too cautious to have three pictures, with an aggregate value of thirty thousand pounds, hanging in an unprotected downstairs room with French windows giving on a terrace." An almost frenzied note came into his voice. "Great Scot! Suppose a burglar—"

"Damn!" said Henderson unexpectedly.

Even Hunt jumped.

Ever since the poker-party, an uneasy atmosphere had been growing. Hunt had picked up an apple from a silver fruit-bowl on the sideboard. He was beginning to pare it with a fruit-knife, a sharp wafer-thin blade which glittered in the light of the wall-lamps.

"You nearly made me slice my thumb off," he said, putting down the knife. "What's the matter with you?"

"It's the ace of spades," said Henderson, still languidly. "That's the second time it's turned up in five minutes."

Arthur Rolfe chose to be dense. "Well? What about it?"

"I think our young friend is being psychic," said Hunt, good-humoured again. "Are you reading characters, or only telling fortunes?"

Henderson hesitated. His eyes moved to Hunt, and then to the wall over the sideboard where Rembrandt's "Old Woman with Cap" stared back with the immobility and skin-colouring of a red Indian. Then Henderson looked towards the French windows opening on the terrace.

"None of my affair," shrugged Henderson.

"It's your house and your collection and your responsibility. But this fellow Butler: what do you know about him?"

Marcus Hunt looked boisterously amused.

"Butler? He's a friend of my niece's. Harriet picked him up in London, and asked me to invite him down here. Nonsense! Butler's all right. What are you thinking, exactly?"

"Listen!" said Rolfe, holding up his hand.

The noise they heard, from the direction of the terrace, was not repeated. It was not repeated because the person who had made it, a very bewildered and uneasy young lady, had run lightly and swiftly to the far end, where she leaned against the balustrade.

Lewis Butler hesitated before going after her. The moonlight was so clear that one could see the mortar between the tiles which paved the terrace, and trace the design of the stone urns along the balustrade. Harriet Davis wore a white gown with long and filmy skirts, which she lifted clear of the ground as she ran.

Then she beckoned to him.

She was half sitting, half leaning against the rail. Her white arms were spread out, fingers gripping the stone. Dark hair and dark eyes became even more vivid by moonlight. He could see the rapid rise and fall of her breast; he could even trace the shadow of her eyelashes.

"That was a lie, anyhow," she said.

"What was?"

"What my Uncle Marcus said. You heard him."
Harriet Davis's fingers tightened still more on the

balustrade. But she nodded her head vehemently, with fierce accusation. "About my knowing you. And inviting you here. I never saw you before this week-end. Either Uncle Marcus is going out of his mind, or. . . will you answer me just one question?"

"If I can."

"Very well. Are you by any chance a crook?"

She spoke with as much simplicity and directness as though she had asked him whether he might be a doctor or a lawyer. Lewis Butler was not unwise enough to laugh. She was in that mood where, to any woman, laughter is salt to a raw wound; she would probably have slapped his face.

"To be quite frank about it," he said, "I'm not. Will you tell me why you asked?"

"This house," said Harriet, looking at the moon, "used to be guarded with burglar alarms. If you as much as touched a window, the whole place started clanging like a fire-station. He had all the burglar alarms removed last week. Last week" She took her hands off the balustrade, and pressed them together hard. "The pictures used to be upstairs, in a locked room next to his bedroom. He had them moved downstairs—last week. It's almost as though my uncle *wanted* the house to be burgled."

Butler knew that he must use great care here.

"Perhaps he does." (Here she looked at Butler quickly, but did not comment.) "For instance," he went on idly, "suppose one of his famous Rembrandts turned out to be a fake? It might be a relief not to have to show it to his expert friends."

The girl shook her head.

"No," she said. "They're all genuine. You see, I thought of that too."

Now was the time to hit, and hit hard. To Lewis Butler, in his innocence, there seemed to be no particular problem. He took out his cigarette-case, and turned it over without opening it.

"Look here, Miss Davis, you're not going to like this. But I can tell you of cases in which people were rather anxious to have their property 'stolen.' If a picture is insured for more than its value, and then it is mysteriously 'stolen' one night—?"

"That might be all very well too," answered Harriet, still calmly. "Except that not one of those pictures has been insured."

The cigarette-case, which was of polished metal, slipped through Butler's fingers and fell with a clatter on the tiles. It spilled cigarettes, just as it spilled and confused his theories. As he bent over to pick it up, he could hear a church clock across the Weald strike the half-hour after eleven.

"You're sure of that?"

"I'm perfectly sure. He hasn't insured any of his pictures for as much as a penny. He says it's a waste of money."

"But—"

"Oh, I know! And I don't know why I'm talking to you like this. You're a stranger, aren't you?" She folded her arms, drawing her shoulders up as though she were cold. Uncertainty, fear, and plain nerves flicked at her eyelids. "But then Uncle Marcus is a stranger too. Do you know what I think? I think he's going mad."

"Hardly as bad as that, is it?"

"Yes, go on," the girl suddenly stormed at him.

"*Say* it: go on and say it. That's easy enough. But you don't see him when his eyes seem to get smaller, and all that genial-country-squire look goes out of his face. He's not a fake: he hates fakes, and goes out of his way to expose them. But, if he hasn't gone clear out of his mind, what's he up to? What can he be up to?"

In something over three hours, they found out.

The burglar did not attack until half-past two in the morning. First he smoked several cigarettes in the shrubbery below the rear terrace. When he heard the church clock strike, he waited a few minutes more, and then slipped up the steps to the French windows of the dining-room.

A chilly wind stirred at the turn of the night, in the hour of suicides and bad dreams. It smoothed grass and trees with a faint rustling. When the man glanced over his shoulder, the last of the moonlight distorted his face: it showed less a face than the blob of a black cloth mask, under a greasy cap pulled down over his ears.

He went to work on the middle window, with the contents of a folding toolkit not so large as a motorist's. He fastened two short strips of adhesive tape to the glass just beside the catch. Then his glass-cutter sliced out a small semicircle inside the tape.

It was done not without noise: it crunched like a dentist's drill in a tooth, and the man stopped to listen.

There was no answering noise. No dog barked.

With the adhesive tape holding the glass so that it did not fall and smash, he slid his gloved hand through the opening and twisted the catch. The weight of his body deadened the creaking of the window when he pushed inside.

He knew exactly what he wanted. He put the tool-kit into his pocket, and drew out an electric torch. Its beam moved across to the sideboard; it touched gleaming silver, a bowl of fruit, and a wicked little knife thrust into an apple as though into someone's body; finally, it moved up the hag-face of the "Old Woman with Cap."

This was not a large picture, and the burglar lifted it down easily. He pried out glass and frame. Though he tried to roll up the canvas with great care, the brittle paint cracked across in small stars which wounded the hag's face. The burglar was so intent on this that he never noticed the presence of another person in the room.

He was an incautious burglar: he had no sixth sense which smelt murder.

Up on the second floor of the house, Lewis Butler was awakened by a muffled crash like that of metal objects falling.

He had not fallen into more than a half doze all night. He knew with certainty what must be happening, though he had no idea of why, or how, or to whom.

Butler was out of bed, and into his slippers, as soon as he heard the first faint clatter from downstairs. His dressing-gown would, as usual, twist itself up like a rolled umbrella and defy all attempts to find the arm-holes whenever he wanted to hurry. But the little flashlight was ready in the pocket.

That noise seemed to have roused nobody else.

393

With certain possibilities in his mind, he had never in his life moved so fast once he managed to get out of his bedroom. Not using his light, he was down two flights of deep-carpeted stairs without noise. In the lower hall he could feel a draught, which meant that a window or door had been opened somewhere. He made straight for the dining-room.

But he was too late.

Once the pencil-beam of Butler's flashlight had swept round, he switched on a whole blaze of lights. The burglar was still here, right enough. But the burglar was lying very still in front of the sideboard; and, to judge by the amount of blood on his sweater and trousers, he would never move again.

"That's done it," Butler said aloud.

A silver service, including a tea-urn, had been toppled off the sideboard. Where the fruit-bowl had fallen, the dead man lay on his back among a litter of oranges, apples, and a squashed bunch of grapes. The mask still covered the burglar's face; his greasy cap was flattened still further on his ears; his gloved hands were thrown wide.

Fragments of smashed picture-glass lay round him, together with the empty frame, and the "Old Woman with Cap" had been half crumpled up under his body. From the position of the most conspicuous bloodstains, one judged that he had been stabbed through the chest with the stained fruit-knife beside him.

"*What is it?*" said a voice almost at Butler's ear.

He could not have been more startled if the fruit-knife had pricked his ribs. He had seen nobody turning on lights in the hall, nor had he heard Harriet Davis approach. She was standing just behind him, wrapped in a Japanese kimono, with her dark hair round her shoulders. But, when he explained what had happened, she would not look into the dining-room; she backed away, shaking her head violently, like an urchin ready for flight.

"You had better wake up your uncle," Butler said briskly, with a confidence he did not feel. "And the servants. I must use your telephone." Then he looked her in the eyes. "Yes, you're quite right. I think you've guessed it already. I'm a police-officer."

She nodded.

"Yes. I guessed. Who are you? And is your name really Butler?"

"I'm a sergeant of the Criminal Investigation Department. And my name really is Butler. Your uncle brought me here."

"Why?"

"I don't know. He hasn't got round to telling me."

This girl's intelligence, even when over-shadowed by fear, was direct and disconcerting. "But, if he wouldn't say why he wanted a police-officer, how did they come to send you? He'd have to tell them, wouldn't he?"

Butler ignored it. "I must see your uncle. Will you go upstairs and wake him, please?"

"I can't," said Harriet. "Uncle Marcus isn't in his room."

"Isn't—?"

"No. I knocked at the door on my way down. He's gone."

Butler took the stairs two treads at a time. Harriet had turned on all the lights on her way down, but nothing stirred in the bleak, over-decorated passages.

Marcus Hunt's bedroom was empty. His dinner-jacket had been hung up neatly on the back of a chair, shirt laid across the seat with collar and tie on top of it. Hunt's watch ticked loudly on the dressing-table. His money and keys were there too. But he had not gone to bed, for the bedspread was undisturbed.

The suspicion which came to Lewis Butler, listening to the thin insistent ticking of that watch in the drugged hour before dawn, was so fantastic that he could not credit it.

He started downstairs again, and on the way he met Arthur Rolfe blundering out of another bedroom down the hall. The art dealer's stocky body was wrapped in a flannel dressing-gown. He was not wearing his eyeglasses, which gave his face a bleary and rather caved-in expression. He planted himself in front of Butler, and refused to budge.

"Yes," said Butler. "You don't have to ask. It's a burglar."

"I knew it." said Rolfe calmly. "Did he get anything?"

"No. He was murdered."

For a moment Rolfe said nothing, but his hand crept into the breast of his dressing-gown as though he felt pain there.

"Murdered? You don't mean the *burglar* was murdered?"

"Yes."

"But why? By an accomplice, you mean? Who is the burglar?"

"That," snarled Lewis Butler, "is what I intend to find out."

In the lower hall he found Harriet Davis, who was now standing in the doorway of the dining-room and looking steadily at the body by the sideboard. Though her face hardly moved a muscle, her eyes brimmed over.

"You're going to take off the mask, aren't you?" she asked, without turning round.

Stepping with care to avoid squashed fruit and broken glass, Butler leaned over the dead man. He pushed back the peak of the greasy cap; he lifted the black cloth mask, which was clumsily held by an elastic band; and he found what he expected to find.

The burglar was Marcus Hunt—stabbed through the heart while attempting to rob his own house.

"You see, sir, " Butler explained to Dr. Gideon Fell on the following afternoon, "that's the trouble. However you look at it, the case makes no sense."

Again he went over the facts.

"Why should the man burgle his own house and steal his own property? Every one of those paintings is valuable, and not a single one is insured! Consequently, why? Was the man a simple lunatic? What did he think he was doing?"

The village of Sutton Valence, straggling like a grey-white Italian town along the very peak of the Weald, was full of hot sunshine. In the apple orchard behind the white inn of the *Tabard*, Dr. Gideon Fell sat at a garden table among wasps, with a pint tankard at his elbow. Dr. Fell's vast bulk was clad in a white linen suit. His pink face smoked in the heat, and his wary lookout for wasps gave him a regrettably wall-eyed appearance as he pondered.

He said:

"Superintendent Hadley suggested that I might—harrumph—look in here. The local police are in charge, aren't they?"

"Yes. I'm merely standing by."

"Hadley's exact words to me were, 'It's so crazy that nobody but you will understand it.' The man's flattery becomes more nauseating every day." Dr. Fell scowled. "I say. Does anything else strike you as queer about this business?"

"Well, why should a man burgle his own house?"

"No, no, no!" growled Dr. Fell. "Don't be obsessed with that point. Don't become hypnotized by it. For instance"—a wasp hovered near his tankard, and he distended his cheeks and blew it away with one vast puff like Father Neptune—"for instance, the young lady seems to have raised an interesting question. If Marcus Hunt wouldn't say why he wanted a detective in the house, why did the C.I.D. consent to send you?"

Butler shrugged his shoulders.

"Because," he said, "Chief Inspector Ames thought Hunt was up to funny business, and meant to stop it."

"What sort of funny business?"

"A faked burglary to steal his own pictures for

the insurance. It looked like the old, old game of appealing to the police to divert suspicion. In other words, sir, exactly what this appeared to be: until I learned (and to-day proved) that not one of those damned pictures has ever been insured for a penny."

Butler hesitated.

"It can't have been a practical joke," he went on. "Look at the elaborateness of it! Hunt put on old clothes from which all tailors' tabs and laundry marks were removed. He put on gloves and a mask. He got hold of a torch and an up-to-date kit of burglar's tools. He went out of the house by the back door; we found it open later. He smoked a few cigarettes in the shrubbery below the terrace; we found his footprints in the soft earth. He cut a pane of glass . . . but I've told you all that."

"And then," mused Dr. Fell, "somebody killed him."

"Yes. The last and worst 'why.' Why should anybody have killed him?"

"H'm. Clues?"

"Negative." Butler took out his notebook. "According to the police surgeon, he died of a direct heart-wound from a blade (presumably that fruit-knife) so thin that the wound was difficult to find. There were a number of his finger-prints, but nobody else's. We did find one odd thing, though. A number of pieces in the silver service off the sideboard were scratched in a queer way. It looked almost as though, instead of being swept off the sideboard in a struggle, they had been piled up on top of each other like a tower; and then pushed—"

Butler paused, for Dr. Fell was shaking his big head back and forth with an expression of Gargantuan distress.

"Well, well, well," he was saying; "well, well, well. And you call that negative evidence?"

"Isn't it? It doesn't explain why a man burgles his own house."

"Look here," said the doctor mildly. "I should like to ask you just one question. What is the most important point in this affair? One moment! I did not say the most interesting; I said the most important. Surely it is the fact that a man has been murdered?"

"Yes, sir. Naturally."

"I mention the fact"—the doctor was apologetic — "because it seems in danger of being overlooked. It hardly interests you. You are concerned only with Hunt's senseless masquerade. You don't mind a throat being cut; but you can't stand a leg being pulled. Why not try working at it from the other side, and asking who killed Hunt?"

Butler was silent for a long time.

"The servants are out of it," he said at length. "They sleep in another wing on the top floor; and for some reason," he hesitated, "somebody locked them in last night." His doubts, even his dreads, were beginning to take form. "There was a fine blow-up over that when the house was roused. Of course, the murderer could have been an outsider."

"You know it wasn't," said Dr. Fell. "Would you mind taking me to Cranleigh Court?"

They came out on the terrace in the hottest part of the afternoon.

Dr. Fell sat down on a wicker settee, with a dispirited Harriet beside him. Derek Henderson, in flannels, perched his long figure on the balustrade. Arthur Rolfe alone wore a dark suit and seemed out of place. For the pale green and brown of the Kentish lands, which rarely acquired harsh colour, now blazed. No air stirred, no leaf moved, in that brilliant thickness of heat; and down in the garden, towards their left, the water of the swimming-pool sparkled with hot, hard light. Butler felt it like a weight on his eyelids.

Derek Henderson's beard was at once languid and yet aggressive.

"It's no good," he said. "Don't keep on asking me why Hunt should have burgled his own house. But I'll give you a tip."

"Which is?" inquired Dr. Fell.

"Whatever the reason was," returned Henderson, sticking out his neck, "it was a good reason. Hunt was much too canny and cautious ever to do anything without a good reason. I told him so last night."

Dr. Fell spoke sharply. "Cautious? Why do you say that?"

"Well, for instance. I take three cards on the draw. Hunt takes one. I bet; he sees me and raises. I cover that, and raise again. Hunt drops out. In other words, it's fairly certain he's filled his hand, but not so certain I'm holding much more than a

401

pair. Yet Hunt drops out. So with my three sevens I bluff him out of his straight. He played a dozen hands last night just like that."

Henderson began to chuckle. Seeing the expression on Harriet's face, he checked himself and became preternaturally solemn.

"But then, of course," Henderson added, "he had a lot on his mind last night."

Nobody could fail to notice the change of tone.

"So? And what did he have on his mind?"

"Exposing somebody he had always trusted," replied Henderson coolly. "That's why I didn't like it when the ace of spades turned up so often."

"You'd better explain that," said Harriet, after a pause. "I don't know what you're hinting at, but you'd better explain that. He told you he intended to expose somebody he had always trusted?"

"No. Like myself, he hinted at it."

It was the stolid Rolfe who stormed into the conversation then. Rolfe had the air of a man determined to hold hard to reason, but finding it difficult.

"Listen to me," snapped Rolfe. "I have heard a great deal, at one time or another, about Mr. Hunt's liking for exposing people. Very well!" He slid one hand into the breast of his coat, in a characteristic gesture. "But where in the name of sanity does that leave us? He wants to expose someone. And, to do that, he puts on outlandish clothes and masquerades as a burglar. Is that sensible? I tell you, the man was mad! There's no other explanation."

402

"There are five other explanations," said Dr. Fell.

Derek Henderson slowly got up from his seat on the balustrade, but he sat down again at a savage gesture from Rolfe.

Nobody spoke.

"I will not, however," pursued Dr. Fell, "waste your time with four of them. We are concerned with only one explanation: the real one."

"And you know the real one?" asked Henderson sharply.

"I rather think so."

"Since when?"

"Since I had the opportunity of looking at all of you," answered Dr. Fell.

He settled back massively in the wicker settee, so that its frame creaked and cracked like a ship's bulkhead in a heavy sea. His vast chin was out-thrust, and he nodded absently as though to emphasize some point that was quite clear in his own mind.

"I've already had a word with the local inspector," he went on suddenly. "He will be here in a few minutes. And, at my suggestion, he will have a request for all of you. I sincerely hope nobody will refuse."

"Request?" said Henderson. "What request?"

"It's a very hot day," said Dr. Fell, blinking towards the swimming-pool. "He's going to suggest that you all go in for a swim."

Harriet uttered a kind of despairing mutter, and turned as though appealing to Lewis Butler.

"That," continued Dr. Fell, "will be the politest way of drawing attention to the murderer. In

403

the meantime, let me call your attention to one point in the evidence which seems to have been generally overlooked. Mr. Henderson, do you know anything about direct heart-wounds, made by a steel blade as thin as a wafer?"

"Like Hunt's wound? No. What about them?"

"There is practically no exterior bleeding," answered Dr. Fell.

"But—!" Harriet was beginning, when Butler stopped her.

"The police surgeon, in fact, called attention to that wound which was so 'difficult to find.' The victim dies almost at once; and the edges of the wound compress. But in that case," argued Dr. Fell, "how did the late Mr. Hunt come to have so much blood on his sweater, and even splashed on his trousers?"

"Well?"

"He didn't," answered Dr. Fell simply. "Mr. Hunt's blood never got on his clothes at all."

"I can't stand this," said Harriet, jumping to her feet. "I—I'm sorry, but have you gone mad yourself? Are you telling us we didn't see him lying by that sideboard, with blood on him?"

"Oh, yes. You saw that."

"Let him go on," said Henderson, who was rather white round the nostrils. "Let him rave."

"It is, I admit, a fine point," said Dr. Fell. "But it answers your question, repeated to the point of nausea, as to why the eminently sensible Mr. Hunt chose to dress up in burglar's clothes and play burglar. The answer is short and simple. He didn't."

"It must be plain to everybody," Dr. Fell went

404

on, opening his eyes wide, "that Mr. Hunt was deliberately setting a trap for someone—the real burglar.

"He believed that a certain person might try to steal one or several of his pictures. He probably knew that this person had tried similar games before, in other country houses: that is, an inside job which was carefully planned to look like an outside job. So he made things easy for this thief, in order to trap him, with a police-officer in the house.

"The burglar, a sad fool, fell for it. This thief, a guest in the house, waited until well past two o'clock in the morning. He then put on his old clothes, mask, gloves, and the rest of it. He let himself out by the back door. He went through all the motions we have erroneously been attributing to Marcus Hunt. Then the trap snapped. Just as he was rolling up the Rembrandt, he heard a noise. He swung his light round. And he saw Marcus Hunt, in pyjamas and dressing-gown, looking at him.

"Yes, there was a fight. Hunt flew at him. The thief snatched up a fruit-knife and fought back. In that struggle, Marcus Hunt forced his opponent's hand back. The fruit-knife gashed the thief's chest, inflicting a superficial but badly bleeding gash. It sent the thief over the edge of insanity. He wrenched Marcus Hunt's wrist half off, caught up the knife, and stabbed Hunt to the heart.

"Then, in a quiet house, with a little beam of light streaming out from the torch on the sideboard, the murderer sees something that will hang him. He sees the blood from his own superficial wound seeping down his clothes.

"How is he to get rid of those clothes? He cannot destroy them, or get them away from the house. Inevitably the house will be searched, and they will be found. Without the blood-stains, they would seem ordinary clothes in his wardrobe. But with the blood-stains—

"There is only one thing he can do."

Harriet Davis was standing behind the wicker settee, shading her eyes against the glare of the sun. Her hand did not tremble when she said:

"He changed clothes with my uncle."

"That's it," growled Dr. Fell. "That's the whole sad story. The murderer dressed the body in his own clothes, making a puncture with the knife in sweater, shirt, and undervest. He then slipped on Mr. Hunt's pyjamas and dressing-gown, which at a pinch he could always claim as his own. Hunt's wound had bled hardly at all. His dressing-gown, I think, had come open in the fight; so that all the thief had to trouble him was a tiny puncture in the jacket of the pyjamas.

"But, once he had done this, he had to hypnotize you all into the belief that there would have been no time for a change of clothes. He had to make it seem that the fight occurred just *then*. He had to rouse the house. So he brought down echoing thunders by pushing over a pile of silver, and slipped upstairs."

Dr. Fell paused.

"The burglar could never have been Marcus Hunt, you know," he added. "We learn that

Hunt's fingerprints were all over the place. Yet the murdered man was wearing gloves."

There was a swishing of feet in the grass below the terrace, and a tread of heavy boots coming up the terrace steps. The local Inspector of police, buttoned up and steaming in his uniform, was followed by two constables.

Dr. Fell turned round a face of satisfaction.

"Ah!" he said, breathing deeply. "They've come to see about that swimming-party, I imagine. It is easy to patch up a flesh-wound with lint and cotton, or even a handkerchief. But such a wound will become infernally conspicuous in anyone who is forced to climb into bathing-trunks."

"But it couldn't have been—" cried Harriet. Her eyes moved round. Her fingers tightened on Lewis Butler's arm, an instinctive gesture which he was to remember long afterwards, when he knew her even better.

"Exactly," agreed the doctor, wheezing with pleasure. "It could not have been a long, thin, gangling fellow like Mr. Henderson. It assuredly could not have been a small and slender girl like yourself.

"There is only one person who, as we know, is just about Marcus Hunt's height and build; who could have put his own clothes on Hunt without any suspicion. That is the same person who, though he managed to staunch the wound in his chest, has been constantly running his hand inside the breast of his coat to make certain the bandage is secure. Just as Mr. Rolfe is doing now."

Arthur Rolfe sat very quiet, with his right hand still in the breast of his jacket. His face had grown

407

smeary in the hot sunlight, but the eyes behind those thin shells of glasses remained inscrutable. He spoke only once, through dry lips, after they had cautioned him.

"I should have taken the young pup's warning," he said. "After all, he told me I would take long chances."

Nicholas Blake
(1904–1972)
THE LONG SHOT

Irish-born Nicholas Blake (C. Day Lewis) once wrote, "Lenin, would you were living at this hour: England has need of you." How this dedicated champion of student radicalism became England's Poet Laureate and a standard-bearer of the English Country House Mystery tradition is one for the books—this book, for example.

The distinguished critic and writer H. R. F. Keating recalls Lewis late in his life saying that he liked the formal restrictions of poetry and detective stories. His hero, Nigel Strangeways, patterned after W. H. Auden, is Oxford-educated and aristocratic, but more finely drawn and cerebral than Wimsey or Albert Campion. Not surprisingly, a knowledge of literature and its history often figures in Blake's plots.

"His Lordship," announced Amphlett as he received me in the hall, "his lordship is in the rookery, sir."

He crooked a little finger at the maid. "Alice, Mr. Strangeways' baggage. We have put you in your old room, sir. I trust you will enjoy your visit."

Did I detect a faint, quite unprofessional lack

409

of conviction in the butler's tone? Why shouldn't I enjoy my visit? Any civilised person is bound to enjoy staying at a beautiful, perfectly run country house, where money is no object. Besides, Gervase was an old friend of mine, and I hadn't seen him for nearly two years.

"I think I'll go straight out, " I said.

"Very good, sir. His lordship has been anticipating your arrival with the keenest pleasure."

I noticed that Gervase had still not succeeded in training dear old Amphlett to disregard his title. Twenty years ago, as a young man, Gervase had had a sort of Tolstoyan conversion. The eldest son of the Earl of Wessex, he had decided to give up his title and be called by the family name, plain Mr. Musbury. Friends, neighbours, relations, servants—all had to toe the line. That was the time he started to run his estate on a co-operative basis.

His struggles to become poor had been singularly unsuccessful, however. His co-operative farming prospered; the fortune left him in securities by his American mother throve on his neglect of it. And if he lost any friends through discarding his title, it may be assumed that they were not worth keeping anyway.

As we walked over the lawn, Amphlett delicately mopped his brow. It was certainly a very hot day for April. The cawing of rooks in the elm trees we were approaching sounded cool as a waterfall. I quite envied Gervase up there; but I didn't much fancy climbing the rope ladder to reach him.

Looking up, I descried a small object, which

presently resolved itself into a ginger-beer bottle on a string descending erratically from the top of the nearest elm.

A young footman silently received it, took a fresh bottle from a silver tray, tied the string round its neck, and gave a signal to haul away. The bottle was drawn up again into the heights, toward a narrow, well-camouflaged platform laid across two of the topmost branches.

"You've got a new footman, I see. A nice-looking young chap."

"Henry gives satisfaction, sir, " said Amphlett gloomily, and not—I thought—with entire conviction.

"Been with you long?" I asked.

"Some eight months, sir."

Henry had held his job, under the exacting Amphlett, for eight months. Well, perhaps I was wrong. Perhaps he did give satisfaction.

"His lordship finds it very hot up there," remarked Amphlett.

I perceive that the reader may be feeling a certain resistance to my narrative. Either this friend of yours was a lunatic, he is saying, or else you're making the whole thing up. That is because he did not know Gervase Musbury.

Gervase was an eccentric who could afford to give his eccentricities a blank cheque and knew how to run them at a profit. Eccentricity, as I see it, is nothing more than the visible track of the libido taking a short cut to the desired object. When Amphlett told me his master was in the rookery, knowing Gervase I never doubted but that he was there for some rational purpose.

411

Equally when I saw the bottle travelling up to that eyrie in the elm top, I accepted it as something quite natural; it was much simpler for Gervase to haul up his ginger-beer than for the footman to scale the rope ladder every time his master wanted a drink.

The ladder began to wriggle. Gervase had seen me and was climbing down—with great agility for a man approaching fifty. He jumped the last six feet, put his hands eagerly on my shoulders, and said, "You've not changed, Nigel."

Nor had he. The piercing blue eyes, the moustache cut like a thicker version of Adolphe Menjou's and appearing to bristle with electricity, the infectious manner of the enthusiast—Gervase was just the same.

"You'd better stay here, Henry," he said to the footman. "I'll be back presently." Then to me, "Henry gives me my bottles at regular intervals. Like a baby."

His blue eyes grew abstracted. "Let me see, Amphlett: who have we staying in the house? I am rather out of touch."

"Your brother and his wife, sir. Mr. Prew. And Miss Camelot."

"Ah, just so." He took my arm. "Better come and meet them. Get it over. Then we can spend the rest of the afternoon watching the rooks. Absorbing, I assure you. I built a nice little hide up there before the nesting season. Fit you in easily."

"No, Gervase, " I said firmly. "There is not room for two on that appalling little platform. And I am not madly interested in the habits of rooks. Since when have you taken up bird-watching?"

412

"Just a relaxation, dear boy, that's all. I got a bit stale this winter, working on a new explosive. MacMaster called me in. Working against time— that's the trouble. We shall have war in two years. Or sooner."

We emerged from the shadow of the elm trees, to be greeted by a small, stoutish man, whose photograph I had seen often enough in the papers. It was Thomas Prew, M.P., a notable defender of lost causes. If Gervase was right, the hardest-fought cause of Prew's life was now as good as lost too, for he was an out-and-out pacifist, who had gone to prison for his convictions in the last war and cried them up and down the country ever since.

I was surprised to find the pacifist Member of Parliament here, and when we left Prew I asked Gervase about it.

"Oh, Tom Prew's an honest man," he said. "Besides, he's an education for my brother. You know what an old war-monger Hector is. He and Tom had quite an argument at dinner the other night. Tom won on a technical knockout. Hector and Diana have barely been on speaking terms with him since. Let's go and find them."

We found them at last in the garage yard, up to the elbows in the engine of their Bentley. I had almost forgotten what a magnificent couple they made. Tall, handsome, golden-haired—there was something leonine about them, both in their restlessness and repose. Hector had all his elder brother's superabundance of energy, but lacked Gervase's many outlets for it: war might well prove his release and *métier*.

Diana I admired without liking; she was too ambitious, too overpowering for my taste. Besides, she was wrapped up in her husband. They gave one, more than any other couple I ever met, the impression of being a team, of physical and mental co-ordination. I felt it again now, watching them as they worked in a sort of telepathic unison over the engine of the car in which they tore restlessly over the face of Europe.

My sensation was obviously shared by the beautiful Miss Anthea Camelot, who had been standing by with an odd-man-out expression on her face. She turned to Gervase with relief—and something more than relief, I fancied. Poor girl, I thought: if you were Circe and Sheba rolled into one, your enchantments would break against Gervase; the name written on his heart is burned too deep for any other woman to erase it.

Though ten years younger than Gervase, I had been for a long time his confidant. I was one of the very few people outside his own family who knew about the tragedy of Rose Borthwick. She had been the daughter of one of his father's tenant farmers. Gervase, in his youth, had fallen passionately in love with her. His father, knowing that Gervase was determined to marry the girl, had managed to have her sent away out of his reach.

There were terrible scenes and a final estrangement between Gervase and his father. Gervase had nearly gone off his head, trying to find Rose again. But all his searches were in vain.

I was still thinking of this sad business a quarter

of an hour later, as we were all at sea on the lawn. Presently the conversation turned to Hitler.

"We should have called his bluff long ago," said Hector Musbury. "If our politicians hadn't all got cold feet—"

"Your politicians have a responsibility, too," said Thomas Prew, in the beautiful deep voice that contrasted so strangely with his dumpy, rather insignificant figure. "Look at that young man"— he pointed toward Henry, who was standing a little distance away, in the shadow of the elm trees. "Multiply him by several millions. Imagine those millions torn, maimed, rotting in the earth . . . Can you wonder if the politicians have cold feet?"

A shade of anger came over Hector's face. "That's just sentimental special-pleading. The alternatives are possible death or certain slavery for us. Evidently some of you people prefer the idea of being slaves."

Diana flicked a warning glance at him, I noticed. Anthea Camelot broke in, "But Mr. Prew wasn't talking about the politicians. He was talking about the people who'd have to be killed. About Henry. Let's see what *he* thinks. Henry!" she called.

The young footman came a few paces forward. There was a piquant blend of respectfulness and irony on his face.

"Henry, would you rather be killed by the Germans or enslaved by them?"

Henry took his time, gazing levelly at us all. "If it comes to that, Miss Camelot," he said at last, "many might think I'm a slave already."

I saw Amphlett flinch. Even for Gervase's

415

equalitarian *ménage*, this was a bit too much. No wonder the old butler had been unconvincing about Henry's giving satisfaction. Diana evidently felt the same.

"Your servants, Gervase," she exclaimed, "seem to enjoy a perpetual Saturnalia."

"You mustn't be hard on Henry," said Anthea Camelot. "After all, he's spent most of the day standing at attention over a tray of ginger-beer bottles. If that isn't slavery, my name is Pharaoh."

I was sitting very near Gervase, and got the feeling that the words he now murmured were for my ears alone. "Youth must have its tests, its ordeals," I heard.

Diana broke in, "Oh, dear, I've left my handkerchief indoors. Henry"—she was the kind of woman who gives orders to servants without bothering to look at them—"fetch the handkerchief from my dressing table."

"My orders are to stay here, madam."

I was afraid there would be an explosion. Gervase evidently intended to give no help: he was glancing quizzically from Diana to the young footman. But Hector was already on his feet, moving toward the house, as though his wife's wish had been communicated to him before she uttered it.

"I'll fetch it," he said.

After tea, Gervase retired up his elm tree again. Hector and Diana set up a target on the lawn and tried to lure the rest of us into archery. But Anthea, well aware no doubt that this particular sport would set off her charms to less advantage than Diana's, indicated that she would not object to my walking her round the rose garden.

416

As we strolled off, in the wake of Amphlett and Henry who were bearing the tea-things back to the house, we noticed Hector and Diana fastening upon a not-too-obviously-enthusiastic Mr. Prew and beginning to instruct him in the art of drawing a six-foot bow.

"The thin end of the wedge," remarked Anthea. "Start off the wee pacifist on a bow and arrow, and he'll soon be romping round with a loaded Tommy gun."

Gervase's rose garden is a charming enough place even when there are no roses out, with its neat grass walks, its fountains and statues, and the box-hedges yielding their fragrance to the sun. Anthea and I sat down on deck chairs, prepared to enjoy each other's company. At least, I was. But it soon became clear that she had brought me here for a purpose.

"You *are* a detective of sorts, aren't you?" she said.

"Of sorts. Why?"

Her eyes followed an early butterfly for a moment. "Oh, everything seems so queer here this time."

"Such as?"

"Well, little Prew wandering about like a lost soul, and Hector quarreling with him, and Diana nagging at Gervase about that new footman, and Gervase sitting up a tree ignoring us all."

And ignoring you in particular, I thought. I said, "It's odd, no doubt. But this always was an odd household."

"Gervase does treat young Henry in an extraordinary way, though, don't you think? Spoiling

417

him half the time, and tyrannising over him the rest. He's hardly let him out of his sight this afternoon, for instance."

"Perhaps it's Henry who's guarding Gervase," I said idly.

"Guarding him!" Anthea gave me a look from her warm, dark eyes. "You'd not say that if— Listen. The other night I came down late to get a book out of the library, and I heard Gervase telling somebody off in the study next door. He was shouting, 'You'll not get any more of my money! I've a better use for it now.'"

"That is interesting. You don't know who he was talking to?"

"No. But any fool could make a good guess. There's only one person in this household who fits the role of blackmailer."

"You're judging Henry on rather flimsy evidence. Why, it might have been Hector. Hasn't Hector been sponging on Gervase most of his life?"

Anthea rose impatiently. I had not taken her seriously enough. Or so she thought. We strolled back to the lawn, where the archers were still at it. Diana made a fine goddess, standing bright-haired with the bow at full stretch. Hector was near her, his hands in the pockets of his tweed jacket. Thomas Prew looked an uninspiring figure beside them.

Diana's arrow flew into the gold. Then she turned to us, her face flushed and excited.

"Now I'll shoot the golden arrow. We used to do it when we were children. Watch, everyone! Henry, you must watch too!"

She made the footman come a little way out from the elm tree and join us on the lawn. Everyone must see her triumph.

She took an ordinary arrow from her quiver and fitted it to the bowstring. "It'll turn to gold in the sky," she said.

Her body bent gracefully back, and she shot straight upward. The dark arrow soared, almost invisible in its speed. The sun had gone down behind the low hill to our west; but, higher up, its rays were still streaming laterally from over the hilltop, so that the arrow was suddenly caught in them, flashed golden, and pursued its course for a little, shining like a gold thread against the sky's deepening blue.

For us, it was a strangely fascinating sight, a moment of pure innocence. Like children, we all wanted to do it. But the lower the sun sank behind the hill, the higher we had to shoot.

After a quarter of an hour only Hector and Diana could get an arrow up into the golden stream. Then Diana failed. Then Hector made a last effort. His arrow just turned gold before it began to wobble, slowly reversed, and streaked down toward the elms just behind us.

We heard it strike a branch, and fall clattering from branch to branch. The sound of its falling grew and grew, was hideously amplified, as if in a nightmare the arrow had turned into a human body hurtling down.

A few seconds later, the body of Gervase Musbury crashed to the ground, only half a dozen yards from where we stood.

It seemed, for a moment, to put into words what

419

we were all thinking, when Anthea Camelot cried out bitterly to Hector, who was standing there, the bow still in his hand, looking stupid and frightened like a child who has broken some treasured ornament. "You've shot him!"

Diana said, in a brisk, motherly sort of voice, "Don't let's get hysterical. Of course Hector couldn't have shot him."

Thomas Prew was staring at the body, an expression of white horror on his face, his mouth moving soundlessly. It must have been some shock in childhood, some spectacle like this of blood and shattered bone, which created the pacifist in him.

Henry was kneeling beside the body, making as if to lift Gervase's head on to his lap. Then he said, dully, "I think his neck's broken."

"I kept telling him that platform wasn't safe," said Anthea, staring up into the treetops. The rooks, which had risen out of them in hundreds, cawing and crawking when the body fell, were beginning to return.

I stepped forward and put my hand on Henry's shoulder. I could feel it trembling. We gazed down at the wreck of Gervase. His face was a queer bluish-pink colour. My heart missed a beat. This was too much; it was grotesque and impossible.

I bent and sniffed at his lips. Then I found, a few yards away on the grass, an object whose fall had been disregarded in the tragic moment—the shattered fragments of a ginger-beer bottle. I picked one of them up. The same scent of peach blossom clung to it as I had smelled on Gervase's lips.

I turned angrily to the cluster of people. "The arrow may have struck him," I said, "and his neck is certainly broken. But what killed him was poison—prussic acid—conveyed to him through that ginger-beer bottle."

An hour later we were all together again, sitting round the table in the dining room. The village constable had taken statements, and was now on guard over the body. A superintendent, police surgeon, and the rest of it were on their way from the county town. In the meanwhile, I had made use of Gervase's keys and had the run of his study, where I had found out one or two interesting things.

I looked round the group at the table. Anthea was crying quietly. Thomas Prew's face remained white, dazed, incredulous. Hector, for some reason, was still holding an arrow and the bow, as though it had frozen to his fingers. Only Diana appeared relatively normal.

"I thought we might clear up a few things before the Westchester police come," I said. "Suicide seems to be out of the question. Gervase had no motive for it, he wasn't that kind of person, and there's no farewell message. So I'm afraid he was murdered."

The four of them stirred, almost as if in relief at knowing the worst. "Somehow the poison was introduced into that bottle," I continued flatly. "Gervase hauled it up, drank it in the ginger-beer—prussic acid works very quickly—and was overcome just at the moment when Hector happened to send up his last arrow, and toppled off the platform."

"But how could the poison—?" began Anthea.

"I've been talking to Amphlett. The ginger-beer is kept in the cellar. Only he and Gervase had keys to the cellar. Gervase's key was on the ring in his pocket. So it's unlikely that anyone but he or Amphlett could have tampered with one of the bottles while they were still in the cellar. Amphlett opened the cellar after lunch, gave half a dozen bottles to Henry, who carried them out on a tray, and locked the cellar door again immediately."

"But Henry was out there beside the tray the whole afternoon," said Mr. Prew.

"Yes. The odd thing is that he admits it. Almost like a sentry on guard, swearing he never left his post. He swears no one could have got at the bottles, except during the couple of minutes after tea when he and Amphlett were carrying the tea-things back to the house."

"Well," said Anthea, "you and I were walking over to the rose garden just then, so we can give each other alibis."

"I suppose Mr. Prew, Hector, and I can do the same," said Diana, in a tone of some distaste, as though giving people an alibi was a vulgar and disgusting thing, like giving them ringworm.

"In that case, no one but Henry or Amphlett could have put the poison into the bottle," said Mr. Prew.

"So it would seem. Logically."

"But Amphlett was devoted to Gervase," said Hector after a pause. "And Henry wouldn't do it.

I mean, he wouldn't murder his own father, would he?"

Anthea gave a gasp of astonishment. It was no surprise to me. I had found a will in Gervase's desk, leaving the bulk of his fortune to Henry Borthwick. There could be little doubt that Henry was Gervase's long-lost child by the love of his youth, Rose Borthwick.

The relationship explained his peculiar treatment of the young man. I remembered him murmuring to me, "Youth must have its tests, its ordeals." There was always method in Gervase's eccentricity. It was quite in character for him to have tested the young man, like the hero in a fairy tale, given him a period of probation, imposing on him the menial duties of a servant.

"So it *was* Henry who was trying to blackmail Gervase," exclaimed Anthea. She told the others what she had heard that night in the library.

"But why," I asked, "should he blackmail Gervase, when Gervase had left him most of his fortune in a will?"

"Is this true?" demanded Diana.

I nodded.

Hector said, "The question about blackmail doesn't seem important now. The point is, Henry *had* a motive for *killing* Gervase. If he knew that Gervase had made a will in his favour, that is."

"We'd better ask him." Before anyone had time to object, I sent Amphlett to fetch Henry. When the young man came in, I asked him, "Did you know Gervase was your father, and was leaving you his fortune?"

"Oh, yes," said Henry, gazing defiantly at us all. "But if you think I murdered him, you're—"

"What else can you expect us to think?"

"I expect you to credit me with some brains. If I'd wanted to kill my father, d'you suppose I'd be fool enough to do it by putting poison in a bottle which points to me as the most likely suspect?"

"There's something in what he says," remarked Mr. Prew. "But who else could have had a motive for—"

"There's yourself for one," I interrupted. "You're a militant pacifist. You heard that Gervase was on the way to perfecting a new explosive. Maybe you wanted to spare humanity the horror of it."

"Oh, but that's fantastic!"

"Then there's Diana and Hector. Diana is an ambitious woman, with a not very rich husband and a very rich brother-in-law. Dispose of the latter, and she'd have the means to gratify all her ambitions—at least, she would as soon as Hector's father dies, and he's a very old man now."

"I think perhaps you had better leave these matters to the police," began Diana icily.

I paid no attention to her. "What Anthea heard in the library that night is significant. It fits the theory that it was Hector, not Henry, who was demanding money from Gervase. Gervase said, 'You'll not get any more of my money! I've a better use for it now.' A better use for it *now*, because he had found his son, Henry. No doubt Hector then asked him what he meant by the last phrase, and was told that Gervase proposed to leave his money to his son."

"In that case, Nigel, you silly ass, what would be the point of my killing Gervase?" Hector was blushing, yet triumphant, like a boy making a decisive point in a school debate.

"None. Unless you did it in such a way as to incriminate Henry. He would be hanged for your crime, and Gervase's fortune in due course would pass to you. And, I must say, if Henry didn't commit the murder, someone took great pains to make it look as if he did. Why—"

We all started, as Anthea burst out hysterically, "Oh, for God's sake stop this! I loved Gervase. Why not say I did it, because—because he wouldn't look at me? Hell hath no fury—"

"Be quiet, Anthea!" I commanded. "I'm not finished with Hector and Diana yet. You see, two rather peculiar things happened which the police may well ask them to explain."

"Well?" asked Diana indifferently; but I could see her curiosity was aroused.

"It was peculiar that you two, who—Gervase told me—were hardly on speaking terms with Mr. Prew, should suddenly become so chummy with him after tea and insist on showing him how to shoot with the bow. But not peculiar if you wanted him to give you an alibi for just then—the only few minutes in the afternoon when Henry wasn't standing by the ginger-beer bottles. Not peculiar if it was absolutely vital for both of you to be able to prove you didn't go near them."

"But, my dear good Nigel, you've admitted, only a few minutes ago, that no one but Henry or Amphlett could have tampered with that bottle. Why pick on us?" said Hector.

425

"I said that logically it seemed so. But Diana did another funny thing. She became matey also with Henry—Henry, whom she'd been treating like dirt up to that point."

Mr. Prew and Anthea had grown tense. They were staring at me as if I was the Apocalypse.

"Yes," I went on, "when she was getting ready to shoot the golden arrow, for the first time, Diana called out to Henry to come and watch. Terribly out of character that was, Diana. But suppose you had to get him away from under the elm trees, get him looking up in the sky like the rest of us, following the course of your arrow, for the seven or eight seconds Hector would need to move the few yards to that silver tray under the elms and substitute a poisoned bottle of ginger-beer for the one that stood there? Hector," I went on quickly, "where's that handkerchief you fetched for Diana during tea? You never gave it to her, did you?"

Hector was angry now, but he gave me a queer smile of triumph, reached in the poacher's pocket of his tweed coat, and took a handkerchief out of it.

"I see what you're driving at, old boy. The idea is that I really went indoors to fetch a bottle of poisoned ginger-beer? Well, I didn't. I just brought the handkerchief. So now," he advanced on me menacingly, "you'll kindly apologise to my wife for—"

I snatched the handkerchief from him and put it cautiously to my nose.

"As I thought. Since when did you start using a perfume of peach blossom, Diana?" I was round the other side of the table from them now. "You

426

fetched both the handkerchief *and* the poisoned bottle, Hector. In that nice big poacher's pocket. The handkerchief was needed to keep your finger-prints off the bottle, no doubt. It was unlucky for you that some of the poisoned ginger-beer leaked out onto it."

Hector and Diana were certainly a good team. I had hardly finished speaking when they were at the door, Hector threatening us with the arrow he had notched on his bowstring.

"If any of you calls out, he gets this arrow in him. Diana, fetch the car."

Diana was out of the door like a flash. Prew, Anthea, and old Amphlett were staring at Hector, dazed out of all movement. I felt like one of the suitors in the banqueting hall when Odysseus turned his great bow on them. Then I heard a scurry of movement behind me.

Henry had snatched up one of the huge, heavy silver dish-covers from the sideboard and, shielding his face and breast with it, was running head-long at Hector. The bow twanged deeply. The arrow clanged against the edge of the dish-cover, ricocheted off, and stuck quivering in the far wall.

Henry's charge brought Hector down. He half killed Hector before we could pull him off. He would have been a good son to Gervase, if Gervase had lived.

I had loved Gervase too. If I hadn't, I don't think I should have played that trick on Hector.

The perfume on the handkerchief I snatched from him was not peach blossom, not the lethal fragrance of prussic acid at all. The handkerchief smelled of nothing more dangerous than fresh linen, though he *had* used it to hold the poisoned bottle.

Yes, it was a very long shot on my part—as long a shot in its way, as that last one of Hector's which had just caught the golden gleam, and then fallen into the treetops where Gervase died.

P. G. Wodehouse
(1881–1975)
JEEVES AND THE
STOLEN VENUS

Variant: *The English Country House Mystery as humor*

The Allingham story was a humorous English Country House Mystery. "Jeeves and the Stolen Venus" is the English Country House Mystery as pure humor. Sir P. G. (Pelham Grenville) Wodehouse, who created Jeeves, the most famous of all gentlemen's gentlemen, was a fancier of the detective story, reading up to 150 a year in later life. On the occasion of the hundredth anniversary of the birth of Conan Doyle he contributed a hilarious send-up of the Great Detective to Punch.

Here, in the Grand Tradition, Aunt Dahlia leads Bertie Wooster and the ever-capable Jeeves into a life of crime. For those of you with a desire to read more of this sort of thing, there is a lively collection of Jeevesiana in Wodehouse on Crime *(New York: Ticknor and Fields, 1981), from which this account was not taken.*

The telephone rang, and I heard Jeeves out in the hall dealing with it. Presently he trickled in.

429

"Mrs. Travers, sir."

"Aunt Dahlia? What does she want?"

"She did not confide in me, sir."

A bit oddish, it seems to me, looking back on it now, that as I went to the instrument I should have had no premonition, if that's the word I want, of an impending doom. Not psychic, that's my trouble.

"Hullo, old blood relation."

"Hullo, Bertie, you revolting young blot," she responded in her hearty way. "Are you sober?"

"As a judge."

"Then listen attentively. I'm speaking from an undersized hamlet in Hampshire called Marsham-in-the-Vale. I'm staying at Marsham Manor with Cornelia Fothergill, the novelist. Ever heard of her?"

"She is not on my library list."

"She would be, if you were a woman. I'm trying to persuade her to let me have her new novel as a serial for the *Boudoir*."

I got the gist. This aunt is the proprietor or proprietress of a weekly paper for the half-witted woman called *Milady's Boudoir*.

"How's it coming?" I asked.

"She's weakening. I have the feeling that one more shove will do the trick. That's why you're coming here for the week-end."

"Who, me? Why me?"

"To help me sway her. You will exercise all your charm—"

"I haven't much."

"Well, exercise what you've got."

I'm not keen on these blind dates. And if life

has taught me one thing, it is that the prudent man keeps away from female novelists.

"Will anyone else be there? Is there any bright young society, I mean?"

"I wouldn't call the society young, but it's very bright. There's Cornelia's husband, Everard Fothergill, the artist, and his father, Edward Fothergill. He's an artist, too, of a sort. You won't have a dull moment. So tell Jeeves to pack your effects."

It surprises many people, I believe, that Bertram Wooster, as a general rule a man of iron, is as wax in the hands of his Aunt Dahlia. They do not know that this woman possesses a secret weapon by which she can always bend me to her will—viz., the threat that if I give her any of my lip she will bar me from her dinner table and deprive me of the roasts and boilers of her French chef, Anatole, God's gift to the gastric juices.

And so it came about that towards the quiet evenfall of Friday the 22nd inst. I was at the wheel of the old sports model, tooling through Hants with Jeeves at my side, the brow furrowed and the spirits low.

Arrival at Marsham Manor did little to smooth the former and raise the latter. Shown into the hall, I found myself in as cozy an interior as one could wish to find—large log fire, comfortable chairs, and a tea-table that gave out an invigorating aroma of buttered toast and muffins. But a single glance at the personnel was enough to tell me that I had struck one of those joints where every prospect pleases and only man is vile.

Three human souls were present, each as out-

431

standing a piece of cheese as Hampshire could provide. One was a small, thin citizen with a beard of the type that causes so much distress—my host, I presumed—and seated near him another bloke of much the same construction but an earlier model, whom I took to be the father. He, too, was bearded. The third was a large, spreading woman wearing the horn-rimmed spectacles which are always an occupational risk for pen-pushers of the gentler sex.

After a brief pause for identification, she introduced me to the gang, and presently Aunt Dahlia blew in, and we chatted of this and that. The Fothergill contingent pushed off, and I was heading in the same direction when Aunt Dahlia arrested my progress.

"Just a second, Bertie," she said. "I would like to show you something."

"And I," I riposted, "would like to know what this job is you say you want me to do for you."

"I'll be coming to that shortly. This thing I'm going to show you is tied in with it. But first a word from our sponsor. Did you notice how jumpy Edward Fothergill is?"

"No. I didn't spot that. Is he jumpy?"

"He's a nervous wreck. Ask me why."

"Why?"

"Because of this picture I'm going to show you. Step this way."

She led me into the dining-room and switched on the light.

"Look," she said.

What she was drawing to my attention was a large oil painting. A classical picture, I suppose

432

you would have called it: stout female in the minimum of clothing in conference with what appeared to be a dove.

"Venus?" I said. It's usually a safe bet.

"Yes. Old Fothergill painted it. He's just the sort of man who would paint a picture of Ladies' Night in a Turkish Bath and call it Venus. He gave it to Everard as a wedding present."

"I like the patine," I said. Another safe bet.

"No, you don't. The thing's a mess. The old boy's just an incompetent amateur. I got the whole strength of it from Cornelia one night. As I say, he gave this eyesore to Everard as a wedding present, and naturally, being devoted to his father and not wanting to hurt his feelings, Everard can't have it taken down and put in the cellar. So he has to sit looking at it every time he has a meal, and he suffers profusely. You see, Everard's a real artist. His stuff's good. Look at this," she said, indicating the picture next to old Fothergill's. "That's one of his things."

I took a steady look at Everard's effort. It, too, was a classical picture, and it seemed to me very like the other one.

"Venus?"

"Don't be an ass. Jocund Spring."

"Oh, sorry. Though, mark you, Sherlock Holmes would have made the same mistake. On the evidence, I mean."

"So now you understand."

"Far from it."

"I'll put it in words of one syllable. If a man can paint anything as good as that, it cuts him to

433

the quick to have to glue his eyes on a daub like the Venus every time he puts on the nosebag."

"Oh, I see that, and the heart bleeds, of course. But I don't see there's anything to be done."

"I do. Ask me what."

"What?"

"You're going to steal that Venus."

"Steal it?"

"Tonight."

"When you say, 'steal it,' do you mean '*steal* it'?"

"That's right. That's the job I alluded to. Good heavens," she said, "you're always stealing policemen's helmets, aren't you?"

I had to correct this.

"Not always. Only as an occasional treat, as it might be on Boat Race night. And stealing pictures is a very different thing from lifting the headgear of the Force."

"There's nothing complex about it. You just cut it out of the frame with a sharp knife. You know, Bertie," she said, all enthusiasm, "it's extraordinary how things fit in. These last weeks there's been a gang of picture thieves working around this neighborhood. They pinched a Romney at a house near here and a Gainsborough from another house. When his Venus disappears, there won't be a chance of old Fothergill suspecting anything. These marauders are connoisseurs, he'll say to himself, only the best is good enough for them. Cornelia agreed with me."

"You told her?"

"Well, naturally. I was naming the Price of the Papers. I said that if she gave me her solemn word that she would let the *Boudoir* have this slush she's writing, shaving her usual price a bit, you would liquidate the Venus."

"You did, did you? And what did she say?"

"She thanked me brokenly, so go to it, boy, and heaven speed your efforts. All you have to do is open one of the windows, to make it look like an outside job, collect the picture, take it back to your room, and burn it. I'll see you have a good fire."

"Oh, thanks."

It was with bowed head and the feeling that the curse had come upon me that I proceeded to my room. Jeeves was there, studding the shirt, and I lost no time in putting him *au courant*, if that's the expression.

"Jeeves," I said, "here's a nice state of things. Do you know what Aunt Dahlia has just been springing on me?"

"Yes, sir. I chanced to be passing the door of the dining-room, and could not but overhear her observations. Mrs. Travers has a carrying voice."

"I suppose I'll have to do it, Jeeves."

"I fear so, sir. Taking into consideration the probability that, should you demur, Mrs. Travers will place sanctions on you in the matter of Anatole's cooking, you would appear to have no option but to fall in with her wishes. Are you in pain, sir?"

"No, just chafing. This has shocked me, Jeeves. Forcing a Wooster to become a picture-pincher! I wouldn't have thought such an idea would ever have occurred to her, would you?"

"The female of the species is more deadly than

435

the male, sir. May I ask if you have formulated a plan of action?"

"Well, you heard the set-up as she envisages it. I open the window—"

"Pardon me for interrupting, sir, but there I think Mrs. Travers is in error. A broken window would lend greater verisimilitude."

"It would also bring the whole ruddy household starting from their slumbers and coming to see what was going on."

"No, sir, it can be done quite noiselessly by smearing treacle on a sheet of brown paper, attaching the paper to the pane, and striking it with the fist."

"But where's the brown paper? Where's the treacle?"

"I can procure them, sir, and I shall be happy to perform the operation for you, if you wish."

"You will? That's very decent of you, Jeeves."

"Not at all, sir. It is my aim to give satisfaction. Excuse me, I think I hear someone knocking."

He went to the door and opened it, and I caught a glimpse of what looked like a butler.

"Your knife, sir," he said, coming back with it on a salver.

"Thank you, Jeeves, curse it." I regarded the object with a shudder. "I wish I could slide out of this binge."

"I can readily imagine it, sir."

After some deliberation we scheduled the kick-off for one o'clock in the morning, when the household might be expected to be getting their eight hours, and at one on the dot Jeeves shimmered in.

"Everything is in readiness, sir."

"The treacle?"

"Yes, sir."

"The brown paper?"

"Yes, sir."

"Then just bust the window, would you mind?"

"I have already done so, sir."

"You have? Well, you were right about it being noiseless. I didn't hear a sound. Then, Ho for the dining-room, I suppose. No sense in putting it off."

"No, sir. If it were done when 'tis done, then 'twere well it were done quickly," he said.

It would be idle to pretend that, as I made my way down the stairs, I was my usual calm, debonair self. The feet were cold, and if there had been any sudden noises I would have started at them. My meditations on Aunt Dahlia, who had let me in for this, were rather markedly lacking in a nephew's love.

However, in one respect you had to hand it to her. She had said the thing would be as easy as falling off a log, and so it proved. She had in no way overestimated the sharpness of the knife with which she provided me. Four quick cuts, and the canvas fell out of the frame. I rolled it up and streaked back to my room with it.

Jeeves in my absence had been stoking the fire. I was about to feed Edward Fothergill's regrettable product to the flames and push it home with the poker, but he stopped me.

"It would be injudicious to burn so large an object in one piece, sir. There is the risk of setting the chimney on fire."

437

"Ah, yes. I see what you mean. Snip it up, you think?"

"I fear it is unavoidable, sir. Might I suggest that it would relieve the monotony of the task if I were to provide you with whiskey and a syphon?"

"You know where they keep it?"

"Yes, sir."

"Then lead it to me, Jeeves."

"Very good, sir."

I was making good progress when the door opened without my hearing it and Aunt Dahlia stole in. She spoke before I knew she was there, causing me to shoot up to the ceiling with a stifled cry.

"Everything all right, Bertie?"

"I wish you'd blow your horn," I said, coming back to earth and speaking with not a little bitterness. "You made me bite my tongue. Yes, everything has gone according to plan. But Jeeves insists on burning the *corpus delicti* bit by bit."

"Well, of course. You don't want to set the chimney on fire."

"That's what he said."

"And he was right, as always. I've brought my scissors. Where is Jeeves, by the way? Why not at your side, giving selfless service?"

"Because he's giving selfless service elsewhere. He will be returning shortly with the whiskey decanter and all the trimmings."

"What a man! There is none like him, none. Bless my soul," said the relative, some minutes later, "how this brings back memories of the dear old school and our girlish cocoa parties. We used

438

to sneak down to the headmistress's study and toast whole wheat bread on the end of pens, with the kettle simmering on the hob. Happy days, happy days. Ah, Jeeves, come right in and put it down well within my reach. We're getting on, you see. What is that you have on your arm?"

"The garden shears, madam. I am anxious to lend all the assistance that is within my power."

"Then start lending. Edward Fothergill's masterpiece awaits you."

With the three of us working away, we soon completed the job. I had scarcely got through my first whiskey and s. and begun on another when all that was left of the Venus, not counting the ashes, was the little bit at the southwest end which Jeeves was holding. He was regarding it with what seemed to me a rather thoughtful eye.

"Excuse me, madam," he said, "did I understand you to say that Mr. Fothergill senior's name was Edward?"

"That's right. Think of him as Eddie, if you wish. Why?"

"It is merely that the picture we have with us tonight is signed 'Everard Fothergill,' madam."

To say that aunt and nephew did not take this big would be paltering with the truth. We skipped like the high hills.

"Give me that fragment, Jeeves. It looks like Edward to me," I pronounced, having scrutinized it.

"You're crazy," said Aunt Dahlia, wrenching it from my grasp. "It's Everard, isn't it, Jeeves?"

"That was certainly the impression I formed, madam."

439

"Bertie," said Aunt Dahlia, speaking in a voice of the kind which I believe is usually called strangled, and directing at me the sort of look which in the old hunting days she would have given a hound engaged in chasing a rabbit, "if you've burned the wrong picture—"

"Of course I haven't," I replied stoutly. "But if it will ease your mind, I'll go and see."

I had spoken, as I say, stoutly, and hearing me you would have said to yourself, "All is well with Bertram. He is unperturbed." But I wasn't. I feared the worst, and already I was wincing at the thought of the impassioned speech, touching on my mental and moral defects, which Aunt Dahlia would be delivering when we foregathered once more.

I was in no vein for another shock, but I got this when I reached journey's end, for as I entered the dining-room somebody inside it came bounding out and rammed me between wind and water. We staggered into the hall together, and as I switched on the lights there, to avoid bumping into pieces of furniture, I was enabled to see him steadily and see him whole, as Jeeves says.

It was old Fothergill, in bedroom slippers and a dressing-gown. In his right hand he had a knife, and at his feet there was a bundle of some sort which he had dropped at the moment of impact, and when I picked it up for him in my courteous way and it came unrolled, what I saw brought a startled "Golly!" to my lips. It dead-heated with a yip of anguish from his. He had paled beneath his beard.

"Mr. Wooster!" he—quavered is, I think, the word. "Thank God you are not Everard!"

Well, I was pretty pleased about that, too, of course.

"No doubt," he proceeded, still quavering, "you are surprised to find me removing my picture by stealth in this way. But I can explain everything."

"Well, that's fine, isn't it?"

"You are not an artist—"

"No, more a literary man. I once wrote an article on What the Well-Dressed Man Is Wearing for *Milady's Boudoir*."

"Nevertheless, I think I can make you understand what this picture means to me. I was two years painting it. It was my child. I watched it grow. I loved it. And then Everard married, and in a mad moment I gave it to him as a wedding present. You cannot imagine what agonies I suffered. I saw how he valued the picture. His eyes at meal times were always riveted on it. I could not bring myself to ask him for it back. And yet I was lost without it."

"So you decided to pinch it?"

"Exactly. I told myself that Everard would never suspect. There have been picture robberies in the neighborhood recently, and he would assume that this was the work of the same gang. And I yielded to temptation. Mr. Wooster, you would not betray me?"

"I wouldn't what?"

"You will not tell Everard?"

"Oh, I see what you mean. No, of course not, if you don't want me to. Sealed lips, you suggest?"

"Precisely."

"Right ho."

"Thank you, thank you. I knew you would not fail me. Well, one might as well be turning in, I suppose, so I will say good night," he said, and having done so, shot up the stairs like a homing rabbit. And scarcely had he disappeared when I found Aunt Dahlia and Jeeves at my side.

"Oh, there you are," I said.

"Yes, here we are. What's kept you all this time?"

"I would have made it snappier, but I was somewhat impeded in my movements by bearded artists."

"By what?"

"I've been chatting with Edward Fothergill."

"Bertie, you're blotto."

"Not blotto, but much shaken. Aunt Dahlia, I have an amazing story to relate."

I related my amazing story.

"And so," I concluded, "we learn once again the lesson never, however dark the outlook, to despair. The storm clouds lowered, the skies were black, but now what do we see? The sun shining and the bluebird working at the old stand. La Fothergill wanted the Venus expunged, and it has been expunged. Voilà!" I said, becoming a bit Parisian.

"And when she finds that Everard's Jocund Spring has also been expunged?"

I h'med. I saw what she had in mind.

"Yes, there's that," I agreed.

"There isn't a chance now that she'll give me that serial."

442

"No, you have a point there. I had overlooked that."

She inflated her lungs, and it could have been perceived by the dullest eye that she was about to begin.

"Bertie—"

Jeeves coughed that soft cough of his, the one that sounds like a sheep clearing its throat on a distant mountainside.

"I wonder if I might make a suggestion, madam?"

"Yes, Jeeves? Remind me," she said, turning to me, "to go on with what I was saying later."

"It is merely that it occurs to me as a passing thought, madam, that there *is* a solution to the difficulty that confronts us. If Mr. Wooster were to be found here lying stunned, the window broken and *both* pictures removed, Mrs. Fothergill could scarcely but assume that he had been overcome, while endeavoring to protect her property, by miscreants making a burglarious entry."

Aunt Dahlia came up like a rocket from the depths of gloom.

"I see what you mean. She would be so all over him for his plucky conduct that she couldn't decently fail to let me have that serial at my own price."

"Precisely, madam."

"Thank you, Jeeves."

"Not at all, madam."

"A colossal scheme, don't you think, Bertie?"

"Supercolossal," I assented, "but with one rather serious flaw. I allude to the fact that I am not lying stunned."

"We can arrange that. I could give you a tiny little tap on the head . . . with what, Jeeves?"

"The gong stick suggests itself, madam."

"That's right, with the gong stick. You would hardly feel it."

"I'm not going to feel it."

"You mean you won't play ball? Think well, Bertram Wooster. Reflect what the harvest will be. Not a smell of Anatole's cooking will you get for months and months and months. He will dish up his Sylphides à la crème d'Ecrevisses and his Timbales de ris de veau Toulousiane and whatnot, but you will not be there to dig in and get yours. This is official."

I drew myself to my full height.

"There is no terror, Aunt Dahlia, in your threats, for. . . how does it go, Jeeves?"

"For you are armed so strong in honesty, sir, that they pass by you like the idle wind, which you respect not."

"Exactly. I have been giving considerable thought, Aunt Dahlia, to this matter of Anatole's cooking, and I have reached the conclusion that the thing is one that cuts both ways. Heaven, of course, to chew his smoked offerings, but what of the waistline? The last time I enjoyed your hospitality I put on a full inch around the middle. I am better without Anatole's cooking. I don't want to look like Uncle George."

I was alluding to the present Lord Yaxley, a prominent clubman who gets more prominent yearly, especially seen sideways.

"So," I continued, "agony though it may be, I am prepared to kiss those Timbales of which you speak goodbye, and I, therefore, meet your suggestion that you should give me tiny little taps on the head with a resolute nolle prosequi."

"That is your last word, is it?"

"It is," I said, turning on my heel, and it was, for even as I spoke something struck me a violent blow on the back hair, and I fell like some monarch of the forest beneath the axe of the woodman.

The next thing I remember with any clarity is finding myself in bed with a sort of booming noise going on close by. This, the mists having lifted, I was able to diagnose as Aunt Dahlia talking.

"Bertie," she was saying, "I wish you would listen and not let your attention wander. I've got news that will send you singing about the house."

"It will be some little time," I responded coldly, "before I go singing about any ruddy house. My head—"

"A little the worse for wear, no doubt. But don't let's go into side issues. I want to tell you the final score. The dirty work is attributed on all sides to the gang, probably international, which got away with the Gainsborough and the Romney. The Fothergill is all over you, as Jeeves foresaw she would be, and she's given me the serial on easy terms. You were right about the bluebird. It's singing."

"So is my head."

"I know. And, as you would say, the heart bleeds. But you can't make an omelette without breaking eggs."

"Your own?"

"No, Jeeves's. He said it in a hushed voice as we stood viewing the remains."

"He did, did he? Well, I trust that in future. . .
Oh, Jeeves," I said, as he entered carrying what
looked like a cooling drink.

"Sir?"

"This matter of eggs and omelettes?"

"Yes, sir?"

"From now on, if you could see your way to
cutting out the eggs and laying off the omelettes,
I should be greatly obliged."

"Very good, sir. I will bear it in mind."

Michael Innes
(b.1906)

DEATH IN THE SUN

Michael Innes (J. I. M. Stewart), the doyen of English mystery writers, has given us an impressive succession of stories, almost all demonstrating a concern for cultural and intellectual questions. A reader in English Literature at Christ Church, Oxford, and visiting professor in both Australia and the United States, he has had a world of experiences to draw upon.

Inspector John Appleby, the hero of his tales, debuted in 1936 in Death in the President's Lodging, *and matched that much-praised achievement in* Hamlet, Revenge *the next year. His rise through the ranks of Scotland Yard to the post of Commissioner of all Metropolitan (London) Police, knighthood, and later retirement is chronicled in these accounts. Even in these final years he remains active, traveling with his wife, Lady Judith, often encountering crime and puzzlement along the way, together with further cultural and intellectual enlightenment. "Death in the Sun" is but a taste of this entertaining educator's craft, a pinch of erudition with a dollop of satire in a savory of the highest order.*

The villa stood on a remote Cornish cape. Its flat roof commanded a magnificent view, but was not

447

itself commanded from anywhere. So it was a good spot either for sun-bathing, or for suicide of a civilized and untroublesome sort. George Elwin appeared to have put it to both uses successively.

He lay on the roof, bronzed and stark naked— or stark naked except for a wrist watch. The gun lay beside him. His face was a mess.

"I don't usually bring my week-end guests to view this kind of thing." The Chief Constable had glanced in whimsical apology at Commissioner Appleby. "But you're a professional, after all. Elwin, as you see, was a wealthy man with unassuming tastes." He pointed to the watch, which was an expensive one, but on a simple leather strap. "Poor devil!" he added softly. "Think, Appleby, of taking a revolver and doing that to yourself."

"Mayn't somebody have murdered him? A thief? This is an out-of-the-way place, and you say he lived here in solitude, working on his financial schemes, for weeks at a time. Anybody might come and go."

"True enough. But there's £5000 in notes in an unlocked drawer downstairs. And Elwin's fingerprints are on the gun—the fellows I sent along this morning established that. So there's no mystery, I'm afraid. And another thing: George Elwin had a history."

"You mean, he'd tried to kill himself before?"

"Just that. He was a hypochondriac, and always taking drugs. And he suffered from periodic fits of depression. Last year he took an enormous dose of barbiturate—again he was naked like this, in a lonely cove. He seems to have had a fancy for

448

death in the sun. But the coast guard discovered him in time, and they saved his life."

Appleby knelt beside the body. Gently, he turned over the left hand and removed the wrist watch. It was still going. On its back the initials *G. E.* were engraved in the gold. Equally gently, Appleby returned the watch to the wrist, and buckled the strap. For a moment he paused, frowning.

"Do you know," he said, "I'd rather like to have a look at his bedroom."

The bedroom confirmed the impression made by the watch. The furnishings were simple, but the simplicity was of the kind that costs money. Commissioner Appleby opened a wardrobe and looked at the clothes. He removed a couple of suits and studied them with care. He returned one, and laid the other on the bed.

He then opened a cupboard and found it crammed with medicine bottles and pill boxes. There could be no doubt about the hypochondria. Appleby started a systematic examination.

"Proprietary stuffs," he said. "But they mostly carry their pharmaceutical name as well. What's tetracycline for, would you suppose? Ah, it's an antibiotic. The poor chap was afraid of infection. You could work out all his fears and phobias from this cupboard. Various antihistamines—no doubt he went in for allergies in a big way. Benzocaine, dexamphetamine, sulphafurazole—terrible mouthfuls they are—in every sense. A suntan preparation. But look, barbiturates again. He could have gone out that way if he'd wanted to—there's enough to kill an elephant, and Elwin's not all that bulky. Endless analgesics—you can bet he was always expecting pain."

Appleby glanced round. "By the way, how do you propose to have the body identified at the inquest?"

"Identified?" The Chief Constable stared.

"Just a thought. His dentist, perhaps?"

"As a matter of fact, that wouldn't work. The police surgeon examined his mouth this morning. Teeth perfect—Elwin probably hadn't been to a dentist since he was a child. But, of course, the matter's merely formal, since there can't be any doubt of his identity. I didn't know him well, but I recognize him myself, more or less—even with his face like that."

"I see. By the way, how does one bury a naked corpse? Still naked? It seems disrespectful. In a shroud? No longer fashionable. Perhaps just in a nice business suit." Appleby turned to the bed. "I think we'll dress George Elwin that way now."

"My dear Appleby!"

"Just rummage in those drawers." The Commissioner was inexorable. "Underclothes and a shirt, but you needn't bother about socks or a tie."

Ten minutes later the body—still supine on the roof—was almost fully clothed. The two men looked down at it somberly.

"Yes," the Chief Constable said slowly. "I see what you had in mind."

"I think we need some information about George Elwin's connections. And about his rela-

450

tives, in particular. What do you know about that yourself?"

"Not much." The Chief Constable took a restless turn up and down the flat roof. "He had a brother named Arnold Elwin. Rather a bad-hat brother, or at least a shiftless one—living mostly in Canada, but turning up from time to time to cash in on his brother George's increasing wealth."

"Arnold would be about the same age as George?"

"That's my impression. They may have been twins, for that matter." The Chief Constable broke off. "In heaven's name, Appleby, what put this notion in your head?"

"Look at this." Appleby was again kneeling by the body. Again he turned over the left hand so that the strap of the wrist watch was revealed. "What do you see on the leather, a third of an inch outward from the present position of the buckle?"

"A depression." The Chief Constable was precise. "A narrow and discolored depression, parallel with the line of the buckle itself."

"Exactly. And what does that suggest?"

"That the watch really belongs to another man—someone with a slightly thicker wrist."

"And those clothes, now that we've put them on the corpse?"

"Well, they remind me of something in Shakespeare's *Macbeth*." The Chief Constable smiled grimly. "Something about a giant's robe on a dwarfish thief."

"I'd call that poetic exaggeration. But the general picture is clear. It will be interesting to discover whether we have to go as far as Canada to come up with—"

Appleby broke off. The Chief Constable's chauffeur had appeared on the roof. He glanced askance at the body, and then spoke hastily.

"Excuse me, sir, but a gentleman has just driven up, asking for Mr. Elwin. He says he's Mr. Elwin's brother."

"Thank you, Pengelly," the Chief Constable said unemotionally. "We'll come down." But when the chauffeur had gone he turned to Appleby with a low whistle. "Talk of the devil!" he said.

"Or, at least, of the villain in the piece?" Appleby glanced briefly at the body. "Well, let's go and see."

As they entered the small study downstairs, a bulky figure rose from a chair by the window. There could be no doubt that the visitor looked remarkably like the dead man.

"My name is Arnold Elwin," he said. "I have called to see my brother. May I ask—"

"Mr. Elwin," the Chief Constable said formally, "I deeply regret to inform you that your brother is dead. He was found on the roof this morning, shot through the head."

"Dead?" The bulky man sank into his chair again. "I can't believe it! Who are you?"

"I am the Chief Constable of the county, and this is my guest Sir John Appleby, the Commissioner of Metropolitan Police. He is very kindly assisting me in my inquiries—as you, sir, may do. Did you see your brother yesterday?"

"Certainly. I had just arrived in England, and I came straight here, as soon as I learned that George was going in for one of his periodical turns as a recluse."

"There was nobody else about the place?"

"Nobody. George managed for himself except for a woman who came in from the village early in the morning."

"Did you have—well, a satisfactory interview?"

"Nothing of the kind. George and I disagreed, so I left."

"Your disagreement would be about family affairs? Money—that kind of thing?"

"I'm damned if I see what business it is of yours."

There was a moment's silence during which the Chief Constable appeared to brood darkly. Then he tried to catch Appleby's eye, but failed to do so. Finally he advanced firmly on the bulky man.

"George Elwin—" he began.

"What the deuce do you mean? My name is Arnold Elwin, not—"

"George Elwin, by virtue of my office I arrest you in the Queen's name. You will be brought before the magistrate, and charged with the willful murder of your brother, Arnold Elwin."

Appleby had been prowling round the room, peering at the books, opening and shutting drawers. Now he came to a halt.

"It may be irregular," he said to the Chief Constable. "But I think we might explain to Mr. Elwin, as we can safely call him, just what is in our minds."

"As you please, Appleby." The Chief Constable was a shade stiff. "But do it yourself."

Appleby nodded.

"Mr. Elwin," he said gravely, "it is within our knowledge that Mr. George Elwin, the owner of this house, was, or is, subject to phases of acute depression. Last year one of these led him to an actual attempt at suicide. That is our first fact.

"The second is this: the wrist watch found on the dead man's hand was not fastened as it would normally have been fastened on the wrist of its owner. The dead man's is a slimmer wrist.

"The third fact connects with the second. The clothes in this house are too big for the dead man. But I think they would fit you very well."

"You're mad!" The bulky man had got to his feet again. "There's not a word of truth—"

"I can only give you what has been in our minds. And now I come to a fourth fact: George and Arnold Elwin were not readily distinguishable. You agree?"

"Of course I agree. George and I were twins."

"Or Arnold and you were twins. Now, our hypothesis is as follows: you, George Elwin, living in solitude in this house, were visited by your brother Arnold, just back from Canada. He demanded money or the like, perhaps under some threat. There was a violent quarrel, and you shot him dead—at close quarters.

"Now, what could you do? The wound was compatible with suicide. But who would believe that Arnold had arrived here, gained possession of your gun, and shot himself? Fortunately there was somebody who *would* readily be believed to

454

have committed suicide, since he was known to have made an attempt at it only a year ago. That somebody was yourself, George Elwin.

"So you, George Elwin, arranged the body of your brother, and arranged the gun, to suggest something fairly close to a repetition of that known attempt at suicide. You strapped your own watch to the dead man's wrist. The clothes in the house would hang loosely on him—but he would be found naked, and who would ever be likely to notice the discrepancy in the clothes?

"The dead body, maimed in the face as it was, would pass virtually unquestioned as George Elwin's. And that is all. You had ceased abruptly to be George, and so had lost what is probably a substantial fortune; but at least you had an identity to fall back on, and you weren't going to be charged and convicted of murder."

"But it's not true!" The bulky man seemed to be in blind panic. "You've framed me. It's a plot. I can prove—"

"Ah," Appleby said, "there's the point. If you are, in fact, George pretending to be Arnold, you'll have a very stiff fight to sustain the impersonation. But, if, as you claim, you are really Arnold, that's a different matter. Have you a dentist?"

"Of course I have a dentist—in Montreal. I wander about the world a good deal, but I always go back to the same dentist. At one time or another he's done something to nearly every tooth in my head."

"I'm uncommonly glad to hear it." Appleby glanced at the Chief Constable. "I don't think," he murmured, "that we ought to detain Mr. Arnold Elwin further. I hope he will forget a little of what has been—well, shall we say, proposed?"

Appleby turned back to Elwin. "I'm sure," he said blandly, "you will forgive our exploring the matter in the interests of truth. You arrived, you know, when we had not quite sorted out all the clues. Will you please accept our sympathy on the tragic suicide of your brother George?"

"You mean to say," the Chief Constable asked half an hour later, "that I was right in the first place? That there was no mystery?"

"None whatever. George Elwin's depression was deepened by the visit of his brother, and he killed himself. That's the whole story."

"But dash it all—"

"Mind you, up to the moment of your charging that fellow with murder, I was entirely with you. And then I suddenly remembered something that didn't fit—that £5000 you found here in an unlocked drawer. If George had killed Arnold and was planning to *become* Arnold—or anybody else—he'd certainly have taken that money. So why didn't he take it?"

"I can see the force of that. But surely—"

"And then there was something else—something I ought to have seen the significance of at once. The dexamphetamine in the medicine cupboard. It's a highly efficient appetite depressant, used for dieting and losing weight. George Elwin was slimming. He'd come down here, I imagine, principally to do so. It was the latest expression of his hypochondria.

"He could lose fourteen pounds in a fortnight,

you know—which would be quite enough to require his taking up one hole in the strap of his watch. And in a month he could lose thirty pounds—which would produce your effect of the giant's robe on the dwarfish thief. George Elwin's first call, had he ever left here, would have been on his tailor—to get his suits taken in."

The Chief Constable was silent for a moment.

"I say!" he said. "We did give that unfortunate chap rather a bad fifteen minutes."

Appleby nodded soberly.

"But let's be thankful," he said, "that one of Her Majesty's judges isn't burdened with the job of giving somebody a bad fifteen years."

457

Ethel Lina White
(1894–1944)
AN UNLOCKED WINDOW

Variant: *The English Country House Gothic Thriller*

The Country House Thriller is truer to its roots than any modern descendant. Early Romantic novels often involved castles or manors that had such overwhelming presence as to dwarf the persons in the book. Threatened girls were understandably terrorized by the occurrences in these places, as was the reader. Its modern counterpart can be equally effective—witness Daphne du Maurier's Rebecca, *one of the greatest mystery novels of all time.*

Ethel Lina White was one of the half-forgotten mistresses of the English suspense novel. Her 1936 novel, The Wheel Spins, *became the basis for Hitchcock's 1938* The Lady Vanishes. Some Must Watch *(1934) became the equally successful* Spiral Staircase *(1945) in the lenses of German-American director Robert Siodmak. Strong recommendations for a name few will recognize.*

I came across this tale in a small collection while reading for this anthology, and could not turn the pages fast enough. It demanded to be included—an excellent example of an undervalued variant of the English Country House Mystery.

459

"Have you locked up, Nurse Cherry?"

"Yes, Nurse Silver."

"Every door? Every window?"

"Yes, yes."

Yet even as she shot home the last bolt of the front door, at the back of Nurse Cherry's mind was a vague misgiving.

She had forgotten—*something*.

She was young and pretty, but her expression was anxious. While she had most of the qualities to ensure professional success, she was always on guard against a serious handicap.

She had a bad memory.

Hitherto, it had betrayed her only in burnt Benger and an occasional overflow in the bathroom. But yesterday's lapse was little short of a calamity.

Late that afternoon she had discovered the oxygen-cylinder, which she had been last to use, empty—its cap carelessly unscrewed.

The disaster called for immediate remedy, for the patient, Professor Glendower Baker, was suffering from the effects of gas-poisoning. Although dark was falling, the man, Iles, had to harness the pony for the long drive over the mountains, in order to get a fresh supply.

Nurse Cherry had sped his parting with a feeling of loss. Iles was a cheery soul and a tower of strength.

It was dirty weather with a spitting rain blanketing the elephant-grey mounds of the surrounding hills. The valley road wound like a muddy coil between soaked bracken and dwarf oaks.

Iles shook his head as he regarded the savage isolation of the landscape.

"I don't half like leaving you—a pack of women—with *him* about. Put up the shutters on every door and window, Nurse, and don't let *no one* come in till I get back."

He drove off—his lamps glow-worms in the gloom.

Darkness and rain. And the sodden undergrowth seemed to quiver and blur, so that stunted trees took on the shapes of crouching men advancing towards the house.

Nurse Cherry hurried through her round of fastening the windows. As she carried her candle from room to room of the upper floors, she had the uneasy feeling that she was visible to any watcher.

Her mind kept wandering back to the bad business of the forgotten cylinder. It had plunged her in depths of self-distrust and shame. She was overtired, having nursed the patient single-handed, until the arrival, three days ago, of the second nurse. But that fact did not absolve her from blame.

"I'm not fit to be a nurse," she told herself in bitter self-reproach.

She was still in a dream when she locked the front door. Nurse Silver's questions brought her back to earth with a furtive sense of guilt.

Nurse Silver's appearance inspired confidence, for she was of solid build, with strong features and a black shingle. Yet, for all her stout looks, her nature seemed that of Job.

"Has he gone?" she asked in her harsh voice.

461

"Iles? Yes."

Nurse Cherry repeated his caution.

"He'll get back as soon as he can," she added, "but it probably won't be until dawn."

"Then," said Nurse Silver gloomily, "we are *alone.*"

Nurse Cherry laughed.

"Alone? Three hefty women, all of us able to give a good account of ourselves."

" *I'm* not afraid." Nurse Silver gave her rather a peculiar look. " *I'm* safe enough."

"Why?"

"Because of *you.* He won't touch me with you here."

Nurse Cherry tried to belittle her own attractive appearance with a laugh.

"For that matter," she said, "we are all safe."

"Do you think so? A lonely house. No man. And two of *us.*"

Nurse Cherry glanced at her starched nurse's apron. Nurse Silver's words made her feel like special bait—a goat tethered in a jungle, to attract a tiger.

"Don't talk nonsense," she said sharply.

The countryside, of late, had been chilled by a series of murders. In each case, the victim had been a trained nurse. The police were searching for a medical student—Sylvester Leek. It was supposed that his mind had become unhinged, consequent on being jilted by a pretty probationer. He had disappeared from the hospital after a violent breakdown during an operation.

Next morning, a night-nurse had been discovered in the laundry—strangled. Four days later, a second nurse had been horribly done to death in the garden of a villa on the outskirts of the small agricultural town. After the lapse of a fortnight, one of the nurses in attendance on Sir Thomas Jones had been discovered in her bedroom—throttled.

The last murder had taken place in a large mansion in the very heart of the country. Every isolated cottage and farm became infected with panic. Women barred their doors and no girl lingered late in the lane, without her lover.

Nurse Cherry wished she could forget the details she had read in the newspapers. The ingenuity with which the poor victims had been lured to their doom and the ferocity of the attacks all proved a diseased brain driven by malignant motive.

It was a disquieting thought that she and Nurse Silver were localized. Professor Baker had succumbed to gas-poisoning while engaged in work of national importance and his illness had been reported in the Press.

"In any case," she argued, "how could—*he*—know that we're left tonight?"

Nurse Silver shook her head.

" *They* always know."

"Rubbish! And he's probably committed suicide by now. There hasn't been a murder for over a month."

"Exactly. There's bound to be another, *soon.*"

Nurse Cherry thought of the undergrowth creeping nearer to the house. Her nerve snapped.

"Are you trying to make me afraid?"

"Yes," said Nurse Silver, "I am. I don't trust you. You forget."

Nurse Cherry coloured angrily.

"You might let me forget that wretched cylinder."

"But you might forget again."

"Not likely."

As she uttered the words—like oil spreading over water—her mind was smeared with doubt.

Something forgotten.

She shivered as she looked up the well of the circular staircase, which was dimly lit by an oil-lamp suspended to a cross-bar. Shadows rode the walls and wiped out the ceiling like a flock of sooty bats.

An eerie place. Hiding-holes on every landing.

The house was tall and narrow, with two or three rooms on every floor. It was rather like a tower or a pepper-pot. The semi-basement was occupied by the kitchen and domestic offices. On the ground-floor were a sitting-room, the dining-room and the Professor's study. The first floor was devoted to the patient. On the second floor were the bedrooms of the nurses and of the Iles couple. The upper floors were given up to the Professor's laboratorial work.

Nurse Cherry remembered the stout shutters and the secure hasps. There had been satisfaction in turning the house into a fortress. But now, instead of a sense of security, she had a feeling of being caged.

She moved to the staircase.

"While we're bickering," she said, "we're neglecting the patient."

Nurse Silver called her back.

"I'm on duty now."

Professional etiquette forbade any protest. But Nurse Cherry looked after her colleague with sharp envy.

She thought of the Professor's fine brow, his wasted clear-cut features and visionary slate-grey eyes, with yearning. For after three years of nursing children, with an occasional mother or aunt, romance had entered her life.

From the first, she had been interested in her patient. She had scarcely eaten or slept until the crisis had passed. She noticed too, how his eyes followed her around the room and how he could hardly bear her out of his sight.

Yesterday he had held her hand in his thin fingers.

"Marry me, Stella," he whispered.

"Not unless you get well," she answered foolishly.

Since then, he had called her "Stella." Her name was music in her ears until her rapture was dashed by the fatal episode of the cylinder. She had to face the knowledge that, in case of another relapse, Glendower's life hung upon a thread.

She was too wise to think further, so she began to speculate on Nurse Silver's character. Hitherto, they had met only at meals, when she had been taciturn and moody.

To-night she had revealed a personal animus against herself, and Nurse Cherry believed she guessed its cause.

The situation was a hot-bed for jealousy. Two women were thrown into close contact with a patient and a doctor, both of whom were bachelors. Although Nurse Silver was the ill-favoured one, it was plain that she possessed her share of personal vanity. Nurse Cherry noticed, from her painful walk, that she wore shoes which were too small. More than that, she had caught her in the act of scrutinizing her face in the mirror.

These rather pitiful glimpses into the dark heart of the warped woman made Nurse Cherry uneasy.

The house was very still; she missed Nature's sounds of rain or wind against the window-pane and the cheerful voices of the Iles couple. The silence might be a background for sounds she did not wish to hear.

She spoke aloud, for the sake of hearing her own voice.

"Cheery if Silver plays up to-night. Well, well! I'll hurry up Mrs. Iles with the supper."

Her spirits rose as she opened the door leading to the basement. The warm spicy odour of the kitchen floated up the short staircase and she could see a bar of yellow light from the half-opened door.

When she entered, she saw no sign of supper. Mrs. Iles—a strapping blonde with strawberry cheeks—sat at the kitchen-table, her head buried in her huge arms.

As Nurse Cherry shook her gently, she raised her head.

"Eh?" she said stupidly.

"Gracious, Mrs. Iles. Are you ill?"

"Eh? Feel as if I'd one over the eight."

"What on earth d'you mean?"

"What *you* call 'tight.' Love-a-duck, my head's that swimmy—"

Nurse Cherry looked suspiciously at an empty glass upon the dresser, as Mrs. Iles's head dropped like a bleached sunflower.

Nurse Silver heard her hurrying footsteps on the stairs. She met her upon the landing.

"Anything wrong?"

"Mrs. Iles. I think she's drunk. Do come and see."

When Nurse Silver reached the kitchen, she hoisted Mrs. Iles under the armpits and set her on unsteady feet.

"Obvious," she said. "Help get her upstairs."

It was no easy task to drag twelve stone of protesting Mrs. Iles up three flights of stairs.

"She feels like a centipede, with every pair of feet going in a different direction," Nurse Cherry panted, as they reached the door of the Ileses' bedroom. "I can manage her now, thank you."

She wished Nurse Silver would go back to the patient, instead of looking at her with that fixed expression.

"What are you staring at?" she asked sharply.

"Has nothing struck you as *strange?*"

"What?"

In the dim light, Nurse Silver's eyes looked like empty black pits.

"To-day," she said, "there were four of us. First, Iles goes. Now, Mrs. Iles. That leaves only two. If anything happens to you or me, there'll only be *one.*"

As Nurse Cherry put Mrs. Iles to bed, she reflected that Nurse Silver was decidedly not a cheerful companion. She made a natural sequence of events appear in the light of a sinister conspiracy.

Nurse Cherry reminded herself sharply that Iles's absence was due to her own carelessness, while his wife was addicted to her glass.

Still, some unpleasant suggestion remained, like the sediment from a splash of muddy water. She found herself thinking with horror of some calamity befalling Nurse Silver. If she were left by herself she felt she would lose her senses with fright.

It was an unpleasant picture. The empty house —a dark shell for lurking shadows. No one on whom to depend. Her patient—a beloved burden and responsibility.

It was better not to think of that. But she kept on thinking. The outside darkness seemed to be pressing against the walls, bending them in. As her fears multiplied, the medical student changed from a human being with a distraught brain, to a Force, cunning and insatiable—a ravening blood-monster.

Nurse Silver's words recurred to her.

" *They* always know." Even so. Doors might be locked, but *they* would find a way inside.

Her nerves tingled at the sound of the telephone-bell, ringing far below in the hall.

She kept looking over her shoulder as she ran downstairs. She took off the receiver in positive panic, lest she should be greeted with a maniac scream of laughter.

It was a great relief to hear the homely Welsh accent of Dr. Jones.

He had serious news for her. As she listened, her heart began to thump violently.

468

"Thank you, doctor, for letting me know," she said. "Please ring up directly you hear more."

"Hear more of what?"

Nurse Cherry started at Nurse Silver's harsh voice. She had come downstairs noiselessly in her soft nursing-slippers.

"It's only the doctor," she said, trying to speak lightly. "He's thinking of changing the medicine."

"Then why are you so white? You are shaking."

Nurse Cherry decided that the truth would serve her best.

"To be honest," she said, "I've just had bad news. Something ghastly. I didn't want you to know, for there's no sense in two of us being frightened. But now I come to think of it, you ought to feel reassured."

She forced a smile.

"You said there'd have to be another murder soon. Well—there *has* been one."

"Where? Who? Quick."

Nurse Cherry understood what is meant by the infection of fear as Nurse Silver gripped her arm.

In spite of her effort at self-mastery, there was a quiver in her own voice.

"It's a—a hospital nurse. Strangled. They've just found the body in a quarry and they sent for Dr. Jones to make the examination. The police are trying to establish her identity."

Nurse Silver's eyes were wide and staring.

"Another hospital nurse? That makes *four*."

She turned on the younger woman in sudden suspicion.

"Why did he ring you up?"

Nurse Cherry did not want that question.

"To tell us to be specially on guard," she replied.

"You mean—he's near?"

"Of course not. The doctor said the woman had been dead three or four days. By now, he'll be far away."

"Or he may be even nearer than you think."

Nurse Cherry glanced involuntarily at the barred front door. Her head felt as if it were bursting. It was impossible to think connectedly. But —somewhere—beating its wings like a caged bird, was the incessant reminder.

Something forgotten.

The sight of the elder woman's twitching lips reminded her that she had to be calm for two.

"Go back to the patient," she said, "while I get the supper. We'll both feel better after something to eat."

In spite of her new-born courage, it needed an effort of will to descend into the basement. So many doors, leading to scullery, larder and coalcellar, all smelling of mice. So many hiding-places.

The kitchen proved a cheerful antidote to depression. The caked fire in the open range threw a red glow upon the Welsh dresser and the canisters labelled 'Sugar' and 'Tea'. A sandy cat slept upon the rag mat. Everything looked safe and homely.

Quickly collecting bread, cheese, a round of beef, a cold white shape, and stewed prunes, she piled them on a tray. She added stout for Nurse Silver and made cocoa for herself. As she watched the milk froth up through the dark mixture and inhaled the steaming odour, she felt that her fears were baseless and absurd.

She sang as she carried her tray upstairs. She was going to marry Glendower.

The nurses used the bedroom which connected with the sick chamber for their meals, in order to be near the patient. As the night-nurse entered, Nurse Cherry strained her ears for the sound of Glendower's voice. She longed for one glimpse of him. Even a smile would help.

"How's the patient?" she asked.

"All right."

"Could I have a peep?"

"No. You're off duty."

As the women sat down, Nurse Cherry was amused to notice that Nurse Silver kicked off her tight shoes.

"You seem very interested in the patient, Nurse Cherry," she remarked sourly.

"I have a right to feel rather interested." Nurse Cherry smiled as she cut bread. "The doctor gives me the credit for his being alive."

"Ah! But the doctor thinks the world of you."

Nurse Cherry was not conceited, but she was human enough to know that she had made a conquest of the big Welshman.

The green glow of jealousy in Nurse Silver's eyes made her reply guardedly.

"Dr. Jones is decent to every one."

But she was of too friendly and impulsive a nature to keep her secret bottled up. She reminded herself that they were two women sharing an ordeal and she tried to establish some link of friendship.

471

"I feel you despise me," she said. "You think me lacking in self-control. And you can't forget that cylinder. But really, I've gone through such an awful strain. For four nights, I never took off my clothes."

"Why didn't you have a second nurse?"

"There was the expense. The Professor gives his whole life to enrich the nation and he's poor. Then, later, I felt I *must* do everything for him myself. I didn't want you, only Dr. Jones said I was heading for a break-down."

She looked at her left hand, seeing there the shadowy outline of a wedding-ring.

"Don't think me sloppy, but I must tell some one. The Professor and I are going to get married."

" *If* he lives."

"But he's turned the corner now."

"Don't count your chickens."

Nurse Cherry felt a stab of fear.

"Are you hiding something from me? Is he—worse?"

"No. He's the same. I was thinking that Dr. Jones might interfere. You've led him on, haven't you? I've seen you smile at him. It's light women like you that make the trouble in the world."

Nurse Cherry was staggered by the injustice of the attack. But as she looked at the elder woman's working face, she saw that she was consumed by jealousy. One life lay in the shadow, the other in the sun. The contrast was too sharp.

"We won't quarrel to-night," she said gently. "We're going through rather a bad time together and we have only each other to depend on. I'm just clinging to *you*. If anything were to happen to you, like Mrs. Iles, I should jump out of my skin with fright."

Nurse Silver was silent for a minute.

"I never thought of that," she said presently. "Only us two. And all these empty rooms, above and below. What's that?"

From the hall, came the sound of muffled knocking.

Nurse Cherry sprang to her feet.

"Some one's at the front door."

Nurse Silver's fingers closed round her arm, like iron hoops.

"Sit down. It's *him*."

The two women stared at each other as the knocking continued. It was loud and insistent. To Nurse Cherry's ears, it carried a message of urgency.

"I'm going down," she said. "It may be Dr. Jones."

"How could you tell?"

"By his voice."

"You fool. Any one could imitate *his* accent."

Nurse Cherry saw the beads break out round Nurse Silver's mouth. Her fear had the effect of steadying her own nerves.

"I'm going down, to find out who it is," she said. "It may be important news about the murder."

Nurse Silver dragged her away from the door.

"What did I say? *You* are the danger. You've forgotten already."

"Forgotten—what?"

"Didn't Iles tell you to open to no one? *No one?*"

473

Nurse Cherry hung her head. She sat down in shamed silence.

The knocking ceased. Presently they heard it again at the back door.

Nurse Silver wiped her face.

"He *means* to get in." She laid her hand on Nurse Cherry's arm. "You're not even trembling. Are you never afraid?"

"Only of ghosts."

In spite of her brave front, Nurse Cherry was inwardly quaking at her own desperate resolution. Nurse Silver had justly accused her of endangering the household. Therefore it was her plain duty to make once more the round of the house, either to see what she had forgotten, or to lay the doubt.

"I'm going upstairs," she said. "I want to look out."

"Unbar a window?" Nurse Silver's agitation rose in a gale. "You shall *not*. It's murdering folly. Think! That last nurse was found dead *inside* her bedroom."

"All right. I won't."

"You'd best be careful. You've been trying to spare me, but perhaps I've been trying to spare you. I'll only say this. *There is something strange happening in this house.*"

Nurse Cherry felt a chill at her heart. Only, since she was a nurse, she knew that it was really the pit of her stomach. Something wrong? If through her wretched memory, she again were the culprit, she must expiate her crime by shielding the others, at any risk to herself.

She had to force herself to mount the stairs. Her candle, flickering in the draught, peopled the walls with distorted shapes. When she reached the top landing, without stopping to think, she walked resolutely into the laboratory and the adjoining room.

Both were securely barred and empty. Gaining courage, she entered the attic. Under its window was a precipitous slope of roof without gutter or water-pipe, to give finger-hold. Knowing that it would be impossible for any one to gain an entry, she opened the shutter and unfastened the window.

The cold air on her face refreshed her and restored her to calm. She realized that she had been suffering to a certain extent from claustrophobia.

The rain had ceased and a wind arisen. She could see a young harried moon flying through the clouds. The dark humps of the hills were visible against the darkness, but nothing more.

She remained at the window for some time, thinking of Glendower. It was a solace to remember the happiness which awaited her once this night of terror was over.

Presently the urge to see him grew too strong to be resisted. Nurse Silver's words had made her uneasy on his behalf. Even though she offended the laws of professional etiquette, she determined to see for herself that all was well.

Leaving the window open so that some air might percolate into the house, she slipped stealthily downstairs. She stopped on the second floor to visit her own room and that of Nurse Silver. All was quiet and secure. In her own quarters, Mrs. Iles still snored in the sleep of the unjust.

There were two doors to the patient's room.

The one led to the nurses' room where Nurse Silver was still at her meal. The other led to the landing.

Directly Nurse Cherry entered, she knew that her fear had been the premonition of love. Something was seriously amiss. Glendower's head tossed uneasily on the pillow. His face was deeply flushed. When she called him by name, he stared at her, his luminous grey eyes ablaze.

He did not recognize her, for instead of "Stella," he called her "Nurse."

"Nurse, Nurse." He mumbled something that sounded like "man" and then slipped back in her arms, unconscious.

Nurse Silver entered the room at her cry. As she felt his pulse, she spoke with dry significance.

"We could do with oxygen now."

Nurse Cherry could only look at her with piteous eyes.

"Shall I telephone for Dr. Jones?" she asked humbly.

"Yes."

It seemed like the continuation of an evil dream when she could get no answer to her ring. Again and again she tried desperately to galvanize the dead instrument.

Presently Nurse Silver appeared on the landing.

"Is the doctor coming?"

"I—I can't get any answer." Nurse Cherry forced back her tears. "Oh, whatever can be wrong?"

"Probably a wet creeper twisted round the wire. But it doesn't matter now. The patient is sleeping."

Nurse Cherry's face registered no comfort. As though the shocks of the last few minutes had set in motion the arrested machinery of her brain, she remembered suddenly what she had forgotten.

The larder window.

She recollected now what had happened. When she entered the larder on her round of locking up, a mouse had run over her feet. She ran to fetch the cat which chased it into a hole in the kitchen. In the excitement of the incident, she had forgotten to return to close the window.

Her heart leapt violently at the realization that, all these hours, the house had been open to any marauder. Even while she and Nurse Silver had listened, shivering, to the knocking at the door, she had already betrayed the fortress.

"What's the matter?" asked Nurse Silver.

"Nothing. Nothing."

She dared not tell the older woman. Even now it was not too late to remedy her omission.

In her haste she no longer feared the descent into the basement. She could hardly get down the stairs with sufficient speed. As she entered the larder the wire-covered window flapped in the breeze. She secured it and was just entering the kitchen, when her eye fell on a dark patch on the passage.

It was the footprint of a man.

Nurse Cherry remembered that Iles had been in the act of getting fresh coal into the cellar when he had been called away to make his journey. He had no time to clean up and the floor was still sooty with rain-soaked dust.

As she raised her candle, the footprint gleamed faintly. Stooping hastily, she touched it.

It was still damp.

At first she stood as if petrified, staring at it stupidly. Then as she realized that in front of her lay a freshly-made imprint, her nerve snapped completely. With a scream, she dropped her candle and tore up the stairs, calling on Nurse Silver.

She was answered by a strange voice. It was thick, heavy, indistinct. A voice she had never heard before.

Knowing not what awaited her on the other side of the door, yet driven on by the courage of ultimate fear, she rushed into the nurses' sitting-room.

No one was there save Nurse Silver. She sagged back in her chair, her eyes half-closed, her mouth open.

From her lips issued a second uncouth cry.

Nurse Cherry put her arm around her.

"What is it? Try to tell me."

It was plain that Nurse Silver was trying to warn her of some peril. She pointed to her glass and fought for articulation.

"Drugs. Listen. When you lock out, you lock *in*." Even as she spoke her eyes turned up horribly, exposing the balls in a blind white stare.

Almost mad with terror, Nurse Cherry tried to revive her. Mysteriously, through some unknown agency, what she had dreaded had come to pass.

She was alone.

And somewhere—within the walls of the house—lurked a being, cruel and cunning, who —one after another—had removed each obstacle between himself and his objective.

He had marked down his victim. *Herself.*

In that moment she went clean over the edge of fear. She felt that it was not herself—Stella Cherry—but a stranger in the blue print uniform of a hospital nurse, who calmly speculated on her course of action.

It was impossible to lock herself in the patient's room, for the key was stiff from disuse. And she had not the strength to move furniture which was sufficiently heavy to barricade the door.

The idea of flight was immediately dismissed. In order to get help, she would have to run miles. She could not leave Glendower and two helpless women at the mercy of the baffled maniac.

There was nothing to be done. Her place was by Glendower. She sat down by his bed and took his hand in hers.

The time seemed endless. Her watch seemed sometimes to leap whole hours and then to crawl, as she waited—listening to the myriad sounds in a house at nightfall. There were faint rustlings, the cracking of wood-work, the scamper of mice.

And a hundred times, some one seemed to steal up the stairs and linger just outside her door.

It was nearly three o'clock when suddenly a gong began to beat inside her temples. In the adjoining room was the unmistakable tramp of a man's footsteps.

It was no imagination on her part. They circled the room and then advanced deliberately towards the connecting door.

She saw the handle begin to turn slowly.

In one bound, she reached the door and rushed on to the landing and up the stairs. For a second, she paused before her own room. But its windows were barred and its door had no key. She could not be done to death there in the dark.

As she paused, she heard the footsteps on the stairs. They advanced slowly, driving her on before them. Demented with terror, she fled up to the top story, instinctively seeking the open window.

She could go no higher. At the attic door, she waited.

Something black appeared on the staircase wall. It was the shadow of her pursuer—a grotesque and distorted herald of crime.

Nurse Cherry gripped the balustrade to keep herself from falling. Everything was growing dark. She knew that she was on the point of fainting, when she was revived by sheer astonishment and joy.

Above the balustrade appeared the head of Nurse Silver.

Nurse Cherry called out to her in warning.

"Come quickly. There's a man in the house."

She saw Nurse Silver start and fling back her head, as though in alarm. Then occurred the culminating horror of a night of dread.

A mouse ran across the passage. Raising her heavy shoe, Nurse Silver stamped upon it, grinding her heel upon the tiny creature's head.

In that moment, Nurse Cherry knew the truth. Nurse Silver was a man.

Her brain raced with lightning velocity. It was like a searchlight, piercing the shadows and making the mystery clear.

She knew that the real Nurse Silver had been murdered by Sylvester Leek, on her way to the case. It was her strangled body which had just been found in the quarry. And the murderer had taken her place. The police description was that of a slightly-built youth, with refined features. It would be easy for him to assume the disguise of a woman. He had the necessary medical knowledge to pose as nurse. Moreover, as he had the night-shift, no one in the house had come into close contact with him, save the patient.

But the patient had guessed the truth.

To silence his tongue, the killer had drugged him, even as he had disposed of the obstructing presence of Mrs. Iles. It was he, too, who had emptied the oxygen-cylinder, to get Iles out of the way.

Yet, although he had been alone with his prey for hours, he had held his hand.

Nurse Cherry, with her new mental lucidity, knew the reason. There is a fable that the serpent slavers its victim before swallowing it. In like manner, the maniac—before her final destruction—had wished to coat her with the foul saliva of fear.

All the evening he had been trying to terrorize her—plucking at each jangled nerve up to the climax of his feigned unconsciousness.

Yet she knew that he in turn was fearful lest he should be frustrated in the commission of his crime. Since his victim's body had been discovered in the quarry, the establishment of her identity would mark his hiding-place. While Nurse Cherry was at the attic window, he had cut the telephone-wire and donned his own shoes for purposes of flight.

She remembered his emotion during the knocking at the door. It was probable that it was Dr. Jones who stood without, come to assure himself that she was not alarmed. Had it been the police, they would have effected an entry. The incident proved that nothing had been discovered and that it was useless to count on outside help.

She had to face it—alone.

In the dim light from the young moon, she saw the murderer enter the attic. The grotesque travesty of his nursing disguise added to the terror of the moment.

His eyes were fixed on the open window. It was plain that he was pretending to connect it with the supposed intruder. She in her turn had unconsciously deceived him. He probably knew nothing of the revealing footprint he had left in the basement passage.

"Shut the window, you damned fool," he shouted.

As he leaned over the low ledge to reach the swinging casement window, Nurse Cherry rushed at him in the instinctive madness of self-defence —thrusting him forward, over the sill.

She had one glimpse of dark distorted features blotting out the moon and of arms sawing the air, like a star-fish, in a desperate attempt to balance.

The next moment, nothing was there.

She sank to the ground, covering her ears with her hands to deaden the sound of the sickening slide over the tiled roof.

It was a long time before she was able to creep down to her patient's room. Directly she entered, its peace healed her like balm. Glendower slept quietly—a half-smile playing round his lips as though he dreamed of her.

Thankfully she went from room to room, un-barring each window and unlocking each door—letting in the dawn.

Philip MacDonald
(1900–1985)
THE WOOD-FOR-THE-TREES

Philip MacDonald was a Scottish writer, later trans-
planted to Hollywood, where he worked on a succes-
sion of scripts, most notably Rebecca *(1940) with*
Hitchcock, several of the Charlie Chan and Mr. Moto
films, and an adaptation of his own 1959 novel, The
List of Adrian Messenger *, with John Huston. The*
last featured his series detective Colonel Anthony
Gethryn, who debuted in The Rasp *(1924), and*
makes his only short-story appearance here.

Gethryn is squarely in the tradition of English
Country House Mystery, especially as it came to in-
fluence the cinema. What distinguishes him, and
MacDonald's work, is a few shudders thrown into
the investigation just when you least expect them.

It was in the summer of '36—to be exact upon
the fifth of August in that year—that the countryside around the village of Friars' Wick in
Downshire, in the southwest of England, was
shocked by the discovery of a singularly brutal
murder.

The biggest paper in the county, *The Mostyn
Courier*, reported the outrage at some length—but
since the victim was old, poverty-stricken, female

but ill-favored, and with neither friends nor kin, the event passed practically unnoticed by the London Press, even though the killer was uncaught.

Passed unnoticed, that is, until, exactly twenty-four hours later and within a mile or so of its exact locale, the crime was repeated, the victim being another woman who, except in the matter of age, might have been a replica of the first.

This was a time, if you remember, when there was a plethora of news in the world. There was Spain, for instance. There were Mussolini and Ethiopia. There was Herr Hitler. There was Japan. There was Russia. There was dissension at home as well as abroad. There was so much, in fact, that people were stunned by it all and pretending to be bored . . .

Which is doubtless why the editor of Lord Otterill's biggest paper, *The Daily Despatch*, gave full rein to its leading crime reporter and splashed that ingenious scrivener's account of the MANIAC MURDERS IN DOWNSHIRE all across the front page of the first edition of August 8th.

The writer had spread himself. He described the slayings in gory, horrifying prose, omitting only such details as were unprintable. He drew pathetic (and by no means badly written) word-pictures of the two drab women as they had been before they met this sadistic and unpleasing end. And he devoted the last paragraphs of his outpourings to a piece of theorizing which gave added thrills to his fascinated readers.

". . . *can it be,* " he asked under the sub-heading "Wake Up, Police!" "*that these two terrible, maniacal, unspeakable crimes—crimes with no motive other than the lust of some depraved and distorted mind, can be but the beginning of a wave of murder such as that which terrorized London in the eighties, when the uncaptured, unknown 'Jack the Ripper' ran his bloodstained gamut of killing?"*

You will have noted the date of the *Despatch* article—August 8th. Which was the day after the *Queen Guinivere* sailed from New York for England. Which explains how it came about that Anthony Gethryn, who was a passenger on the great liner, knew nothing whatsoever of the unpleasant occurrences near Friars' Wick. Which is odd, because—although he'd never been there before and had no intention of ever going there again after his simple mission had been fulfilled—it was to Friars' Wick that he must make his way immediately the ship arrived at home.

A quirk of fate: one of those odd spins of the Wheel.

He didn't want to break his journey to London and home by going to Friars' Wick, or, indeed, any other place. He'd been away—upon a diplomatic task of secrecy, importance, and inescapable tedium—for three months. And he wanted to see his wife and his son, and see them with the least possible delay.

But there it was: he had in his charge a letter which a Personage of Extreme Importance had asked him to deliver into the hands of another (if lesser known) P.O.E.I. The request had been made courteously and just after the first P.O.E.I. had gone out of his way to do a service for A. R. Gethryn. *Ergo*, A. R. Gethryn must deliver the letter—which, by the way, has nothing in itself to do with this story.

So, upon the afternoon of August the eleventh, Anthony was driving from the port of Normouth to the hamlet of Friars' Wick and the country house of Sir Adrian Le Fane.

He pushed the Voisin along at speed, thankful they'd managed to send it down to Normouth for him. The alternatives would have been a hired car or a train—and on a stifling day like this the thought of either was insupportable.

The ship had docked late, and it was already after six when he reached the outskirts of Mostyn and slowed to a crawl through its narrow streets and came out sweating on the other side. The low gray arch of the sky seemed lower still—and the grayness was becoming tinged with black. The trees which lined the road stood drooping and still, and over everything was a soft and ominous hush through which the sound of passing cars and even the singing of his own tires seemed muted.

He reduced his speed as he drew near the Bastwick cross-roads. Up to here he had known his way—but now he must traverse unknown territory.

He stopped the car altogether, and peered at a signpost. Its fourth and most easterly arm said, with simple helpfulness, "FRIARS' WICK—8."

He followed the pointing arm and found himself boxed in between high and unkempt hedgerows, driving along a narrow lane which twisted up and across the shoulder of a frowning, sparsely-wooded hill. There were no cars here; no traffic of any kind; no sign of humanity. The sky had grown more black than gray, and the light had a gloom-laden, coppery quality. The air was heavy enough to make it difficult to breathe.

The Voisin breasted the hill—and the road shook itself and straightened out as it coasted down, now steep and straight, between wide and barren stretches of heathland.

The village of Friars' Wick, hidden by the foot of another hill, came upon Anthony suddenly, after rounding the first curve in the winding valley.

Although he was going slowly, for the corner had seemed dangerous, the abrupt emergence of the small township—materializing, it seemed, out of nothingness—was almost a physical shock. He slowed still more, and the big black car rolled silently along the narrow street, between slate-fronted cottages and occasional little shops.

It was a gray place, sullen and resentful and with something about it at once strange and familiar; an air which at the same time fascinated and repelled him; an aura which touched some sixth sense and set up a strange tingling inside him . . .

He recognized the feeling but wasn't sure if it were genuine; it might have been induced by a combination of the weather and his personal irritation at having to come so far out of his way from London and home.

He reached the end of the main and only street of Friars' Wick, the point where the small church faces the inn across a traditional triangle of emerald grass. Here he stopped the car. He knew he must be within a mile or so of LeFane's house, and the easiest way to find out was to ask.

He looked around for someone to ask. He saw there was no human being in sight—and for the first time realized there had been none at all since he had come around the hill and into the village.

Something hit the leather of the seat beside him with a small, smacking sound. A single florin-sized raindrop.

He looked up at the sky. Now it was so close, so lowering, that it seemed almost to brush the tops of the big elms behind the white-fronted inn. A spatter of the big drops hit the dust of the road, each one separated by feet from its fellows. He realized he was waiting for thunder.

But no thunder came—and no relief. The coppery light was greener now, and the hush almost palpable.

And then he saw a man. A man who stood beside the out-buildings of the inn, some twenty yards away.

He was an ordinary-looking man. He fitted his surroundings, yet seemed to stand out from them in sharp relief.

He wore a shapeless hat, and a shapeless coat, and he had a shotgun under his arm.

Anthony felt an increase of the odd tingling. He looked back along the gray street and still saw no one. He looked at the man again. He looked the other way and saw for the first time the cluster of oaks on the rise away to his left; saw too, above the oaks, the chimneys of a big house.

He drove off. He followed his eyes, and sent

the car up another twisting lane and came presently to imposing wrought-iron gates.

The gates stood open, and he turned the Voisin into them—and at once was in a different world. Outside, the land had been dead and tired and sterile, but here it was lush and well-groomed and self-conscious. A hundred feet above, and still half a mile away, he could see the chimneys and the rambling Tudor building beneath them.

There came another flurry of the outsized raindrops, and he thought of stopping and closing the car. He slowed and as he did so his attention was attracted by something off the road to his right. A figure which stood under one of the trees and looked at him. A large and square and gauntly powerful figure, as motionless as the man in the deserted village had been.

He stared, and for some reason stopped the car. The figure was clad in nondescript clothes, and it was with something of a shock that he realized it was a woman's.

He went on staring—and it turned abruptly and strode off into the shadows of a copse . . .

There were no more raindrops and he drove on, toward the lawns and gardens and the house itself . . .

When the rain came in earnest, it was a solid sheet of water, a deluge. It started almost as soon as Anthony was in the house—while, in fact, he was being greeted by his hostess, who was blondish and handsome and just verging upon the haggard. She was ultra-smart and over-nervous. She laughed a great deal, but her eyes never changed. She was, it appeared, Mrs. Peter Crecy, and she was also the daughter of Sir Adrian LeFane. She swept Anthony away from the butler and took him to a room which was half-library, half-salon, and wholly luxurious. She gave him a drink and sprayed him with staccato, half-finished sentences. He gathered that he couldn't see her father just yet—"the man, as usual, doesn't seem to *be* anywhere . . ." He gathered that he was expected to stay the night— "But you *must*—my parent gave the strictest orders . . ."

So he murmured politely and resigned himself, helped no little by the sight of the rain beyond the mullioned windows.

He was given eventually into the care of a black-coated discretion named Phillips, who led him up stairs and along corridors to a sybaritic and most unTudor-like suite.

He bathed luxuriously and when he had finished, found his trunk unpacked, his dinner clothes laid out. In shirt-sleeves, he walked over to a window and looked out and saw the rain still a heavy, glittering, unbroken veil over the half-dark world. He lit a cigarette, dropped into a chair, stretched out his long legs, and found himself wondering about the village of Friars' Wick and its odd and ominous and indescribable air. But he didn't wonder either long or seriously for, from somewhere below, he heard the booming of a gong.

He put on his coat and slipped LeFane's letter into his breast-pocket and made a leisurely way downstairs.

He had expected a dinner which would at the most have a couple of other guests besides himself.

492

He found instead, when he was directed to the drawingroom, a collection of eight or ten people. They were clustered in the middle of the room, and from the centre of the cluster the voice of Mrs. Peter Crecy rose and fell like a syncopated fountain.

"Well, that's settled!" it was saying. "Not a word about it—too frightfully macabre! . . ."

Anthony made an unobtrusive entrance, but she saw him immediately and surged towards. She was contriving paradoxically to look handsomer and yet more haggard in a black-and-gold evening gown. She led him on a tour of introduction. He met, and idly catalogued in his mind, a Lord and Lady Bracksworth (obvious Master of Fox Hounds—wife knits); a Mr. and Mrs. Shelton-Jones (obvious Foreign Office—wife aspiring Ambassadress); a Professor Martel (possible physicist, Middle-European, bearded, egocentric); a Mr. and Mrs. Geoffrey Dale (newspaper-owner, leader-writing wife)—and then, an oasis in this desert, his old friend Carol Dunning.

She was sitting in an enormous, high-winged chair and he hadn't seen her until Mrs. Crecy led him towards it.

"And—Miss Dunning," said Mrs. Crecy. "The novelist, of course . . . But I believe you know each other—Carol Rushworth Dunning—"

"Hi, there!" said Miss Dunning refreshingly. A wide and impish smile creased her impish and ageless and unmistakably American face.

"What would happen," asked Miss Dunning, "if I said, long time no see?"

493

"Nothing," Anthony said. "I concur. *Too long.*"

He noted with relief that Mrs. Crecy had left them. He saw a servant with a tray of cocktails and got one for Miss Dunning and another for himself.

"Thanks," said Miss Dunning. "Mud in your eye!" She took half the drink at a gulp and looked up at Anthony. "If the answer wasn't so obvious, I'd ask what brought you into this *galère?*"

Anthony said, "Same to you." He reflected on the letter in his pocket. "And what's obvious? Or has the Diplomatic Service—"

He broke off, looking across the room at a man who hadn't merely come into it, but had effected an entrance. A tall, slight, stoop-shouldered person with a velvet dinner jacket, a mane of gray hair, and a certain distinction of which he was entirely aware.

"Enter Right Centre," Anthony said to Miss Dunning. "But who? I've lost my program."

She looked at him in surprise. "Curiouser and curiouser," she said. "So the man doesn't know his own host. That's him—Sir Adrian LeFane in person. Old World, huh?"

"Well, well," said Anthony, and stood up as LeFane, having hovered momentarily over the central group with a courtly smile of general greeting, came straight towards him.

"Colonel Gethryn?" He held out a slim white hand, beautifully shaped. "I trust you'll forgive me for not being here to welcome you. But"— the hand sketched a vague, graceful movement in the air— "I was forced to be elsewhere . . ." The

494

hand came down and offered itself again and Anthony shook it.

"Out, were you?" said Miss Dunning. "Caught in the rain?"

"Not—ah—noticeably, my dear." LeFane gave her an avuncular smile. "I regard myself as fortunate—"

But he never told them why—for at that moment his daughter joined them, words preceding her like fire from a flame-thrower. She was worried, it seemed, about someone, or thing, called "Marya"—you could hear the "y"—who, or which, should have put in appearance.

She led her parent away—and again Anthony was relieved. He looked at Miss Dunning and said:

"Who is Marya, what is she? Or it, maybe? Or even he?"

"Dax."

"An impolite sound." Anthony surveyed her. "Unless—oh, shades of Angelo! Do you mean the sculptress? The Riondetto group at Geneva? The Icarus at Hendon?"

"Right!" Miss Dunning looked at the door and pointed. "And here she is . . ."

Striding from the door towards the advancing LeFane was a gaunt giant of a woman. Despite her size—she must have topped six feet—and her extraordinary appearance—she wore a strange, flowing, monk-like garment of some harsh, dark-green material—she was impressive rather than ludicrous. Her crag-like face gave no answer to the best of LeFane's smiles, but she permitted herself to be steered towards the group around

Mrs. Crecy, and in a moment seemed to become its pivot.

"Well?" said Miss Dunning.

"Remarkable," said Anthony. "In fact, I remarked her a couple of hours ago. She was under a tree. Looking."

"Like what?" Miss Dunning wanted to know.

But she wasn't answered. Two more people were entering the room—a well-built, pleasant-faced man of thirty-odd, with a tired look and what used to be called "professional" appearance; a small, angular, weatherbeaten little woman, with no proportions and a face like a happy horse.

Once more Anthony looked at Miss Dunning, and once more she enlightened him.

"Human beings," said Miss Dunning. "Refreshing, isn't it? Local doctor and wife. I like 'em." She looked at her empty glass and handed it to Anthony. "See what you can do," she said.

But he had no chance to do it. Mrs. Crecy swooped, and he was drawn towards Marya Dax and presented, and surveyed by strange dark eyes which seemed to be all pupil and were almost on a level with his own.

He murmured some politeness, and was ignored. He turned away and was pounced upon again, and found himself meeting Dr. and Mrs. Carmichael. Looking at the woman's freckled, equine face, he was assailed by a flicker of memory.

He shook hands with the husband, but they hadn't said a word to each other when the wife spoke.

"You don't remember me, do you?" She looked up at Anthony with bright, small eyes.

"That's the worst thing you can do to anyone, Min!" her husband chided her affectionately. "You ought to be ashamed of yourself."

"If you'll let me have a moment, I'll tell you," Anthony said—and then, "It's some time ago— and I remember pigtails—of course! You're Henry Martin's daughter."

"There!" Mrs. Carmichael caught hold of her husband's arm. "He did it!"

"And he'd have done it before," said Carmichael, smiling at her, "only he couldn't see Little Miss Moneybags as the wife of a country sawbones." He patted her hand.

"Colonel Gethryn," said Mrs. Carmichael, "I'm going to trade an old acquaintance. I'm going to ask you a—an indiscreet question. I—"

Her husband moved his broad shoulders uncomfortably. "Please, Min, go easy," he said.

"Don't be silly, Jim. You've *got* to try—and Colonel Gethryn won't mind."

She looked up at Anthony like an earnest foal. "Will you?"

Anthony looked down at the appealing face. "I shouldn't think so," he said, and was going to add, "Try me out," when dinner was announced and the party began to split into their pairs and he found, with pleasure, that he was to take in Miss Dunning.

The meal, although heavy and of ceremonious splendor, was excellent, and the wines were beyond reproach. So that Anthony found time passing pleasantly enough until, as he chatted with Miss Dunning beside him, he heard his name emerge from what appeared to be a heated argument lower down the table.

". . . Surely Colonel Gethryn's the one to tell us that!" came the husky voice of Mrs. Carmichael. "After all, he's probably the only person here who knows anything about that sort of thing."

Anthony, as he was obviously meant to, turned his head. He found many eyes upon him, and said to Mrs. Carmichael, "What sort of thing? Or shouldn't I ask?"

"Crime, of course!" Mrs. Carmichael looked as if she were pricking her ears forward. "Crime in general and, of course, one crime in particular. Or two, I should say."

Anthony repressed a sigh. He said, hopefully, "If they're new and British-made, I'm afraid I can't help you. I've been away for months, and only landed this afternoon. I haven't even seen an English paper for a fortnight."

With a smile alarming in its area and determination, Mrs. Crecy cut into the talk. She said:

"How fortunate for you, Mr. Gethryn. So abysmally dull they've been! And I think it's a *shame* the way these people are trying to make you talk shop . . ."

She transferred the ferocious smile to little Mrs. Carmichael, who shriveled and muttered something about being "terribly sorry, Jacqueline," and tried to start a conversation with Lord Bracksworth about hunting.

But she was cut off in mid-sentence by Marya

Dax, who was sitting on Adrian LeFane's right, and therefore obliquely across the table from Anthony. Throughout the meal she had sat like a silent, brooding Norn but now she leaned forward, gripping the edge of the table with enormous, blunt-fingered hands, and fixing her dark gaze on Anthony, she said, in a harsh contralto:

"Perhaps you have no need to read the papers. Perhaps you can smell where there is evil."

It was neither question nor statement and Anthony, smiling a smile which might have meant anything, prepared to let it lie.

But the Foreign Office, in the person of Mr. Shelton-Jones, saw opportunity for conversation.

"An interesting thought, Miss Dax, " said Mr. Shelton-Jones, turning his horn-rimmed gaze upon the Norn. "Whether or not the trained mind becomes attuned, as it were, to appreciating the *atmosphere*, the *wavelength*—perhaps I should call it the *aura*—which might very well emanate from wrongdoing."

The Norn didn't so much as glance at Mr. Shelton-Jones: she kept her dark gaze fixed upon Anthony's face.

But Mr. Shelton-Jones was undaunted and now he too looked at Anthony.

"What do you say, Mr. Gethryn?" he asked. "*Is* there a criminal aura? Have you ever known of any—ah—'case' in which the investigator was assisted by any such—ah—metaphysical emanation?"

Anthony sighed inwardly; but this was too direct to leave unanswered. He said, "You mean what the Americans might call a super-hunch? I'm no professional, of course, but I have known of such things."

The Press joined in now, in the slender shape of Mrs. Dale.

"How *fas*-cinating!" she said. "Could you possibly tell us—"

"Please!" Anthony smiled. "I was going on to say that the super-hunch— the 'emanation'—is utterly untrustworthy. Therefore, it's worse than useless—it's dangerous. It has to be ignored."

Surprisingly, because he had been silent throughout the meal, it was the bearded physicist Martel who chimed in now. He jutted the beard aggressively in Anthony's direction, and demanded, "Unt why iss that?" in a tone notably devoid of courtesy.

Anthony surveyed him. "Because," he said coolly, "one can never be sure the impact of the super-hunch is genuine. The feeling might very well be caused by indigestion."

There were smiles, but not from the Professor, who glared, grunted, and turned back to his plate.

Someone said, "But seriously, Colonel Gethryn—"

Anthony said, "I am serious." The topic couldn't be dropped now, so he might as well deal with it properly. He said:

"I can even give you a recent instance of what I mean . . . I was at the Captain's dinner on the *Guinivere* last night. I drank too much. I didn't get quite enough sleep. And when I landed, the current deluge was brewing. Result, as I drove through Friars' Wick, which I'd never seen before, I had the father and mother of all super-hunches. The countryside—the village itself—the fact that there didn't happen to be anyone about —the black sky—everything combined to produce a feeling of"—he shrugged—"well, of evil. Which is patently absurd. And almost certainly, when you think of the Captain's dinner, stomachic in origin."

He was surprised—very much and most unusually surprised—by the absolute silence which fell on the company as he finished speaking. He looked from face to face and saw on every one a ruling astonishment. Except in the case of Professor Martel, who scowled sourly and managed at the same time to twist his mouth into a sardonic smile of disbelief.

Someone said, "That's—*extraordinary*, Colonel Gethryn!"

Martel said, "You ssay you haff not read the paperss. But you haff hear the wireless—perhaps . . ."

Anthony looked at the beard, then at the eyes above it. He said, "I don't know what that means . . . Just as well, no doubt."

Marya Dax looked down the table at Martel, examining him with remote eyes. She said, to no one in particular, "That man should be made to keep quiet!" and there was a moment of raw and uncomfortable tension. Mrs. Crecy bit at her lips as if to restrain them from trembling. Adrian LeFane propped an elbow on the table and put a hand up to his face, half-hiding it.

Miss Dunning saved the day. She turned to Anthony beside her with semi-comic amazement

501

wrinkling her goblin face. She said, on exactly the right note:

"Remarkable, my dear Holmes!" And then she laughed exactly the right laugh. "And the odd thing is—you don't know what you've done. Maybe you'd better find out."

The tension relaxed, and Anthony said, "I seem to have caused a sensation." He looked around the table again. "It could mean there *is* something"—he glanced at the Norn—"evil-smelling in Friars' Wick."

There was a babble of five or six voices then, all talking at once, and through them, quite clearly, came the husky eagerness of Mrs. Carmichael's.

". . . most wonderful thing I ever heard of! Colonel Gethryn, do you realize you've *proved* what Miss Dax was saying."

Anthony looked at Mrs. Carmichael and smiled. "That isn't proof," he said. "Might be coincidence. The Captain's dinner was—lavish."

But Mrs. Carmichael wasn't to be deterred. "You've got to hear," she said. "You've *got* to!" She spoke to her husband across the table. "Jim, tell him all about it."

A worried look came into Dr. Carmichael's tired, nice-looking face. He cast a glance towards his hostess, but she said nothing, and Mrs. Carmichael said, "Go *on*, Jim!" and Mrs. Dale said, "Please, Doctor!" and he capitulated.

He looked across the table at Anthony. "I'm deputed for this," he said, "because I happen to look after the Police work in this part of Downshire. Most of the time the job's a sinecure. But lately—"

He blew out his cheeks in a soundless little whistle and proceeded to tell of the two murders which had so much exercised the Press, particularly the *Despatch*. He was precise and vaguely official. He merely *stated*—but yet, and although it was no news to them, everyone else at the table was absolutely silent. They were, for the most part, watching the face of Anthony Ruthven Gethryn.

Who said, when the statement was over, "H'mm! Sort of Ripper Redivivus." His face had offered no signs of any sort to the watchers. It had, as he listened, been as completely blank as a poker player's, with the lids half-closed over the green eyes.

Dr. Carmichael said slowly, "Yes, I suppose so. If there are any more—which I personally am afraid of—although the Chief Constable doesn't agree with me . . . ."

"He doesn't?" Anthony's eyes were fully open now. "Who is he?"

"Major General Sir Rigby Forsythe." Acid had crept into the doctor's tone. "He 'can't see his way' to calling in Scotland Yard. He considers Inspector Fennell and myself 'alarmists.' He—" Dr. Carmichael cut himself off abruptly with a grimace of impatience.

But Anthony finished the sentence for him. "—refuses to realize that two brutal murders, apparently carried out by a sexual maniac, could possibly be the beginning of a series. That it?"

"Precisely!" Dr. Carmichael brightened at this

ready understanding. "And he goes on refusing to realize, in spite of the fact that Fennell's tried a hundred times to show him that as the death of either of those poor women couldn't conceivably have benefited anyone, the murders must have been done by a maniac." A faint expression of disgust passed over Dr. Carmichael's face. "A peculiarly revolting maniac! And maniacs who've found a way of gratifying their mania—well, they don't stop . . ."

"For mysself," came the harshly sibilant voice of Professor Martel, "I do not think a maniac." He was sitting back in his chair now, the beard tilted upward. "I think a public benefactor."

He paused and there came the slightly bewildered silence he had obviously expected. He said:

"Those women! Thosse creaturess! I haff sseen them both while they were alife. They sserved no purposse and they were hideouss! The worlt is better less them."

Now the silence was shocked. It was broken by Marya Dax. Again she looked down the table towards Martel, and again seemed to examine him. She said:

"There is one hideous thing here with us. It is your mind." She ceased to examine the man, and went on. "No human body," she said, "is completely without beauty."

"Oh, come now, my dear Miss Dax," said Lady Bracksworth surprisingly, in a mild but determined little voice. "Although I have nothing but sympathy"—she darted a look of dislike towards Martel— "for those poor unfortunate women, I must say that at least one of them—Sarah Paddock, I mean—was a truly disgraceful object."

The Norn turned slow and blazing eyes upon this impudence.

"This woman," said the Norn, "this Paddock —I suppose you did not ever look at her hands?" She said, "They were dirty always. They were harsh with work. But they were beautiful."

"An interesting thought indeed!" said Mr. Shelton-Jones. "Can beauty in the—ah—human frame be considered, as it were, in *units*—or must it be, before we recognize it, a totality of such units?"

Mrs. Carmichael said, "I think Miss Dax is right." She looked over at her husband. "Don't you think so?"

He smiled at her, but didn't answer and she said insistently, "Isn't she right, Jim? You think she is, don't you?"

"Of course she is," Carmichael said. He looked around the table. "In my profession I see a great many human bodies. And I see a great many"—he looked at Mr. Shelton-Jones —"beautiful 'units' in otherwise ugly specimens. For instance"—he looked at Marya Dax — "I particularly noticed poor Sarah Paddock's hands."

Mr. Shelton-Jones settled his spectacles more firmly astride his nose. "But, my dear sir—if I may be permitted to support my original contention—what beauty can there be in a 'beauty-unit' if such a unit is a mere island, as it were, in an ocean of ugliness?" Obviously prepared for debate, he leaned back in his chair, fixing his gaze upon Dr Carmichael.

Carmichael said, "Plenty. You can't deny, for instance, that Sarah Paddock's hands were beautiful in themselves." He seemed nettled by the Parliamentary manner of Mr. Shelton-Jones. "Suppose Miss Dax had modelled them!"

"Then," Mr. Shelton-Jones blandly observed, "they would have been apart from their hideous surroundings."

"Euclidian," said Anthony. "Some of the parts may or may not be equal to their total."

But Dr. Carmichael went on looking at Mr. Shelton-Jones.

"All right," said Dr. Carmichael. "Suppose you saw magnificent shoulders on a —on an extreme case of *lupus vulgaris*. Would the horrible condition of the face and neck make the shoulders repulsive too?"

"The whole picture would be—ah—definitely unpleasing." Mr. Shelton-Jones was blandness itself and the Norn turned her dark, examining gaze upon him.

Color had risen to Dr. Carmichael's face. He stared hard at Mr. Shelton-Jones and said:

"Let's try again. Do you mean to tell me that if you saw Titian hair on a typical troglodytic head, you'd think it was ugly, because of its setting?"

"I agree with the doctor," said the Norn. "The other killed woman—her name I forget—was worse formed than the first. But the shape of her skull was noble."

"Umpf-chnff!" remarked Lord Bracksworth. "That'd be the fortune-tellin' one, the Stebbins woman . . . D'ja know, I was talkin' to that Inspector-fellah s'mornin', and he was tellin' me that when they found her, this old gal—"

At the head of the table Adrian LeFane sat suddenly upright. He brought his open hand violently down upon the cloth, so that the glasses beside his plate chimed and jingled.

"Please!" His face twisted as if with physical pain. "Let us have no more of this—this—intolerable *ugliness!"*

It was about an hour after dinner—which, thanks mainly to the social genius of Miss Dunning, had ended on a subdued but embarrassing note—that Mrs. Carmichael, her husband in attendance, contrived to corner Anthony in a remote quarter of the vast drawing-room.

He had just come in after a visit to Adrian LeFane's study, where he had at last delivered the letter which had nothing to do with this tale. He allowed himself to be cornered, although he would much rather have talked with Miss Dunning, because there was something desperately appealing in the filly-like gaze of Mrs. Carmichael.

She said, "Oh, please, Colonel Gethryn, *may* we talk to you!" Her long, freckled face was as earnest as her voice.

Anthony said, "Why not?"

Carmichael said, "Oh, Min, why insist on worrying the man?" He gave Anthony a little apologetic smile.

"Because it's worrying *you*, darling!" Mrs. Carmichael laid a hand on her husband's arm, but went on looking at Colonel Gethryn.

"Jim's terribly upset," she said, "about that

507

horrid old Chief Constable. He thinks—I mean, Jim does—that the Downshire police can't possibly catch this dreadful murderer unless they get help from Scotland Yard. And they can't get it unless the Chief Constable asks for it . . ."

Her husband interrupted. "For heaven's sake, dear, Gethryn knows all about that sort of thing!"

She paid no attention to him. She said to Anthony, "And what I was going to ask you: we wondered if there was any way—any way at all— you could use your influence to—"

She left the sentence in midair as she caught sight of a servant approaching her husband.

"Dr. Carmichael," said the man. He lowered his voice, but his words came clearly. "Excuse me, sir, but there's an important message for you." A curious blend of horrified dismay and cassandrine pleasure showed through his servitor's mask. He said:

"Inspector Fennell telephoned. There's been another of these dreadful murders. He wants you to come at once, sir, to Pilligrew Lane, where it comes out by Masham's . . ."

"Just around the next corner," said Dr. Carmichael, and braked hard.

Beside him, Anthony grunted—he never has liked and never will like being driven.

The little car skidded around a sharp turn and into the mouth of a lane which lay dark and narrow between a high hedge and the looming backs of three great barns.

Through the steady, glittering sheet of the rain, a group of men and cars showed ahead, barring

508

the way completely and standing out black in the glare of headlights.

Carmichael stopped his engine and scrambled out. Anthony followed and felt the sweeping of the rain down over him and the seeping of viscous mud through his thin soles. He followed Carmichael towards the group and a figure turned from it, advancing on them and flashing an electric torch—a man in a heavy black storm-coat and the flat, visored cap of a uniformed Police Inspector.

Carmichael said, "Fennell, this is Colonel Gethryn—" and didn't get any further because the man, having darted a look at Anthony, turned back to him in amazement.

"But, Doctor," said Inspector Fennell in a hoarse and confidential whisper, "Sir Rigby's done it already. Did it last night, without saying a word to me. Called London and got the Commissioner, and turned up, after I'd phoned him about this, all complete with a Detective-Inspector who'd just arrived from the Yard!"

Carmichael stared as if he couldn't believe his ears, and Anthony said to Fennell, "Who did they send? Hobday?"

Fennell said, "That's right, sir," and led the way towards the group in the light.

They slithered after him through the mud, and in a moment Hobday was looking at Anthony and saying, "Good Lord, sir, where did *you* drop from?"

And then there was a word with Sir Rigby Forsythe, who seemed somewhat taken aback by Anthony's presence, and a moment or so of waiting

509

while the photographers finished their work over what lay in the ditch against the hedge.

Anthony said, "This new victim? I suppose it's a woman—but what kind? Was she another local character?"

Fennell said, "Yes, she's a woman all right, sir. And it's—it's horrible, worse than the others." He glanced towards the ditch and quickly away again. He seemed to realize he had strayed most unprofessionally from the point, and cleared his throat. "I don't think she's—she was a local, sir. So far nobody's recognized her. Seems to've been one of those gipsy basket-menders. She had an old horse and cart—prob'ly was just passing through on her way to Deyning."

Hobday said, "If it hadn't been for the horse, we wouldn't have known yet. But a farm laborer found it wandering and began to look for its owner."

The photographers finished their work, and one of them came up to the Chief Constable and saluted. "All through, sir," he said, his voice shaky and uncertain.

Sir Rigby Forsythe looked at Anthony, then at Carmichael and the others. His weatherbeaten face was lined and pallid. He said, "You fellahs go ahead. I've seen all I need." He stood where he was while Fennell, visibly conquering reluctance, led the way with Carmichael, and Hobday and Anthony followed.

The headlights of the police cars cut through the water-drenched darkness. They made a nightmare tableau of the thing which lay half in and half out of the ditch. Anthony muttered, "God!"

and the usually stolid Hobday drew in his breath with a little hiss. Carmichael, his face set and grim, dropped on his knees in the oozing mud. He made a cursory examination.

Then he stood up. "All right," he said. "We can move her now," and then, helped by Anthony and Hobday, lifted the thing and set it upon clean wet grass and in merciful shadow. He straightened the saturated rags of its clothing, and then suddenly dropped on one knee again and said, "Anyone got a torch?"

Hobday gave him one, and he shone the light on the head, and gently moved the heavy, mud-covered mass of red hair away from the features it was covering.

"Just wondering whether I'd ever seen her," he said. He kept the light of the torch on the face, and it stared up at them, washed cleaner every moment by the flooding rain. It was a brutish, sub-human face, and although it was distorted by death and terror, it could have been little more prepossessing in life.

Carmichael shook his head. "No," he said. "They're right. She's a stranger round here." He switched off the torch, but Anthony said, "Just a minute," and took it from him and knelt beside the body himself and switched the light on again and peered at the throat, where a darkness like a big bruise showed in the hollow below the chin.

But after a moment, he too shook his head. "No. It's a birthmark," he said, and Carmichael peered at it and said, "Yes. Or possibly an old scar."

They stood up, and Hobday took the torch and

knelt in his turn and began slow, methodical examination.

Anthony said, "Silly question, I know, but about how long since death?" A little cascade of water tumbled from his hat-brim as he bent his head to button his raincoat, which had come undone.

Carmichael said, "Oh—very loosely, and subject to error—not more than five hours, not less than two."

Anthony looked at his watch, whose glowing figures said eleven forty-five, and found himself calculating times. But this didn't get him anywhere, and he was glad when, thirty minutes later, he found himself being driven back to LeFane's house by Carmichael. He said to Carmichael on the way:

"You see, it's definitely not my sort of thing. Mass murders are mad murders, and mad murders, in the ordinary sense of the word, are motiveless. Which makes them a matter for routine politico-military methods. At which I'm worse than useless, while men like Hobday are solid and brilliant at the same time."

Carmichael smiled. "I'm glad you're both here—Hobday and yourself. I'll sleep better tonight than I have for a week."

They reached the house and were no sooner in the big hall than they were surrounded. They were plied with drinks and food, and besieged with questions. Was it really another of the *same* murders? Where had it happened? Was the victim the same *sort* of person? Did they think the murderer would be caught this time? Wasn't there something terribly *wrong* with police methods when things like this were allowed to go on? Wouldn't it be a good idea to have a curfew, or a registration every day of the movements of every man, woman and child in the district?

Mr. Shelton-Jones said, "An interesting point. How far may the liberties of the individual be restricted when such restriction is—ah—for the purpose of protecting the community?"

Miss Dunning said, "Human beings are terrifying, aren't they?" and shuddered a little.

Professor Martel said, "I woult like to know— wass thiss one usseless and hideouss like the otherss?"

Mrs. Carmichael said, "Oh, *had* Sir Rigby sent for Scotland Yard *already?* Oh, thank *goodness!*"

Everyone said something. Except Adrian LeFane and Marya Dax. And they were not present.

Anthony, throwing aside civility, at last forced his way upstairs. It seemed to him that he was even more grateful than the Carmichaels for the advent of Detective-Inspector Hobday.

He made ready for bed and then, smoking a last cigarette and wondering how soon in the morning he could decently leave, strolled over to a window.

The rain had stopped now and a pale moon shone through clouds onto the sodden earth. By the watery light he saw a figure striding up the steps of a terrace beneath him, making for the house. It was tall and powerful and square-shouldered and unmistakable in spite of its shapeless coat and headgear.

513

He watched it until it was out of sight beneath him. He heard a door open and close.

He went over to the bed and sat on the edge of it and finished the cigarette. He pondered. He stubbed out the cigarette at last and got into bed. After all, if sculptresses liked to walk at night, why shouldn't they?

But he knew he would stop on his way home tomorrow and have a word with Hobday.

He went to sleep.

It was six o'clock on the next afternoon. He had been in London and at home since one. He sat in the library at Stukely Gardens with his wife and his son.

A violent storm had replaced yesterday's deluge. It had raged intermittently over London and the whole south of England since early morning, and still the hard, heavy rain drove against the windows, while thunder rumbled and great flashes of lightning kept tearing the half-darkness.

Master Alan Gethryn gave his approval of the weather. "It sort of makes it all small and comf't-able in here," he said, looking up from the jigsaw puzzle strewn about the floor.

Anthony said, "I know exactly what you mean," and looked at his wife, who sat on the arm of his chair.

Master Alan Gethryn pored over the puzzle—an intricate forest-scene of which he had only one corner done. He sighed and scratched his head, and then suddenly laughed.

"It's like what Mr. Haslam's always saying," he said—and Lucia looked at Anthony and explained *sotto voce*, "Master at the new school," and then said to her son, "What d'you mean, old boy?"

He looked up at her, still smiling. "He's *always* saying, 'You chaps can't see the wood for the trees.'" He chuckled. "Like this puzzle . . ."

Sublimely unconscious of the effect his words had made upon his father, he returned to his labors.

But Lucia, watching her husband's face, was concerned. She had to wait until her son had left them and gone supperwards, but the moment the door had closed behind him, she stood over Anthony and looked down at him and said:

"What's the matter, darling? You've got that look. What did Alan say?"

Anthony reached up a long arm and pulled her down onto his knees. "He gave me an idea— unintentionally, of course." He kissed her. "A damned nasty, uncomfortable idea. I'd like to forget about it."

Lucia said, "You know you won't. So you'd better tell me."

Anthony said, "Suppose I wanted to kill someone—let's say, your Uncle Perceval. And suppose his demise would benefit me to such an extent that I was afraid a nice straight murder would inevitably point to me. And suppose I were that most dangerous of madmen, the secret megalomaniac, and utterly ruthless to boot. So suppose I started a wave of apparently insane slaying, and got well going with three murders of middle-aged clubmen I didn't know at all—and then killed Uncle Perceval in exactly the same way—

515

and then killed three more middle-aged clubmen! The police would be chasing a madman with an extraordinary quirk. They wouldn't dream of chasing me!"

"What loathsome thoughts you do have!" Lucia turned her head to look at his face. "Oh, Anthony—is that just an idea? Or do you think it's what's happening in Downshire?"

"Oh, just an idea," said Anthony slowly. "It doesn't fit . . ."

She dropped a kiss on his forehead and stood up. She said, "I'll get you a drink. And after that, my lad, you've got to change—we're due at the Dufresnes' by eight. White tie."

She started to cross the room, then checked. She said:

"What on earth did Alan say that gave you that dreadful notion?"

Anthony looked at her. "My dear girl!" he said. "'You can't see the wood for the trees' . . ."

Lucia shivered, went out of the room, came back with his drink, and very soon herded him upstairs.

Forty-five minutes later she walked into his dressing-room. He was tying his tie, and he saw her in the mirror and said, "You know, Americans really develop the possibilities of our language. Baby, you look like a million dollars!"

She said, "I love you. But we're going to be late and then I won't."

He put the finishing touches to the bow. "Get my coat, beldame," he said, and started to distribute keys and money and cigarette case among his pockets.

516

Lucia crossed towards the big wardrobe. Beside it was Anthony's trunk, and on a nearby chair a neat pile of the clothing with which he had traveled. Something about the pile caught Lucia's eye, and she stopped and looked down at it. She said, "Whatever happened to this dinner jacket?"

"Rain last night," Anthony said. "White'll see to it."

She smiled. Carefully she picked something from the shoulder of the black coat. She said, "He ought to've seen to this, oughtn't he? Before *I* saw it?"

She went towards him, carrying her hands in front of her, one above the other and a good two feet apart.

"Magnificent!" said Anthony. "Most impressive! But what's the role?"

She came close to him. She moved her hands and there was a glint of light between them.

He saw a long hair of glittering reddish-gold.

He said, "Not Guilty, M'lud," and looked at the hair again.

He said, "Nobody at LeFane's had that color. Or length . . ."

He said, "Good *God!*"

He jumped across the room and snatched at the telephone.

And two minutes later was being informed that, owing to storm-damage, all the trunk lines to Downshire were out of order . . .

He began to tear off the dress clothes.

He said, "Get them to bring round the car! Quick!"

517

Little Mrs. Carmichael lay on the rather uncomfortable couch in the livingroom of Dr. Carmichael's rather uncomfortable house. She was pretending to read but really she was listening to the thunder.

She wished Jim hadn't had to go out on a call, especially on a night like this. She thought about Jim and how wonderful he was. Although it was two years now since they'd been married, she was happier than she had been on her honeymoon. Happy—and proud. Proud of Jim, and proud of herself, too; proud that she didn't mind uncomfortable sofas and cups with chips in them and a gas fire in the bedroom. Proud of her cleverness —her really heaven-inspired cleverness—in realizing right at the start, even before they were married, that a man of Jim's caliber couldn't possibly bear living on his wife's money . . .

The thunder was far away now, and almost casual. Little Mrs. Carmichael dozed . . .

She was awakened by the sound of a key in the front door—Jim's key. She heard Jim's step in the hall and jumped up off the sofa and went to the door to meet him—and then was shocked by his appearance as he threw it open just before she reached it. He had his hat on still, and his raincoat. They were both dark and dripping with water. He was frowning, and his face was very white, there was a look in his eyes she'd never seen before.

She said, "Jim! What is it, dearest? What's *happened?*"

"Accident," he said. "I ran over someone . . ."

He pulled the back of his hand across his forehead so that his hat was pushed back and she noticed, with utter irrelevance, the little red line which the brim had made across the skin.

He said, "Come and help me, will you? Put on a coat and run out to the car. He's in the back seat." He turned away and strode across the hall to the surgery door. "With you in a minute," he said.

She ran to the hall cupboard and dragged out a raincoat. She tugged open the front door and hurried down the path, the uneven brick slippery under her feet.

The gate was open and through the rain she could see the dark shape of Jim's car. She stumbled towards it and pulled open the door and the little light in the roof came on.

There was nothing in the back seat.

Bewildered, she turned—and there was Jim, close to her.

She started to say something—and then she saw Jim's face—

It *was* Jim's face—but she almost didn't recognize it. And there was something bright in his hand, something bright and sharp and terrifying.

She screamed—and suddenly everything went very fast in front of her eyes, the way things used to go fast in films when she was a child, and there was a shouting of men's voices, and something heavy like a stone swished through the air past her and hit Jim on the head, and he fell down and the bright steel thing dropped out of his hand, and two men ran up, and one of them was Colonel Gethryn and the other knelt over Jim, and Colonel

519

Gethryn put his arms around her as she swayed on her feet, and the black wet world spun dizzily faster and faster . . .

"But there isn't anything complex about it," said Anthony. "It started when my son gave me the 'can't-see-the-wood-for-the-trees' idea. And then Lucia found that long, magnificent, red-gold hair on my dinner-jacket. And that's all there was to it . . ."

The others said a lot of things, together and separately.

He waited for them to finish, and then shook his head sadly.

He said, "My dear people, that hair was tantamount to a confession by Dr. James Carmichael, duly signed, attested and registered at Somerset House. I might never have realized it, of course, if Alan hadn't handed me 'wood-for-the-trees.' But as I'd evolved the notion of hiding one murder with a lot of other murders—well, it was completely obvious. Carmichael, whose wife was rich and plain and over-loving, fitted everything. He was a doctor. He could travel about. He—"

"But *why* did the hair necessarily point to him?"

"Because it must have come from the third body. Because no one at LeFane's had hair even remotely red. Of course, it was caked with mud and colorless when it got onto my coat, but by the time it dried—"

"Hold it! Hold it! I *still* don't see how it pointed to the doctor!"

"I'm surprised at you!" Anthony surveyed the speaker with real astonishment.

"After all, you were there at LeFane's. You heard Carmichael arguing with that horn-rimmed intellect from the Foreign Office. Don't you remember him talking about *Titian hair on troglodytes?*"

"Why, yes . . . But—"

"Don't you realize he talked *too soon?* He said that nearly two hours *before* they found the third murderee. And the third murderee was a brute-faced redhead!"

Christianna Brand
(1907–1988)
THE MAN ON THE ROOF

That irascible old smoothie Inspector Cockrill, detective of the Kent police, appears in one of the most celebrated English mysteries ever written: Green for Danger *(1944), set in a London operating theater during the Blitz. It was made into one of the most celebrated of all mystery films, with the incomparable Alastair Sim as Cockrill, in 1946.*

Christianna Brand (Mary Christianna Milne Lewis), the last of the grandes dames of traditional English writing, was, like Josephine Tey, a connoisseur's writer. Her plots are intelligently premeditated, rich in atmosphere, keenly observed, and subtly set forth. She died as this anthology was being prepared, much loved and now much missed.

Sergeant Crum, who, with the assistance of only a fledgling constable, runs the tiny police station in the village of Hawksmere, rang up Chief Inspector Cockrill in Heronsford. "It's the Duke, sir. Phoned to the station and says he's going to shoot hisself."

"The Duke? What Duke? Your Duke, up at the castle?"

Sergeant Crum took a leisurely moment to reflect that in his own small neck of the woods they were hardly so rich in the gilded aristocracy as to necessitate discrimination. Inspector Cockrill, however, had not waited for an answer.

"What have you done about it?"

"Tried to get my constable, sir. Gets his dinner in the village, he does, being his home is there—the Sardine Tin, they call it these days, since the old people—"

"Yes, well, never mind your constable's domestic arrangements—"

"—and they told me he'd suddenly rushed off," continued Crum placidly. "Said he'd heard a shot or something of that. *They* hadn't heard nothing, but the old people are getting a bit—"

"Well, get after him fast, for goodness' sake! I'll be there in half an hour at latest."

The sergeant pursued his unhurried way and at the North Gate leaned out of his car to question the lodgekeeper—and, learning that His Grace had gone down a two–three hours ago towards South Lodge, cursed himself mildly for not having thought of that and started on the long haul round the castle walls to what had once been the opposite entrance. South Lodge, of course! Fisher couldn't have heard a shot fired up at the castle.

The constable met him at the little wooden gate of the graveled path that led up to the lodge, clinging as though for support to his bicycle. Over his large, rather handsome young face was spread a strange pall of grey. He said, "He's dead, Sarge."

"Dead? He's done it?"

"Seems like it. He's lying on the floor in the parlor. Lot of blood around."

"You're sure? You didn't make certain?"

"Door's locked, sir. I looked in at the window, but it's too small to get through. And anyway—"

"I was held up. Started for the castle first. You came here direct?"

"Yessir. I heard the shot, I guessed what it might be. I knew he'd be here— I saw him this morning, turning in at the gate. So I got on me bike and came over."

The lodge was in fact a lodge no longer. In the not too distant past, its magnificent wrought-iron gates had been removed and the gap bricked up except for a small postern door. And the high wall ringing the castle and its grounds, rebuilt in a curve that now left the little house standing outside on its own, in an expanse something under an acre of dull, flat land, was at present covered in a blanket of Christmas snow about two inches deep. A hedge completed a sort of high ring around the building, with a break in it to admit of a small wooden gate leading up to the tiny porch over the front door.

The redundant lodgekeeper had been allowed to remain in residence until the accession of the present Duke about three years ago, when he had been evicted with his poor old wife, so that His Grace, whose single bleak passion was the collection and destruction of butterflies, might convert the place into a sort of playroom for himself and his hobby. Considering that there must, up at the castle, be at least seventy rooms which might equally have served his purpose, the dispossessed might be forgiven for suggesting resentfully—but not to the Duke—that a nook might have been created for him there.

Now, in the light snow, two narrow lines, clearly the marks of the constable's bicycle tires, led up and away from the front door—the return journey having apparently been decidedly wobbly. There was no other mark in the snow.

"No sign of his footsteps."

"No. It hadn't started snowing when I saw him going in through the gate." For whatever reason, the constable had lost more color. "That was a couple of hours ago."

"Oh, well." Sergeant Crum abandoned a secret hope that by delaying his errand until the Inspector should come, he might shift onto other shoulders the onus of the whole alarming affair, for sudden death is not a commonplace in quiet little Hawksmere, nestling under the calm shadow of the castle up the hill. He started off through the light flurry of swirling snow, some vague instinct suggesting that it might be well to avoid the tracks of the bicycle tires. You could see where the constable had propped his machine against the wall of the house and gone up the two or three steps. Snow was shuffled as his footprints came down and appeared to move round to the right.

"I ran round to the side window," said Fisher, following his glance. He indicated a small window to their left. "You can't see in so well from there."

"Yes, well, you'd know, wouldn't you?" said Sergeant Crum.

The door was secured by a Yale lock, the sort that clicks shut of itself, to be opened, when the door is closed, only by its own particular key. "Mm," said the sergeant. He tramped in the constable's footsteps leading round the house, and returned with his rugged countryman's visage the same curious shade of grey. "Certainly *looks* very dead," he said uncomfortably and lifted up his heart in a wordless prayer.

The prayer was answered. There came the throbbing of a car in the snowbound stillness and Chief Inspector Cockrill stood at the little gate. For once his shabby mackintosh was not trailing over one shoulder but was worn with his arms in the sleeves, and pushed back upon his noble head with its spray of fine grey hair was the inevitable ill-fitting hat. Inspector Cockrill is known to pick up any hat that happens to be at hand, to the considerable inconvenience of the true owner. Anything that does not actually deafen and blind him is perfectly acceptable to the Terror of Kent.

He remained for a long time intently surveying the scene: the little house in its flat white circle of snow, ringed in by the wall and the hedge so as to be almost invisible to anyone not looking in over the gate. Nice setting for a locked-room mystery, he thought: which God forbid! Fortunately, it appeared to have been a good, straightforward suicide, heralded in advance by the gentleman himself. And from what he had heard, there would be few to mourn the passing of the sixth Duke of Hawksmere—very few indeed.

A pretty little building, almost fairylike in its present aspect, its highly ornamental pseudo-Gothic façade aglitter with its dusting of snow.

527

An octagonal room, flat-roofed, with a small side window where the lodgekeeper might sit watching for the first signs of approaching vehicles all ready to leap out and open the gates. Into this room, the door opened directly. There was an opposite door leading to the back of the house—two or three small rooms and the household offices. Only the front had been designed to be seen. The rest was cut off and hidden away behind it, considerably less decorative in appearance. The room was furnished only with a desk and a trestle table, upon which were distributed the tools of the Duke's preoccupation, a typewriter, and sheaves of paperwork. There was no other furniture in the house.

Inspector Cockrill stood quietly, taking it all in. The door leading to the other rooms was locked and bolted on this side. There could be nobody else in the house unless they had entered by a back door or window: and in fact there was nobody there. The body lay across the front door, so that, upon entering, one saw nothing but the head and shoulders (turned away from the door) and an outflung hand and arm. The shot had gone through the right temple and out through the other side of the head, somewhat higher up; a bullet was lodged much where one would have expected it to be, high up on the post of the opposite door. An open thermos jug stood on the desk with a puddle of cooling coffee left inside, and there was a piece of foil that had evidently been wrapped round a packet of sandwiches. The time was still early afternoon.

It was almost an hour before, having set in motion the wheels of investigative law, Mr. Cockrill decided: "Well, I'd better go up to the castle and see them there." But before he went, he summoned the constable to stand before him—very pale, hands hanging faintly twitching at his sides. "So, boy. Fish your name is, is it?"

"Fisher, sir," said the constable, hardly daring to contradict.

Inspector Cockrill conceded the point. "Well, now, once again—you heard this shot?"

"Having me dinner I was, sir, at home with me gran and grandad and Mum and Dad and all. And I heard this shot and I thought, the old bastard has done it at last. I mean," said the constable in a terrible hurry, "His-Grace-has-done-himself-in-at-last, sir!"

"You knew of this habit of the Duke's of constantly threatening suicide?"

"Being as he often rang up the station—which he did today, sir."

"Mm. Who else heard the shot?"

"Well, no one, Mr. Cockrill, sir. Gran and Grandad, they're a bit deaf and me mum and dad was arguing and the kids all quarreling, kicking up a row as usual. Besides—"

"Besides?"

"They'd've only said good riddance, and to leave things be."

"Oh?" said Cockie coldly. "Why would they have said that?"

"Well, account of—I mean, nobody liked the

old—I mean, nobody liked the Duke, sir, did they?"

"You, however, stifled your feelings and dashed off to his assistance?"

"Only me duty, sir," said Constable Fisher.

"How did you know he'd be here?"

"Well, I saw him arriving," the constable explained. "And he always did spend most of the day here, brought down his sangwidges and coffee and that."

"And seems to have consumed them. Does that strike you as rather odd?"

"What, like 'the prisoner ate a hearty breakfast'?"

The Inspector bent upon him an appreciative eye. "Exactly. Who eats up his lunch before he sets about killing himself?"

"If a gentleman had—well, like moods, sir. And it was a while ago: the coffee's gone quite cold."

"Yes, well . . . Now once again, Constable. You were at this door within six or seven minutes of your hearing the shot? The door was locked. You went round to the window and looked through. The window round at the side of the room, not to this one next to the door, which is nearest."

"You can't see the whole room from the little window, sir. Even from the other one, I couldn't see much. But I could see a good bit of him. I— well, I got a bit rattled, sir, seeing him lying there like that, sort of dead like."

"Very dead like," said Cockie sardonically. "You didn't think of going in and trying to resuscitate him?"

530

"But he was dead, sir. His head—" He puffed out his cheeks and put a hand over his mouth.

"You'll get used to it," said the Inspector, more kindly. "It shakes one, the first time. So you got on your bike and rode back to the gate? A bit wobbly, those tire marks, the returning ones."

"Yes, well, I was a bit—I didn't know what to do, sir, till the sergeant came."

"In other words, you lost your head."

To Sergeant Crum he said, grumbling: "A wretched young rookie! The Duke of Hawksmere, no less, announces his forthcoming suicide and who's on the spot? This great, green baby of a rookie constable, not yet dry behind the ears." He glanced up at the castle frowning down, formidable, upon them from the hilltop. "God knows what on earth the Duchess is going to say . . ."

What the Duchess in fact said was, comfortably, "Oh, well, he was always threatening suicide, *wasn't* he? His farewell notes simply litter the place. If the police had always had someone important at the ready, no other work would have got done at all." But that poor boy, she added, must have been scared stiff, all on his own, having to cope. "And you say it's not really quite so simple?"

Not simple at all. But for the moment he dodged it. He said, gratefully: "Your Grace takes it very calmly."

They sat in her private room with its charming pieces of period furniture, made cozy by large, comfortable armchairs. The Duchess had always seemed to him, in many ways, like a comfortable armchair herself: warm and well cushioned and

531

to all the world holding out welcoming arms. "Well, yes—I can't pretend to be heartbroken, he was only a fairly remote cousin, you know, and such a misery, poor man!" Her son, the young Duke, had died in an accident up at his University three years ago and his cousin succeeded to the title.

"I stayed on here at the castle with him, though I longed to retire to the Dower House and be on my own. But he was a mean man, he cared nothing for the estate and the people—he was doing a lot of harm all over the place. Now his brother will succeed him and he's a very different kettle of fish. He loves it, and Rupert, his boy, and darling little Becca, they really do care about it, too. And what a change for them! Poor as church mice they all were till Cousin Hamnet inherited. Everyone thinks that if you belong to a great old family like ours, you must naturally be rich, but of course, apart from the title, that needn't be so at all. And they certainly weren't." It was on account of this, she believed, that Hamnet had never got married; though now, as a matter of fact, there were murmurs about his doing so.

"So Hamnet was pretty happy to succeed?"

"Well—not happy as we've seen. He was not a happy man. A depressive, I suppose the psychiatrists would say, and he certainly got no joy out of being Duke of Hawksmere. But there *is* a joy, you know, in being at the center of it all and caring about the land—running it properly, looking after the people, one's own people. It sounds condescending, referring to them as 'our people,' but they do become like one's own, so many have been for generations with the family. One gets very protective towards them, and I'm thankful to say that Will, the new Duke, and darling Rupert and Becca have the feeling very strongly. I must confess," said the Duchess, "that I've loved it all. Even the bazaar-opening I've secretly rather enjoyed."

"Nobody opens a bazaar like Your Grace," said Cockie handsomely.

"Well, a new Grace will be opening them now, and they're all so happy to be here—now forever. The children were here a lot in their school hols, inseparable friends with the family down at South Lodge. Poor Dave, a bad attack of calf-love, it was rather touching, all great hands and feet and blushing like a peony every time she came near him."

Inspector Cockrill, unfamiliar with any South Lodge family and ignorant of whoever Dave might be, preferred to probe a little further into the family of the new Duke. "They're all staying here at the moment, I understand?"

"Yes, for Christmas. I'm so happy having them here."

"A handsome pair, I believe. Tall, are they? Take after their father?"

"Oh, my dear, no—*ants!* I mean, compared with my own beautiful son, they seem so dark and little."

"Pretty lightweight, are they?"

"Both of them." She looked at him warily. "Why should you ask? You've got something up your sleeve, you old devil! You've been holding out on me."

"No, no," said the Inspector, "I just wanted to get the facts from you, unprejudiced. And so I have. And in return I'll offer Your Grace a fact, which I wouldn't do for most people, so please keep it absolutely to yourself." But he could hardly bring himself to speak it aloud. "Have you ever heard, Duchess, of a locked-room mystery?"

"You mean like detective stories? Doors bolted, windows barred, wastes of untrodden—" She broke off, incredulous. "You don't mean it? The lodge down there in the middle of all that snow?"

"The constable rode up to the front door on his bike. He walked a little way round to a side window and back. He rode back down to the gate. He and his sergeant then walked up to the house. *I* walked up to the house. Apart from those footsteps coming and going and the two lines coming and going of the bicycle tires there isn't a break in the whiteness all round about that place. Ringed round by the wall and the hedge, the lodge sitting like a cherry in the middle of an iced cake. Not a single sign."

"Oh, well," said the Duchess, "what's really so odd about that? Naturally, he'd have let the door close when he went into the lodge—the Duke, I mean. And in this weather he'd keep the windows shut. He went down before the snow began. Had this gun with him—presumably in case he came on suicidal at any time, which he was always doing; and he did come on suicidal. He rang up the police station as usual, sat down and composed yet another note, and this time, for a change, poor old Ham, he really did shoot himself. I mean, you say he was just lying there?"

"Almost right across the doorway," said Cockie. "Right hand flung out, fingers curled as though the gun had just fallen from them. The first thing you saw as you pushed open the door —his hand with his fingers half curled. Death instantaneous, shot at very close range, and no question of one of these medical freaks when a man moves about a bit, even walks a little distance after death. He died at once and lay where he had fallen."

"And in fact the constable even heard the shot. So where's the mystery?" said the Duchess reasonably. "Where's your locked room?"

"The locked room is the lodge," said Cockie, "locked in, as it were, in all that untrodden snow. A man dead in the lodge, very recently dead, death instantaneous, from a gunshot wound at very close range. And the mystery is very easy to state and not at all easy to answer. The mystery is, where is the gun—?"

"Where—?"

"—because it isn't lying there close to his right hand where it ought to be, and it isn't anywhere else in the lodge, and it isn't anywhere outside in all the snow." The cigarette held in his cupped hand sent its pale smoke spiraling up between his fingers, and he flung the butt suddenly, with an almost violent movement, into the heart of the flickering fire. "So damn the blasted thing," he said. "Where the hell *is* it?" And apologized immediately, "I beg Your Ladyship's pardon!"

"Oh, no, don't apologize," said the Duchess. "I do see. It's dreadful for you." Well, and dreadful for all of them, she added with growing recognition of what it must mean.

For if the Duke of Hawksmere hadn't shot himself at last, who had done it for him?

And how did that person get away?

And what did he do with the gun?

They sat for a long time in silence, thinking it over. The Chief Inspector said at last, reluctantly: "There seems to be only the one possible solution."

"Mm," said the Duchess. She looked at him rather unhappily. "Are you thinking what I'm thinking?"

"Just a question of what on earth could have been the motive," said the Inspector, shrugging.

"Motive? Oh!" She looked quite horrified. "You're not thinking what I'm thinking after all, Cockie." And what he *was* thinking was absolutely, absolutely, said the Duchess earnestly, "abso*lutely wrong.*"

The handful of men at the disposal of the police had been supplemented by carefully selected village helpers, and at South Lodge there was much pushing and thrusting and beating about hedges and ditches in search of the missing weapon. Result: exactly nil. By now, in the magical way that such things happen, the local press at least had got wind of the affair and their reporters had come swarming over in a fever of excitement from the neighboring small towns: doubtless Fleet Street would soon be upon them. Already they were creating a dangerous nuisance, slouching about in the inevitable filthy old mackintoshes, humped under the weight of swinging cameras, trampling all over the sacred ground.

"Couldn't do much about it," said the Inspector's own sergeant, Charlie Thomas, from Heronsford. "What with the search and all, there aren't enough men to keep them back. It's like a blob of mercury, you think you've got them all under your thumb and suddenly they're scattering into little blobs all over the place again. But anyway, with fresh snow falling we couldn't do much more in the way of investigation, Chief. All the tracks are disappearing and we'd sorted out every last detail of what might have been a clue."

The Inspector stood for a long, long time looking outside at the ring of wall and hedge surrounding the flat expanse of white, tramped round through the churned-up snow to the window through which Constable Fisher had peered, trembling, for his first sight of the Duke's dead body. (Later the constable had been hoisted up by way of the same window frame to look over the many-spired parapet for any sign of the revolver. "No, Sarge," he had reported, "nothing up here!" From no other vantage point could it have been thrown there.)

And no gun anywhere else in the house. Not in the room where the Duke had died nor in the empty rooms out at the back. The connecting door had been locked and bolted from this side, all the windows and the back door had been similarly fastened—boarded up in most cases. It was as though someone, having made all safe from within, had come out into the octagonal room and locked the intervening door behind him. Nor was there any sign of anyone having been in the back of the house for many long months. Inspector Cockrill gave vent to a satisfied sigh. He liked things to be exact.

It was late evening when, having left in charge trusted henchmen of his own, he collected his sergeant and drove with him back to Heronsford. The night was dark but star-lit, all aglitter where the headlights picked out the leafless twigs of the hedges, frost-laden. He sat in the passenger seat, the cigarette smoke curling up through his nico-tined fingers. "Well, then, Charlie—what do you make of it?"

"Not a lot," said the sergeant, eyes on the un-rolling white ribbon of the road.

"Sealed room. No marks in the snow that aren't accounted for."

"Time of death?" prompted the sergeant.

"The doc says very recent. Works out at about the time young Fish says he heard the shot."

"Fisher," said Charlie.

"I don't know why I keep thinking it's Fish. Well—so?"

"Well, so there are questions to be asked," said the sergeant. "No acrobatic leaps possible, or tra-peze acts or any of that stuff: the distances between the lodge and anything else are much too great. So number one would be, could anyone have been hiding in the lodge? Answer—we searched it thor-oughly, even the roof outside, and positively there was not. Well, we were looking for the gun, but if a man had been there we'd hardly have missed him.

538

"Question two—and this one I know you're a bit fond of: why were the returning bicycle marks so wobbly? Answer—the wretched lad was scared out of his wits, having been first on the scene and found the Duke dead—his hands were probably shaking like jellies on the handlebars. Even Crum observed that he was pale and distressed. Question three, then: did he really hear the sound of the shot?—no one else did. Answer—sure enough, we have only his word for it. Question four then is: was it really the Duke who telephoned the station? And the answer to that is that Sergeant Crum, who took the message, is so thick he would never think to question it.

"Number five: why did Crum then bat off up to the castle when the constable was supposed to have heard the shot from his home, which he couldn't possibly have done if it had been fired up at the castle? That gets the same answer—the man is as thick as two planks. Question six: did the Duke really write the suicide note which was propped up on the desk? Answer—yes, probably, but it could have been written under coercion. Finally—and this is the sixty-million-dollar one —how did the murderer get away, taking the gun with him? Answer—

"Or answers . . ."

"Pretty obvious, Mr. Cockrill, don't you think? Only one way, really. Different versions of the same, depending upon who the murderer *was*."

"Except in the case of the one I think of as number four."

"Four?" said the sergeant, almost as though

they were playing a word-game. "I've only got three."

Inspector Cockrill ran over them, ascribing to each a motive or motives. "I've only just now decided to add in this fourth one. In that case, the motive could be anything: His Late Grace was a deeply unlovable man." They sat silent a little while, musing over it all, while the little car crept across the light carpet of snow—in this narrow, little-used byroad hardly disturbed at all. The sergeant said at last: "It's odd that with the first three the motive in each case seems to be vicarious—if by that I mean, on behalf of other people."

"Well, I'd hardly say that: other people would benefit, certainly. In the first, it would certainly seem so vicarious, as you call it, as to be very hard to believe." He added rather gloomily that they mustn't forget that the Duchess appeared to have a candidate of her own and one without even a motive. "And that makes five."

The sergeant was hardly impressed. "Oh, well, sir—the Duchess!"

The Inspector had sat all this time nursing the enormous hat on his bony knees. Now, as they reached his gate, he scrambled out, clapping it back onto his head. "Yes, well—'the Duchess' you say, my lad. But the Dowager Duchess of Hawksmere, let me tell you, is an exceedingly shrewd old bird. And I'm a bit scared of her. There's nothing she'd stop at to protect 'our people,' let alone her own family." He slammed-to the door of the car and stood hunting through the pockets of the disreputable old mac in search of his keys. "Oh, thank goodness, here are the damn

540

things. I'm in need of a hot drink and bed. Good night, Charlie. Go off home now and sleep well. Tomorrow is another day."

Another day. For all but the late Duke of Hawksmere, lying so quiet and stiff in his metal cold-box, split like a herring to reveal his body's secrets: with nothing to disclose, however, but the recent consumption of a sandwich meal, and a gunshot wound in the head . . .

The new day was less than gladdened for Inspector Cockrill by the arrival of the Chief Constable of the county. A choleric, ex-military man, he huffed and puffed a good deal, unable to face the gro-tesquerie of a locked-room mystery right there in their midst, and for comfort settled on the solid facts relating to the missing weapon. Well, yes, said Inspector Cockrill, a common enough type of weapon left over from the last war—impossible to say how many ex-officers might, for one reason or another, have failed to hand back their revolvers at the conclusion of hostilities. The passage through bone, explained the experts, would make it difficult to ascribe the bullet to any one partic-ular gun.

"Was the late Duke known to have possessed such a revolver?"

"If you recall, Sir George, you yourself under-took to question him on the subject."

"Yes, well, so I did call on him and ask him. But delicately, you know, stepping very delicately. He hardly seemed to know what I was talking about. But he certainly didn't deny that he had such a weapon."

Very helpful, reflected Cockie.

"Well, you can't march in with a sniffer-dog and search a place like the castle," said the Chief Constable huffily. Besides, he added, these people who were always threatening suicide never really did it.

"Nosir," said Cockie in the authentic accents of Police Constable Fisher at his most wooden. He explained the probable difficulties in ascribing the bullet to the late Duke's, or indeed to any revolver.

"Which, anyway, you've lost," the Chief Constable reminded him sourly.

"Oh, yessir, so we have," said the Inspector, more in the Sergeant Crum line this time. Sort of thing that could happen to anyone, the voice suggested.

At first light, the search for the missing gun had begun again—village people, tremendously eager and helpful, said Cockie. Although, he added limpidly, none of them had liked the Duke, most of them having understandable grudges against him. To tenants so long accustomed to the cherishing rule of the Dukes of Hawksmere, with the family arms around "our people," he had seemed a mean, to them a dangerous man.

The Chief Constable was as appalled as the Inspector could have wished. "Good God, man, they'll all be on the side of the killer! You don't know *who* may have found the thing and be harboring it somewhere. They must be taken off at once—search them, search their homes, search every house in the village!"

He stumped off angrily to wreak further havoc from the comfortable ambiance of the Heronsford police station and Chief Inspector Cockrill was able to give out, with a lightened heart, that these arbitrary orders came not from himself—as if he would—but from the Chief Constable in his unwisdom. He must, however, have considerably overrated his superior's enthusiasm—Sir George would never have contemplated an intrusion into the castle itself.

The search there was more easily concluded than might have been expected—by anyone but the Inspector himself. "Under some papers in a drawer of the late Duke's desk," he explained to the Dowager Duchess. "Surprise, surprise!" he added sardonically.

"*Not* a surprise," said the Duchess. "After all, it may not be the one that was used. I hear the bullet may not prove to be traceable. Perhaps he didn't have this one with him. He presumably didn't always lug one around with him."

"So how did he propose to shoot himself down at the lodge? He rang up the station and said he was about to do so."

"Well, someone rang up the station. Would Sergeant Crum necessarily have questioned the voice? And there'd be suicide notes all over the place. Whoever it was could just have used one of those."

"Your Grace ought to be in my job," said the Chief Inspector, respectfully.

"Do you know, Cockie," said the Duchess on a note of not very sincere apology, "in this particular case, I really believe I should."

543

Mr. Cockrill felt in duty bound to report to his Chief Constable, though by no means to unravel matters clearly for him. "Her Grace put the gun there herself, of course, as I knew she would."

"The *Duchess?*"

"The Dowager. It was in a package sent up with her letters this morning. Well, of course, her post has been prodigious. Posted last night here in Hawksmere. Everyone's been in and out of the village, in and out of Heronsford, up and down to London like yoyos, lawyers and so forth: a Duke doesn't die like ordinary men, let alone get himself murdered. The post alone may tell us something," suggested Cockie. "Don't you think?"

It patently told the Chief Constable nothing whatsoever. He huffed and puffed and went off at a tangent. "Why should the Duchess do such a thing?"

"Protecting her family?"

"For heaven's sake—her family! You're not suspecting the new Duke of Hawksmere in a business like this?"

"He had everything to gain. But, well, no—"

"Well, then, young Rupert. You wouldn't—"

"His father has succeeded the sixth Duke. He is now heir to the title. And he loves the place and the people on the estate deeply. The family own half the county. He was horrified by the way the late Duke was treating them. And he was threatening to marry and get an heir for himself. We have to consider young Rupert."

"Good heavens, Cockrill, I shall never live this down!"

"Or there's the girl," continued Cockie remorselessly. "She felt the same about it all. And of course her parents now become Duke and Duchess instead of being just hard-up nobodies."

Sir George looked as though spontaneous combustion were just around the corner. The daughter of the Duke! Or the heir to the dukedom! But comfort was at hand. He demanded triumphantly, "Just explain to me how either of them could have got away from the building? The tire marks, the footmarks, are all accounted for, and there are no others. So how could either of those young people have got away from the place?"

Oh, well, as to that, said Cockie, tremendously offhand, one could think of three or four explanations in each case; surely Sir George must have worked them out for himself? And he suddenly caught sight of Charlie Thomas and must rush off and join his sergeant, if Sir George would excuse him. . .

To Charlie, he said: "I can't resist pulling the old buffer's leg."

"You'll get yourself into trouble one of these days, Boss," said the sergeant, laughing. But what on earth, he wondered, was going to happen next?

"What will happen next," said Cockie prophetically, "is that a letter will arrive, suggesting a new and totally unexpected suspect and a new and totally unexpected method of getting away from the lodge—snow surroundings, bike marks, footprints, and all."

And duly the letter arrived and was handed over to them by the Duchess herself. "In this morning's post. Addressed to me. The postmark? But, Cockie dear, you've no notion what the mails have been like — with the Duke's death, you know, all the business letters and the sympathetics, poor loves, so tricky for them to know just what to say! I mean, 'So sorry to hear that your cousin has been murdered. Whatever will you do about the funeral? Yours affectionately, Aunt Maude.' The children are reading through them in fits of giggles, they are so naughty! But as to the postmarks, I'm afraid we just slit all the envelopes open and threw them away. It's not like the Americans who put their addresses on the back—I never get used to it. But out they've gone, and with this sort of cheap writing paper there wouldn't be a matching envelope, we'd never trace which belonged to which."

Nor had the typewriter proved traceable to anyone in or around Hawksmere. Probably done in a pretense of testing a demonstration model somewhere up in London, Cockie thought. A very old trick. Style, predictably illiterate.

"Dear Dutchess," ran the letter, "I am well away now and soon will be abroad so to save truoble for others I confes to the murder of tghe duke of Hawksmear he was a relaiton of yuors but he was a dead rotter and he deseved to die. I went doun befor the sno began he let me in I told him he mite as well comit suiside but he siad he would not now as he was hopeing to het marrid he did not seam to have a gun but I had bruoght one

546

along with me in case. I cuold not make him write a suiside note but there was one rihgt there on the desk just lying about.

"By now it was snoing and I pushed the gun in his back and mad him ring up the police station and say he was going to shoot hisself then I put tghe gun near his head and shot him. When I opend the door it was very quite I haerd a bycicle bell and I went back and closed the door when I hared the person go away I cam out and I saw footsteps in the snow going round the house and I followed them and there was a window. I climbed up by the window on to the roof and when the jurnalists cam crowding round I showed myself and a policeman came and hauled me down so I said I only wanted to get a shot of the snow with the footmarks, as if I was a jurnalist and they quit beleived me. I better say I saw a policeman was being hoisted up to see if tghe gun was on the roof, so I lay up against the parapet where he would be leaning over to look and unles he bent right over he wuld not see me and he did not he only calld out no gun here. That is all. There was a lot of peeple hated tghe duke long before he was a duke and I was one of them. Yuo need not look any feurther."

"Well, well, well," said Cockie, handing over this effusion to his sergeant. "What did I tell you?" He went on down to the lodge and summoned the constable. "Well, now, Fish—"

"Fisher, sir," said the constable a trifle desperately.

"All right, never mind that. You were the man sent up to see if the gun had been thrown onto

547

the flat roof of this room. Why did you choose to climb up via the side window?"

"It couldn't have been thrown from any other point, sir. There's a porch over the front steps and there weren't any other marks in the snow."

"The gun could have slithered back and come to rest just under the parapet. You didn't think to hook yourself right over the edge and look downwards and inwards?"

"The gun wouldn't have done that, Mr. Cockrill, sir." He made a chucking movement with his hand. "It would slither away, sir, not backwards. But anyway, with the snow it would probably just stay where it fell. So it would be about in the middle of the roof. And it wasn't."

"So if a man were hiding close up under the parapet where you looked over—?"

"I could well have missed seeing him," Fisher admitted. "I wasn't looking there." And come to think of it, he suggested, a man *had* tried to climb up on the roof—two or three in fact—but each time been hauled back before he got there. "Them journalists, sir. If anyone got far enough, he would have seen if a gun had been thrown up there."

In fact, several of the culprits had been traced but none admitted having got up as far as the roof, and the consensus had been that this was true. Still, it might be well for Cockrill to scan the newspapers for press photographs of the snowy ground, taken from a high angle. . .

He came back to Constable Fisher. "The late Duke had a good many enemies? You yourself hardly loved him, I daresay?"

The constable's air of ease gave way to pallor

548

and tensed-up fingers. "I never hardly set eyes on him, sir. Him being the Duke and all."

"Till the day before yesterday?"

"And by then he was dead, sir."

"Yes, so he was. It must have been a shock, peering in at that close-shut window? Now, tell me again— why that particular window?"

"You can't see right into the room from the nearer one, sir. Not into the whole of the room."

"No you can't, can you? But how did you know that?"

"Well, sir, being as my gran and grandad used to live here—"

"They *lived* here?" said Cockrill, and glanced with a sort of gleam towards his sergeant. "They *lived* here? And were chucked out by the Duke, I suppose? And had to squash in with the rest of your big family, all in one little cottage—the old folks cranky and carping, I daresay, as old people are when they see too much of the young—your parents resentful and answering back, all those noisy brothers and sisters worse than ever, and everyone miserable. In other words— the Sardine Tin!"

"Except I think it must be more peaceful, sir, in a sardine tin."

No wonder, reflected the Inspector, that I kept thinking of him as Fish. "Never mind your constable's domestic arrangements," he had said, choking off Sergeant Crum's ill-timed explanations, and all that time . . . "All right for the moment, then, Fisher." But to Charlie he said: "Well, Sarge—the simplest explanation, after all? It was only that being more or less strangers to these parts we had no idea that such a motive existed. But now—"

A shot that nobody else had heard. Down to the lodge on one's bicycle and up to the front door. The Duke, placidly consuming sandwiches, is easily persuaded to admit the uniformed figure of the local rozzer. Some excuse—the police require the handing over of the revolver which His Grace is understood to have illegally in his possession. Gun in hand, force the telephone call to the police station. With any luck, Sergeant Crum will go batting off up to the castle, thus giving one more time. Force the production of the suicide note and then—one shot and it's done.

It's done: but all of a sudden, it's horrible. Back away to the open front door, gun in hand, having forgotten in one's panic to throw it down beside the outflung hand. Stand there, shaking, trying to wipe off one's fingerprints and—horror!—the door is blown shut by the whirl of the wind that is sending the snowflakes aflurry and one is locked out on the step with the gun in one's hand! Round to the window in hopes it may open sufficiently to throw the gun into the room. But it is tightly closed—and at any moment Sergeant Crum may arrive!

Down to the gate, then, awobble with nervousness, on one's bike and when the hue and cry goes forth, join eagerly in. For who will think of looking in the pocket of the heroic discoverer of the crime, for the weapon which brought it about?

Nervous? Yes, of course he would be nervous. But so what? A man is dead whom all the world detested, Gran and Grandad can come back to the cozy little home, Mum and Dad will be free and happy again, and the pack of younger brothers and sisters will be safe from the ceaseless censure of the older generation and settle down happily once more. Her Grace can move out to the dear little Dower House, the new Duke is a kind and generous man, Rupert, friend of one's childhood, will be heir to the dukedom, and long-loved Becca will be rich and happy and always down here at Hawksmere to be adored from afar. And how grateful, could they have known, would everyone for miles around have been to the begetter of all this happiness . . .

But first the gun. One cannot carry it around in a uniform pocket, and where to hide it in the narrow confines of the village to which one is now restricted? Post it off to the castle, then, with a message to the Duchess, "Please put this back where it belongs, for all our sakes." Her Grace must recognize that the thing has been done by someone here on the ducal estates, by one of "our people." Her Grace won't make trouble for anyone who will throw themselves upon her mercy, and Her Grace knows very well how to protect herself . . .

Charlie Thomas had been mulling it over, muttering at intervals into the recital, "Mm, mm." Now he said: "And the letter?"

"Ah," said Cockie, for the first time losing confidence a little. "The letter."

"Very interesting, that letter. Not in fact the work of an illiterate. The mistakes are deliberate. A writer who spells 'brought' as 'bruoght' knows what letters there are in that difficult word. A true illiterate would write 'brort' or something. And this isn't an accomplished typist. It's easy to hit a *g* when you intended an *h* and he keeps putting *tghe*. But Fisher types very well and I don't think he's bright enough to have thought all this up. So that would bring us to—"

"The new heir," said Cockie none too happily. "Young Rupert."

"It's one thing for a lad to want to help his grandparents to get back their old home," said Charlie. "But Rupert's dad becomes a Duke, they're all in the money, and, what's probably the most important point, 'our people' will be safe from the tyrant, who was threatening to marry and spawn a breed of mini-tyrants forever."

"So how do you suggest he got away, leaving no trace in the snow? You don't suggest that Rupert was the man on the roof?"

"There never was any man on the roof, sir, *was* there? Just some damn journalist, trying to be cleverer than the rest; and *he* was hauled down and whoever he may have been, he wasn't Rupert. But we've both thought of ways in which someone other than Fisher could have got away from the lodge . . ."

There was the sound of hooves chiff-chuffing across the grass and a light voice exhorted: "Now, darlings, be good horses and just stay there!" and, with a thump at the door, the two young people came into the room.

"Look here, Inspector, you're *not* accusing poor Dave of murdering Cousin Ham?" demanded Lady Rebecca on a note of scorn.

An ant she might be, but a very pretty ant, the

cloud of dark, soft hair crowned by a shabby little riding bowler. The brother was as dark and scarcely taller, very slender, and no less shabbily fitted out. Poor as church mice, the Duchess had said, and clearly their late cousin had not been generous with handouts, despite his sudden acquisition of title and great wealth. Inspector Cockrill said mildly: "Are you referring to Police Constable Fisher?"

"Yes—we've just met him in the lane, and he's petrified."

"If he did kill the Duke, that would be fairly natural."

"He no more killed the Duke than I did!" Rupert said.

"In fact, my boy, we were just discussing that very possibility. That you *did*"

"*Me?* What a lot of rubbish! Why on earth should I want to kill rotten old Cousin Hamnet?"

"Just because he *was* rotten old Cousin Hamnet."

The brother and sister were leaning back negligently against the edge of the table, feet crossed in their well worn riding boots. "Good lord," said Rebecca, "you're not going to suggest that he was the man on the roof, beloved of our Aunt Daisy —the Duchess Daisy," she elaborated. "And if you are, how did he get away from the lodge without leaving great humping footprints in the snow?"

"Well," said the Inspector easily, "we had an idea that he might have used a bicycle."

"Oh, that's great!" said Rupert. "I haven't even got a bicycle."

"But your dear friend Dave—he had a bicycle."

It rocked them a little, but the boy said nonchalantly enough, "Don't tell me—let me guess. I borrowed Dave's bicycle."

"At gun-point," suggested Becca, mocking, her pretty little nose in the air.

"Or by cajolement. He would be very much on your side."

"You seem to have a simple faith in the trustworthiness of your force," said Rupert.

"Well, but—to such a good friend. And it does all seem to fit."

"It doesn't fit at all," said Rebecca. "We were together the whole afternoon, out riding." She saw as she spoke the weakness of this double alibi and added, "My Aunt Daisy saw us from the window. She'll tell you so."

"I'm sure she will," said the Inspector drily.

Rebecca slid down from her perch on the table edge. "So we'll be going home now because I can assure you that Dave didn't do it and neither did Rupert, so just *don't* be silly about it."

"No, indeed, since you put up so convincing a case. On the other hand," suggested Cockie, "you leave yourself undefended."

"*Me?*" said Becca as her brother had said before her.

"You had exactly the same possible motives as your brother. One or the other of you came down here before the snow fell—"

"Why one or the other—why not both of us?"

"Because only one person could have ridden away on that bicycle, with or without Constable Fisher." The sergeant opened his mouth to speak, but Mr. Cockrill quelled him. "You came down here before the snow fell, one or the other of you. You started a long argument with your cousin about the running of the estate—about his possible marriage, perhaps. But it was all no good. You lost your temper, the gun was lying around as usual, ready for use if the fancy took him— and you picked it up. By that time the snow had fallen, but while you stood panicking on the doorstep, there appeared the gallant Saint Dave to the rescue on his trusty bicycle. No need in your case, Lady Rebecca, for any gun-pointing or even cajolement: up you scramble and, wobbling a bit with the extra weight and general insecurity, you duly arrive at the gate. Off you scarper and the friend of your childhood is left, rather scared, but glowing with the knowledge that he has saved— well, I'll still say one or other of those he loves."

"Not bad," said Rupert with a determined air of superiority, but looking, all the same, a little pale. "But surely there must be other candidates, not just Becca and me?"

"There aren't, you know. Your father is too big and heavy to have shared a bike with Fisher, who's a big chap too—I've tried an experiment and the bicycle broke down—and what's more, he has an alibi rather more convincing than that of a brother and sister out riding, watched by Her Grace, your cousin Daisy. Someone from round about? Well, the police aren't entirely idiots, you know, whatever you may believe to the contrary, and we've made very thorough investigations—you can count them all out."

"So you seriously think you have a case against us—against one of us?"

"Or Constable Fisher," said Cockie placidly.

Rupert slid down and stood beside his sister. "Well, we'll be going now, if you'll excuse us. You can bring the handcuffs up to the castle any time. Come on," he said to his sister. "We'll go and lay this mouse at the feet of our ever present help in times of trouble and see what *she* has to say to Mr. Cockrill about it."

The Inspector waited until the shuffle of hooves had trotted off into silence. Then he stretched himself. "Well, Charlie, at least we've got that off our chests." And perhaps another time, he added laughing, his sergeant would refrain from breaking out into expostulation when his superior officer dropped a clanger.

"It was you saying that only one person could have ridden away on the bike—with or without Fisher. Of course, anyone who had ridden the bike up to the lodge could just have ridden it back again—and any bike, for that matter, it needn't be Fisher's. The tire marks were snowed over before we really got at them."

"Well, it doesn't matter either way. The tracks were made by the constable: he'd seen into the room, he described it to Sergeant Crum. The tire marks were made by him, riding his own bike— quite possibly giving a lift back to the gate to someone of a fairly small physique. And we've eliminated everyone except that precious pair." He heaved himself up and shrugged on his dreadful old mac, thrust that hat onto his head, and gave it a thump which brought it down over his eyes. "Damn the thing, it never used to be as big as this," he said, irritably shoving it up to his forehead. "I'll get on up to the castle now and, in my turn, place my poor mouse at the feet of Her Ladyship. Who, however, is their cousin and not their aunt."

"Does it matter?" said Charlie, surprised.

"Not a bit," said the Inspector and folded himself, mac and hat and all, into his little police car. "See you, Sarge!"

"In one piece, I hope," said Charlie rather doubtfully.

The Duchess of Hawksmere met him in the vast hall, where she stood surrounded by his trio of suspects. "Oh, Cockie—how nice to see you! Now you, my loves," she said to the young ones—apparently without affectation on either side, including among her loves the village constable—"go off and get some coffee and buns or something and don't make any more fuss." One freckled hand on the bannisters, she began to haul herself up the stairs. "Sorry to be so slow, Inspector, but my arthritis is giving me hell today." At the door of her sitting room, she ushered him in. "Find a chair for yourself, but first pour me a drop of vodka, like an angel, and help yourself to whatever you like. And no nonsense about being on duty and all that—we're both going to need it, I promise you."

The Chief Inspector thought that upon his side, at any rate, this would certainly prove only too true. He cast the mac and hat upon a chair and

557

sat down with her before the agreeably flickering fire. "Well, Duchess?"

"Well, Cockie! I thought you'd come up after the kids, with all their dramas, and here you are, and we can settle down and have a real good yat."

Only the Duchess of Hawksmere, reflected the Inspector, would refer to a serious discussion of a murder in the family as a good old yat. "I have to walk circumspectly, my lady."

"Oh, not with me. I mean nobody ever does: it's because I'm so dreadfully uncircumspect myself. So I thought," she suggested with her own particular brand of authority and humility, "would it be possible for you to outline for me the cases you have against all these young people? Because I really do think I can help you, you know."

He thought it over. It was all highly unconventional, but he, no more than Her Grace, had never been, would never be, a slave to that sort of thing. Moreover, he was curious about her own so-far-undisclosed candidate. "If it honestly will go no further?"

"Cross my heart and wish to die," said the Duchess, making a sign upon her well upholstered bosom.

"Well, then . . ." Somewhat gingerly and with many ifs and ands, he outlined one by one his suspicions of the young heir, Rupert, and his sister, the Lady Rebecca. "And then as to Fish—"

"Fisher," said the Duchess. "I do think it's so hurtful to get people's names wrong. I do it all the time myself, but I'm old so it doesn't count. Besides, I call everyone darling, such an actressy habit, I simply hate it: but at least they don't realize that half the time it's because I can't think who on earth they are!"

"Duchess, you are trying to charm me," said Cockie severely.

"Am I? Well, perhaps I am—I never know I'm doing it. But we need a little gaiety in all this awfulness, don't we? So, well then, that brings us to the man on the roof—the letter."

Chief Inspector Cockrill expatiated at length upon the letter. Don't let's be silly about that, was the unexpressed burden of his reflections. Aloud he said: "We know that that was just a diversion."

"But a very potent diversion, Chief Inspector, wouldn't you say? I mean—hardly to be denied outright, at least with any certainty. No possible proof for or against, is there?" She fixed him with a quizzical look which told him that he might as well be a bazaar that Her Grace was about to open. He knew he was at her mercy—and would love every minute of it. "But first, Cockie dear—another drink?"

"Not another drop, Duchess, thank you."

"Oh, but you must, or *I* can't. And you know that I can't get weaving till I'm in vodka up to the ankles. I get so tired," said the Duchess, looking as wan as every evidence of robust health would allow, "and when I'm tired, my mind simply won't work—I'm helpless."

It seemed to Inspector Cockrill highly desirable from his own point of view that Her Grace should remain without reviving vodka, but she had him in thrall. He reluctantly poured out two small rations ("Oh, Cockie, for goodness' sake!") and more generously topped them up. "So now, my dear, what are we to do? Because you know perfectly well that my two young ones couldn't possibly have killed the man, and neither could poor, dear Dave. So we come back to the letter. And who wrote the letter."

"You wrote the letter yourself, Duchess, and posted it on one of your necessary expeditions up to London. Or didn't post it at all—just 'found it' among your letters."

"Well, what a thing to suggest! But really very perspicacious of you, Cockie. Yes, of course. I thought it might come in nicely for covering every eventuality: because if you could just settle for that—only keeping it to yourself, of course—and never be able to find a trace of the murderer, well, who could say a word against you?"

"My Chief Constable, for one, could say a word against me and would, most vociferously."

"Oh, that pompous old fool! Nobody will listen to a word he says; you just leave him to me. All you need do is cast about like mad, dragging in Scotland Yard and Interpol and all that lot, trying to trace the letter, trying to ferret out all Hamnet's old enemies, which after all would take you back twenty or thirty years—and finally give up and say the case is closed or whatever the expression is."

"No case is ever closed," said Cockie severely.

"Well, keep it a bit open, but just never solve it. Because what the letter says is true. Millions of people simply hated poor old Ham, long before he was ever a Duke. He was a misery to himself, always saying he wanted to die, never having the courage to get around to doing it. And now the lovely man on the roof has done it for him and everyone will simply love him for it and never want him to be caught at all."

"Except me, " said the Chief Inspector somberly.

"Well, I do call that rather lacking in appreciation of my efforts to help you!"

"You don't suppose that *I'd* be content with some cooked-up nonsense, no one ever knowing the truth?"

"Well, but someone does know the truth, don't they, Cockie? I mean, I've told you all along, haven't I? *I* do."

"Your Grace has never had the goodness to divulge it to *me*."

"Oh, Cockie, how cross and sarcastic! Well, I'll divulge it now. But only," said the Duchess, downing the last of her second vodka tonic, "if you promise, promise, promise never to do anything about it."

"Are you asking me to let a criminal go free?"

"No, I'm not. I don't think there is any criminal—except the man on the roof. I think Hamnet did at last really go ahead and commit suicide. Ate his lunch, thought things over—he was always a bit dyspeptic after meals—and reached for the gun. And then—" She put out her pudgy hand with its carefully tended, varnished nails and touched his own nicotined fingers. "Trust me. You'll be grateful to me, honestly you will. I'm not practicing any deceit upon you —and it will solve everything."

You are old, he thought, and stout and arthritic

and nowadays no beauty, but damn you—"All right," he said grudgingly. "So?"

"So—that boy, Cockie. You kept on saying it yourself—to be first on the scene of the bloody death of the Earl of Hawksmere, no less—a baby, a great, raw green rookie of a baby policeman, not yet dry behind the ears. In a total panic—wouldn't he be? What he said was the truth, my dear—he heard the shot, leapt on his bike, and pedaled like a lunatic down to the lodge and up through the snow to the front door. And the door was open. Hamnet always left an escape route—rang up in advance so that if ever he did take the plunge, someone could get there in time to haul him back to life. The door was open—how would anyone have heard the shot if it had been fired from behind sealed-up windows and doors? He looked inside and the first thing he saw was the Duke's head, dreadfully wounded, and the revolver lying there, fallen from the dead hand. So—what would any of us do? He panicked and, in an automatic impulse, bent down and picked up the gun."

"Oh, my God!" said the Inspector.

"Yes, it was a bit Oh-my-God, wasn't it, since the number-one lesson a policeman is taught is never ever to touch anything at the scene of the crime. He would have thrown it down at once, I daresay, but another lesson came into his mind as he began to calm down—watch out for fingerprints! He got out his hankie or whatever and started wiping his own off the gun and—horror of horrors—there comes a flurry of wind and the door blows shut!"

"Leaving him locked out, with the gun still in

his hands. Nips round to the side window to see if he can throw it back in, but the window's tight shut. So he shoves the thing into his pocket and, very nervous, wobbles back to the gate, and when Sergeant Crum arrives—not the most observant of men—goes into his act. The door was closed, he could only see the body by looking in through the window . . ."

"Yes. Well, there you are, Cockie—and there *he* was, poor wretched boy, and just think of his state of mind. Marching about all evening searching for the weapon when all the time it was in his uniform pocket. And now, for days, he'll be kept on duty in the village—and where in little Hawksmere can such a thing remain hidden for any length of time, with everyone searching for it? So what does he do? He posts it off to me. Of course, he can't be sure I've guessed the truth, but people have got into a sort of habit of thinking I'll cope. And that's all, really, except for the lovely, convenient man on the roof, made up for you by me."

He sat almost paralyzed in the deep armchair, looking at her smiling face. "Constable Fisher lost his head and just picked up the gun. Is this what you really believe?"

"It's the simple truth, my dear. And simple is the word."

"He's admitted it?"

"I haven't asked him. It was so obvious."

Not to the assembled forces of the law, it hadn't been. "But to prefer to be suspected of murder—?"

"He could always tell the truth in the end."

"Why not have told it from the beginning?"

563

"My *dear*," said the Duchess, "You'd have had his guts for garters."

He leapt to his feet. "One thing's for certain—I'll have them now."

"Yes, well—the only thing is, if this story gets out you'll look a bit of a fool, old love, won't you?"

Chief Inspector Cockrill, the Terror of Kent—a bit of a fool, right here on his own patch. "Hey, now, Duchess, if you *don't* mind —"

"Oh, but I do mind," she said. "I don't like to think of you looking foolish." And she pleaded, "Let the boy go! He's been through a bad time, you can be pretty sure of that; he won't do it again. There's nothing against Rupert and Becca, there's been no crime! This is what actually happened and that's the end of it. But the man on the roof—there he is, all worked out so nicely for you and it all hangs together perfectly, now doesn't it? Someone out of the past caught up with the wicked Duke and you never had a hope in hell of catching up with the someone from the past. Gradually the whole affair will fade and Chief Inspector Cockrill, for a miracle, has failed to Get His Man; but for the rest, everyone is happy." And one couldn't help thinking, said the Duchess, confiding to the fireplace, that it is less humiliating to fail to solve a very difficult case than to have failed to solve such a very simple one as a young officer losing his head.

"No one must ever know," said the Inspector; and it was capitulation.

"Good heavens, no. I'll talk to Dave Fisher and tell him what I've guessed and that to save his skin I've played a naughty game all round, and just to pipe down and never get it into his head to confess because he'd get me into trouble. I could even suggest that you rather suspect that this might have happened, but you have to investigate every possibility."

"Except the right one," said Chief Inspector Cockrill rather stiffly. He collected his droopy mackintosh from the back of the chair, clapped the hat on his head, and hastily removed it, in the presence of Her Ladyship. "And honestly—not one word of this to anyone?"

"Oh, not a word," vowed the Duchess, even now casting about in her mind for someone one could safely confide in. For really it had been rather a bit of fun. "But I *told* you."

"You told me—?"

"That in this case, I really should have been in your job," said the Duchess. She too rose. "I say, Inspector—what about one more little one? I really think we could do with it. Do join me!"

Inspector Cockrill paused a moment and then cast down his hat and coat again. "Do you know, Duchess—I think I will," he said.

Cyril Hare
(1900–1958)

THE DEATH OF AMY ROBSART

Cyril Hare (Alfred Alexander Gordon Clark) was one of a number of English jurists who wrote mystery stories. Henry Cecil, Michael Gilbert, and John Mortimer, the creator of Rumpole of the Bailey, *are others that come to mind quickly. Like other writers in this collection, Hare could write a classical English Country House Mystery in the Grand Manner, and did in* An English Murder *(1950).*

This late-in-the-cycle story is not far afield, but the reader will now be struck by the fact that the cast of characters of the Country House has changed: included now are foreigners, movie types, and entrepreneurs. Are the original inhabitants turning over in the family plot? They need not, for the tale is an old and familiar one: murder most foul in a setting most fair.

I

Gus Constantinovitch was an Englishman. His passport said as much when he went abroad. His name, indeed, hinted at Russia or Greece, his complexion suggested the Levant, his nose proclaimed Judea. As for his figure, it was as cosmopolitan as the restaurant meals that were responsible for it. But anybody who had seen him standing by the door of the music-room of his house at Ascot, rolling a cigar from one corner of his mouth to the other, or heard the crisp monosyllables in which he took leave of his guests, would have been excused for thinking him American. For this his profession was responsible. As Chairman and Managing Director of Cyclops Films Ltd., the organization which was (in his own words) to beat Hollywood at its own game, he had adopted, quite naturally, the badges of his tribe.

The party in honour of the trade showing of "Amy Robsart—the film magnificent" was slowly petering out. Gus from his station at the door surveyed his few remaining guests with lack-lustre eyes. It was impossible to tell from his expression whether either party or film had proved to his liking. The long room was almost empty, its windows open to the sultry July night. A Strauss waltz was being played on the gramophone, but only one couple still gyrated in the middle of the polished floor—a slim young man in evening clothes and a fair, white-faced girl with tired eyes who wore Amy Robsart's flowing Tudor dress. In a corner a lank young woman with a predatory face was sitting talking to a superbly handsome giant of a man.

"She's a pretty little thing, isn't she?" she said, indicating the dancer.

"Who do you mean—Camilla?" he asked. "Why, Lady Portia, she's lovely."

Lady Portia Fanning's mouth gaped in a tigerish smile.

"Yes, Mr. Brancaster, I had noticed during the evening that you thought as much. What does your wife think about it?"

Teddy Brancaster looked across the room to the bar, where his wife and one or two men were standing.

"We can leave Geneviève out of it," he said, reddening.

"Of course. Besides, she's French, and they look at these things differently from you Americans, don't they? Otherwise I should have expected her to look for consolation to that young man with her now. What is his name—Bartram, isn't it?"

"Dick Bartram's all right."

"I'm sure he is. But we were talking about Camilla Freyne—have you seen her film?"

"No. I was on the set this morning, and this afternoon I was practising dives in the swimming-pool here."

"Has Gus got his own swimming-pool?"

"Sure. In the garden. A very good one, too."

"How sweet! Too, too Hollywood! But does a champion like you need to practise?"

"Every day, Lady Portia, if I'm not to lose my form."

"How wonderful of you! Well, you didn't miss much—the film, I mean. Your Camilla may be all you think her, but as an actress she's the world's worst."

"Maybe."

She looked at her watch.

"I must go. Can't I give you a lift home, Mr. Brancaster?"

"No, thank you. I am staying here, you know."

"Of course, I forgot. Perhaps I shall see you in London some time, if Mrs. Brancaster will allow?"

She went up to her host.

"Good night, Mr. Constantinovitch. It's been such a delightful party, and I'm sure the picture will be a great success."

"Good night, Lady Portia. Happy to have you at my house."

The waltz came to an end. Camilla's partner bowed his thanks and took his leave. No sooner had he gone than in a flutter of long skirts she was across the room to where Teddy Brancaster was standing.

"Now I'm going to dance with you, Teddy," she said. "Put on another record, just for you and me—please." She looked up to his face like a small girl at the window of a sweetshop.

As if by magic, Geneviève, who had been standing contentedly during the dance among the group at the bar, materialized at her husband's side.

"She should not dance any more, Teddee," she declared. "But see how tired she is!"

"Sure," said Teddy equably. "Time little girls were in bed, Camilla." His voice, as he turned to her, took on an altogether new quality of warmth and tenderness.

"Oh, what's the use of going to bed when you can't sleep?" Camilla pouted. "I haven't slept properly for ages." She passed the back of her hand across her eyes with a gesture simple as a child's. "Not since I started work on the picture."

Gus Constantinovitch had joined the group.

"And the picture's finished now," he said. "You'll sleep sound tonight, Camilla. That's what you're in my home for, to sleep sound."

"But I want to dance, Gus. Just one more little dance with Teddy."

Teddy shook his head.

"It's too late for dancing," he said. "I guess I'll have a dip in the swimming-pool before I turn in."

"I too," broke in Geneviève. "I will come with you swimming, Teddee."

"Sure you will," said Teddy sardonically. "You'll follow me round anywhere, won't you, Geneviève? Well, let's go get our bathing things."

"I'll come too," Camilla declared. "Bathing by moonlight—lovely!"

"You're going to bed," said Teddy firmly. "Besides, there's no moon tonight, no stars neither. It's as dark as pitch."

"Ah, but that makes it better still! To dive into the dark, when you can see nothing! That's what Amy Robsart did, wasn't it? Just fell in the dark, and it was all over." Her voice trailed away uncertainly.

"Camilla!" Gus spoke sharply. "Here, Mrs. Brancaster, take her upstairs to her room. You know where it is, don't you? Next door to yours. And see that she doesn't come down again."

Geneviève took her by the arm. For a moment it seemed as if she would try to resist, but the

571

Frenchwoman had a grip of iron, and she gave way meekly enough.

"That's a good girl," said Gus paternally. "Go to bed now, and your Uncle Gus will come and tuck you up."

They made an odd couple as they moved together to the door—the fragile girl, wilting under her Tudor magnificence, and the active, muscular young woman beside her. Teddy Brancaster seemed to feel the contrast as he stared after them.

"I'll go change," he said abruptly.

Among the group at the cocktail bar Dick Bartram was watching them too.

"She's very handsome," someone said.

"Pity she can't act."

"Act? Why, I bet she could if she ever tried."

"I like that! Hasn't she been trying hard enough these last six months?" Dick blushed painfully.

"Oh—you mean Camilla! I—I thought you were talking about—"

There was a chorus of laughter, which made his cheeks redder than ever.

"My poor chap!" said the man who had spoken first. "Don't waste your young love in that quarter. Geneviève's a one-man's woman. Haven't you noticed that?"

"Pity her husband's not one woman's man," said another.

"Oh, I shouldn't worry. The fair Geneviève can be relied on to protect herself. A stiletto in her garter for any rivals—that's her type."

Without a word Dick left them and walked out of the room.

"And there goes the best cameraman in England," was the comment from the bar. "Well, if Gus goes on turning out tripe like his last opus, he'll soon be out of a job."

"Will America look at it, do you think?"

"Not a hope. I saw Souderberg after the show today, and he told me—"

"Gus was looking pretty green tonight, I thought."

"That doesn't prove anything. He always does. It's his British blood boiling in his veins."

"I hear there's been some trouble down at the studio. They've had a Scotland Yard man in."

"Oh, that's nothing. Some bright cashier been embezzling while the going's good."

"Where's Gus got to? He was here just now."

"Counting his losses, I expect. Well, here's luck."

Teddy Brancaster strode in, his magnificent brown body clad only in a pair of bathing trunks, a towel over his arm.

"Is Geneviève down yet?" he asked.

"My dear Apollo, was ever a woman ready when you expected her? Of course not."

Teddy went into the hall and called up the stairs.

"Hi, Geneviève! Are you coming?"

Geneviève appeared on the landing.

"Coming soon, Teddee!" she cried.

A bedroom door opened just behind her, and Camilla's white face appeared.

"Please, may I come too? Please, Teddy, just this once!"

Teddy smiled and shook his head.

"You shall not come!" said Geneviève with decision, and the door closed.

"I'm going down now," said Teddy. "See you at the pool, then. So long!"

From a chair in an alcove in the hall Dick Bartram, sick with envy, saw him go. Then he moved to the foot of the staircase.

"Geneviève!" he called softly.

II

Some twenty minutes later the last guests reluctantly decided that it was time to be going. They had damned *Amy Robsart* in general and Camilla's performance in particular, down to the last detail. They had cheerfully canvassed the prospects of a similar fiasco for the film which Teddy Brancaster was rehearsing, and they had almost exhausted their host's abundant supplies of drinks. At this point Gus again entered the room.

"Gus, old man, it's time I was going. It's been a great party."

"Glad you enjoyed it, Tom."

"Good night, Gus. That little Freyne girl is a real find. You'll make a big hit with *Amy Robsart*. All the boys think the same."

"Sure I hope so, Mike, I hope so."

"Good night, old boy. We've overstayed our welcome, I'm afraid."

"Not a bit, Jimmy. Always happy to see you."

"Good night . . . Good night . . ."

"Hey, you fellows! Anybody seen my wife about?"

Teddy Brancaster came in by the french window, his skin glistening with water drops, his bare feet leaving damp marks on the parquet floor.

"Hullo! It's Apollo back again! Didn't she keep her date with you, Teddy?"

"Nope. I've been swimming around the last quarter of an hour and she never came along."

"Too bad, Teddy. Quite a new experience for you to be jilted, isn't it? Sorry we can't stay for the end of the drama, but we're just off. Good night."

Teddy grinned cheerfully.

"Good night, you fellows. Guess I'll go look for her."

"Hope there's no bloodshed when you find her, anyway."

The guests took their noisy departure. Teddy followed them into the hall and went upstairs. A moment or two later he was down again. Gus was standing in the hall and Teddy looked down at him with troubled eyes.

"Gus, she isn't in her room. What's happened to her, d'you think?"

"I shouldn't worry, Teddy. Maybe she stayed in Camilla's room to help her sleep. I'll go and see, if you like."

"But she said she was coming swimming," Teddy objected.

"I'll go and look, all the same," said Gus, and mounted the stairs.

Teddy remained for a moment irresolute.

"Were you looking for me, Teddee?" said a voice behind him.

He spun round as if he had been shot. Geneviève

575

and Dick Bartram had just emerged from a little sitting-room on the further side of the hall.

"I'm sorry I didn't come with you, Teddee," she began, but he cut her short. He had gone deathly pale, his eyes blazed.

"You . . . !" he exclaimed. "You . . . !" He seemed incapable of saying more.

"But what is the matter, Teddee?"

"What's the matter? Weren't you coming swimming with me? Where have you been? What have you been doing? And who—oh, my God!"

But Geneviève had found her tongue.

"Ah, so it is like that, is it?" she exclaimed. "So the great Teddee is become jealous all at once, is it not? And all because I did not come the moment I was wanted, eh? Is it so often you want me, then? Have I ever complained to you about your Rosa, your Kitty, and now your Camilla? You know now what it is to feel what I have felt, then? That is good!"

"You little bitch!"

"Look here, Brancaster," began Bartram, "you're not to speak to your wife in that way. And if you suggest that she and I—"

"Be quiet, Dickee. This is my affaire."

"Hold your tongue, both of you, I—"

A fresh voice cut in above the noise of the dispute. Gus's voice, urgent with alarm.

"Stop that noise, for God's sake! Something is wrong here!"

All three were suddenly silent.

"Camilla's not in her room," said Gus. "And —and her window's wide open!"

It was an appreciable time before anyone spoke

again. Gus came slowly down the stairs. His shallow face was as expressionless as ever, but his fingers twitched incessantly as they grasped the banister rail and his feet stumbled uneasily at every step. When he reached the foot of the stairs, it was as if a spell had been broken, and everyone began to talk at once.

"Camilla!" groaned Teddy. "No, it's not possible!"

"*Ah, la pauvre fille!*" exclaimed Geneviève. "*Elle est somnambule sans doute. C'est ça que j'ai toujours cru!*"

Dick said simply:

"Did you look in her bathroom, Gus?"

"I looked," Gus answered. "It was empty. Her clothes were all over the room and her bed hadn't been slept in."

Once more silence fell on the little group—an oppressive silence in which each looked at the others in growing perplexity and fear.

"But what do we wait for?" said Geneviève suddenly. "We must search—the house, garden, everywhere!"

"The garden!" said Dick. "Have you got a torch anywhere, Gus? Come on, quickly, for God's sake!"

But it was Teddy who led the blind rush through the garden door behind the staircase to the back of the house.

To eyes coming direct from the brilliantly lighted hall the garden was in utter darkness, and the party halted in momentary uncertainty on the threshold. From the open door behind them a broad shaft of light illuminated a section of the terrace which ran the length of the house, and a little of the lawn beyond. Their shadows wavered against the background of white stone and vivid green.

"To the right," said Dick. "That's where her window is, isn't it? Hurry up with that torch, Gus!"

But before the torch could be found, and while their eyes were still straining to accustom themselves to the dark, Teddy had seen something dully white against the surrounding blackness.

"There! There!" he cried, and ran in its direction.

The others heard the patter of his bare feet as he went towards it, heard the sharp intake of his breath as he reached it. Then Gus's fumbling fingers found the switch of the electric torch and the whole scene was revealed.

Teddy was kneeling beside the body of Camilla Freyne, a pitiful crumpled heap upon the wide stone terrace. Her bare arms and legs gleamed alabaster white in contrast to the dark-blue bathing dress which was her only covering. Her face was so hideously mutilated as to be scarcely recognisable. From a dreadful wound in the head the blood had soaked through the towel on which it lay, staining the stone a dull red.

Teddy was weeping unashamedly.

"Camilla! Camilla, darling!" he sobbed. "Why did you do it? I loved you! I loved you! I'd have given my life for you—Camilla!"

"Teddee!" Geneviève's voice was shrill. "Teddee, get up! There is nothing you can do."

Teddy rose to his feet. His grief-distorted face

disappeared from the circle of light. In the darkness his voice sounded hollow.

"Sure, there's nothing we can do—nothing at all! Amy Robsart fell in the dark, that's all—and now I suppose you're happy!"

"How dare you!" cried Dick.

"Be silent, all of you!" Gus commanded. "Have you no reverence? Dick, you will please go and telephone for a doctor and the police."

"A doctor and a policeman!" echoed Teddy bitterly. "They'll be mighty useful! Will they give me Camilla back again? Ask them that! Ask them—" He sobbed afresh.

"Teddy," said Gus, with an air of authority, "you will go indoors. In my study there is brandy. Drink some. And do not come out again. Geneviève, you will stay here with me till help comes. It is not good for the dead to be alone."

III

It was a brilliantly fine morning. The sun, flaming out of a cloudless sky, penetrated into the room where Gus lay, sleepless. He rose from his bed and went to the window. The room occupied a wing built on to one end of the house, and from where he stood he could look along the whole length of the terrace. It was a placid, smiling scene, with nothing at first sight to remind him of the events of the night before. Only at one point on the terrace a single flagstone was covered with a rough piece of sacking. Gus averted his eyes from it hastily. The poor broken body of Camilla had

579

been taken away overnight under the orders of a doctor who had murmured remarks about multiple head injuries and shock, and a police sergeant who had been a miracle of sympathy and calm. About the house in which she had been the guest of honour a few hours before nothing of her remained except an ugly red stain, protected from the elements by an old half sack.

As Gus watched, two men came into his view round the further end of the house. One of them was the kindly sergeant of the night before. The other was a tall, broad-shouldered man in grey tweeds, with a fierce military moustache. As they walked round the corner they appeared to be deep in conversation.

". . . Danish bacon!" the one in tweeds was saying. "It's all very well, Parkinson, but when I come into the country I don't expect to be given Danish bacon!"

"I know, sir," said the sergeant sympathetically, "but it's like that everywhere nowadays. When I was a boy—er—here we are, sir!"

They had arrived at the piece of sacking. The sergeant pulled it away and together they looked at what lay beneath. Then he replaced it.

"You see where it lies, sir," he demonstrated. "Now, if anyone was to fall, or dive from that window above us, this is just where you would expect them to pitch."

"So I see," replied the other. "But, strictly speaking, you couldn't fall from the window. You would have to get on the balustrade outside it."

"Exactly. But that's easy done."

"No doubt."

580

"You've seen the body, I suppose, sir?"

"Yes, I called at the mortuary on the way here."

"Well, sir, it certainly looks a simple enough case to me. This young lady, according to all accounts, was in a bad state of nerves. They often are, them actresses, you know. She takes it into her head that she wants to bathe last night—to dive into the dark, as he puts it. She's told she's not to, and put to bed. Then she gets up, sleepwalking like, if you follow me, pops on her bathing dress, and dives out of window."

"It seems simple, certainly."

"Why, sir, it's plumb natural, if you ask me. And I'll tell you another thing. This girl's been acting a part called Amy Robsart. Now Amy Robsart, so far as I can make out, is killed much the same way, only it wasn't a window she fell out of—"

"I know. I've read the book."

"It isn't a book, it's a film. But I daresay it's much the same thing. What I'm getting at is that with her in a bad state of nerves and all, she'd be quite likely not to know whether she was herself or whether she was Amy Robsart, and behave accordingly, if you follow me?"

"Amy Robsart didn't wear a bathing dress, did she?"

"That's true, sir, she didn't. But I reckon the young lady got into a proper muddle about things and forgot that."

"Very likely."

A door in the house opened, and Teddy Brancaster, dressed—or rather undressed—for swimming, came out on to the terrace. He stopped when he saw the two men.

"Good morning," said Sergeant Parkinson. "You're up early."

"I'm always up for a dip before breakfast when your English climate allows it," said Teddy. He looked hard at the man in tweeds. "Haven't I seen you before?" he asked.

"This is Inspector Mallett of Scotland Yard," the sergeant explained. "He has been doing some investigation at the Cyclops Studios, and he was good enough to come along this morning and help us."

"Pleased to meet you," said Teddy. "Well, if you gentlemen will excuse me, I'll be going."

"Perhaps you will give me a moment or two later, when you have had your breakfast," said Mallett.

"Surely."

The giant strode away across the lawn. He struck a narrow stone path that ran in the direction of a little shrubbery, and, following it, disappeared from view. A moment later the detectives heard the thud of a springboard, followed by a splash.

"A fine figure of a man, that," was Parkinson's comment. "It's easy to see that he keeps himself in 'good condition.' Makes men like us look quite flabby, doesn't it, sir?"

"At all events, I haven't got black circles under my eyes at this time of day," said Mallett in an aggrieved tone.

"Well, sir, we must make allowances for that. I don't expect he had much sleep last night. He

582

was in a terrible state when I came in—crying and howling fit to burst himself, he was."

"Really? Suppose we go indoors now?"

They passed into the house. A scared house-maid fled at their approach.

"That reminds me," said Mallett. "What about the servants last night? Did they hear anything?"

"They had all gone to bed," Parkinson explained. "They sleep in a wing on the other side of the house. The guests at the party were looking after themselves. It was what they call a Bohemian party, I'm told—meaning that they could all drink as much as they liked without any servants to tell tales on them."

"I see. Now which way do we go?"

The sergeant led the way upstairs. He stopped before a door on the first-floor landing and un-locked it with a key which he took from his pocket.

"This is her room," he said. "Nothing has been touched."

It was a room of medium size, lit by one large sash window giving on to the garden. The bed was made, but had not been slept in. On it, and on the armchair at its foot, was distributed Camilla's finery of the night before—the heavy, embroidered Elizabethan gown and the stomacher stiffened with whale-bone contrasting strongly with the gossamer silk underwear of the twentieth century. The built-in wardrobe hung open. On the dressing-table a pearl necklace and some rings lay scattered. From an open powder bowl a faint scent permeated the room. To the right an open door led into the bathroom. Here, in contrast to the disorder of the bedroom, all was neatly arranged. The towels were folded; the sponges, hard and dry, in orderly array; and the bath mat, neatly centered, showed no sign of having been disturbed since the servant laid it down. The window, a small one, was closed.

Mallett took in everything with a few quick glances. Then, returning from the bathroom to the bedroom, he went to the window. It was open at the bottom, and, leaning through, he looked out for a few moments. Outside the window was a balustrade, some two feet high, which ran the entire length of the house. Between this and the window was a small space, just sufficient for a man to stand in.

His survey completed, Mallett withdrew his head.

"Have you looked out of here?" he asked Parkinson.

"No, sir. It was dark when I was here last night, of course."

"Have a look now."

The sergeant did so.

"Well?" Mallett said. "Did you notice anything?"

"I did, sir."

"Yes?"

"The place where the body was found is not under this window, sir. It is farther along to the right."

"What does that convey to you?"

"Why, sir, it looks as if the young lady had walked along the balustrade that way before she fell off."

"Why should she?"

584

"Isn't that just the kind of thing a sleep-walker would do, sir? Walk along a dangerous place until she lost her footing? I'm sure I've heard of that sort of thing happening more than once."

"Sleep-walking . . . H'm . . . And where did she sleep, Sergeant?"

Parkinson looked at the bed, and flushed a little.

"She fell asleep in the chair, very likely," he suggested.

"On top of her undies? Well, that's always possible, though one would expect them to be more crumpled. But there's one thing you haven't accounted for."

"Indeed, sir?"

"If she went sleep-walking, as you suggest, why was her head wrapped in a towel when she was found?"

"Good Lord, sir! Why didn't I think of that at once? Of course, that explains it. It wasn't sleep-walking at all, but just plain suicide!"

"I don't quite follow."

"Why, sir, don't you see the pea sigh cology of the thing?"

"The what?"

"The pea sigh cology, sir."

"Oh, the pea. . . No, I'm not sure that I do."

"Why, it's quite plain to me. Look here, sir. The young lady wants to kill herself. She makes up her mind to throw herself out of window. Then when it comes to the point she finds that she hasn't the nerve. So what does she do? She blindfolds herself with the towel, so that she can't see what's coming to her, if you follow me—"

"I do, Sergeant, I do."

585

"And just walks along the edge till she falls off, so taking herself by surprise in a manner of speaking. Am I right?"

"You may be, Sergeant. By the way, which window was it that she was found under?"

"Mr. and Mrs. Brancaster's bedroom, sir. That's next door to this, with just the bathroom in between."

"I see. Well, there doesn't appear to be anything further that we can do up here. We had better go downstairs now and see what the people in the house can tell us."

IV

In the dining-room the detectives found Teddy Brancaster finishing his breakfast. He had changed into a grey-flannel suit which set off his magnificent proportions to advantage.

"You are all alone, I see," said Mallett.

"As you see," assented the American gravely.

"Is Mrs. Brancaster breakfasting in bed?"

"I expect so. I haven't seen her this morning."

"How is that?"

"Well, if it interests you, I slept in my dressing-room last night—if you can call it sleeping," he added bitterly.

"When were you last in her bedroom?"

Teddy looked surprised at the question, and reflected a little before answering.

"Why, I guess it must have been before dinner last night," he said slowly.

586

"But didn't you go up there to look for her when you came in from bathing?"

"Sure, I did. I forgot that. She wasn't there."

"Can you tell me," the inspector pursued, "whether the window was open or shut when you went in?"

"Shut."

"Are you sure of that?"

"Positive."

"Do you know that it was under that window that Miss Freyne's body was found?"

"Is that so?" said Teddy slowly. "No, I did not know it."

"It occurred to me that she might perhaps have fallen from that window last night, but if you are right in your recollection that the window was shut it doesn't seem possible, does it?"

"It certainly does not."

"And you still say the window was shut?"

"I do, sir."

"When you went up to change last night, you didn't hear anything suspicious?"

"I did not go up to change last night. Gus lets me use the cloak-room down here as a changing room. It's more convenient for the pool, as I'm in and out all day."

"Thank you. That may be important. Now I must ask you about another thing altogether: was there something of a quarrel between you and your wife last night?"

Teddy's face darkened.

"There was," he admitted.

"Things were not altogether happy between the two of you?"

"Well—you've heard of film-stars' marriages not turning out well before now, I suppose?"

"Film-stars' marriages don't often last as long as yours, Mr. Brancaster. Let me see, six years, isn't it?"

"You seem to know a lot about me, Inspector."

"You must remember that I have been carrying out a fairly thorough investigation at the studios, and I have found it necessary to examine the lives of pretty well everyone connected with it."

"You British are certainly thorough," said Teddy with a faint smile.

"We try to be. And your American police are not very far behind when we ask them for assistance. Now I find that since your marriage your name has been—connected, shall we say—"

"Connected will do very well."

"—with a number of women. There was Rosa Layton, for example. She was killed in an accident, wasn't she, Mr. Brancaster?"

"She was drowned in a boating accident—yes."

"Then there was Kitty Cardew."

"Sure. Poor Kitty, she died from an overdose of Veronal."

"Was your wife jealous of these women?"

"Of them—and others. Yes."

"Was she jealous of Miss Freyne?"

"She most certainly was."

"Has it ever occurred to you, sir, that there might be some connection between these various accidents?"

Teddy Brancaster sat silent for a moment, staring at his plate. Then he said between clenched teeth, "Never—until now."

Dick Bartram came into the room. Teddy gave him a curt "Good morning!" and rose to his feet.

"I must be getting along to the set," he announced. "If you gentlemen want me again you know where to find me."

Bartram meanwhile had sat down at the table and was attacking a grapefruit with a gloomy air. He paid no attention to the other two men until Mallett addressed him.

"You know who I am, I think?" he began.

"Certainly. You're the Scotland Yard man, aren't you? How is your work at the studios going?"

"Pretty well. But that isn't what I'm here for today."

"No?"

"I am looking into the circumstances of the death of Camilla Freyne."

Dick pushed away his plate and looked up with interest.

"Do you really think," he asked, "that there may be something to—to look into, as you put it?"

"Every case of sudden death has to be investigated, naturally."

"But do you think that this case is—is something that needs special investigation?"

"I think it possible."

"Then I shall give you all the assistance in my power, of course. That is," he added, "if you don't mind my going on with my breakfast while I do it."

"Please do. . . . Your coffee smells remarkably good, if I may say so."

"Gus has it specially imported from Costa Rica. Would you care for a cup?"

"Well, since you press me. . . . Thank you. . . . Yes, that is certainly excellent coffee. Costa Rica, you say? I'll make a note of it."

"Would you care for some, Sergeant?"

"I thank you, no, sir," said Parkinson virtuously. "I drink tea myself."

"Now, sir," said Mallett, putting down his cup with an air of satisfaction. "I just want to put a few questions to you about your movements last night."

"They were very restricted movements, Inspector."

"After Miss Freyne had gone upstairs what did you do?"

"I stayed at the bar in the music-room for a short time and then went into the hall."

"Yes?"

"I remained there till after Brancaster had gone out to the swimming-pool—"

"While you were in the hall, did you hear Mr. Brancaster speaking to his wife?"

"Yes, and I heard her speak to him and to Miss Freyne."

"You heard Miss Freyne's voice too?"

"Yes."

"No doubt about it?"

"None at all. I have had the job of photographing Miss Freyne every day for the last two or three months, and I'm not likely to be mistaken about her face or her voice or her scent or anything that is hers."

"Quite. Then what did you do?"

"As soon as Brancaster was out of the house I called upstairs to Geneviève. She came down immediately. I took her into the smoking-room next door to the hall and there we stayed till Brancaster came back."

"You did not leave the room during that time?"

"No."

"From where you were could you have heard anybody going up or down the stairs?"

"I think not. We heard Teddy's voice when he came in, but he was talking pretty loud."

"What were you and Mrs. Brancaster doing in the smoking-room?" asked the inspector suddenly.

Bartram answered without a tremor.

"I was trying to persuade Geneviève to come away with me."

Parkinson blew out his cheeks and looked shocked, but Mallett pursued, unruffled, "Did you succeed?"

"No," said Dick bitterly. "Nothing that I could say would induce her to leave that hulking brute of a husband of hers. I don't know what women can be made of. He has treated her disgracefully —neglected her for a simpering little doll who thinks she's an actress because she's got a pretty face—"

He stopped abruptly.

"Sorry," he murmured. "I forgot—she's dead. I shouldn't have spoken of her in that way. I daresay she didn't know what she was doing. She was very young, and infatuated with him. But she was breaking the heart of a woman worth ten of her, and I couldn't forgive her."

There was a pause, and then the inspector said in a matter-of-fact way:

"It comes to this, then, Mr. Bartram. You and Mrs. Brancaster were alone together from the time that Miss Freyne, so far as we know, was last seen alive to the time when she was found to be missing?"

"Yes."

"And there is nobody, apart from Mrs. Brancaster, who can verify—Oh, good morning, Mr. Constantinovitch."

Gus's sallow face had appeared in the doorway.

"Good morning," he said. "You wished to see me, Inspector?"

"If you please. But it will keep till after you have breakfasted."

"I do not breakfast," said Gus, rubbing his great paunch reflectively.

"Once, perhaps, but for many years—no, I do not breakfast."

"You have my sympathy. Then in that case—"

"Come this way, please."

The two men followed him into his study, a tiny room almost entirely filled by an enormous Louis XV desk, littered with papers. Gus sat down before it and sighed heavily.

"And what have you to tell me, Inspector?" he asked.

"The position is serious," answered Mallett. "The defalcations are on an even larger scale than was thought at first. They have been cleverly made, and very cleverly concealed."

"Ah . . . ! It is that fellow Sneyd, I suppose?"

"It would appear so."

"We must prosecute, of course. But what good will that do us? All this is most unfortunate, Inspector, especially coming at this time. It puts the Cyclops set in a very difficult position. I say it within these four walls, but the position is difficult."

"Your organisation suffered a loss of a different kind last night," Mallett observed.

"The poor Camilla! Indeed, yes! An artist," said Gus sententiously, "whom the British film industry could ill afford to lose."

"Did your company insure her life?" Mallett asked abruptly.

"Certainly. We insure all our stars while they are under contract to us."

"What was Miss Freyne's contract?"

"For three years, at three hundred pounds a week. She was only beginning, you know," he added, as if in apology for the beggarly figure.

"And the insurance?"

"Twenty thousand pounds."

"So her death was not entirely a loss from the point of view of your company," suggested Mallett.

"One must look on the bright side, even of the greatest tragedy," Gus agreed.

"What were you doing last night," was the inspector's next question, "between the time when Miss Freyne went to bed and the time when you went to her room and found it empty?"

"After she had gone to bed," was the reply, "I stayed a little in the music-room and looked at my guests—those who remained. They all seemed to be enjoying themselves without me, so I left them

593

and came in here, where I remained until just before Mr. Brancaster came back from his swim. There were some figures and reports that I wanted to look at."

"Figures and reports relating to *Amy Robsart?*"

"Yes. My secretary had left them during the evening."

"They were not very satisfactory, were they?"

Gus made a deprecatory gesture.

"The preliminary bookings were disappointing," he admitted.

"Miss Freyne's tragic death will, however, give the film some assistance, I suppose?"

"We shall have some very useful publicity from it, I have no doubt."

"Thank you, Mr. Constantinovitch. I think that is all I want to know."

Mallett and Parkinson left the room.

"You certainly do know how to make them talk, sir," said Parkinson admiringly. "Now I suppose it's Mrs. Brancaster's turn to be put through it?"

"Mrs. Brancaster? No, I hardly think I need trouble her yet. I think I shall go for a walk in the garden. I've hardly seen it so far."

"The garden, sir? Oh yes, just so—the garden. Can I assist you in any way?"

"I don't think I need trouble you. I am sure you have plenty to do elsewhere."

"Since you mention it, sir, I have. Good day, sir!"

The sergeant left the house, and Mallett stepped out alone into the sunshine.

The garden was not a horticulturist's paradise. Its principal attraction was the well-kept lawn which stretched broad and green for some eighty yards from the terrace. This was flanked on either side by some tasteless beds of antirrhinums and fuchsias, and at the further end by leaden statuettes intended to give an olde worlde atmosphere, and succeeding only too well. Beyond it, to the right, a rustic sundial formed the focal point of an unenthusiastic rose-garden, which was separated from the lawn by the path which led to the swimming-pool.

This path Mallett followed. It took him to the little shrubbery behind which he had seen Teddy Brancaster disappear that morning. Here it sloped steeply downwards, serpentined aimlessly left and right, and ended abruptly at the edge of the pool.

The pool was not large—some fifty feet long by twenty broad, its length running in the same direction as the path, but it was well equipped, with a high diving-board, water-climb and spring-board, all at the deep end of the pool where Mallett now found himself. He stopped, one foot on the spring-board, and gazed meditatively into the clear water, through which the pattern of the blue-and-white-tiled bottom wavered and sparkled. Lifting his eyes he saw at the other end of the pool another man, apparently similarly engaged. From his clothes it could be guessed that he was a gardener, and from his expression that he did not care much for his job. Mallett walked over towards him.

"Good morning," he said.

The man acknowledged his presence by a stare and a sniff.

"This is a pretty place you've got down here," the inspector went on genially.

"So 't oughter be with all the money it cost," was the answer.

"Ah! Expensive, was it?"

"Cost a packet to make and costs a packet to run. Money no objeck! And can I git any money for my 'ouses? Can I get s'much as a bundle of pea-sticks without there's Gawd Almighty's row first? No, it's always the same thing. 'Jenkins, I can't afford it!' 'Jenkins, the garden costs too much money!' But 'is lordship's loverly swimming-bath—that's quite another pair o' shoes!"

He spat disgustedly into the water. Mallett's face must have shown what he felt, for he added:

"Oh, you needn't worry! I'm going to clean her out now."

"It doesn't look as if it needed it."

"Needed it? Of course it doesn't need it. But that makes no difference. Twice a week it 'as to be done, while 'is mightiness is in residence. That's nice work for an Englishman, ain't it? Swilling out a bath for a pack of foreign-born film actors. Company's water, mind you! Waste of money, waste of time, I calls it."

"How long does it take?"

"Two hours to empty, four hours to fill. And the time spent in the scrubbing of it out."

"How is it emptied?"

"I'll show you. It's just over where you're standing. See? There's a cock 'ere. You turn it *that* way, and she starts to empty. Then when you want to fill 'er, you turn that cock there. That's all."

"Thanks very much. Now I wonder if you could

596

do something for me. Perhaps I had better tell you who I am . . ."

Mallett continued to talk to the man for a full quarter of an hour, and then left him gloomily regarding the receding waters with the evident intention of doing no further work until the pool was empty.

On returning to the house, Mallett went straight to the little study. Gus was busy on the telephone. As he put down the receiver and turned to the inspector he displayed a countenance decidedly more cheerful than it had been an hour previously.

"You were quite right, Inspector," he said. "The publicity value of this business—this sad tragedy, I should say, is going to be very great. Greater than I had imagined, and I think that I should know something about publicity. Already I have given three interviews by telephone to press representatives, and now I think that the trade will begin to find that there is more in *Amy Robsart* than they had bargained for." He rubbed his hands. "Was I not right when I said that one must always look on the bright side?" he added.

"You were," the inspector admitted. "Now, Mr. Constantinovitch, there is only one more thing I should like you to do for me. I am going now, and shall not return until this evening. Can you arrange for all the people who slept in the house last night to be here then?"

"That can be done, Inspector. What time will you wish to see them?"

"I will be here at ten o'clock."

"Very good. Hullo? Yes? Mr. Constantinovitch speaking . . . Certainly I will give a message to

597

your readers. 'The tragic death of the glamorous young star at the very moment of attaining the pinnacle of fame in a performance which experts acclaim as . . .'"

Mallett left Gus to the telephone and made his way to the police-station. Sergeant Parkinson greeted him eagerly.

"Can I help you in any way, sir?" he asked.

"Yes," said Mallett. "You can tell me where the offices of the local water company are."

Parkinson looked somewhat disappointed.

"I'll take you round myself," he said. "But I meant—that is, I hoped—well, I thought there would be something you wanted *done*, if you follow me."

"I'm afraid not—at the present, at any rate. But I'd like you to meet me outside Mr. Constantinovitch's house at ten o'clock this evening. Perhaps there will be something to be 'done' then."

Mallett would vouchsafe no more, and he parted from Parkinson at the offices of the water company. Here he interviewed an intelligent young engineer, who from being bored and suspicious became as the interview went on more and more interested, and finally very busy indeed.

V

It was an uneasy party that awaited Mallett's visit in the music-room that evening, after a dinner that had been eaten for the most part in silence. Gus, who was by a good deal the most self-possessed of the four, proposed a game of poker. He was a good player at all times, and on this occasion the others were no match for him. Geneviève seemed listless and preoccupied, Dick was nervous, Teddy out of temper with his cards, his companions and himself. It was a positive relief to all of them, except Gus, who had pocketed a good deal of his guests' money, when on the stroke of ten Inspector Mallett was announced.

"I think you know everyone here," said Gus, "except Mrs. Brancaster."

Mallett bowed to her. She inclined her head languidly and then looked away. Mallett stood in the middle of the room and cleared his throat.

"As you all know," he said, "I am enquiring into the circumstances of the death of Miss Camilla Freyne. There will have to be an inquest, of course, and you, who were the only persons in or about the place at the time, will all be essential witnesses. There are reasons, which I cannot go into now, why it is important that I should know exactly what were the movements of each of you between the time when Miss Freyne left this room and the moment when she was found outside the house."

"But we've told you all that already," Dick objected.

"I agree. But at the same time there are some points which I should like cleared up, and I think they can best be cleared up by your helping me, so far as possible, to reconstruct the events of last night—in so far as you were respectively concerned in them. I want everyone to go through

599

the same actions in the same order and in the same place as they did last night. Is that agreed?"

There was a murmur of assent.

"Very good, then. We start from the moment when Mr. Constantinovitch asked Mrs. Brancaster to take Miss Freyne to bed. Where were you standing?"

"Here," said Gus.

"Very good. Mrs. Brancaster, go and stand there too, please. Were you with them, Mr. Brancaster? Then stand with them also. Where were you, Mr. Bartram?"

"By the bar, at the other end of the room."

"Then go there, please. Now, Mrs. Brancaster, what did you do?"

"I left the room with Camilla, *so*."

"Did you follow, Mr. Brancaster?"

"Not at once."

Mallett followed Geneviève to the door. She walked up the stairs and stopped at the door of Camilla's room.

"I went in for a moment or two to talk to her," she explained.

"Go in there, then," said Mallett from the hall.

"Go in? In there? I cannot—I will not. It is not good in there."

Mallett shrugged his shoulders.

"Very well," he said. "Then stand at the door till it is time to come out. Now, Mr. Brancaster?"

Teddy came out of the music-room.

"This was where I went to the cloak-room and got into my bathing-kit," he said.

"Then go there now," said the inspector.

"And change my clothes?"

"Certainly. I want to see how long it takes you."

"Will any old bathing trunks do, or must it be the same ones?" asked Teddy sarcastically.

"That is of no importance. Who moves next?"

"I came out of the room just after Brancaster," said Dick, moving accordingly, "and sat in the hall, *here*."

From above, Geneviève's voice was heard.

"I leave this room now, and go to my own."

"Very good, Mrs. Brancaster."

Gus walked across the hall.

"I am going to my study to look at papers," he said.

A pause ensued, during which nobody moved. Mallett ran quickly up the stairs, surveyed the hall from the landing and came down again. Then Teddy came in, wearing his bathing trunks.

"Here I am, Sherlock," he announced. "Where do I go from here?"

"Wherever you went last night."

Teddy took a few steps into the music-room and back again.

"I'm looking for my wife," he explained.

"He call me, and I come out here," said Geneviève from above. "Then Camilla open her door, and I shut her back, so."

"And I go off for my swim," said Teddy, walking into the music-room again.

"Stay there a moment, Mr. Brancaster. What do you do, Mr. Bartram?"

"Call for Mrs. Brancaster."

"Without going upstairs?"

"Yes."

"Then come down, Mrs. Brancaster."

601

Geneviève came down.

"Now we go to the smoking-room," she said.

Mallett saw them go and then went into the music-room where Teddy was waiting.

"What next?" asked Teddy.

"Which way did you go?"

"Through here," he said, indicating the french windows.

"Then let's go."

Mallett walked with him out into the garden. The moon was up and they could see their surroundings clearly.

"It was pitch dark last night, of course," Teddy explained.

"But you knew your way well enough?"

"Sure. You just follow the path. It runs straight from here."

"We'll follow it, then."

Teddy shrugged his shoulders and they walked on together. When they reached the clump of bushes he stopped.

"That's all there is to it," he said. "I just run down here and dive in."

"We'll run, then," said the inspector amiably.

They reached the edge of the pool together.

"Dive in," said Mallett.

"Here, what's the great idea?" said Teddy violently.

Before them in the moonlight, the pool gleamed bare, polished, empty.

"Did you dive in last night?" Mallett asked in a new and terrible voice. "Or did somebody else —somebody who didn't know, who couldn't see, that she was diving into an empty pool?"

From the shadows behind them Sergeant Parkinson silently approached and stood at Brancaster's shoulder.

"You knew that it was empty," Mallett continued. "You had emptied it yourself. You arranged for your wife to come here last night, so that she might kill herself in the dark. You waited here, and saw her, as you thought, plunge to her death down there. You climbed down into the pool, wrapped her head in your towel, so that the blood drops might not betray you and carried the body back to beneath your wife's window, turning on the water to fill the pool again before you left. Then you went into the house and began asking where your wife was. It wasn't till you found her that you knew the truth—that it was not your wife but Camilla Freyne who had followed you—that you had killed the woman for whose sake you wanted to murder your wife. Is that not true?"

Teddy was shuddering convulsively, and his breath came in quick gasps.

"Sure, it's true," he muttered over and over again. "Sure, it's true—true. I killed her—I killed her! The only girl I ever loved—I killed her! Leave me go!"

As Mallett's hand closed upon his shoulder, he swung round, drove him off with a tremendous blow in the face, knocked Parkinson fairly over and made a rush for the spring-board. He leapt in the air, came down with all his weight upon its end and soared into the sky. In the moonlight his brown body gleamed for an instant as it turned in a perfect jack-knife dive, to crash head first on to the tiled floor below.

Ruth Rendell
(b. 1930)

FEN HALL

Ruth Rendell is one of a handful of mystery writers who were subject to "the new Agatha Christie" speculation that occupied readers following that lady's death. She is, of course, not the new Agatha Christie. There will be none, just as there will be no new Ruth Rendell when this commanding figure passes from the scene.

"Fen Hall" marks a further departure from the classic Country House format. The characters are more carefully drawn and diminished in stature. Their story is told in the shadow of the great Country House. The house is an anachronism, but a powerful one. It contends with a new style of mystery fiction, one that Rendell has mastered as thoroughly as Agatha Christie mastered the tone of her time. Will mystery readers in 2025 grow as nostalgic for the Inspector Wexford stories as today's readers do for Poirot? Very likely, as long as great mystery writing gives pleasure.

When children paint a picture of a tree they always do the trunk brown. But trees seldom have brown trunks. Birches are silver, beeches pewter colour, planes grey and yellow, walnuts black and the bark of oaks, chestnuts and sycamores green with lichen. Pringle had never noticed any of this until he came to Fen Hall. After that, once his eyes had been opened and he had seen what things were really like, he would have painted trees with bark in different colours but next term he stopped doing art. It was just as well, he had never been very good at it, and perhaps by then he wouldn't have felt like painting trees anyway. Or even looking at them much.

Mr. Liddon met them at the station in an old Volvo estate car. They were loaded down with camping gear, the tent and sleeping bags and cooking pots and a Calor gas burner in case it was too windy to keep a fire going. It had been very windy lately, the summer cool and sunless. Mr. Liddon was Pringle's father's friend and Pringle had met him once before, years ago when he was a little kid, but still it was up to him to introduce the others. He spoke with wary politeness.

"This is John and this is Roger. They're brothers."

Pringle didn't say anything about Roger always being called Hodge. He sensed that Mr. Liddon wouldn't call him Hodge any more than he would call *him* Pringle. He was right.

"Parents well, are they, Peregrine?"

Pringle said yes. He could see a gleam in John's eye that augured teasing to come. Hodge, who was always thinking of his stomach, said:

"Could we stop on the way, Mr. Liddon, and buy some food?"

Mr. Liddon cast up his eyes. Pringle could tell he was going to be "one of those" grown-ups. They all got into the car with their stuff and a mile or so out of town Mr. Liddon stopped at a self-service shop. He didn't go inside with them which was just as well. He would only have called what they bought junk food.

Fen Hall turned out to be about seven miles away. They went through a village called Fedgford and a little way beyond it turned down a lane that passed through a wood.

"That's where you'll have your camp," Mr. Liddon said.

Of necessity, because the lane was no more than a rough track, he was driving slowly. He pointed in among the trees. The wood had a mysterious look as if full of secrets. In the aisles between the trees the light was a greenish-gold and misty. There was a muted twittering of birds and a cooing of doves. Pringle began to feel excited. It was nicer than he had expected. A little further on the wood petered out into a plantation of tall straight trees with green trunks growing in rows, the ground between them all overgrown with a spiky plant that had a curious prehistoric look to it.

"Those trees are poplars," Mr. Liddon said. You could tell he was a schoolteacher. "They're grown as a crop."

This was a novel idea to Pringle. "What sort of a crop?"

"Twenty-five years after they're planted they're cut down and used for making matchsticks. If they don't fall down first. We had a couple go over in the gales last winter."

Pringle wasn't listening. He had seen the house. It was like a house in a dream, he thought, though he didn't quite know what he meant by that.

Houses he saw in actual dreams were much like his own home or John and Hodge's, suburban Surrey semidetached. This house, when all the trees were left behind and no twig or leaf or festoon of wild clematis obscured it, stood basking in the sunshine with the confidence of something alive, as if secure in its own perfection. Dark mulberry colour, of small Tudor bricks, it had a roof of many irregular planes and gables and a cluster of chimneys like candles. The windows with the sun on them were plates of gold between the mullions. Under the eaves swallows had built their lumpy sagging nests.

"Leave your stuff in the car. I'll be taking you back up to the wood in ten minutes. Just thought you'd like to get your bearings, see where everything is first. There's the outside tap over there which you'll use of course. And you'll find a shovel and an axe in there which I rely on you to replace."

It was going to be the biggest house Pringle had ever set foot in—not counting places like Hampton Court and Woburn. Fen Hall. It looked and the name sounded like a house in a book, not real at all. The front door was of oak, studded with iron and set back under a porch that was dark and carved with roses. Mr. Liddon took them in the back way. He took them into a kitchen that was exactly Pringle's idea of the lowest sort of slum.

He was shocked. At first he couldn't see much because it had been bright outside but he could smell something dank and frowsty. When his vision adjusted he found they were in a huge room or cavern with two small windows and about four hundred square feet of squalor between them. Islanded were a small white electric oven and a small white fridge. The floor was of brick, very uneven, the walls of irregular green-painted peeling plaster with a bubbly kind of growth coming through it. Stacks of dirty dishes filled a stone sink of the kind his mother had bought at a sale and made a cactus garden in. The whole place was grossly untidy with piles of washing lying about. John and Hodge, having taken it all in, were standing there with blank faces and shifting eyes.

Mr. Liddon's manner had changed slightly. He no longer kept up the hectoring tone. While explaining to them that this was where they must come if they needed anything, to the back door, he began a kind of ineffectual tidying up, cramming things into the old wooden cupboards, sweeping crumbs off the table and dropping them into the sink. John said:

"Is it all right for us to have a fire?"

"So long as you're careful. Not if the wind gets up again. I don't have to tell you where the wood is, you'll find it lying about," Mr. Liddon opened a door and called, "Flora!"

A stone-flagged passage could be seen beyond. No one came. Pringle knew Mr. Liddon had a wife, though no children. His parents had told him only that Mr. and Mrs. Liddon had bought a marvellous house in the country a year before and he and a couple of his friends could go and camp in the grounds if they wanted to. Further information he had picked up when they didn't know he was listening. Tony Liddon hadn't had two halfpennies to rub together until his aunt died and left him a bit of money. It couldn't have been much surely. Anyway he had spent it all on Fen Hall, he had always wanted an old place like that. The upkeep was going to be a drain on him and goodness knows how he would manage.

Pringle hadn't been much interested in all this. Now it came back to him. Mr. Liddon and his father had been at university together but Mr. Liddon hadn't had a wife then. Pringle had never met the wife and nor had his parents. Anyway it was clear they were not to wait for her. They got back into the car and went to find a suitable camping site.

It was a relief when Mr. Liddon went away and left them to it. The obvious place to camp was on the high ground in a clearing and to make their fire in a hollow Mr. Liddon said was probably a disused gravel pit. The sun was low, making long shafts of light that pierced the groves of birch and crab apple. Mistletoe hung in the oak trees like green bird's nests. It was warm and murmurous with flies. John was adept at putting up the tent and gave them orders.

"Peregrine," he said. "Like a sort of mad bird."

Hodge capered about, his thumbs in his ears and his hands flapping. "Tweet, tweet, mad bird. His master chains him up like a dog. Tweet, tweet, birdie!"

"I'd rather be a hunting falcon than Roger the lodger the sod," said Pringle and he shoved Hodge and they both fell over and rolled about grappling on the ground until John kicked them and told them to stop it and give a hand, he couldn't do the lot on his own.

It was good in the camp that night, not windy

610

but still and mild after the bad summer they'd had. They made a fire and cooked tomato soup and fish fingers and ate a whole packet of the biscuits called iced bears. They were in their bags in the tent, John reading the *Observer's Book of Common Insects*, Pringle a thriller set in a Japanese prison camp his parents would have taken away if they'd known about it, and Hodge listening to his radio, when Mr. Liddon came up with a torch to check on them.

"Just to see if you're OK. Everything shipshape and Bristol fashion?"

Pringle thought that an odd thing to say considering the mess in his own house. Mr. Liddon made a fuss about the candles they had lit and they promised to put them out, though of course they didn't. It was very silent in the night up there in the wood, the deepest silence Pringle had ever known, a quiet that was somehow heavy as if a great dark beast had lain down on the wood and quelled every sound beneath under its dense soft fur. He didn't think of this for very long because he was asleep two minutes after they blew the candles out.

Next morning the weather wasn't so nice. It was dull and cool for August. John saw a Brimstone butterfly which pleased him because the species was getting rarer. They all waked into Fedgford and bought sausages and then found they hadn't a frying pan. Pringle went down to the house on his own to see if he could borrow one.

Unlike most men Mr. Liddon would be at home because of the school holidays. Pringle expected to see him working in the garden which even he could see was a mess. But he wasn't anywhere about. Pringle banged on the back door with his fist—there was neither bell nor knocker—but no one came. The door wasn't locked. He wondered if it would be all right to go in and then he went in.

The mess in the kitchen was rather worse. A large white and tabby cat was on the table eating something it probably shouldn't have been eating out of a paper bag. Pringle had a curious feeling that it would somehow be quite permissible for him to go on into the house. Something told him—though it was not a something based on observation or even guesswork—that Mr. Liddon wasn't in. He went into the passage he had seen the day before through the open door. This led into a large stone-flagged hall. The place was dark with heavy dark beams going up the walls and across the ceilings and it was cold. It smelled of damp. The smell was like mushrooms that have been left in a paper bag in the back of the fridge and forgotten. Pringle pushed open a likely looking door, some instinct making him give a warning cough.

The room was enormous, its ceiling all carved beams and cobwebs. Even Pringle could see that the few small bits of furniture in it would have been more suitable for the living room of a bungalow. A woman was standing by the tall, diamond-paned, mullioned window, holding something blue and sparkling up to the light. She was strangely dressed in a long skirt, her hair falling loosely down her back, and she stood so still, gazing at the blue object with both arms raised, that for a moment Pringle had an uneasy feeling that she wasn't a woman at all but the ghost of a woman. Then she turned round and smiled.

"Hallo," she said. "Are you one of our campers?"

She was at least as old as Mr. Liddon but her hair hung down like one of the girls' at school. Her face was pale and not pretty yet when she smiled it was a wonderful face. Pringle registered that, staring at her. It was a face of radiant kind sensitivity, though it was to be some years before he could express what he had felt in those terms.

"I'm Pringle," he said, and because he sensed that she would understand, "I'm called Peregrine really but I get people to call me Pringle."

"I don't blame you. I'd do the same in your place." She had a quiet unaffected voice. "I'm Flora Liddon. You call me Flora."

He didn't think he could do that and knew he would end up calling her nothing. "I came to see if I could borrow a frying pan."

"Of course you can." She added, "If I can find one." She held the thing in her hand out to him and he saw it was a small glass bottle. "Do you think it's pretty?"

He looked at it doubtfully. It was just a bottle. On the window sill behind her were more bottles, mostly of clear colourless glass but among them dark green ones with fluted sides.

"There are wonderful things to be found here. You can dig and find rubbish heaps that go back to Elizabethan times. And there was a Roman settlement down by the river. Would you like to see a Roman coin?"

It was black, misshapen, lumpy, with an ugly man's head on it. She showed him a jar of thick bubbly green glass and said it was the best piece of glass she'd found to date. They went out to the kitchen. Finding a frying pan wasn't easy but talking to her was. By the time she had washed up a pan which she had found full of congealed fat he had told her all about the camp and their walk to Fedgford and what the butcher had said:

"I hope you're going to wash yourselves before you cook my nice clean sausages."

And she told him what a lot needed doing to the house and grounds and how they'd have to do it all themselves because they hadn't much money. She wasn't any good at painting or sewing or gardening or even housework, come to that. Pottering about and looking at things was what she liked.

" 'What is this life if, full of care, we have no time to stand and stare?' "

He knew where that came from. W. H. Davies, the Super-tramp. They had done it at school.

"I'd have been a good tramp," she said. "It would have suited me."

The smile irradiated her plain face.

They cooked the sausages for lunch and went on an insect-hunting expedition with John. The dragonflies he had promised them down by the river were not to be seen but he found what he said was a caddis, though it looked like a bit of twig to Pringle. Hodge ate five Mars bars during the course of the afternoon. They came upon the white and tabby cat with a mouse in its jaws. Undeterred by an audience, it bit the mouse in two and the tiny heart rolled out. Hodge said faintly, "I think I'm going to be sick," and was. They still resolved to have a cat-watch on the morrow and see how many mice it caught in a day.

By that time the weather was better. The sun didn't shine but it had got warmer again. They found the cat in the poplar plantation, stalking something among the prehistoric weeds John said were called horse tails. The poplars had trunks almost as green as grass and their leafy tops, very high up there in the pale blue sky, made rustling whispering sounds in the breeze. That was when Pringle noticed about tree trunks not being brown. The trunks of the Scotch pines were a clear pinkish-red, as bright as flowers when for a moment the sun shone. He pointed this out to the others but they didn't seem interested.

"You sound like our auntie," said Hodge. "She does flower arrangements for the church."

"And throws up when she sees a bit of blood, I expect," said Pringle. "It runs in the family."

Hodge lunged at him and he tripped Hodge up and rolled about wrestling among the horse tails. By four in the afternoon the cat had caught six mice. Flora came out and told them the cat's name was Tabby which obscurely pleased Pringle. If she had said Snowflake or Persephone or some other daft name people called animals he would have felt differently about her, though he couldn't possibly have said why. He wouldn't have liked her so much.

A man turned up in a Land-Rover as they were making their way back to camp. He said he had

615

been to the house and knocked but no one seemed to be at home. Would they give Mr. or Mrs. Liddon a message from him? His name was Porter, Michael Porter, and he was an archaeologist in an amateur sort of way, Mr. Liddon knew all about it, and they were digging in the lower meadow and they'd come on a dump of nineteenth-century stuff. He was going to dig deeper, uncover the next layer, so if Mrs. Liddon was interested in the top, now was her chance to have a look.

"Can we as well?" said Pringle.

Porter said they were welcome. No one would be working there next day. He had just heard the weather forecast on his car radio and gale-force winds were promised. Was that their camp up there? Make sure the tent was well anchored down, he said, and he drove off up the lane.

Pringle checked the tent. It seemed firm enough. They got into it and fastened the flap but they were afraid to light the candles and had John's storm lantern on instead. The wood was silent no longer. The wind made loud sirenlike howls and a rushing rending sound like canvas being torn. When that happened the tent flapped and bellied like a sail on a ship at sea. Sometimes the wind stopped altogether and there were a few seconds of silence and calm. Then it came back with a rush and a roar. John was reading Frohawk's *Complete Book of British Butterflies*, Pringle the Japanese prison-camp thriller and Hodge was trying to listen to his radio. But it wasn't much use and after a while they put the lantern out and lay in the dark.

About five minutes afterwards there came the

strongest gust of wind so far, one of the canvas-tearing gusts but ten times fiercer than the last; and then, from the south of them, down towards the house, a tremendous rending crash.

John said, "I think we'll have to do something." His voice was brisk but it wasn't quite steady and Pringle knew he was as scared as they were. "We'll have to get out of here."

Pringle put the lantern on again. It was just ten.

"The tent's going to lift off," said Hodge.

Crawling out of his sleeping bag, Pringle was wondering what they ought to do, if it would be all right, or awful, to go down to the house, when the tent flap was pulled open and Mr. Liddon put his head in. He looked cross.

"Come on, the lot of you. You can't stay here. Bring your sleeping bags and we'll find you somewhere in the house for the night."

A note in his voice made it sound as if the storm were their fault. Pringle found his shoes, stuck his feet into them and rolled up his sleeping bag. John carried the lantern. Mr. Liddon shone his own torch to light their way. In the wood there was shelter but none in the lane and the wind buffeted them as they walked. It was all noise, you couldn't see much, but as they passed the plantation Mr. Liddon swung the light up and Pringle saw what had made the crash. One of the poplars had gone over and was lying on its side with its roots in the air.

For some reason—perhaps because it was just about on this spot that they had met Michael Porter—John remembered the message. Mr. Liddon said OK and thanks. They went into the house through the back door. A tile blew off the roof and crashed on to the path just as the door closed behind them.

There were beds up in the bedrooms but without blankets or sheets on them and the mattresses were damp. Pringle thought them spooky bedrooms, dirty and draped with spiders' webs, and he wasn't sorry they weren't going to sleep there. There was the same smell of old mushrooms and a smell of paint as well where Mr. Liddon had started work on a ceiling.

At the end of the passage, looking out of a window, Flora stood in a nightgown with a shawl over it. Pringle, who sometimes read ghost stories, saw her as the Grey Lady of Fen Hall. She was in the dark, the better to see the forked lightning that had begun to leap on the horizon beyond the river.

"I love to watch a storm," she said, turning and smiling at them.

Mr. Liddon had snapped a light on. "Where are these boys to sleep?"

It was as if it didn't concern her. She wasn't unkind but she wasn't involved either. "Oh, in the drawing room, I should think."

"We have seven bedrooms."

Flora said no more. A long roll of thunder shook the house. Mr. Liddon took them downstairs and through the drawing room into a sort of study where they helped him make up beds of cushions on the floor. The wind howled round the house and Pringle heard another tile go. He lay in the dark, listening to the storm. The others were asleep, he could tell by their steady breathing. Inside the bag it was quite warm and he felt snug and safe. After

618

a while he heard Mr. Liddon and Flora quarreling on the other side of the door.

Pringles's parents quarrelled a lot and he hated it, it was the worst thing in the world, though less bad now than when he was younger. He could only just hear Mr. Liddon and Flora and only disjoined words, abusive and angry on the man's part, indifferent, amused on the woman's, until one sentence rang out clearly. Her voice was penetrating though it was so quiet:

"We want such different things!"

He wished they would stop. And suddenly they did, with the coming of the rain. The rain came, exploded rather, crashing at the windows and on the old sagging depleted roof. It was strange that a sound like that, a loud constant roar, could send you to sleep . . .

She was in the kitchen when he went out there in the morning. John and Hodge slept on, in spite of the bright watery sunshine that streamed through the dirty diamond window panes. A clean world outside, new-washed. Indoors the same chaos, the kitchen with the same smell of fungus and dirty dishcloths, though the windows were open. Flora sat at the table on which sprawled a welter of plates, indefinable garments, bits of bread and fruit rinds, an open can of cat food. She was drinking coffee and Tabby lay on her lap.

"There's plenty in the pot if you want some."

She was the first grown-up in whose house he had stayed who didn't ask him how he had slept. Nor was she going to cook breakfast for him. She told him where the eggs were and bread and butter. Pringle remembered he still hadn't returned her frying pan which might be the only one she had.

He made himself a pile of toast and found a jar of marmalade. The grass and the paths, he could see through an open window, were littered with broken bits of twig and leaf. A cock pheasant strutted across the shaggy lawn.

"Did the storm damage a lot of things?" he asked.

"I don't know. Tony got up early to look. There may be more poplars down."

Pringle ate his toast. The cat had begun to purr in an irregular throbbing way. Her hand kneaded its ears and neck. She spoke, but not perhaps to Pringle or the cat, or for them if they cared to hear.

"So many people are like that. The whole of life is a preparation for life, not living."

Pringle didn't know what to say. He said nothing. She got up and walked away, still carrying the cat, and then after a while he heard music coming faintly from a distant part of the house.

There were two poplars down in the plantation and each had left a crater four or five feet deep. As they went up the lane to check on their camp, Pringle and John and Hodge had a good look at them, their green trunks laid low, their tangled roots in the air. Apart from everything having got a bit blown about up at the camp and the stuff they had left out, soaked through, there was no real damage done. The wood itself had afforded protection to their tent.

It seemed a good time to return the frying pan. After that they would have to walk to Fedgford for some sausages—unless one of the Liddons offered a lift. It was with an eye to this, Pringle had to admit, that he was taking the pan back.

But Mr. Liddon, never one to waste time, was already at work in the plantation. He had lugged a chain saw up there and was preparing to cut up the poplars where they lay. When he saw them in the lane he came over.

"How did you sleep?"

Pringle said, "OK, thanks," but Hodge, who had been very resentful about not being given a hot drink or something to eat, muttered that he had been too hungry to sleep. Mr. Liddon took no notice. He seemed jumpy and nervous. He said to Pringle that if they were going to the house would they tell Mrs. Liddon—he never called her Flora to them—that there was what looked like a dump of Victorian glass in the crater where the bigger poplar had stood.

"They must have planted the trees over the top without knowing."

Pringle looked into the crater and sure enough he could see bits of coloured glass and a bottleneck and a jug or tankard handle protruding from the tumbled soil. He left the others there, fascinated by the chain saw, and went to take the frying pan back. Flora was in the drawing room, playing records of tinkly piano music. She jumped up, quite excited, when he told her about the bottle dump.

They walked back to the plantation together, Tabby following, walking a little way behind them like a dog. Pringle knew he hadn't a hope of getting that lift now. Mr. Liddon had already got the crown of the big poplar sawn off. In the short time

621

since the storm its pale silvery-green leaves had begun to wither. John asked if they could have a go with the chain saw but Mr. Liddon said not so likely, did they think he was crazy? And if they wanted to get to the butcher before the shop closed for lunch they had better get going now.

Flora, her long skirt hitched up, had clambered down into the crater. If she had stood up in it her head and shoulders, perhaps all of her from the waist up, would have come above its rim, for poplars have shallow roots. But she didn't stand up. She squatted down, using her trowel, extracting small glass objects from the leafmould. The chain saw whined, slicing through the top of the poplar trunk. Pringle, watching with the others, had a feeling something was wrong about the way Mr. Liddon was doing it. He didn't know what though. He could only think of a funny film he had once seen in which a man, sitting on a branch, sawed away at the bit between him and the tree trunk, necessarily falling off himself when the branch fell. But Mr. Liddon wasn't sitting on anything. He was just sawing up a fallen tree from the crown to the bole. The saw sliced through again, making four short logs now as well as the bole.

"Cut along now, you boys," he said. "You don't want to waste the day mooning about here."

Flora looked up and winked at Pringle. It wasn't unkind, just conspiratorial, and she smiled too, holding up a small glowing red glass bottle for him to see. He and John and Hodge moved slowly off, reluctantly, dawdling because the walk ahead would be boring and long. Through the horse

622

tails, up the bank, looking back when the saw whined again.

But Pringle wasn't actually looking when it happened. None of them was. They had had their final look and had begun to trudge up the lane. The sound made them turn, a kind of swishing lurch and then a heavy plopping, sickening, dull crash. They cried out, all three of them, but no one else did, not Flora or Mr. Liddon. Neither of them made a sound.

Mr. Liddon was standing with his arms held out, his mouth open and his eyes staring. The pile of logs lay beside him but the tree trunk was gone, sprung back roots and all when the last saw cut went through, tipped the balance and made its base heavier than its top. Pringle put his hand over his mouth and held it there. Hodge, who was nothing more than a fat baby really, had begun to cry. Fearfully, slowly, they converged, all four of them, on the now upright tree under whose roots she lay.

The police came and a farmer and his son and some men from round about. Between them they got the tree over on its side again but by then Flora was dead. Perhaps she died as soon as the bole and the mass of roots hit her. Pringle wasn't there to see. Mr. Liddon had put the plantation out of bounds and said they were to stay in camp until someone came to drive them to the station. It was Michael Porter who turned up in the late afternoon and checked they'd got everything packed up and the camp site tidied. He told them Flora was dead. They got to the station in his

623

Land-Rover in time to catch the five-fifteen for London.

On the way to the station he didn't mention the bottle dump he had told them about. Pringle wondered if Mr. Liddon had ever said anything to Flora about it. All the way home in the train he kept thinking of something odd. The first time he went up the lane to the camp that morning he was sure there hadn't been any glass in the tree crater. He would have seen the gleam of it and he hadn't. He didn't say anything to John and Hodge, though. What would have been the point?

Three years afterwards Pringle's parents got an invitation to Mr. Liddon's wedding. He was marrying the daughter of a wealthy local builder and the reception was to be at Fen Hall, the house in the wood. Pringle didn't go, being too old now to tag about after his parents. He had gone off trees anyway.

P. D. James
(b. 1920)
A VERY DESIRABLE RESIDENCE

Rendells' great rival, if any rivalry can be said to exist, must be P. D. James (Phyllis Dorothy James White), another introspective writer engaged in psychological study.

This story comes from Winter's Crimes *(No. 8), the important annual series chronicling the pageant of contemporary mystery short fiction. One has not achieved stature as an English crime writer until a story has been collected into one of these engaging anthologies.*

"A Very Desirable Residence" may well be the tale that closes the tradition. As in "Fen Hall," the house is a reminder of the past. The characters, like Rendell's, are ordinary to the point of depression. They have none of the grandeur and allure of those who once dominated the property. They are the survivors of the Grand Tradition, but only survivors.

When the great stories of this era are collected, it may well be into a collection called "Great English Town Flat Mysteries." James would be a cornerstone of such a collection. So would Rendell, and Fremlin and Yorke and others whose writing rings true with contemporary familiarity, well observed.

Lord and Lady Ferncliffe, Lord Peter, and Mr. Holmes will not be found there. They are gone, but hardly forgotten. Luckily, they can be summoned forth again simply by turning a page.

During and after Harold Vinson's trial, at which I was a relatively unimportant prosecution witness, there was the usual uninformed, pointless and repetitive speculation about whether those of us who knew him would ever have guessed that he was a man capable of scheming to murder his wife. I was supposed to have known him better than most of the school staff and my colleagues found it irritatingly self-righteous of me to be so very reluctant to be drawn into the general gossip about what, after all, was the school's major scandal in twenty years. "You knew them both. You used to visit the house. You saw them together. Didn't you guess?" they insisted, obviously feeling that I had been in some way negligent, that I ought to have seen what was going on and prevented it. No, I never guessed; or, if I did, I guessed wrong. But they were perfectly right. I could have prevented it.

I first met Harold Vinson when I took up a post as junior art master at the comprehensive school where he taught mathematics to the senior forms. It wasn't too discouraging a place as these teaching factories go. The school was centered on the old 18th century grammar school, with some not too hideous modern additions, in a pleasant enough commuter town on the river about twenty miles southeast of London. It was a predominantly mid-

626

dle-class community, a little smug and culturally self-conscious, but hardly intellectually exciting. Still, it suited me well enough for a first post. I don't object to the middle-class or their habitats; I'm middle-class myself. And I knew that I was lucky to get the job. Mine is the usual story of an artist with sufficient talent but without enough respect for the fashionable idiocies of the contemporary artistic establishment to make a decent living. More dedicated men choose to live in cheap bed-sitting rooms and keep on painting. I'm fussy about where and how I live so, for me, it was a diploma in the teaching of art and West Fairing Comprehensive.

It only took one evening in Vinson's home for me to realise that he was a sadist. I don't mean that he tormented his pupils. He wouldn't have been allowed to get away with it had he tried. These days the balance of power in the classroom has shifted with a vengeance and any tormenting is done by the children. No, as a teacher, he was surprisingly patient and conscientious, a man with real enthusiasm for his subject ("discipline" was the word he preferred to use being something of an intellectual snob and given to academic jargon) with a surprising talent for communicating that enthusiasm to the children. He was a fairly rigid disciplinarian, but I've never found that children dislike firmness provided a master doesn't indulge in that pedantic sarcasm which, by taking advantage of the children's inability to compete, is resented as particularly unfair. He got them through their examinations too. Say what you like, that's something middle-class kids and their parents appreciate. I'm sorry to have slipped into using the word "kids", that modern shibboleth with its blend of condescension and sycophancy. Vinson never used it. It was his habit to talk about the alumni of the sixth. At first I thought it was an attempt at mildly pretentious humour, but now I wonder. He wasn't really a humorous man. The rigid muscles of his face seldom cracked into a smile and when they did it was as disconcerting as a painful grimace. With his lean, slightly stooping figure, the grave eyes behind the horn-rimmed spectacles, the querulous lines etched deeply from the nose to the corners of his unyielding mouth, he looked deceptively what we all thought he was—a middle-aged, disagreeable and not very happy pedant.

No, it wasn't his precious alumni whom he bullied and tyrannised over. It was his wife. The first time I saw Emily Vinson was when I sat next to her at founder's memorial day, an archaic function inherited from the grammar school and regarded with such reverence that even those masters' wives who seldom showed their faces at the school felt obliged to make an appearance. She was, I guessed, almost twenty years younger than her husband, a thin, anxious looking woman with auburn hair which had faded early and the very pale transparent looking skin which often goes with that colouring. She was expensively and smartly dressed, too incongruously smartly for such a nondescript woman so that the ill-chosen, too fashionable suit merely emphasised her frail ordinariness. But her eyes were remarkable, an unusual grey green, huge and slightly exophthalmic under the arched narrow eyebrows. She seldom turned them on me but when, from time to time, she gave me a swift elliptical glance it was as astounding as turning over an amateurish Victorian oil and discovering a Corot.

It was at the end of founder's memorial day that I received my first invitation to visit them at their home. I found that they lived in some style. She had inherited from her father a small but perfectly proportioned Georgian house which stood alone in some two acres of ground with lawns slanting green down to the river. Apparently her father was a builder who had bought the house cheaply from its impoverished owner with the idea of demolishing it and building a block of flats. The planning authority had slapped on a preservation order just in time and he had died in weeks, no doubt from chagrin, leaving the house and its contents to his daughter. Neither Harold Vinson nor his wife seemed to appreciate their possession. He grumbled about the expense; she grumbled about the housework. The perfectly proportioned façade, so beautiful that it took the breath, seemed to leave them as unmoved as if they lived in a square brick box. Even the furniture, which had been bought with the house, was regarded by them with as little respect as if it were cheap reproduction. When at the end of my first visit I complimented Vinson on the spaciousness and proportions of the dining-room he replied,

"A house is only the space between four walls. What does it matter if they are far apart or close together, or what they are made of? You're still in a cage." His wife was carrying the plates into the kitchen at the time and didn't hear him. He spoke so low that I scarcely heard him myself. I am not even sure now that I was meant to hear.

Marriage is both the most public and the most secret of institutions, its miseries as irritatingly insistent as a hacking cough, its private malaise less easily diagnosed. And nothing is so destructive as unhappiness to social life. No one wants to sit in embarrassed silence while his host and hostess demonstrate their mutual incompatibility and dislike. She could, it seemed, hardly open her mouth without irritating him. No opinion she expressed was worth listening to. Her small domestic chat—which was, after all, all she had—invariably provoked him by its banality so that he would put down his knife and fork with a look of patient resigned boredom as soon as, with a nervous preparatory glance at him, she would steel herself to speak. If she had been an animal, cringing away with that histrionic essentially false look of piteous entreaty, I can see that the temptation to kick would be irresistible. And, verbally, Vinson kicked.

Not surprisingly they had few friends. Looking back it would probably be more true to say that they had no real friends. The only colleague of his who visited from the school, apart from myself, was Vera Pelling, the junior science teacher, and she, poor girl, was such an unattractive bore that there weren't many alternatives open to her. Vera Pelling is the living refutation of that theory so beloved, I understand, of beauty and fashion journalists in women's magazines that any woman if she takes the trouble can make something of her appearance. Nothing could be done about Vera's pig-like eyes and non-existent chin and, reasonably enough, she didn't try. I am sorry if I sound harsh. She wasn't a bad sort. And if she thought that making a fourth with me at an occasional free supper with the Vinsons was better than eating alone in her furnished flat I suppose she had her reasons, as I had mine. I never remember having visited the Vinsons without Vera although Emily came to my flat on three occasions, with Harold's approval, to sit for her portrait. It wasn't a success. The result looked like a pastiche of an early Stanley Spencer. Whatever it was I was trying to capture, that sense of a secret life conveyed in the rare grey-green flash of those remarkable eyes, I didn't succeed. When Vinson saw the portrait he said:

"You were prudent, my boy, to opt for teaching as a livelihood. Although, looking at this effort, I would say that the choice was hardly voluntary." For once I was tempted to agree with him.

Vera Pelling and I became oddly obsessed with the Vinsons. Walking home after one of their supper parties we would mull over the traumas of the evening like an old married couple perennially discussing the inadequacies of a couple of relatives whom we actively disliked but couldn't bear not to see. Vera was a tolerable mimic and would imitate Vinson's dry, pedantic tones.

"My dear, I think that you recounted that not very interesting domestic drama last time we had supper together."

"And what, my dear, have you been doing with yourself today? What fascinating conversation did

631

you have with the estimable Mrs. Wilcox while you cleaned the drawing-room together?"

Really, confided Vera, tucking her arm through mine, it had become so embarrassing that it was almost enough to put her off visiting them. But not quite enough apparently. Which was why she, too, was at the Vinsons' on the night when it happened.

On the evening of the crime—the phrase has a stereotyped but dramatic ring which isn't inappropriate to what, look at it as you will, was no ordinary villainy—Vera and I were due at the school at 7 P.M. to help with the dress rehearsal of the school play. I was responsible for the painted blackcloth and some of the props and Vera for the make-up. It was an awkward time, too early for a proper meal beforehand and too late to make it sensible to stay on at school without some thought of supper, and when Emily Vinson issued through her husband an invitation to both Vera and me to have coffee and sandwiches at 6 o'clock it seemed sensible to accept. Admittedly, Vinson made it plain that the idea was his wife's. He seemed mildly surprised that she should wish to entertain us so briefly—insist on entertaining us was the expression he used. Vinson himself wasn't involved with the play. He never grudged spending his private time to give extra tuition in his own subject but made it a matter of rigid policy never to become involved in what he described as extramural divertissements appealing only to the regressed adolescent. He was, however, a keen chess player and on Wednesday evenings spent the three hours from nine until midnight at the local chess club of which he was secretary. He was a man of meticulous habit and any school activity on a Wednesday evening would, in any case, have had to manage without him.

Every detail, every word spoken at that brief and unremarkable meal—dry ham sandwiches cut too thick and synthetic coffee—was recounted by Vera and me at the Crown Court so that it has always intrigued me that I can no longer visualise the scene. I know exactly what happened, of course. I can recount every word. It's just that I can no longer shut my eyes and see the supper table, the four of us seated there, imprinted in colours on the mind's eye. Vera and I said at the trial that both Vinsons seemed more than usually ill at ease, that Harold, in particular, gave us the impression that he wished we weren't there. But that could have been hindsight.

The vital incident, if you can call it that, happened towards the end of the meal. It was so very ordinary at the time, so crucial in retrospect. Emily Vinson, as if uneasily aware of her duties as hostess and of the unaccountable silence which had fallen on the table, made a palpable effort. Looking up with a nervous glance at her husband she said:

"Two such very nice and polite workmen came this morning—" Vinson touched his lips with his paper serviette then crumpled it convulsively. His voice was unusually sharp as he broke in:

"Emily my dear, do you think you could spare us the details of your domestic routine this evening? I've had a particularly tiring day. And I am trying to concentrate my mind on this evening's game." And that was all.

The dress rehearsal was over at about nine o'clock, as planned, and I told Vera that I had left a library book at the Vinsons' and was anxious to pick it up on the way home. She made no objection. She gave the impression, poor girl, that she was never particularly anxious to get home. It was only a quarter of an hour's brisk walk to the house and, when we arrived, we saw at once that something was wrong. There were two cars, one with a blue light on the roof, and an ambulance parked unobtrusively but unmistakably at the side of the house. Vera and I glanced briefly at each other then ran to the front door. It was shut. Without ringing we dashed round to the side. The back door, leading to the kitchen quarters, was open. I had an immediate impression that the house was peopled with large men, two of them were in uniform. There was, I remember, a policewoman bending over the prone figure of Emily Vinson. And their cleaning woman, Mrs. Wilcox, was there too. I heard Vera explaining to a plain-clothes policeman, obviously the senior man present, that we were friends of the Vinsons, that we had been there to supper only that evening. "What's happened?" she kept asking. "What's happened?" Before the police could answer Mrs. Wilcox was spitting it all out, eyes bright with self-important outrage and excitement. I sensed that the police wanted to get rid of her, but she wasn't so easily dislodged. And, after all, she had been first on the scene. She knew it all. I heard it in a series of disjointed sentences:

634

"Knocked on the head—terrible bruise—marks all over the parquet flooring where he dragged her—only just coming round now—human fiend—head resting on a cushion in the gas stove—the poor darling—came in just in time at 9:20—always come to watch colour TV with her on Wednesday night—back door open as usual—found the note on the kitchen table." The figure writhing on the floor, groaning and crying in a series of harsh grunting moans like an animal in travail, suddenly raised herself and spoke coherently.

"I didn't write it! I didn't write it!"

"You mean Mr. Vinson tried to kill her?" Vera was incredulous, head turning from Mrs. Wilcox to the watchful, inscrutable faces of the police. The senior officer broke in:

"Now Mrs. Wilcox, I think it's time you went home. The ambulance is here. An officer will come along for your statement later this evening. We'll look after Mrs. Vinson. There's nothing else for you to do."

He turned to Vera and me. "If you two were here earlier this evening, I'd like a word. We're fetching Mr. Vinson now from his chess club. But if you two will just wait in the sitting-room please."

Vera said:

"But if he knocked her unconscious and put her head in the gas oven, then why isn't she dead?"

It was Mrs. Wilcox who replied, turning triumphantly as she was led out:

"The conversion, that's why. We're on natural gas from this evening. That North Sea stuff. It

635

isn't poisonous. The two men from the Gas Board came just after nine o'clock."

They were lifting Emily Vinson on to a stretcher now. Her voice came to us in a high querulous wail.

"I tried to tell him. You remember? You heard him? I tried to tell him."

The suicide note was one of the exhibits at Vinson's trial. A document examiner from the forensic science laboratory testified that it was a forgery, a clever forgery but not Mrs. Vinson's writing. He couldn't give an opinion on whether it was the work of the husband, although it was certainly written on a page taken from a writing pad found in the desk in the sitting-room. It bore no resemblance to the accused's normal writing. But, in his view, it hadn't been written by Mrs. Vinson. He gave a number of technical reasons to support his view and the jury listened respectfully. But they weren't surprised. They knew that it hadn't been written by Mrs. Vinson. She had stood in the witness box and told them so. And they were perfectly clear in their own minds who had written it.

There was other forensic evidence. Mrs. Wilcox's "Marks all over the parquet floor" were reduced to one long but shallow scrape, just inside the sitting-room door. But it was a significant scrape. It had been made by the heels of Emily Vinson's shoes. Traces of the floor polish which she used were found, not on the soles, but on the sides of the scraped heels and there were minute traces of her shoe polish in the scrape.

The fingerprint officer gave evidence. I hadn't realised until then that fingerprint experts are mostly civilians. It must be a dull job, that constant and meticulous examination of surfaces for the tell-tale composites and whirls. Hard on the eyes I should think. In this case the significance was that he hadn't found any prints. The gas taps had been wiped clean. I could see the jury physically perk up at the news. That was a mistake all right. It didn't need the prosecution to point out that the taps should have shown Mrs. Vinson's prints. She, after all, had cooked their last meal. A cleverer murderer would merely have worn gloves, smudging any existing prints but ensuring that he left none of his own. It had been an over-precaution to wipe the gas taps clean.

Emily Vinson, quiet, distressed but gallant, obviously reluctant to testify against her husband, was remarkably competent in the witness box. I hardly recognised her. No, she hadn't told her husband that she and Mrs. Wilcox had arranged to watch the television together shortly after nine o'clock. Mrs. Wilcox, who lived nearby, usually did come across to spend a couple of hours with her on Wednesday nights when Mr. Vinson was at his chess club. No, she hadn't liked to tell Mr. Vinson. Mr. Vinson wasn't very fond of inviting people in. The message came over to the jury as clearly as if she had spelt it out, the picture of a downtrodden, unintellectual wife craving the human companionship which her husband denied her, guiltily watching a popular TV show with her cleaning woman at a time when she would be certain that her husband wouldn't catch them out. I

637

glanced at his proud, unyielding mask, at the hands clutched over the edge of the dock, and imagined what he was thinking, what he would have said.

"Surely you have enough of domestic trivia and Mrs. Wilcox's conversation, hardly exciting I should have thought, without inviting her into your drawing-room. The woman should know her place."

The trial didn't take long. Vinson made no defence except to reiterate stubbornly, eyes fixed straight ahead, that he hadn't done it. His counsel did his best, but with the dogged persistence of a man resigned to failure, and the jury had the look of people glad to be faced, for once, with a clear cut case they could actually understand. The verdict was inevitable. And the subsequent divorce hearing was even shorter. It isn't difficult to persuade a judge that your marriage has irretrievably broken down when your husband is serving a prison sentence for attempted murder.

Two months after the decree absolute we married and I took over the Georgian house, the river view, the regency furniture. With the physical possessions I knew exactly what I was getting. With my wife, I wasn't so sure. There had been something disturbing, even a little frightening, about the competence with which she had carried out my instructions. It hadn't, of course, been particularly difficult. We had planned it together during the sessions when I was painting her portrait. I had written and handed her the fake suicide note on the paper she had supplied a few days before our plans matured. We knew when the gas was due to be converted. She had, as instructed, placed the note on the kitchen table before scraping the heels of her shoes across the polished floor. She had even managed beautifully the only tricky part, to bang the back of her head sufficiently hard against the kitchen wall to raise an impressive bruise but not sufficiently hard to risk bungling the final preparations; the cushion placed in the bottom of the oven for the head, the gas tap turned on and then wiped clean with her handkerchief.

And who could have imagined that she was such a consummate actress? Sometimes, remembering that anguished animal cry of "I tried to tell him. I tried to tell him," I wonder again what is going on behind those remarkable eyes. She still acts, of course. I find it remarkably irritating, that habit she has particularly when we are in company, of turning on me that meek, supplicating, beaten dog expression whenever I talk to her. It provokes unkindness. Perhaps it's intended to. I'm afraid I'm beginning to get rather a reputation for sadism. People don't seem to want to come to the house any more.

There is one solution, of course, and I can't pretend that I haven't pondered it. A man who has killed another merely to get his house isn't likely to be too fastidious about killing again. And it was murder; I have to accept that.

Vinson only served nine months of his sentence before dying in the prison hospital of what should have been an uncomplicated attack of influenza. Perhaps his job really was his life and without his precious alumni the will to live snapped. Or perhaps he didn't choose to live with the memory of his wife's great betrayal. Beneath the petty tyranny, the impatience, the acerbity, there may have been love of a kind.

But the ultimate solution is barred to me. A month ago Emily explained, meekly, like a child propounding a problem, and with a swift sidelong glance, that she had written a confession and left it with her solicitor.

"Just in case anything happens to me, darling."

She explained that what we did to poor Harold is preying on her mind but that she feels better now that all the details are written down and she can be sure that, after her death, the truth will at last be known and Harold's memory cleared. She couldn't have made it more plain to me that it is in my interest to see that I die first.

I killed Harold Vinson to get the house; Emily to get me. On the whole, she made the better bargain. In a few weeks I shall lose the house. Emily is selling it. After all, there's nothing I can do to stop her; the place belongs to her not me.

After we married I gave up the teaching post, finding it embarrassing to meet my colleagues as Emily's husband. It was not that anyone suspected. Why should they? I had a perfect alibi for the time of the crime. But I had a dream that, living in that perfection, I might become a painter after all. That was the greatest illusion of all.

So now they are taking down from the end of the drive the board which states "This Desirable Residence For Sale." Emily got a very good price for the house and the furniture. More than enough to buy the small but pretentious brick box on an executive estate in North London which will be my cage from now on. Everything is sold. We're taking nothing with us except the gas stove. But, as Emily pointed out when I remonstrated, why not? It's in perfectly good working order.

James Miles

THE WORCESTER ENIGMA

Before we part, one final adventure—a return to those days of hope and glory when the welfare of the nation often rested in the secure hands of Mr. Sherlock Holmes.

This time a rather extraordinary problem confronts us, one of Holmes's lesser known cases, but one that involves one of England's most baffling mysteries.

The chimes of Big Ben sound outside the window. The clatter of carriages is heard in Baker Street below. The evening fog gathers. A figure emerges from the shadows and approaches the door to 221B. . . .

Dear Sirs,

Enclosed please find the manuscript "The Worcester Enigma" and cover letter. It was recently found among the papers of my grandfather's estate. Owing to its subject matter, I thought you might find it suitable for publication in your magazine.

Sincerely,
James M———

May 3, 1936
Dr. Thomas M——
Sansome Walk
Worcester, England
Dear Tom,

So good to see you again after all these years. You looked remarkably fit after so many years. Usually I find affairs of that kind a dreadful bore, but I must say I enjoyed our chat immensely.

You asked about Holmes's cases involving Worcester, and the other day, while consulting my files, I found the enclosed. It had been my intention for some time to publish the matter of the Worcester Enigma, but I found, after several attempts to set it down, that it was just too technical for general consumption. Also it includes mention of a certain bodily fluid that the public has never found acceptable in literature no matter how tastefully presented.

Finally and most honestly, it was in this affair, that Holmes showed me up, so to speak, in my own profession—an embarrassment I have little desire to circulate among my readers.

Therefore I am sending this manuscript to you. It is still in very rough form, lacking that final polish I try to give my published accounts. Peruse it at your leisure. I have no desire to see it returned.

My best to you and Kate.

Most sincerely,
John [Watson]

It was late in the season of '88 that we repaired to the sitting-room at 221B Baker Street following a matinee performance of *Traviata* at Covent Garden. Holmes had been at great pains to point out the shortcomings of the Violetta, a Miss Maud Palmerston, distant relative to Sir Charles Halle.

"Miss Palmerston," Holmes remarked, applying a bow to his violin as he paced about the room, "achieved the dubious distinction of making it appear that Verdi's unfortunate heroine died as a result of a three-hour bout of asthma. Indeed, she seemed so strangulated and short-of-breath, that I fully expected you to spring from your seat to render medical assistance."

I buried my eyes in the evening newspaper, trying to lose the memory of that ghastly ordeal.

"Watson," my friend continued, etching a flawless account of a Paganini caprice, "it occurs to me that, if England remains a land without music, it is most likely because the muse is so ill-treated here. I know of your fondness for Parry, and those abominable concoctions of Stainer, but even you must admit England has failed to produce a first-class musical figure since Henry Purcell."

"Come now, Holmes. I think you exaggerate," I remonstrated, setting the paper aside. "What of the light operas of Sullivan? I have heard a kind word from your lips on their merits."

"Yes, yes," he said impatiently, "but surely you would not rank them alongside the works of Mozart and Signor Verdi— Hallo, what's this?"

Holmes had stopped at the window and was looking into the street below. I joined him in time to catch a glimpse of a solidly-built man of military bearing, staring up at our quarters uncertainly, through the gathering mists of evening.

Holmes stepped back into the room and resumed his musings upon the violin. He struck up a rather distinctive theme of falling intervals that I recalled hearing him play on previous occasions.

"You see, Watson, how easily it falls on the ear. I am quite certain this is owing to its correspondence to certain electrical and circulatory pulsations within the brain."

Mrs. Hudson's rap at the door announced our visitor below.

Holmes nodded without interest and began to restate his theme. "I fear these subtleties of musicality have escaped the English ear. At least the ear of Miss Palmerston, who was rewriting Verdi's music to its detriment. Ah, listen to that, Watson. So devilishly simple, yet so pleasing to the ear. Would you not agree, sir?"

He turned suddenly to face our visitor, who appeared on the threshold.

The poor fellow was clearly taken aback. "I fear, sir, you have me at a disadvantage."

I observed that our guest was much younger than had been my initial impression, no more than thirty I should have thought. He had a prominent, squared nose, a full moustache that threatened to encircle his head, and a high forehead above eyes that were warm, yet mixed with melancholy and mischief. I took him at once for a country squire—staunch and sturdy, bright and bucolic—the embodiment of all that distinguishes the English at their best.

Holmes set his instrument aside, and indicated a chair near the fire.

"As we were engaged in serious discourse on the nature of music, I thought that, perhaps you, as a serious and accomplished musician, might offer a theory of your own."

"Extraordinary," the younger man exclaimed, seating himself. "But how could you know?"

"Simple deductive reasoning," Holmes declared, taking up a briar from the side table. "From the flecks of white linen upon the left shoulder of your jacket, I would say you are in the habit of placing a handkerchief there. Therefore I must conclude that you play the violin. From the closely cropped appearance of your fingernails, I presume this is not a casual preoccupation. From the distinctive pads on the palmar surfaces of your hands, I would also deduce that you are adept at a keyboard instrument. From the peculiar marks on the sole of your boot, just revealed as you crossed your legs, I assume that keyboard instrument to be the organ. Therefore the ink stains on your cuff are the result of manuscript work, most assuredly musical composition."

"Astounding," our guest said, sitting forward again, "you are every bit as good as Alice led me to believe."

"Quite so, but I doubt that you have travelled all the way from Worcestershire just to have me guess at your profession."

"I see I can have no secrets from you," our guest chuckled, quite pleased.

Holmes puffed patiently at his pipe, waiting for our guest to proceed.

"It is like this, Mr. Holmes. I am a musician, a music teacher from Worcester. Also a composer of some very modest achievement. Recently I have fallen in love with one of my students, Miss Caroline Alice Roberts, the daughter of Major-General Sir Henry Gee Roberts. I should tell you that we intend to be married, but . . ."

He stopped speaking, and began to fumble at his waistcoat, ostensibly for a smoke.

"There are problems," Holmes interjected, helping the fellow through what was clearly a difficult spot.

"Yes, I am afraid so," he admitted, abandoning his search. "You see, I have very little money of my own, largely what I make from instruction, and a few shillings here and there from the local concerts. It is not much, I fear. Alice's parents are quite well off, and, not surprisingly, they are opposed to the union. They would prefer Alice marry Mr. Adrian Fox-Fordyce, the son of the local M.P. Adrian is more ambitious, and more solidly grounded in matters they feel are important to Alice's well-being."

Holmes nodded sympathetically.

"I love Alice, Mr. Holmes. And she loves me. She has been my inspiration, made me more than myself. Two nights ago at Alice's urging, I determined to ask for her hand in marriage. I knew what General Roberts would say, but I was resolved to set the matter forth.

"Unfortunately, there was a terrible scene. I am afraid we both fell to shouting. I left the house abruptly. Later Alice sent word that her father had taken ill. Apparently he suffers from a touch of sugar diabetes, and it must have gone out of control. He is gravely ill, and Lady Roberts blames me for bringing it on."

Holmes nodded, and relit his pipe. "A most unfortunate affair, but I fail to see where I can be of assistance."

"I spoke to Alice again this morning, and she is of the opinion that there may be foul play involved. According to one of the servants, General Roberts had returned from London the day of these unfortunate occurrences in a state of agitation and distress. My suit only served to disturb him further. Later in the evening, General Roberts and his wife were to dine with Sir Gregory Fox-Fordyce, but they returned home early when the General complained of not feeling well. Alice says the Fox-Fordyces have been pressing for her marriage to Adrian. Sir Gregory has suffered recent financial losses as the result of unsound investments. The marriage would be advantageous to him."

Holmes arose and went over to the window. "And I take it Alice feels Sir Gregory might have had something to do with her father's sudden illness."

"Alice does not care for Sir Gregory, Mr. Holmes. She feels he is a heartless man who would do anything to advance himself. With General Roberts incapacitated, Alice feels her mother might be easily pressured into the union. Lady Roberts has been utterly dependent on her husband for years. With him gone . . . well, I think you can see what I am driving at."

"Indubitably," Holmes said. "I take it there is a doctor on the case."

"Yes, Dr. Harvey. A prominent local man. Very highly regarded. Retired from a Harley Street practice for reasons of health. He came as soon as the General took ill."

"Very good, Watson. I think we should leave at once." He turned to our guest again. "Bye the bye, in her haste, Mrs. Hudson neglected to give us your name."

"My apologies, gentlemen," said the man, offering his hand. "The name is Elgar. Edward Elgar."

We boarded the last train from Paddington Station, arrived in Worcester in the dead of night, and lost no time in proceeding directly to Elgar's flat in the suburb of Malvern, some eight miles southeast. I found myself nodding off at several opportunities, but Holmes was exhilarated by the challenge, and conversed at great length with young Elgar by a fire laid upon our arrival.

Finally, at dawn, we set out across the flat verdant countryside of Worcestershire, to the Robertses' residence, Hazeldine House, in Redmarley d'Abiot. We were announced and shown in directly to Miss Alice Roberts, a fine figure of womanhood, whose face nevertheless reflected the sacrifice of sleep that the present calamity had demanded. She was, I surmised, a few years older than Elgar, yet her manner was most gentle and charming. She was not, I would say, a truly beautiful woman, but there was a measure of strength and spirit in her carriage that made her seem so. She greeted us warmly, in spite of the earliness of the hour.

"I am so glad you have come," she said by way of greeting. "Dr. Harvey is here. Father is unchanged. I finally persuaded Mother to get some sleep, poor dear. She has not taken this at all well. I trust 'Edoo' has explained the situation."

She moved to his side, and took his hand affectionately as she spoke.

"Yes," Holmes said, "but there are one or two questions which remain. What was the nature of your father's trip to London the day of his illness?"

"I am not certain. I believe he was to look into certain business matters, and meet some friends at his club."

"Did you see your father after he returned from the Fox-Fordyce dinner later in the evening?"

"Yes, just briefly. He was quite agitated and upset. He complained of headache, refusing, at first, Mother's request to send for Dr. Harvey. Later, however, he changed his mind, and sent for him himself."

"When did you next see your father?"

"Not until much later. Father retired to his study until Dr. Harvey arrived. His condition deteriorated quite rapidly. We were fortunate Dr. Harvey came as promptly as he did."

"I take it your father is on good terms with Sir Gregory."

"From all outward appearances. Mother said the evening was quite cordial, although Father felt

651

Sir Gregory most indelicate in raising the issue of marriage in a social setting. I suppose that 'Edoo' has told you that it has been my parents' wish that I marry Adrian. Well, I have nothing against Adrian. He is, in fact, a sweet and harmless person. But I have told them that, if I am not permitted to marry 'Edoo,' I shall not marry at all. And that is final."

Her eyes flashed defiance, and from the set of her mouth, I knew this was a woman who meant what she said.

Our conversation was interrupted by the appearance of a tall, elegantly attired man in a dark suit, carrying a medical bag. The man, whom I took to be Dr. Harvey, bowed slightly in our presence. Even in the Midlands countryside, he carried an air of Harley Street hauteur.

"Miss Roberts, may I have a word with you?" he inquired most properly. "I have some bad news. There is no change in your father, in spite of all my efforts. I think you should inform your mother to prepare herself for the worst."

Anguish and sorrow registered strongly on Miss Roberts's face. Elgar held her tenderly, hiding the tears.

"I must return to my surgery," the doctor continued, "but I shall stop by later in the morning, as soon as I am able. Meanwhile, I have given Miss Jenkins further instructions. She is a most capable woman. Do not hesitate, however, to send word if you should need me."

"I take it then, that General Roberts is in irreversible diabetic coma," Holmes inquired, stepping forward.

"I do not believe we have been introduced," the doctor said, drawing back, regarding my friend like an unsavory bit of suet.

"Allow me to introduce myself. I am Sherlock Holmes, a friend of General Roberts."

Dr. Harvey's face betrayed his surprise. His mouth dropped slightly, his starchy manner precipitously.

"I have heard of you, sir," he said quite civilly. "You must forgive any rudeness. I am quite tired. The General's illness has been a strain on everyone."

"No doubt. Can you enlighten me as to the details of the General's illness?"

"I was summoned to the house at nine-thirty by a message saying General Roberts was complaining of headache and malaise. About a year ago, I discovered a mild diabetic condition on routine examination. When I saw him the other night in his study, it was immediately apparent that the disease had advanced to an alarming degree. He became lethargic and unresponsive. I could barely get him to his bed. I have tried every measure I know to reverse the condition, but to no avail. I fear the situation is almost hopeless."

"Have you any idea what caused the disease to advance so relentlessly?"

"None, but it is my experience that this is often the case with diabetes."

"I see," Holmes said, thoughtfully. "Is it possible that he could have ingested something, accidentally perhaps, that might have brought this on?"

653

"I do not see what you are driving at, Mr. Holmes."

"I have been told that your patient returned early from a dinner engagement. I wondered if he might have encountered something there that might have adversely affected his diabetes."

"Oh I see," the doctor said, rubbing his chin studiously. "I had not, in all candour, considered that possibility. I suppose it is possible, but I cannot think what that substance might have been. The General was very careful about his diet."

"I wonder if I might trouble you to see General Roberts. I would stay no longer than a few minutes."

Dr. Harvey appeared ready to offer objection, but instead gave his approval.

"Is it permissible for my friend Dr. Watson here to accompany us? He is a trusted friend, and I would value his presence."

Harvey hastily agreed, and we followed him out of the sitting room into the hall, up a large central staircase and into a darkened room at the top.

The air was stale with the odour of sickness, and heavy curtains had been drawn across the windows, giving a funereal appearance. A large mahogany bed, hung with a canopy, commanded the far end of the room. Illumination came from a solitary lamp on a table by the side of the bed, where a nursing sister, in a freshly starched gown with a new gold watch pinned at the bodice, sat reading from a small book. She rose quickly as Dr. Harvey entered and spoke to her in the most discreet of tones.

I was barely able to make out the faint outlines

of an elderly man through the sheer curtain drawn about the sickbed. His respirations were slow and deep. His face, or what I could see of it, was pale and bloodless.

Dr. Harvey reached under the bed and retrieved a small specimen jar which he brought over to us.

"See here," he said. "High amounts of sugar in spite of complete dietary deprivation."

He took some drops of Benedict's reagent and dropped it into the specimen. The urine turned quite dark in colour, confirming the severity of the patient's disease.

"What is the meaning of this?" a woman's voice demanded stridently. "Dr. Harvey, you said my husband was permitted no visitors, not even family, and yet you turn this sickroom into a reception hall."

A woman, whom I took to be Lady Roberts, was standing in the doorway, supported by a maid. Her face was drawn and haggard, the features severe and exaggerated. She cut off all attempts at explanation, ordering us summarily from the house. Even Alice Roberts's entreaties were to no avail.

Once outside, Holmes thanked the physician, shaking hands most cordially with him, before re-entering Elgar's trap. The young musician was clearly distressed, though he said nothing as he took up the reins.

"Too bad, Holmes," I said, as we made our way across the rural landscape. "Bad business, this diabetes. I fear there's little to be done."

"Watson, you disappoint me. The problem lies

before us quite clearly. A devilish matter. We must act quickly."

"Great Scott. Then you do suspect foul play."

"In its most chilling form. There's not a moment to lose. Mr. Elgar, if you would be so kind, I must proceed at once to the nearest telegraph office. You must return to your flat and await any word from Hazeldine House."

My friend fell silent again, enrapt in his thoughts. Once on our journey, I caught him putting a fingertip to his lips, but I was too exhausted to take in its significance.

I seized the opportunity for a nap on the couch in the front room of Elgar's flat, as we awaited Holmes's return. It was a hard, uncomfortable piece of furniture, a fact I failed to notice until I awoke several hours later. Elgar was seated at his piano, improvising a piece he had written for Miss Roberts called *Salut d'Amour*. He played it through several times, and I recall thinking it a charming piece of sentiment.

We passed the afternoon speaking of musical matters, watching the clock above the mantel.

At dusk, Holmes came in excitedly.

"Quickly, we must return to Hazeldine House. I only hope we are in time to avert tragedy."

We moved with great dispatch, completing the nine-mile journey in half the time of our morning traversal. Holmes burst into the house without waiting to be announced, and bounded up the stairs to the sickroom. Lady Roberts confronted him at the head of the staircase, with tones that were icy and sharp.

656

"Who gives you the right to break into this house like a common criminal?"

"My apologies, Lady Roberts, but if you value the life of your husband, you will stand aside."

Without further delay, Holmes swept past her into the sickroom beyond. "That won't be necessary," he said, taking a syringe from the hand of a surprised Miss Jenkins. "Mr. Elgar, will you take charge of this woman?"

He turned to me, in earnest. "Now, Watson, look closely, do you see what is wrong?"

I looked down at the comatose patient, and immediately grasped the situation.

"But, of course, Holmes. The respirations. They are not rapid and shallow, as they should be in a diabetic coma!"

"Precisely," he said, moving to the head of the bed. "Now, if you will assist me . . ."

He leaned down, and began to study the posterior portion of the patient's scalp.

"Ah ha," he exclaimed, exposing a wound beneath the white hair. "The true cause of General Roberts's coma."

Lady Roberts was aghast. Her face could not have reflected greater surprise if Holmes had produced the Star of India.

"But, Holmes," I said, "the sugar in the urine. We saw it ourselves."

"Yes, put there for our benefit by Dr. Harvey, as our attention was drawn to General Roberts. Outside, after shaking hands, little granular particles adhered to my hand—particles that were sweet to the taste. I realized then that he had put sugar into the specimen as he was taking it from under the bed."

"But I do not understand this," Lady Roberts protested. "Dr. Harvey and my husband were good friends. They had even embarked on a financial venture together."

Holmes acknowledged Lady Roberts, drawing the curtain back from the window before he answered.

"Yes. The same venture in which your neighbor Sir Gregory Fox-Fordyce recently lost substantial sums. I took the liberty of cabling the London Medical Society to see what I could learn of Dr. Harvey's retirement from their number. I learned that there had been some improprieties involving the finances of several of his elderly patients. Nothing, unfortunately, that could ever be proved in a court of law. The victims were reluctant to press charges. So a deputation from the Medical Society confronted him with their findings, and forced him to yield his practice.

"Your father," Holmes continued, turning to Alice Roberts, "apparently learned of this on his trip to London. That is why he returned so distraught. When he summoned Dr. Harvey to the house, it was to confront him with this knowledge, not to seek medical attention. Dr. Harvey panicked, and struck your father on the head, then fabricated this entire diabetes matter, until he could decide on a course of action.

"He knew he would eventually have to do away with your father to protect himself. Fortunately, he was never able to bring himself to it."

"And a fine mess 'e's left me in," whined Miss

658

Jenkins, standing almost forgotten in Elgar's grasp.

"Yes, I fear so. He never did tell me how he induced you to prolong the coma with injections of morphia whilst he temporized."

Miss Jenkins shrugged pathetically. "I suppose I knew all along that 'e never meant to marry me. Where's 'e now?"

"Gone from Worcester. That I can assure you. At least the Roberts name has been spared the notoriety of a prolonged and public trial."

The figure in the bed began to stir.

Holmes turned to me. "Chin up, old fellow. I believe General Roberts will be requiring the care of a first-class physician, and I would most heartily commend your services."

Several years later, in the spring of '99, an envelope arrived by post containing two box seats to the June 19 concert at St. James Hall. The prominent work on the program was to be a new set of variations on an original theme by Edward Elgar. Alice Elgar added a note indicating that it was of the utmost importance to her husband that we be in attendance.

It was, I need not remind you, a concert unlike any other in English history. The *Enigma Variations* were cheered most enthusiastically, and our friend was obliged to take several bows from the stage before being allowed to retire.

Holmes was most effusive in his praise of the composition, and told the Elgars so when we met them later that evening at the Belgravia.

"So good of you to come," the composer said,

659

pumping Holmes's hand most enthusiastically. "I trust you understand my indebtedness to you for my success tonight."

Holmes suddenly began to whistle a tune out loud, in the lobby of the Belgravia, an appalling gesture that struck me as decidedly ill-mannered. Our friend, however, seemed rather delighted.

"Ah, then you've got it," he said. "I have recalled the theme many times since I heard you play it that evening in Baker Street. So pleasing to the ear, as you said. I determined to use it as the basis for my thirteen *Enigma Variations* depicting my friends, yet hesitated to state it outright, as I could not claim it as my own."

"But it is yours, most assuredly," Holmes said graciously. "The theme rightfully belongs to any first-class musical figure who could transform it into a work of genius that speaks the language of England so all may appreciate it. Accept it as a grateful gift from your most devoted admirer, Sherlock Holmes. But, if I might be allowed one small suggestion it would be that you allow the theme of your *Enigma Variations* to remain a secret. I have found, my dear Elgar, that as much as a good tune, the English love a good mystery."

Editor's note: Edward (later Sir Edward) Elgar (1857–1934) is generally regarded as the first major English composer to appear in over two centuries, and the most popular composer the country ever produced. In 1889 he married Caroline Alice Roberts. The marriage endured until her death in 1920. Although best known for his Pomp and Circumstances Marches, *it was the* Enigma Variations *(1889) which estab-*

lished his international reputation. The Variations, a series of portraits in music (including a self-portrait), are built around a principal theme that is never stated by itself. The source and significance of this theme were never revealed by Elgar during his lifetime, and its identity remains a mystery that intrigues scholars even to this day.